North Woods

By Daniel Mason

The Piano Tuner
A Far Country
The Winter Soldier
A Registry of My Passage upon the Earth

North Woods

❄

A NOVEL

Daniel Mason

RANDOM HOUSE

New York

Published in the United States by Random House, an imprint and division of Penguin Random House LLC, New York.

RANDOM HOUSE and the HOUSE colophon are registered trademarks of Penguin Random House LLC.

Published in the United Kingdom by John Murray Press, a Hachette company.

Photo credits: Page 123: Lucian Turner, National Anthropological Archives, Smithsonian Institution, [06549100]. Page 129: Daniel Huntington, Courtesy of the Century Association, New York. Page 159: Kate Wolff. Page 177: Courtesy of the Vermont Historical Society. Page 205: Courtesy of University of Michigan Library. Page 261: Courtesy of the Wellcome Collection. Page 363: artist unknown, likely Mark Jefferson; courtesy of the Eastern Michigan University Archives.

LIBRARY OF CONGRESS CATALOGING-IN-PUBLICATION DATA

Names: Mason, Daniel (Daniel Philippe)
Title: North woods: a novel / Daniel Mason.
Description: First Edition. | New York: Random House, [2023]
Identifiers: LCCN 2022056687 (print) | LCCN 2022056688 (ebook) |
ISBN 9780593597033 (Hardback) | ISBN 9780593597057 (Ebook)
Classification: LCC PS3613.A816 N67 2023 (print) |
LCC PS3613.A816 (ebook) | DDC 813/.6—dc23/eng/20221205
LC record available at lccn.loc.gov/2022056687
LC ebook record available at lccn.loc.gov/2022056688

International ISBN 9780593730621

Printed in the United States of America on acid-free paper

randomhousebooks.com

2 4 6 8 9 7 5 3 1

FIRST U.S. EDITION

Book design by Simon M. Sullivan

For Ariana and Selah

. . . to build a fire on Ararat with the remnants of the ark.

Nathaniel Hawthorne, *The American Notebooks*

Contents

CONTENTS

North Woods

One

THEY had come to the spot in the freshness of June, chased from the village by its people, following deer path through the forest, the valleys, the fern groves, and the quaking bogs.

Fast they ran! Steam rose from the fens and meadows. Bramble tore at their clothing, shredding it to rags that hung about their shoulders. They crashed through thickets, hid in tree hollows and bear caves, rattling sticks before they slipped inside. They fled as if it were a child's game, as if they had made off with plunder. My plunder, he whispered, as he touched her lips.

They laughed with the glee of it. They could not be found! Solemn men marched past them with harquebuses cocked in their elbows, peered into the undergrowth, stuffed greasy pinches of tobacco into their pipes. The world had closed over them. Gone was England, gone the Colony. They were Nature's wards now, he told her, they had crossed into a Realm. Lying beneath him in the leaves, in the low hollow of an oak, she arched her neck to watch the belted boots and leather scabbards swinging across the wormy ceiling of the world. So close! she thought, biting his hand to stifle her joy. Entwined, they watched the stalking dogs and met their eyes, saw recognition cross their dog-faces, the conspiring shiver of their tails as they continued on.

They ran. In open fields, they hid within the shadows of the bird flocks, and in the rivers below the silver veil of fish. Their soles peeled from their shoes. They bound them with their rags, with bark, then lost them in the sucking fens. Barefoot they ran through the forest, and in the sheltered, sappy bowers, when they thought they were alone, he drew splinters from her feet. They were young and they could run for hours, and June had blessed them with her berries, her untended farmer's carts. They paused to eat, to sleep, to steal, to roll in the rustling meadows of goldenrod. In hidden ponds, he lifted her dripping from the water, set her on the mossy stone, and kissed the river streaming from her tresses and her legs.

Did he know where he was going, she asked him, pulling him to her, tasting his mouth, and always he answered, Away! North they went, to the north woods and then toward sun-fall, trespassing like fire, but the mountains bent their course and the bogs detained them, and after a week they could have been anywhere. Did it matter? Rivers carried them off and settled them on distant, sun-warmed banks. The bramble parted, closed behind them. In the cataracts, she felt the spring melt pounding her shoulders, watched him picking his way over the streambed, hunting creekfish with his hands. And he was waiting for her, winged in a damp blanket which he wrapped around her, lowering her to the earth.

They had met in, of all places, church. She had known of him, been warned of him, heard that he stirred up trouble back in England, had joined the ships only to escape. Fled Plymouth, fled New Haven, to settle in a hut on Springfield's edge. They said he was ungodly, consorted with heathens, disappeared into the woods to join in savage ritual. Twice she'd seen him watching her; once she met him on the road. This was all, but this was all she needed. She felt that she had sprung from him. He watched her through the sermon, and she felt her neck grow warm beneath his gaze. Outside, he asked her to meet him in the meadow, and in the meadow, he asked her to meet him by the river's bank. She was to be married to John Stone, a minister of twice her age, whose first wife had died with child. Died beaten with child, her sister told her, died from her wounds. On the shore, beneath the watch of egrets, her lover wrapped his fingers into hers, made promises, rolled his grass sprig with his tongue. She'd been there seven years. They left that night, a comet lighting the heavens in the direction of their flight.

From a midwife's garden: three potatoes. Hardtack from the pocket of a sleeping shepherd. A chicken from a settler's homestead, a laying chicken, which he carried tucked beneath his arm. My sprite! he called his lover in the shelter of the darkness, and she looked back into his eyes. He was mad, she thought, naked but for his scraps of clothing, his axe, his clucking hen. And how he talked! Of Flora, the dominion of the toad and muck-clam, the starscapes of the fireflies, the reign of wolf and bear and bloom of mold. And around them, in the forest, everywhere: the spirits of each bird and insect, each fir, each fish.

She laughed—for how could there be space? There'd be more fish than river. More bird than sky. A thousand angels on a blade of grass.

Shh, he said, his lips on hers, lest she offend them: the raccoon, the worm, the toad, the will-o'-the-wisp.

They ran. They married in the bower, said oaths within the oaken hollow. On the trees grew mushrooms large as saddles. Grey birds, red snakes, and orange newts their witnesses. The huckleberries tossed their flowers. The smell of hay rose from the fern they crushed. And the sound, the whir, the roar of the world.

They ran. The last farms far behind them; now only forest. They followed Indian paths through groves hollowed by fire, with high green vaults of celestial scale. On the hottest days, they climbed the rivers, chicken on his shoulder, her hand in his. Mica dusted her heels like silver. Damselflies upon her neck. Flying

7

squirrels in the trees above them, and in the silty sand the great tracks of cats. Sometimes, he stopped and showed her signs of human passage. Friends, he said, and said that he could speak the language of the people this side of the mountains. But where were they? she wondered. And she stared into the green that surrounded them, for fear was in her, and loneliness, and she didn't know which one was worse.

And then, one morning, they woke in the pine duff, and he declared they were no longer hunted. He knew by the silence, the air, the clear warp of summer wind. The country had received them. In the Colony, two black lines were drawn through two names in the register. The children warned of thrashings if they spoke of them again.

They reached the valley on the seventh day. Above them, a mountain. Deer track led through a meadow that rose and narrowed northly, crossed through the dark remnants of a recent fire. A thin trail followed a tumbling brook to a pond lined with rushes. Across the slope: a clearing, beaver stumps and pale-green seedlings rising from the rich black ash.

Here, he said.

Songbirds flitted through the burn. They stripped their last rags, swam, and slept. It was all so clear, so pure. From his little bag, he withdrew a pouch containing seeds of squash and corn and fragments of potato. Began to pace across the hillside, the chicken following at his feet. At the brook, he found a wide, flat stone, pried it from the earth, and carried it back into the clearing, where he laid it gently in the soil. Here.

Anonymous, The "Nightmaids" Letter

ON the 7th of July, came the heathens in great number, upon the village in the middle of the night. And I was awake with my babe when I saw fire at the stockades and heard shots and shouting. Then my husband woke, and bid me hide with the child. Swiftly, he ran to lock the door, but then they breachd it and struck him down and murderd him, still in his nightclothes. Then came one and orderd me to follow, but such was my fear I could not move, though the house was burning and cinders were falling from the rafters. I thought I should prefer to die with my husband than go with these murderous creatures, but the heathen grabbd me and my babe. Outside the fires made it light as day. I saw my kin and neighbours slaughterd, my brother-in-law cut down before my eyes, my cousin shot, his belly slit, they fell on us like beasts on sheep. In the snow were scatterd chairs and rakes and other things that people fought with. Then a panic seemd to come upon the heathens, for they calld to one another and, shouting, they ran to the breach in the stockade. Then was I taken by the one who first seizd me, and I had but stockings and no boots. With me were my neighbours and some carryd children and some wore nothing but their bedclothes. When we stoppd I lookd back, I could see the village burning, and in the light my neighbours' weeping faces. Then our captors came and commanded us to follow. Through the woods they marchd us, there were six Indians and twenty capturd, but none made escape, so woeful were our hearts and so forbidding was the wilderness.

Near me was my cousin, and she was weeping, and she told me all were gone, my father slayn, my mother slayn, my sister slayn—for she had seen them hatcheted. Then I prayd to God that He might take me, but I had displeasd Him and he wishd me to suffer longer on this earth. Each step took me farther from my home and into the darkness of the forest. Then dawn came and they bid us march faster, for they feard we would be discoverd. I was so benumbd, I wishd to lie down, but those that falterd were beaten, I but held my babe and tried to give him suck. In the afternoon we rested, and, seeing that many of us had only stockings on our feet, our captors made us shoes of birch bark. Then night came and they bound us together by hand and foot. And sleep came not to my eyes, for all night I thought only of my sorrows. I listend to my cousin praying for one who might save us, *break the jaws of the wicked, and pluck the spoil out of his teeth.* I tried to join, but my spirit was so oppressd that only cries came from my mouth. And this was the first night, and in the morning, when we were walking, my neighbour J—— came and said, Let us run, no fate can be worse than this. But I did not dare, and God blessd me in my wisdom, for shortly after noon I heard Indian shouts and saw a body crashing through the brush and they after him, and we were made to stop and wait, and all of us prayd that he might escape and bring help or at least save his own life. And though it was warm we were cold and shaking, and one of the heathens said, Think! Who has brought this suffering upon you? Who has made you wait here? And no sooner had he said this than there appeard the one who'd given chase, and he wiped his bloody hatchet on the moss and said, This be a lesson. And we walkd on, and night came, and this was the second night we slept in the muck, and in the morning I saw my babe was sick and not sucking, and I thought, He died, but still his body was warm when I pressd him to me. And such was my pain for my child that I could not feel my own pain, I walkd as if it was a dream, and sometimes I stumbld and fell. Then my friends would help raise me, for they too knew what fate would befall me if I delayd. This was the third day, but little I remember, for come evening, I began to feel weak and feverish, and all night I coughd. And in the morning, my captor came, and I knew he would kill me, but his blood lust had ebbd, for he went and conferd with another, and this one came down from his horse and they lifted me upon it. I did not know why he showd me this compassion, perhaps we were not many now, and they were displeasd with what they would get for ransom. And we walkd until night and stoppd beneath a ledge, but the heathen said, Come, and led my horse down a trail. Then I was weeping, and he said in English, Why do you cry, and I, I want to return to my people, and he, They are not your people anymore. And this filld me anew with terror, and truly, I thought to run so he would kill me and my child, for now I knew I would never see my home again. And I thought bitterly upon the words of Jeremiah, *But shall he die in the place whither they have led him captive, and shall see this land no more.* Then we came upon a clearing beneath a mountain, and there I saw what seemd to be a hut of log and stone, and a chicken in the yard, and there, my master whistld and the door opend, and an old woman most strange came out, she was dressd in skirts and blankets like an Indian, but her face was English and she spoke both English and the heathen's tongue. And after some words I did not understand, my captor left me with this one. Come, she said, and took me in. It was a small house, with one room, and there was a hearth and she stoked the fire, then she strippd me and wrappd me in a blanket with my babe. Then she took my wet clothes and hung them above the fire and brought a broth and I drank, and then she gave some to my child, who took it and began to cry, and she said, Quick, give it your breast. And my child took it and such was my relief that for a moment I forgot my sorry plight. Then, when my babe had finishd feeding, I drank again though the broth smelld unwholesome, I did not question, so far had I come in my hunger that I might drink from the spoon of the heathen's friend. I slept and late that night I awoke, I was with fever and now a thought came upon me that the woman would harm me. This fancy grew stronger until all reason had left me, I knew she would kill me and my child or give it to the D——l. I rose and there next to the hearth was the poker and I got it and stood above the demon, I would have killd her but my child began to wail. Then I went to my babe and fed him but I kept the poker, and the woman must have seen though it was dark, for she said, Come, foolish child, I am not a witch, and she went and came back with a book, and I saw it was a Bible. And she gave her names, both her Christian name and Indian name, for she had fled the Colony with her husband many years ago and lost him in that forsaken wilderness, and marryd a Praying Indian and lost him too. And I knew her name and his name for I oft heard whisper of these Godless fleeing people, though I thought them dead. And were you marryd with this husband before God? I askd her, for I had seen she did adorn herself as would the wicked, with a ring of silver on her finger. Or was it the D——l who shaped that omen to your skin? You are sick, she said, and I said, I know a sinner! and she, Only God knows who has a true heart, and I, But God has given me the ability to see. Then your eyes have scales, said she. And she was sitting next to me, for she had crossd the room in the darkness. Oh! said I. *Will you require of us a song?* And a hand touchd my head and she said that I was raving, and I knew then that she had poysond me. I ran out but I was naked and fell and then she was beside me. Godly woman! she cried. You flee without your child! Come! Then the fever was upon me fully, for days I ravd, and when I came about she said a fortnight had passd. And I did not know if it was a fortnight, but when I held my babe, I saw how he had grown. Look, she said, while you ravd I pressd him to your breast. And he was well and smiled handsomely, but I had heard of false children, made of the D——l's clay, and when she went, I checkd him for marks of stitching that would show the seams. And he was wailing, for it was cold, and the old woman came back and said, Come, why do you distress him so? Then I askd might we pray together and she took the Bible and when we reachd those words *As for man, his days are as grass: as a flower of the field, so he flourisheth. For the wind passeth over it, and it is gone; and the place thereof shall know it no more,* then I began to weep. And she leand close and I saw she wore a necklace with charms of bone and iron. Put off thy ornaments from thee! I thought to cry, but I had been softend by her verses. And I askd, Is the heathen who took me truly your friend? and she said, The one who savd you is my friend. Then anger filled me, and I said, And is he who slayd my father your friend, and is he who slayd my sister? And she said, Has he not a father and a sister who were also slayn? And I hated her but she did not say more, instead she went out and I heard the sound of an axe and she came in and said, Will you just drink my broth? so I went out and carryd the wood inside. Then she took me and showd me how she livd, how she kept dried meat and corn and acorn meal in the loft above. And in a shed she showd me the baskets for fishing, and the traps, and these she showd me how to set out in the wood. Then dark fell and we went back and ate and I thought how the last time I broke bread was with my family who was dead, and I wept bitterly, and when I saw she had nothing to say, I askd, Will you not comfort me? and she said, I do not have the comfort which you seek. So my misery was great, but in the morning again there was work, though I did not forget my sorrow. Now I had been there a month. Each day I expected my captor to return, and no longer did I fear for my life, but that he would make me live among them and become an enemy of my own people. When I askd my mistress what would become of me, she said she did not know, perhaps they would trade me for one of theirs that had been taken, as for each of us there were a hundred of them that had been stolen from their homes. Now that I was strong, I thought again of running, but I feard a worse fate were I capturd. In the garden, there were beans, and corn, and squash, for long ago, she said, there was a beaver pond and so the land was rich. And she taught me to set snares for rabbits, and which of the mushrooms we might eat and which ones she calld nightmaids that we were to avoid for they were poyson. And sometimes I spoke with my mistress of other things. I askd her, if she lovd the Indians so, why did she not go and live with her second husband's people? To this she answerd that sometimes in the winter she went to them, but most had died from the pestilence, and this was her home, the land was good. Then she spoke freely, she told me of the rites and dances, and the beasts of the place. And I told her this sounded like the D—l talking, but she took me out when it was night, and said, Come, don't you notice? But there was nothing save the mountain and the forest, and this I told her. No, she said, listen, and we were quiet, and suddenly there it was, pacing, and there are no words to describe it, I do not lie. And fear oppressd my heart, but my mistress comforted me, for had not He promisd, *For every beast of the forest is mine?* Then we went back, and time passd, maybe three weeks, and the days were the same, and we both wonderd what had happend to my captor, when there arrivd a party, and lo! they were not Indians but three English scouts, and such was their surprise when they saw me with my babe. And my spirit leapt though I knew none by name, but they knew my story, for some of our captives had been ransomd, and told them I'd been taken. And I wept because it paind me to recall my dear husband and my family. As for my mistress, now was I afrayd that they might slay her, so I said that she was a Christian who had been marryd to a Praying Indian, that she continued to bring light to these dark forests. I saw she had removd her ring and necklace to her pocket. Then we welcomd them and brought them food and one of them, he bid me sit near him and from his pockets took an apple and invited me to taste. And I laughd, and said, Who am I, Eve? for he frightend me so. That night, we slept up in the loft, and my mistress closd the trapdoor, and movd over it some boards and I knew that it was so that none would come to us unchastely. The next morning, before the sun rose, they went out, and when they came back it was evening and they were laughing and I askd what made them so. Then the one who had offerd me the apple reachd into his bag, and there, wrappd in leaves, was a hand, small like a child's. Tomorrow, he said, they would leave to bring more soldiers, for the boy had told them the location of the village and they would avenge the murders of our people. Then it was time to eat, so my mistress went out into the garden and I could see that she was weeping. When she returnd I went to her, she did not let me prepare the supper, but sent me up into the loft. Then she came to me and closd the door again. She had her axe. Downstairs, the men were eating, and she said, You must understand what is about to happen must happen so that there is no more bloodshed. And I must have lookd afraid for she said, It is so the Evil stops. And I was crying and nodded, but I did not understand, I saw she had put back on her ornaments, and she said, It is what is right, and from below us came a groaning, and a scrape of chair, and plates crashing, and a body on the floor was heaving. Then a second groan rose and a third and one of them screamd that they'd been poysond and we heard the ladder creak and there was pounding on our door. There we went and tried to block them from coming up, but with their guns they hammerd and broke it open. Then my mistress went with her axe and struck one, but the other had his musket and shot her through her good heart and killd her and I took her axe. The man came and as God is my witness, I acted only to defend my child. Then I took his musket and went and found one retching who in his agony had pushd his way outside. I thought he was dead but he came at me and God did not forsake me, but steadyd my hand. Then, I was wailing, my child wailing, but I feard I must work swiftly for others would come and find them. I strappd my child to my back and got the shovel and went out into the meadow above the house and dug and didn't stop until dawn and then I went and draggd the bodies through the high wet grass. There I buryd them, the men together and my mistress nearer to the house, and prayd for their souls, that they might be forgiven for their sinning. And this I write and swear to be true, for I must leave and I cannot bear my secret any longer. May you that find it know what happend here, in this time of great conflict, in the Colony of Massachusetts, by she who briefly calld this place her home.

Two

IT is late August when the woman bundles up her child, closes the door to the cabin, and follows the trail to the edge of the clearing, where she stops to look back before she vanishes into the woods. Deer, lifting their heads above the goldenrod, watch her depart, and then move cautiously toward the garden. Across the valley comes a thrumming, rumbling sound, as a flock of passenger pigeons draws its curtain over the sky.

Days pass. Snakes settle into the warm coves between the stones. A wolf pack gathers briefly in the lee of the cabin; the pups chase white butterflies by the pond. In the garden, the squash grows plump on thundershower, the trailing beans swarm up the cornstalks, the corn ripens in its husk. Butterflies alight upon the swaying sprays of boneset, and milkweed pods split open and begin to spill their tuft.

In the meadow, beneath soft mounds of earth, lie the bodies of the woman and three men, and in the belly of the man who offered the apple to the woman with the child, is a piece of apple core with three remaining seeds.

No one comes. No soldiers. Not the man who brought the woman to the place. In the garden, the beanstalks wither in the heat, the squash rots, and rust infests the ears of corn.

Colors change. Yellow creeps down from the mountain and slips into the veins of the hornbeams, red limns the oaks and maples, and in the understory, violet consumes the lemon-yellow wings of the viburnum. Leaves fall upon the brook that splits the hillside like a tear in the fabric of the earth.

In the soil, the mold and the worm find the bodies of the woman and the men.

Rain comes, patters on the remaining canopy, runs down the upstretched branches of the oaks and elms, foams about the hemlock trunks and slides into the dirt. It soaks the soft earth about the bodies, the ground swells with the water, the hillside slumps, the body of the man who offered the apple to the woman is brought closer to the surface and then into the light. A new rain bares his head and shoulders, until it looks as if he is trying to crawl out.

Rats, flies, and pecking birds now do their work.

Then it is winter. Snow falls and covers the bones of the man who offered the apple to the woman, buries him up to his crown. Field mice run through the icy corridors beneath the snow, voles nose the frozen litter, and the snorting of the weasels echoes through the hollows.

Months pass, and on a single warm and windswept night, the rains come again and wash away the snow.

The wolves return, the pups now tall and winter-thin. In the mud, they find the carcass of the man who offered the apple to the woman, dance about it, barking, and drag it farther up the hill.

It grows warmer, until the water that gathers in the hoofprints of the deer no longer freezes in the night. Now, in the place that was once the belly of the man who offered the apple to the woman, one of the apple seeds, sheltered in the shattered rib cage, breaks its coat, drops a root into the soil, and lifts a pair of pale-green cotyledons. A shoot rises, thickens, seeks the bars of light above it, and gently parts the fifth and sixth ribs that once guarded the dead man's meager heart.

The sapling grows through summer. By the end of August, it has eighteen leaves and is the same height as the haunches of a lynx.

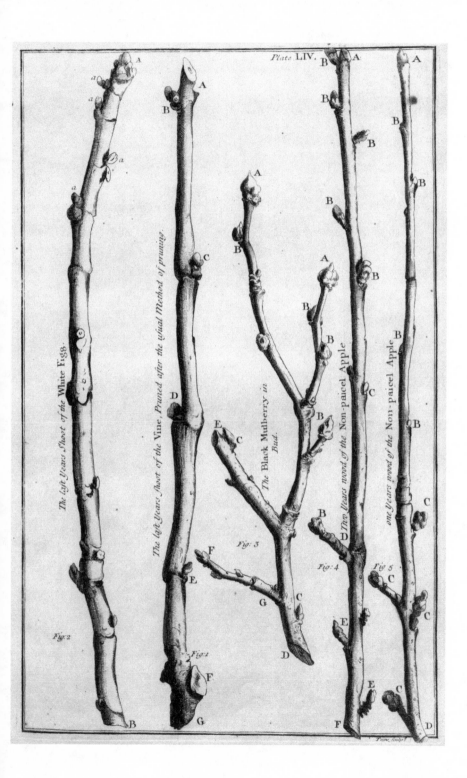

Plate LIV.

The last Years Shoot of the White Figg.

The last Years Shoot of the Vine, Pruned after the usual Method of pruning.

The Black Mulberry in Bud.

Two Years wood of the Non-paicel Apple

one Years wood of the Non-paicel Apple

Fig. 1

Fig. 2

Fig. 3

Fig. 4

Fig. 5

"Osgood's Wonder," Being the Reminiscences of an Apple-Man

Dedication
To my most beloved daughters, to whom I entrust this letter of
VALEDICTION, by an Orchardist going to war.

AUTUMN arrives again in all her glory, and yet the moment of
crisis is upon us. From her heights, the hawk looks down and sees
the tiny ranks of marching men. Tomorrow I must leave my farm,
my orchards, your sweet company. Ten and four years have we
made this our Arcadia. I have watched you grow alongside the
apples. Once I had foresworn the battlefield and consecrated my
affections to our fruit, but circumstance now demands I leave Pomona's arms and go directly to the fields of Mars.

It is my intent and expectation that, come winter, I will return
to these hills to join you once again, and that this letter will prove
unnecessary. But I have been to battle many times before, and cannot delude myself as to the danger. If at times my words seem
hasty, it is because I must complete my valediction before I depart
at daybreak. My hope is that, though it be written under distressed
circumstances, it will be but the first chapter of a great book I will
one day complete.

On My Origins and Why I Became an Apple-Man

Of our family and my early history, I need not waste these fleeting midnight hours. My uncle has written an account of the Osgoods of Northamptonshire; I refer all readers to it. Know that we are of the martial Osgoods. There is not a family in England who has served more nobly, and I, too, would have remained on the fields of our sweet Albion forever, had my first wife not died with child. Though already grey in hair, I had little left to retain me. I came to America for war, found love again, served proudly in the French and Indian conflicts. Through the 48th Foot, I rose to Major, and there was talk that I was destined for Colonel, General even, when the Spirit came upon me and produced my fateful decision, being to leave the drill, the march, the song of fife and drum, the smell of gunpowder, and devote myself entirely to apples.

How did this come to pass? Might I locate, in my passage through the world, the spark that struck the kindling of the fancy of my soul? Was there, on those back rivers of the St. Lawrence, some watery Road to Damascus? It was a deathbed dream that moved me, but dreams too must have their causes. Was it, in my faraway childhood, a pretty farmer's daughter, who handed me a sun-warmed fruit and placed the slumbering seed within my heart? The water-colored cards that taught me my alphabet? The pyramids of bounty that overflowed our village market stalls?

A kiss somewhere, on someone's lips still wet with cider?

The serpent that tempts us all?

Or was it simply this: that the French soldier I surprised behind his bulwark on that fatal day upon the Plains of Abraham was slicing a sweet pippin with his bayonet when he rose and thrust it up into my chest?

Of My Wounding and the Dream That Followed

They tell me that the blade passed between my ribs and gently kissed my heart. That were it not for all the cries, the shots, the screaming cannister, one might have heard its steely beat. An inch more, and I would have been lost forever. But God had noticed me. Or simply, pressing His brush to the unfolding scene of battle, He bent the fabric of His canvas, and saved my life.

The last that I recall was the apple splitting with a crunch. It was Rumbold, my batman, who saw me fall and brought me to the surgeon's tent. When I awoke, wind was whipping through the open flaps; nearby another man lay screaming. Rumbold sat at my cot-side, and by his expression, I knew what was expected. Giving myself over to death, I asked that I be commended to my wife and daughters, lay back, and slept.

And dreamed: That I was back in England, walking through a vast green field, when I came over a hill and found myself before a tree. Children dressed in white were playing, running along the branches like little squirrels, each with an apple in a hand. Curious, they scampered down to me, and when I asked what they were eating, they told me that I had reached the tree that fed the souls. Would I like one? they asked. Yes! For I ached so with hunger. I stretched out my arms, but I was only in a field tent, dark, cold, the tent flap snapping in the wind that came across the plain.

Rumbold was waiting, and handed me a letter, from my sister, Constance.

Dear Charles, It is with a heavy heart that I inform you . . .

I read it slowly, unbelieving that a God so merciful would protect his soldiers, and not his soldiers' wives.

On My Return to Albany and the Fateful Decision Made There, and the Arguments Levied Against It

I spent the winter convalescing at the Quebec garrison. When I was at last well enough to endure the journey, I travelled back to Albany, where I found my own house empty and my daughters living with my sister.

It had been two years since I had seen these dear children, and they approached me warily at first, and then, with a leap, they hurled themselves upon me. They now were four. Identical born, Nature had preserved them as mirror images, with golden curls and rosy lips. They had dolls and play toys, and a cat, and they asked if I had killed anyone, and might I show them my wound, and had I heard that mother had left us? Now she was watching over them from Heaven; and they pulled me by the hands to show me the small memorial in the yard.

That night, when they were asleep, I sat in the parlour with my sister, her husband, and my brother, John, who had served beside me in Quebec.

They asked me what I would do now that I was home.

I told them of the dream. When I finished, my sister reached across the table and touched my hand. She was a great interpreter of dreams, knew all their meanings, and this one was obvious: I had been granted a vision of Eternity. The dream-child was my wife, the apple her devotion.

"But I woke before I tasted," I told her, and she nodded sagely and explained it meant that it was the will of God that I should live.

My brother asked when I would return to the garrison. The rumour was that I was due a promotion before the year was up; he had heard this from no less than Amherst's cousin, who had a lovely sister, a beauty, now of marrying age.

And I had seen her, and knew this was so. But at that moment,

I felt not joy, but a new pain in my chest, though it had healed so neatly during my weeks of recuperation. Distinctly I now recall the vision of my own reflection in the cupboard window. I wore, in those days, my sideburns long, and my wavy hair combed neat against my head. The white ruffle beneath my chin gave off the strange impression that I was somehow cloud-borne. And perhaps I was! For God *had* willed me to live, but it was more than that. Since the Plains of Abraham, my passion had only grown. I had tasted every apple that had crossed my path between Quebec and Albany. I turned to them. God had willed me to raise an orchard, I said.

On My Purported "Madness," and the Question of What Is a Lunatick?

Take a man in perfect health, and let him assert against the general opinion, and you will find such man accused of deviancy, or error, or madness. Such was my fate: that my sister and brother, while pretending to listen patiently to my dreams, were in fact conspiring behind my back. At that time, I was wont to wander the city, meditating on my future course, and it was upon my return from one of these rambles, that I found my house mysteriously empty except for my siblings. My daughters, Constance had me understand, had been taken on an excursion, which was the better, for I was to be visited by one Dr. Arbuthnot, who had agreed to my examination at half past three. I had no time to object, for the hall clock chimed the half-hour and was answered by an arrogant little knock. Now, if only the man had been as wise as he was punctual. Indeed, I knew of his reputation, both that which he flaunted, as a great surgeon of the War, and that which was whispered among the soldiers, as "Dr. Wrong-o-Leg." A reasonable man might, then and there, have refused him, and yet I was aware that it behooved me to pretend to cooperation. Therefore, I

girded myself to suffer this idiot, and smiled warmly, and welcomed him into my sitting room, while Constance ordered up
some biscuits. The doctor was in a buoyant mood, having just
come from a bleeding, in which he had taken off three litres and
seen the child return most miraculously to health. It was further
proof, he said, that illness persisted because the physician did not
confront it aggressively, and, perhaps because he knew I was a
military man, he employed the most martial language: what was
needed was to launch a full assault upon my fancy, hunt every last
vestige of the offending humour as one would the most heinous
traitor, and treat it without—and here he slammed the coffee
table—mercy.

Of course, I should have walked out right there, but his imperi-
ous manner so irritated me that I became set on defying him. Bleed
me! I told him, rolling up my sleeve.

Ah, but bleeding was for *general* lunacy, he said, whereas mine
was most particular—a *pomomania*, so to speak, a madness for
fruit alone. And he explained that a soldier who has lain out in the
field for hours will find his circulation altered by natural miasmas.
Thus the spleen was tilted off its axis, and, via a sympathy, began
to act upon the circulation of the lymph, which acted on the blood,
the blood on the phlegm, the phlegm on the bile, the bile on the *jus
gastrique*, and so on, eventually imparting its momentum to the
fluids of the cord. From there it was but a skip to the brain, lengthening the medulla oblongata and tugging open the recently
discovered lesser operculum, the "guardhouse" of the cerebrum,
through which raced fancies, notions, images, and even—and here
he whispered in a low voice—passions, or, as they say in French,
passions.

However, this was not the cause of my troubles.

"No?"

Dr. Arbuthnot shook his head quite gravely. After all, we all had
errant fancies, notions, images, passions. Indeed, last night, while

he was . . . Well, it mattered not what he was doing . . . But he fancied for a moment that his wife was his wife's sister, while they looked nothing alike! No, the danger was the premature *closing* of the operculum, and the subsequent trapping of said fancies, notions, images, and passions, which like rabbits, like hamsters, like—God forbid, rabbit and hamster together—entranced by that state of such promiscuity that might attend any shared enclosure within tight quarters, such as travelling with a lady in a warm, sultry, jostling carriage . . . Well we got the idea—it was a matter of augmentation, fecundation, intermingling, producing even more fanciful fancies, notional notions, passionate notions, fanciful passions, &c, &c, &c, the effect being, well—and with a flurry and flourish, he indicated—*me*.

"I'm sorry?"

"You," said the doctor. "This."

I told him that I did not follow.

Again, he began to muster his argument, but my brother interrupted. "And this dreaded . . . operculum . . . Might it be removed?"

"Remove the lesser operculum!" Arbuthnot nearly threw over the table in astonishment, and for a long time, he laughed with heaves that shook his teary jowls. And he had thought he'd heard everything!

We waited. Briefly, I hoped my siblings had seen that this man was loonier than I.

"Removed? My God, no!" said Arbuthnot at last. "But *opened* . . ."

The treatment apparently had been worked out long before the discovery of the lesser operculum itself. The key was to *coax* it open, with treats; it was quite fond of bread soaked in "raccoon seed" that had been bound for three days to the udders of an unwashed ewe. One needed but to inhale the mixture and the vapors locked up behind the operculum would flee faster than a horde of prisoners through an open prison gate.

Fortunately, he had a sample with him.

"Well?" asked my sister. By then I was so relieved that he would neither bleed nor purge me that I happily leaned forwards towards the vial that he'd withdrawn from his coat.

"Now inhale," said Arbuthnot. "Deeply."

For a long time, I inhaled. What none knew was that I had recently obtained, from my daughters, a most dreadful grippe, which had left my smelling apparatus entirely dysfunctional. Around me, I could see the faces of my family grow pale. There was a thump from the parrot cage. Even the doctor's eyes began to stream.

"And how will we know when the lesser operculum has opened?" coughed Constance at last.

But here the authorities differed. Laurentius described a puff of smoke, and Hundertius the dropping, from the nostril, of a little grain, while the famed Anthius proclaimed—and to this belief Arbuthnot subscribed—that Folly had no physical form at all.

"We will know," said Arbuthnot, "when he no longer thinks of fruit."

"It is not mad to think of fruit," said I.

"You be quiet," said Constance.

"Sniff, man," said John.

And I sniffed for a long time, until my sister fainted, for a ripe old ewe it was.

"Can't you just bleed him?" asked my brother.

And if you wonder why I have gone on so long about this story, it is that you might see which man among these was the ass, and recall it against any future slander against my sanity.

On Setting Out and What I Found

Proclaimed incurable, I was recommended to the madhouse, but my family knew well the dangers of such an incarceration to our name, so I was left to roam.

For my war service, I had been given a tract of land by the

Foxkill, but it took only a single visit to the neighbouring farms to realize that it was too flat, too wet for apples. So I left the girls with Constance and set out looking for new land, and because I was already well into my fifth decade of life and did not have much time left for error, I decided that I must seek the tree first and the land would follow. And a natural tree it must be. Many were the grafted varietals available in the nurseries of Albany, but I wouldn't have them. No pampered English import, no effete Continental still reeking of the paws of some French *fruitier*. Mine would be wild, American! Around it I would build my new life.

And so, that very month, as the carts began to make their way to village markets, I set out on horseback with Rumbold at my side.

And I came to realize that the country was overflowing: scraggly crab-trees grown up from cores tossed off in roadside culverts, ranks of stately Newtown Pippins, unnamed heirlooms growing in solitude in a settler's yard. How profligate America was with her apples! How had I never noticed? Less than two centuries ago, not a seed had touched the soil, and now they were everywhere, dropped by bare-armed boys with juicy chins, gentry passing in their carriages, lovers who in distant fields had hurled the cores and turned to different past-times. They grew from pigs—t, cows—t, dogs—t, fishs—t, sprung from raven droppings on the forking branches of the chestnuts. My God! Until that moment, I had never noticed; it was as if one might subtract all matter but the apple tree and still see, in what remained, the contours of the world.

And I tasted all of them. For two weeks, I tasted, I made my way through Albany and Ghent, across the hills and valleys between the Hudson and the Connecticut, scouring markets, interrogating puzzled farm girls with my questions about varieties and soil. Twice, discovering some resplendent, solitary tree of fruit unlike any I had ever tasted, I approached the nearest hovel and made an offer for the land. Both times, they refused me. For why would they trust this stranger with his servant lingering behind him? It was *their* patch, *their* tree, the benediction granted for *their* stewardship. *Their* land.

An American tree, of American soil: if this was the first innovation that would lead me to glory, my second was to fill my pockets with coins and follow the children. They all had a tree, the children did—a sprawling coppice in the graveyard depths, a silver dryad with her many-marbled fingers, a dell matron with long arms drooping her burden to the earth. They showed me trees with oblong red-black fruit or tight, smooth spheres as white as pearls, fruit with russeting as thick as potato skin around the sweetest crackly flesh. And then, far up a valley where a thin string of farms had pierced the howling wilderness, a snub-nosed boy, perhaps sensing easy prey, haggled another penny for his services, and led me on a long and winding path deep into woods.

Ah, how I recall it as if it were yesterday! The thickets were so dense I had to leave my horse with Rumbold. The mist was drinking-thick, the path was stony, serpentine, vanishing into a meadow like an illusion, before emerging, just as illusory, in the wet cowlick of a wind-blown field. Leaving the meadow, we entered a final grove of oak and chestnut. The land rose slowly, then steeply, and at the point of this inflection, I could see a little cabin, and I readied for another settler to tell me off his land. Or worse, I thought, registering the gathering evening, the silence into which the whistling boy had fallen: Perhaps my guide had scented more than a penny to be found on this stranger, and had led me to a brigands' den. And it would end here in the dark woods, my pockets empty, a thief's stiletto in my heart.

But still I followed. Drizzle became rain. I could barely see the bounding boy; at times I had but the dark parting through the ferns to guide me. I reached the cabin. Most strange—this home of log and stone, with wooden beams that once had held a roof, now fallen. More ferns grew from the walls, vines curled around the broken wood, and asters bloomed amidst the rubble. But I did not have time to inspect it further, for the boy was whistling again and I followed him past the cabin, to the tree.

The ground beneath was two apples deep, and they fizzed and popped as I approached. Animals had picked clean the lowest branches, the wind was blowing through the surrounding birches, the boughs swayed. Nearby, a single rain-wet apple beckoned. I reached; it slipped beyond my fingers. Another wind: again the apple rose, up, up, higher, and, at the height of its curve, it seemed to pause as if considering the worthiness of its petitioner, and swung down into my hand.

Thin veins of crimson ran through its spring-green flank. Faint streaks of russeting, a blush that seemed to change in colour as I raised it in the failing light. When I bit into it, I had the sense of tasting not only with my tongue, but deep within my palate, a scent more than a flavour, as light as lemon blossoms, before a second wave came spreading through like syrup. What in heaven was this? I wondered. An apple, of course, an apple in all ways, and yet I had never eaten an apple like this. No one had ever eaten an apple like this.

Erratum: the boy had tasted, the little sandaled creature now eyeing me from where he crouched upon a fieldstone. I wanted to weep.

I felt the forest watching as I reached up to take another apple. Then I paused. The house was empty, the ground thick with rotting windfall, and still I felt as if I were trespassing on another's bounty. So I took just four more: for Constance, for Alice, for Mary, and one for Rumbold, who must be cold and worried back on the road. Then one more for myself.

It was pitch-black when I reached the place where we'd started. Rain streamed over my servant's hat. Grinning stupidly, I held up the fruit and said, simply, "I found it." Then I rummaged in my pocket for another penny, but the boy was gone.

On the Land: Its Proprietors, and Purchase

The land was part of a grant made to a minister, Carter, to bring him to the nearby town of Oakfield: five hundred acres, of which, in the past two decades, he'd cleared a bit more than a dozen. How happily he parted with the bosky uplands that rose behind his farm! As to the cabin, we could find no clue to its prior inhabitants. It was not of any form common to the Natives who had lived there before the town had claimed it, while the custom of the recent settlers of the country was to raise a wooden frame. Nor could I find any record of it at the County, where the tract maps showed only a few trees and a fanciful decorative panther. But besides the pacing beast, nothing. Sometimes, said the Register of Deeds, they turned up abandoned homesteads; the land was hard, and few endured upon their errands. But I had no need to worry about another claimant. In the eye of the Great and General Court of Massachusetts, the deed was clear, the cabin did not exist. Perhaps among the Indians there was someone who knew the answer, but most of them were gone.

I purchased it there, in the Register's office, the Reverend Carter's rosy tongue emerging from his beard to lick the nib before he signed. Then I rode to Albany, stopping only for a short night's sleep in a crowded wayside inn, joining in drink with the men I now could call my neighbours.

It was evening of the following day when I arrived back at my sister's. I was still in the doorway when the words came tumbling: the house, the land, the tree. By then I had it all planned out. We would begin to build that month, and plant there in the spring.

She followed me into the parlour. "But the girls . . ."

Ah, but I'd decided many miles back. They would come with me—it would be better there, away from the city's leering tradesmen, the untethered migrants moving up the valley, tempting girls with promises of frontier life. And I'd bring Rumbold, and our old servant Anne.

My sister shook her head. She didn't understand, she said. So far away? And I had a tract by the Kill that could grow anything!

"Not anything!"

I rustled through my bag and removed one of the apples.

"What's that?"

Ah, but to her great dismay she knew the answer.

I smiled.

"You have bought five hundred acres for an apple tree. In New England."

"Taste it," I said. Though in the dark room, absent the dew, the wind, the fruit that rested in my fingers seemed but a meagre offering.

She shook her head again.

"Taste it," I cried.

A tear ran down her cheek. Truly: fancy had taken me!

"Taste it."

"But you will starve," she said. "You will be killed by bears, by wolves."

"Taste it!"

"Then leave the girls with me," she said.

And as if they had been summoned, I heard a shuffling behind me and turned to see them staring wide-eyed at the dusty apparition standing before their weeping aunt.

"See, you have wakened them," said Constance. And then, in a firm, commanding voice: "Alice, Mary, back to sleep."

Poor Constance! She had forgotten that an officer of the French and Indian campaigns was not just a soldier, but a diplomat, trained to recognise even the most fleeting opportunities to forge alliances. Often far from our command, surrounded by tribes with shifting affinities, those of us who led our companies into Quebec that season were forced to seek help at every turn, even if it was just to find a path across a frozen pass, or skirt an enemy camp. We were experts at the science of allegiance, at bribery, at pressing any advantage we could find.

I reached into my bag for the last remaining apples. Into the air: one, two. Stem over calyx.

"Alice, Mary: catch!"

On Our Removal to the Country

Passion sometimes gets the better of Reason. What made a wood hospitable to an apple tree, did not mean that it might so readily accommodate a man. If the settler who had once raised his cabin did so with log and stone, I had all modern conveniences with which to advance construction. What I wanted, however, was a road. It was but a mile from the carriage road that ended at the Minister's, but oh, what a mile! The memory of my arrival had condensed the journey into a scramble; barely did I recall that it was hardly passable by horse. This in turn brought a challenge of personnel. Such was the swarming into the wilderness during those years, that it was nigh impossible to find an idle hand, and in the end I had to settle for a motley gang I gathered from the Albany docks: five Dutchmen of visage each more criminal, a Spaniard who spent his leisure whittling with a vengeful intensity, and a pair of Negroes, Sam and Thomas, whose origin I saw not my business to enquire; the scars that glistened in the autumn heat told me enough.

Sam had brought his wife, Betsy, who served as camp cook and general preserver of civilization, for, were it not for her severe enforcement, our group would have immediately dissolved into drunkenness and villainy. But no iron fist could stay such ruffians forever. By mid-month, one Dutchman had stabbed the other, and the Spaniard had vanished with the Minister's housemaid. It was sheer fortune that I secured a carpenter in nearby Oakfield, who arrived with his gang at our site and set about raising the house with swift efficiency, while my remaining crew helped clear the fields and dig the well.

John Carpenter was the name of the carpenter—God works in odd ways, for he came from a family of cobblers. Puzzled was he over the cabin, and reckoned to reduce it to a garden wall, but I'd have none of that. History haunts him who does not honour it. In England, our manse turned up Roman coins with regularity. Piecing through the wreckage, we were able to surmise that once it consisted of a single room and sleeping attic. There were fragments of a rough-hewn table, the rusted head of an axe, and in the corner, a dusty chest delivered up a copy of a Bible. It was very fragile, with many writings in the margins, but small and difficult to decipher, save for quotes from Scripture, suggesting our prior lodger had not been some brutish settler, but, rather, a devout, God-fearing man.

By then, Mr. Carpenter had acceded to my desire to leave the place's ghosts in peace, and when we had raised the roof again, he stuccoed the walls and laid a floor, opening but a single passage to connect the cabin to the new house, itself of simple construction, two stories high, and three bays wide, with a roof that rose steeply to a central chimney and descended to a single story in the back. And Providence smiled on us, for the day our Carpenter brought the windows up from Oakfield and secured them was the night of our first frost.

She looked then much as she does now: a clean façade of lemon yellow, with white shutters on the windows and a tall black door. A home of perfect symmetry, were it not for the ell on her left flank. In the dooryard, we planted the sapling that would one day grow into the noble elm that now stands forty feet and gives us shade in summer.

It was then that I returned to Albany to fetch my furniture and daughters.

On the Growth of My Orchard

And so it was that my little family came to settle in this remote station in the north woods. I will admit that there were days when I faltered in my conviction. How I recall the miserable cold that accompanied our journey, the rude inn where we took shelter. An icy rain had fallen on the day of our arrival, the world was cloaked in glass, the girls stared wide-eyed at the crystal palace that awaited. From behind us in the sleigh, the furniture creaked its protest; the piano hammers leapt against the strings. Oh, I thought, would I had waited until summer, to reward them with limpid streams and wild berries! To take such tender children from their home seemed nothing less than extirpation. And so that their father might pursue his fancy?

What had I done?

But the die was cast, and work awaited.

How swiftly did the months then follow! We took our cuttings of the tree in February, grafted them in March, and planted them in April. By summer, a neat square of a hundred little saplings was rising beneath their Mother's watchful gaze. The first gave fruit the third autumn of our sojourn; the following year, some forty-seven trees were blossoming, and the fifth lifted our census to ninety-three.

The September of that year, I gathered 2,397 apples, less the taxes imposed by my coterie. We were ready to bring them to market.

The question then arose of what to call our apple. Nature cares not of the names imposed by men, and yet one must mull carefully, for the farmer who does not keep vigilant, will find appellation thrust upon him. Mr. Lee, of Bettsbridge, has not been served by the popular name given to his pale, paired, wrinkly codlings; nor Mr. Palmer his long brown fruits of such alarming taste.

By then both the snows of winter and long summer evenings

had left my daughters and me many an hour to consider the name by which the world would come to know our apple. My girls, who had learned to graft before they learned their letters, could not be counted on for their vocabulary, but what they lacked in learning, they made up in instinct. As I read to them the list of varieties in *The Pomological Manual,* they hurrah'd their favorites, Mary's earnest gaze brightening each time I lighted upon a Royal or a Regal, while her impish sister cast her vociferous vote for the Winter Monster, the Hogsnout, and the Bright Young Maid. None fully won their hearts, however; nor did the tradition of using place-names meet their approval. No, the apple's name should be our family's own, for, barring the snotty ragamuffin, we'd been the first to taste it. But what? Swiftly did my daughters dispense of Osgood's Pippin as too ordinary, Osgood's Nonpareil as too immodest, Osgood's Rose too floral, Osgood's Prize too presumptuous, Osgood's Belle too Gallic, Osgood's Harvest too matter-of-fact. Osgood's Red didn't do justice to the hints of green that made it so lovely. Osgood's Dessert sounded like a pastry, while Osgood's Sugar ignored the complexity of the fruit. I need not comment on the sad fate of Osgood's Wife.

Many nights we played this game. For a while, we settled upon the Osgood Beauty, and the Osgood Glory was a durable selection, before the girls eventually dismissed it as too martial. Defeated, I even considered, simply, Osgood's Apple. Slowly, the novelty of the search began to dim. Increasingly, we passed our evenings reading, or singing, and Mary's voice could conjure angels, while Alice on the fife brought joy to all who heard. Together we composed many a ballad about our woods, and the animals within. But still, I pondered on my apple. Was this my *pomomania?* Too many times had I been mismeasured: call a man mad once and he will be forever vigilant. But what could satisfy me? For a Fruit is a Thing, while that which I was searching for was nothing less than that which could transcend the tangible, speak to astonishment, invoke not only pleasure, but the perception of something vast, supernal, nothing less than enchantment itself.

Which, in my greatest eloquence, I at last propounded to my little audience.

"You mean *Wonder*?" they asked, at once.

Some Notes Concerning Technique

Long have I thought that I should write a book on technique, as I have learned much over the years that may aid others in their orchards. For now, I will simply state, for the record, my position on some of the great debates of our profession.

Pruning should be done in moderation. There are those who would remove crossing branches, and others who might trim the young trees to assure a regular form. If this is your want, then who am I to deny you, but as my head bears an unruly mane, so I prefer my trees. The dead branch might meet my saw, but I am cautious in my amputations, for even dead branches serve purposes, and who knows if it is not the nesting bird that over-watches your garden?

The gall of a green lizard does not prevent rot.

A painted tree is an abomination; they should be adorned only in Moss and Lichen.

Placing a stone in the forks of a tree branch is a child's charm; it should not be practiced systematically. Like all charms, it will lose its Magic when it becomes a Method.

Beware the shell-less snail.

There is not a fence that will keep out the porcupine; to try is folly. One must pay one's taxes, sometimes.

Wilkinson's Phosphate is a false promise that presses a tree into an untimely maturity. Similarly, Powell's Ash is a fraud. Contrary to the claims on the label, Pliny's Bisphosphate was not developed by the Pliny of the *Natural History*, but Pliny Norton, of Worcester, who is deliberately opaque concerning this distinction.

On the topic of fertilizer, here I will admit a brief confession. Some dozen years ago, I became aware that a Mr. Fludd, of Bettsbridge, was slandering me in the marketplace, repeating the tired accusations of Lunacy. Of course, I knew the cause of his campaign was envy. Many years before, Fludd, having been convinced that he might find his wealth in farming, had tricked a group of Indians into giving up a sizeable property with the promises of future payments. When, as one might have expected, such monies never materialized, and the Indians lodged an objection with the Great and General Court, Fludd circulated a rumour that the men were harassing his daughter, had stolen from the garrison stores, and so forth, the effect being that the ire of a local militia was raised, and the Indians, by then living in meagre circumstances, were met one night by an angry mob that killed one as an example and chased the rest, first to the small mission at Corbury Junction and then onwards. His territory secured, Fludd set about establishing one of the largest farms in the district, and while the land yielded, it did so poorly—pest took his corn, his cows got green-tit, and one of his farmhands died from a poisoned potato. Still, the sheer vastness of the estate more than compensated, and yet old Fludd was not to be satisfied, having staked his pride on the cultivation of apples. By then the Osgood Wonder had established itself as the nonpareil of the district, and one day Fludd approached me with an offer to buy cuttings from my tree. I refused, and told him that my fruit would have nothing to do with his bloody business. He skulked away, and I had thought the matter finished when one morning I was in the garden and I noticed some severed branches and immediately understood that I'd been robbed.

Now, I was not worried by competition. By then, the Wonder had proved itself utterly incapable of transplantation—whatever magical connection held it to this soil meant that elsewhere it was but a common, unremarkable fruit. Nevertheless, the theft rankled, and when I confided in Rumbold, he was equally outraged. Together we hatched a plan of revenge, most perfect, but requiring us to wait three years to implement, until the stolen Wonders fruited over at Fludd farm. Then, once the old thief had realized, to his fury, that the much-anticipated tree was but a mealy codling on his cursed soil, I sent Rumbold to his parts, where he befriended Fludd's gardener, drank with him, and one night, in a state of pretended inebriation, whispered the formula of the "great fertilizer" that was the secret of my success.

"Truly?" asked the gardener.

"And sometimes he has me participating," said my faithful batman.

Which is why, to this day, if you are passing the Fludd property on a morning, and you look into his apple orchard, you will see the diligent farmer, his wife, their three daughters, and their grandchildren, all squatting red-faced and bare-bottomed at the base of the accursed apple tree, thinking this will be the s—t that brings them fame at last.

On Bachelorhood

At times, a question has been raised about my bachelorhood. Would it not be easier, I have been asked, to take a wife?

A casual answer may be found in that I *was* twice married, loved my two wives dearly, and mourned deeply upon their passing. Often I am stirred by the memories of Julia's sweet lips and Hannah's figure, and wish that we might have grown old together, and compared our worries and our aches.

To mourn a lost friend, however, is not the same as wishing for another. *Pomona* is my mistress. Too often I have sensed, in the hungry gaze of the Albany widow or the lonely farmer's wife, a plan to tame me. But how can she who has not had her breast pierced by a bayonet sweetened with an autumn pippin understand my passion?

This said, I would be remiss not to share several observations on bachelorhood and the temptations of marriage.

Indeed, the young man in search of a bride, would be well advised to consider apple cultivation. Open any of our chivalric narratives, and you will conclude that it is the knight that is most desired by the female of the species. Well, I have been a soldier, and I am well familiar with the shy eyes that gaze out at a passing regiment from gently parted curtains, but can assert that there is nothing like the sight of an apple to ignite the female imagination. Is it an accident that our artists chose none other than *Malus domestica* to depict the forbidden fruit which tempted Eve? Was not Eve herself in fact a *cutting*, taken from Adam's rib?

Still, I was an old man of fifty when I came to this place, and no great beauty. Time had creased my brow, garlanded my chin with several companions, and furred both ear and nostril generously against the cold. And yet, I had been here but one season, when the maid of V——, my neighbour, having tasted of the fruit, offered to help me with its harvest, tried to tickle me in the orchard, and asked, more than once, if she might climb the ladder while I secured it, an offer which I turned down, well suspecting what sight she had in store should I look up.

No matter the temptation, I have always put my garden first. Have I dallied? Perhaps, but I will not stoop to tell of it. I know the rumours as to how I obtained cuttings of the Striped Pearmain of Mrs. Kirkpatrick, who guarded her husband's prize-winning trees after his death. Of this, I will venture no comment that might besmirch the reputation of that good lady; the enchantments of the grove should in the grove remain.

On the Raising of Daughters; and the Judgement of Paris, and How It Might Have Ended Differently

Busy we were in our industry, Mary fierce in her vigilance against marauders, Alice gently laying out the fruit so that it would not be bruised. But many were the quiet hours of midwinter when there was little to do but sing or talk. Mary and Alice (say it quickly, *Malus!*) never tired of hearing how the hedgehog carries apples on his quills, or the pelican mulls hers in her pouch to make a cider for her young. And how many times I told them of the legend of Hera's gardens, planted with golden apples, gifts from the goddess Gaia on her wedding day, guarded by the Hesperides and a hundred-headed dragon at the garden's gates! It was a great marvel for them to hear how Heracles was sent there in his Labors, to steal three apples, something our fawns accomplish every day.

But their favorite story was that of the Judgement of Paris, for which I had woven a delightful version, which I recommend to anyone who loves a fruity myth.

A banquet was held in celebration of the marriage of Peleus and Thetis. All the gods and goddesses were invited save Eris, Goddess of Discord, who, jealous of having been excluded from the festivities, swept down from the heavens and tossed upon the table an apple on which was written TEI KALLISTEI, "For the Fairest." Of course, Hera and Athena and Aphrodite each argued for the honour, until Zeus, weary of such bickering, ordered Hermes to yoke them together and carry them to Mount Ida to be judged by the shepherd Paris.

And Hermes did, and, pushing forward the bickering women, handed over the apple and whispered into Paris's ear that he must choose.

And how I would look back and forth between my daughters— as little ones of seven, young girls of ten, and budding maids of twelve—and hold the Wonder out before them, equidistant (for a father must not play favorites), and cry *"Tei kallistei!"* And each in turn would reach for it, shouting, "I! I! The fairest! It is I!" But each time I would pull it back, as Paris must have done, as the goddesses jostled and elbowed and made their famous offers: glory, empire, the hand of the most beautiful woman in the world.

"Which did he choose?" I would ask them, as I ask you, my reader: which—*kleos, tyrannos, eros*—would you?

"Helen!" my daughters would cry, for they knew the story, knew the abduction and the war that would follow. But always with laughter in their eyes.

For they knew, this time, the tale was different.

"Wrong," I would say, and, palming the Wonder, I would take a bite. "In this version, Paris chooses the apple."

On Riddling

Another great past-time of mine was the writing of riddles, and I am told that some of these have gone on to become famous in our district. As one cannot trust literary posterity to children, I here include my favorites.

Green of girth
And hair but one
Brown in frost and red in sun
(The answer: an apple!)

Fat red man
Hanging by one hand
Sways in the wind that blows down on the land
(Also an apple.)

Eye but no head
Skin but no hands

Flesh but no bones
Children she has none
Until she's dead and gone

(This was less popular among the wee ones, but remains a personal favorite. The answer, also, is "apple.")

Finally, these two call on the passage of time.

White at dawn
Green at noon
Red at vespers
Brown in death

and

Sniff her in April
Bite her in September
Come Father Frost
And we will
Sip her in December

Apple and apple! Anne and Rumbold feel the last one should be reserved for those of a riper age.

Some Apple Lore and New Interpretations

The Greeks were not the only ones to give the apple mythical status. It was a tradition in the old country for young men, on Twelfth Night, to go into the orchards with bowls of wassail, and pour the cider mixture over the tree roots in hope of a good crop.

Now, I had long been skeptical of this practice, for was not my Wonder proof that no such rite was needed? Alone she had grown and fruited, with no reveller to douse her skirts. And yet I can recall the day I came upon my tree, and the cider-y odor of those rotting apples that fizzed beneath my feet. Was this not a wassailing? Might not the apple wassail its neighbour? Might not *our* rites be but those copied out of Nature? What kind of offering have you left, friend? Might we all not learn to wassail, in spirit, if not with fruit, then with words or deeds?

This no doubt ancient practice has been said by some authorities to be related to an older myth of the so-called Apple Tree Man, that spirit said to reside in the oldest tree in the orchard, guardian of her fertility and of the health and well-being of its inhabitants generally. And while I do not believe the legend of the Man who leads the wassailer to a golden treasure (for what use is gold to an orchardist when he has his trees?), I have come to the opinion, generally, that he who does good to the land shall be protected, while he who trespasses upon her will be met with most violent return.

Concerning My Decision to Go to War (or, a Lamentation on the Brevity of the Life of Man Compared to That of His Trees)

Dawn approaches. Though the sky is dark, I can sense about the house, the stirrings of morning. Looking back upon these notes, I see that what has gone unmentioned are those very events that necessitated this writing. War has come! And once I had thought I had finished with her entirely! But if one finds no mention of Politics in these pages, no Acts, no Dates and Declarations, it is because this is a History of Trees, not Men. That is, *it was*. But now the pitch has risen so that even deep within my woods I hear it. In the market, the calls of apple-mongers have been drowned out by the dueling tirades. Militias practice, and though the war is far away, man seems to will the fight upon these peaceful hills. When asked to take a side, I claim allegiance to my Wonder. But whereas once they chuckled at an old man in his dotage, now they demand to know my loyalties. What can I answer? My very blood is suspect. Even if I were to pretend to Rebel sympathies, there are too many who know the deep English roots of Osgood stock.

Thus, when my brother came thundering up the road with Orders promising me my old Battalion, I turned back towards my orchard that I might ask for her advice.

For a quarter of my life I have toiled here. Still my old tree flourishes above her children, now themselves tall enough to give me shade. How I wish that I had come here sooner. That I might have watched my orchard grow, my trees enlace their branches. Sought new varieties and crossed them with my old. Learned what other wonders this earth could yield.

And yet, I know my work is done here. I have found my corner of the world, planted home and garden; both are thriving. Having sown my seeds, I must defend them. I do not trust the rabble that thinks the land is theirs, and not vice versa. The Indians too fear the revolt. Like them, I have seen the swarming men, their locust's harvests. Like them, I join our King.

Today we march east, to reconnoitre outside Albany. Rumbold, as ever, will watch over me. With luck, I will return by Christmas, and will not miss another season.

But if not: Alice, Mary! Remember, always: she is an eating-apple, never press her into cider. Beware the waxwing as you would the worm, and do not over-prune, even if the trees grow shaggy. My testament is simple: this all is yours to hold together. Soon you'll be of age to welcome suitors. May they share your affection for this piece of earth.

Mary: be gentle with the porcupines. They are thieves, but they are also Nature's creatures. Alice: do not forget your fife!

Three

OVER the course of the forty-one years since the death of their father, Alice and Mary Osgood, joint proprietors of the locally known apple of that name, had lived a life which seemed, at least to others, unchanging. In some ways this was an accurate assessment. As twins and spinsters, they had but a single birthday to celebrate; by virtue of their isolation, they received few invitations. They still slept on the same straw-stuffed mattress they had slept on as children, woke each morning with the crowing of the rooster, winced at their cricks (neck, Mary; back, Alice), swung out of bed into the skirt and blouse and jacket laid out on a bedside chair, and went downstairs. They walked softly, a habit from their childhood, though there had been no one else, for years, to wake.

There were of course, occasional exceptions—the rare night one might spend alone if the other were waylaid by a snowstorm, or the weeks of illness in which one, and then the other, stayed in bed. But such variance was rare. If life, as the man said, was a song, theirs was more refrain than verse. And yet to have claimed that a warm spring morning walking over earth carpeted with apple blossoms was somehow the same, substantively, spiritually, as a cold winter noon spent pruning, or a harvest evening heavy with the smell of juice and hay—this would have betrayed an ignorance not only of country life, but of the thousand seasons—of frogsong, of thunderheads, of first thaws—that hid within the canonical Four.

Similarly, a neighbor, looking upon the sisters' persons, might also have remarked on the fidelity with which Nature had duplicated her creations, and considered it unnecessary to differentiate the two. But this also would have betrayed a failure of imagination. For while Alice and Mary looked so similar that there were times, passing before a mirror, or staring down into a quiet pool, that one might smile at the image in greeting—nevertheless, they had, over the years, both become aware of a fundamental and widening difference between them.

And had they been asked—though they were never asked—they would have both said that their recognition of the difference had arrived one warm September morning of their fifth year in the north woods, when, standing side by side, they'd watched their father ceremoniously pick the first apple of the season, consider it for a moment, and then, with a twinkle in his eye, cry, "For the fairest!" and hold it out to them in his hand. And that would have been it, a joke upon the tale they'd heard so many times, about a vengeful goddess and the judgement of a handsome prince. They would have raced to grab it, laughing, knocking the apple from his fingers, falling upon the warm earth, each knowing that whoever grabbed it would share it with her sister.

That was how it was supposed to happen, how it had happened each time before. That fateful year shouldn't have been different, had they both not sensed that, in the briefest instant before their father realized his error, he had turned, almost imperceptibly, to Alice.

For Alice *was* the fairest. They were the same, with the same pale eyes, the same apple cheeks that still shone through sunbrowned skin, the same lips which on their father had seemed oddly cherubic, the same curls hidden in the same bonnet, the same callused hands and muscle-knotted calves. They were the same height—tall enough to reach an apple which might escape a fawn but not its mother; the floor creaked to the same pitch beneath their feet. And yet, somehow, from the earliest days, even before their father's error, they both had known that there was something in Alice that the world took notice of, and this same thing was not in Mary. Had it been there in the beginning? Neither could recall their mother beyond a dwindling, coughing presence in a nightgown; their nursemaids, for what they could recall, were careful to dole out both reward and punishment in equal measure. They had flanked their father on the journey to the mountains, from *that* life, to *this* one, and if Alice had espied a family of deer the first morning of their waking, Mary had seen a bobcat slinking past the apple tree. They did not know this, but there were times their father stood above their bed and marveled at the way they even breathed together, and when they woke, all four eyes opened at once.

And yet, they knew. What a charming child! a visitor might say of Alice; while Mary, if she was noticed, was *prudent, clever, wise.* Their father's gaffe, then, came less as a surprise than as a confirmation. For years—indeed, forever—Alice would carry with her both the memory and the emotion that came with it—first joy and love, then, followed on its heels, a shame and sorrow and a worry for her sister. And Mary, also for years—indeed, forever—would find excuses to drag her sister before the mirror, as part of one game or another, to laugh at the strangeness of the duplication, but secretly to study. She saw it, she couldn't see it, and it pained her to think that there was something perceived mostly by others. But she also realized, as did Alice, that when they were alone together, the memory of the moment vanished, and they could become, again, the same.

❉   ❉   ❉

They were four when they came to the place in the north woods, and although later in life neither could recall the journey, by then they had repeated the story so many times that it seemed fresh in their minds: the snow kicked up by the struggling horses, the creaking sled, the strings of the piano faintly jingling. They spoke of the night spent in the crowded inn near Corbury Junction that since had developed an unsavory reputation; the druidic, white-cloaked hemlocks that lined the long road from Oakfield; the distant farmhouses of their new neighbors, the people and possibilities that lay within. And they recalled—and this they truly could see with clarity—the moment that they reached the meadow, for a freezing rain had coated every sprig of winter grass with ice thick as their fingers, and the sun was splintered by a thousand prisms, and as they dropped from the carriage to race the horse, they felt and heard and saw the shattering of glass.

Years later, veterans of so many winters, they would look back upon their removal to the mountains as an act of folly, and laugh and shake their heads at the disasters that might have befallen such an unseasoned crew. Had their father considered the dark, cold nights that they would spend with horse and Anne and Rumbold all, sleeping by the kitchen's hearth? The long road to town to buy provisions? The stalking wolves that howled after the storms? But they had few wants, and they feared nothing. The hill above the house seemed built for the sleds that Rumbold fashioned them. And in the center of the field, there stood the tree whose fruit they'd tasted that preceding autumn, on the day their father had returned, wild-eyed, hair aflame, coated with dust.

From the beginning, it was the apple that had defined their days. From Albany, their father had brought a dozen books on gardening, from Evelyn to *The Pomological Manual*, which he consulted nightly as if it were the Bible. It would be many years before they understood that such an enterprise—to leave one's home and venture off to raise an orchard—was considered by others to be eccentric. All adult life seemed eccentric, and the nights they read aloud from Pliny seemed as normal as those they passed in psalm, Mary singing, father on piano, Alice on her fife. From the beginning, they knew the tasks awaiting them. A single tree does not an orchard make, their father warned them, and when their first February came, they watched him gently cut a hundred scions from the bare tips of the apple's branches, and helped him carry them inside the house.

There, in the dining room and parlor, they'd set out a hundred little burlap sacks of earth, each bearing a rootstock purchased from a nursery in Oakfield. And their father showed them how he cut each stock so that it fitted neatly against each cutting, and they helped him bind the pair with bandages (their little field hospital!), and slathered them with a grafting wax from tallow, beeswax, and rosin that hardened in the winter air.

It was Mary who woke first to find the miracle that spring, and nudged her sister awake to see the budding apples. Each time they came inside over the weeks that followed, it seemed as if they were entering a lush, enchanted world, so different from the one outside. How they wished that they could keep the trees indoors with them! But then their father said the earth had thawed and it was time to plant, and they carried out the saplings one by one, while he and Rumbold dug holes in ranks that striped the slope. "Forward!" their father bellowed when he saw them flagging, bugling with a curled hand and conjuring for them a future life of boundless pie and sauce.

And then it was June. Bright, creamy flowers bloomed on the chestnuts. Buttercups appeared on the waysides, and light-brown frogs gathered in the mornings by the ponds. Some days their father had them help him in the garden, but he had Rumbold and then a hired farmhand, and so he took them walking in the forest until they came to know the paths, and then he let them go alone.

There were many walks, but one that was their favorite. A path ran up from the house, through the stumpy field where wild squash and potato grew in summers. At the entrance to the woods, the trail split and turned, gave off other trails, and sometimes seemed to disappear entirely, before it reappeared in unexpected places. The secret, they learned, was that they just needed to keep going to find the winding paths converge again.

Even in summer, the forest was cool. White-tailed deer browsed in the fern and snakeroot. They walked side by side until they reached a fallen trunk, and Alice, without breaking stride, leapt up, keeping pace with her sister, dropping as she reached the up-turned roots. Side by side again they continued, until they reached another log, this time on Mary's side. And now *she* vaulted onto it while Alice walked below.

Their first stop was a brook that tumbled over blue-grey ter-races. There the trees wore thick moss stockings, and the ferns splayed their fronds neatly, like fingers. A scramble up the stones brought them to a pool beneath a cataract that sometimes trickled and sometimes coursed with spray and thunder. Here the stones along the path were so high they had to help each other climb them, and as time passed, they came to name it "the Giant's Stair-case." In the smooth bark of a beech, above the viburnum, they carved their names. Squirrels perched like sentries on the rocks and watched them strip and dive into the water, and each year, they dared each other to jump from greater heights.

From the brook, another deer path continued up the mountain at a gentler angle. Along the way, they'd stop to rest inside the hollow of an oak where they imagined Indian mothers sheltered with their children, and later, when they were older, they reckoned Indian boys would come and kiss their sweethearts. From the oak, a path led back down to the house, but on days they weren't needed they took a second route that scaled a jumble of ferny boulders they came to call "the Danger" and crossed into a forest of a differ-ent character, with rocky soil and low, sinuous trees that barely rose above the whortleberry and laurel. Sometime not too long before, there'd been a fire, and the trunks of pine and oak were black and interspersed with sassafras with funny mitten leaves.

This, they called "the Fire of London," and from there it was a short scramble to a barren knoll, where the trees thinned out and a view opened to the valley. There they could see the top of the mountain above, and the dark-green patches of the hemlock groves, the tall crowns of chestnuts and swaying oaks.

They called the mountain "Blue Mountain," because that was its color when they first saw it, though, depending on its mood, it could be bright green or black or purple, or silver after an ice storm, or white with snow, or gold with sun. If they climbed a rocky outcrop, they could see their home, the growing orchard, and beyond, the farm of the Minister, and each year, as he sold another parcel down the valley, they saw new patches opening in the forest, and smoke rising from the fires set to clear the fields. In the summer, thunderheads came marching, right to left, and they would sit and watch the slinking shadows and the scouring rain, until they became great connoisseurs of cloud-shape, and waited with mounting anticipation for the rains to sweep across their perch.

By then, they had usually been gone so long, that one or the other would worry that their father would be angry, though as they grew older, and taller, and their strides longer, they began to realize that their travels were never quite so far as they had seemed when they were small.

There were two ways to return. They might retrace their steps, or descend in the direction of the declining sun, through a stretch of forest that seemed older and grander, with trees so large that, even standing on each other's shoulders, they couldn't see above a fallen trunk. Because it was often evening when they arrived there, it seemed even darker and more mysterious than the other dark, mysterious stations of their walk, and their father, who also loved it, named it, after Merlin's wood of legend, "Brocéliande."

❖   ❖   ❖

In their ninth year, warned by Anne that the girls were growing wild, their father declared they needed schooling, and would be attending classes with the Minister, who had just opened a class-room in his home.

He had announced it in church one Sunday, and their father, who was rarely in attendance, had heard it from Anne, who always was. So he bought the girls new shoes and bonnets, and walked them to the Minister's house.

There were twelve other children in the class, from four fami-lies. The day was divided into subjects: Scripture, Penmanship, Geography, Mathematics, and History, though it quickly became apparent that the Minister knew little about Geography, History, and Mathematics. For Penmanship, they copied proverbs written on the blackboard—

Temptation ruins many.

Idle hands are the devil's workshop.

The wicked live for rebellion; they shall be severely punished.

—while "Scripture" consisted mostly of the Minister's expostula-tion of a theory that had arrived to him that winter, that the events of the Bible had actually transpired in New England.

It hadn't taken him long to work out the details. Moses had been placed in a basket of cattails and hidden by the banks of the Connecticut River; the remnant of the Flood could still be found in Lakes Pontoosuc and Winnipesaukee; the Behemoth of Job was a moose; winter sumac was the burning bush as seen by Moses; and the first Beast of Revelation was not one creature, but a wolf pack, which explained its many heads. As for the Red Sea, he'd found a pond near Shadd's Falls where the tannins from the hem-locks turned the water the color of claret, and in winter, if one crawled out on the creaking surface, one could look down and see a tangle of an "Egyptian chariot," that had long been mistaken as a capsized mail coach from New York.

Once, he took them high into the woods to show what looked like a deer skeleton beneath a fallen bone-white birch, but in fact was Jonah and the whale.

He laughed, he read aloud, he pointed at the heavens. And yet they both perceived, within his triumphs, a touch of tragedy. Alice thought he needed a new wife, but Mary blamed his theory, and said he knew that it was nonsense, but he was in too deep. So he just went piling it with more nonsense, like burying a pile of old manure with fresh. In fact, she said, the theory was probably the reason his wife had died, from despair.

In any case, each day the class went back home and reported what they had learned to their parents, who measured this education against the loss of the labor, and soon the only children remaining were Alice and Mary, the Minister's son, and a poor thing named Abigail, who passed the entire lesson sleeping with her head upon her desk. No one bothered to wake her, even when the Minister, seized by a realization, would stop mid-sentence and send them out so he could think.

This left the sisters with the Minister's son.

George Carter Jr. was seven when they first met him, and an expert in the country. From his father, he had inherited a name and the preacher's rhetorical mode of the sermon, but beyond this, was a different creature altogether: tatter-shirted, dirt-fingered, a bit raunchy of the nose. He had a slight speech impediment, though this did nothing to stop him from talking. And while the father's boots were always polished, the son had long ago disposed of them entirely, not out of poverty, but because the Indians "didn't need 'em either," an assertion he maintained no matter how many times the sisters reminded him of moccasins.

He knew the locations of sixteen bear dens, the name of the ugliest dog in Massachusetts, the best blueberry swamps, and which trees smelled like wintergreen and which like almonds. He even had some of his own money, for he collected leeches and sold them to a middleman in Oakfield, who marked them up and sold them to a Boston surgeon to feed upon the high-bred asses of his fancy clientele.

And he knew the people too. After the Minister's was the house of Robert Jones, a higgler of knickknacks and thingumbobs, who drank straight from the bung, hung a sign from his fence saying "Smallpox" to keep away the tax assessor, and was prone to threatening intruders, even if they were just walking down the road. Then Efraim Ash, who had the "best land" but the "worst luck," for his wife had gone mad from eating an eggplant, and once he'd shot a catamount, but hadn't killed it, and the creature came and slaughtered all his horses in revenge. After came the van Hassels, a Quaker couple who'd moved up from the Hudson even before the Minister, had a daughter married to an Oakfield tanner, and liked to grapple in the barn muck when they thought no one was around.

The girls didn't understand this at first, blamed George's impediment, and when he explained further, they didn't believe him. So one day when the Minister was seized mid-lesson by his realization that Lot's wife was a salt lick and dismissed the children so that he could work out the implications of his discovery, they followed George down the road, where they hid in the van Hassels' woodlot for half the morning, slapping midges and calling him a liar. For Anne had explained to them the means by which husband and wife consecrate their eternal bond, and Mary was explaining piously how God Himself was present at the sacred moment of begetting, when there was the sound of the door and the farmer led his wife across the yard into the barn.

George waited, "to give 'em time to get it started." When, at last, the sound of bleating rose across the yard, he whispered

"Now!" and led them, bent like stalking braves, across the grass, to where he'd placed, during a prior viewing, a stone so he could reach a knothole. Inside, Mr. van Hassel had Mrs. van Hassel on her knees. Both were naked except for their boots. He brayed with each heave, and her great breasts swung so far that they slapped up against her face. The girls took turns peering.

"'Em likes to pretend 'em two are animals," said George, in anticipation of the natural question, for the van Hassels lived alone, and owned a four-poster bed that was the envy of the valley and presumably could have accommodated such a ceremony. He took his place, squinted, studied the scene with an appraiser's eye, and then turned back to the sisters. "'Em's goats today," he said, thought for a moment, and added, "Varies, though."

Then Mary looked again, and then Alice, and then George again, rotating, until each grew tired of balancing on the stone.

"Got stamina," said George, as if in apology, but the girls had turned their attention to a pair of blister beetles engaged in the same act as the van Hassels, though far more delicately.

"Should we catch frogs?" George asked them.

"Yes!"

Another time, he took them to meet an Indian.

This too the sisters thought was a tall tale, but five miles down the road was a thin path they'd never noticed, and at the end of it they found a cabin. How disappointing! they both thought, for they had been imagining a wigwam, strung with bearskin blankets. Instead, the door opened, and out came an old man dressed just like their father. George Carter presented them as "Miss Mary Osgood and Miss Alice Osgood" and the Indian as "Mr. Joe Walker," though when the man repeated his name, it didn't sound like "Joe Walker" at all.

They sat outside. A woman came, dressed in sun-faded gingham, with long grey hair in braids, and Joe spoke to her in what sounded like Indian, and she went back inside and brought out a cake, which was just like any other English cake, and he even had cups like the cups English people had. But his face was definitely an Indian's face, thought both Mary and Alice. They ate. Mostly George Carter talked, and told Joe about where they had been, though he left out the part about the van Hassels. Then he asked Joe if he'd ever eaten rattlesnake and porcupine, and before Joe could answer, George explained to the sisters how the Indians prepared them with chokeberries and currants. Also, he explained the names of the tribes from the area, and how many of them had been massacred. He said that all people talked about was how Indians would scalp women and children, but the way he looked at it, he would probably do the same if someone—say, the Swedish—were to come and sicken his family and kick them off their land. "I'd give it to 'em Swedish good," he told Joe.

Joe didn't say much. He waited with great forbearance while George was doing his explaining, and only once—when the sisters said they lived in the house at the top of the road—did he seem curious, and asked them if they knew about the previous owners. But they didn't, except for the story their father told about discovering the place, and the axe head that he'd refitted with a handle, and the old Bible which he didn't let them touch because it was so fragile. In any case, George didn't shut up. And Mary, whose longing for precision and clarity extended even into language, thought that there really should be a word for this particular kind of explaining boys did to girls, while Alice watched the old man and felt a kinship with someone who had learned to untether part of himself and let it roam, while the rest of him was bound by circumstance. At last, when George had finished explaining King Philip's War—"the bloodiest of the bloody"—he abruptly asked if they could see the pharmacy, and Joe led them inside his house. There were no skins or scalps there either, but a small shelf of books, with tattered and missing covers, and tables and benches on which were arranged sheaves of herbs, and piles of little flowers. The girls were quiet, astonished by the array. There was a doctor in town, but he prescribed garlic for everything, while Joe's collection looked like they had wandered into a second meadow, only sorted.

How different the woods must seem to him! thought Alice, and Mary instantly felt a surge of competition, for there were plants there that she didn't know at all.

At the edge of the table was a great pile of flowers the girls recognized as gravel root or purple boneset, and Joe explained he made a tincture which he sold for typhus, sprains, and heartbreak.

Heartbreak, interrupted George, came from bee stings. There was a girl who died of it in Oakfield: his father had ministered at the funeral. She'd swollen up to the size of a sow, before she went. "Near burst," he said, and shook his head somberly.

How terrible, thought Alice, but Mary had lost all patience. "Comes from longing," she said. "Any fool can tell you."

And the three children turned to Joe, who began to speak, but then, deciding otherwise, kept his silence, as if they were on their own to figure this one out.

When the girls were thirteen, the Minister died, and left the house in the care of his old servant Jenny, and George Jr. was sent to live with family in Boston. Now the nearest school was fifteen miles away, so the Major decided to educate the girls himself, though he liked teaching about as much as they liked studying. And it was pruning season. Already they were fierce workers, could handle a plow, pluck a chicken faster than their father, and thought nothing of reaching inside a cow to turn a calf.

By then the saplings were nine-year-old trees, and fruitful, and the Wonder had a reputation. Some afternoons still found them together on their old walks, but more often Alice went alone. The farm seemed smaller as she grew older, and there were times when she needed to escape. On the hottest days, she lay on a bed of moss in the darkness of Brocéliande. Ferns as high as ostrich feathers waved above patches of partridgeberry. She brought her fife and *Fifer's Companion*, but mostly she was silent. Birds sang from the branches. The moss was cool and soft, and sometimes she would open her blouse and lie against it, or lift her skirts, to feel it against her legs. Her thoughts would wander, to the young men and women she'd met over the years, and she wondered how they passed their days, if they also felt so cold in the winter and so listless in the heat.

From Anne, she'd learned to sew, and in the summer of her sixteenth year, without her father or her sister knowing, she bought a bolt of pink chintz in Oakfield, and sewed a pair of matching dresses, with frilled cuffs and a ruffle over the rump. Her father was delighted by them, and to commemorate the harvest, he hired a painter to paint the sisters' portraits, each holding a gleaming Osgood Wonder. Mary cooperated, but later said she thought the dresses were frivolous, and refused to wear hers again, even when they were invited to a dance in Bettsbridge.

For why should they dance? asked Mary. Their father played piano beautifully, and with her voice and Alice's fife, and the ballads they composed together in the manner of the old country, they had a surfeit of music. And there was so much work.

And she preferred to work, loved work, loved her father's praise for her strength and mind for business, the assiduous guard she took against the waxwings who came to eat the apple blossoms, marching through the orchard with a shotgun in her arms. She read the *Agricultural Record* even before her father, and at night, she told Alice about the newest varieties, and her plans to make the Osgood Wonder known throughout the world.

She designed a long flail for gathering chestnuts faster, a basket that she wore on her back, and at seventeen she announced that, since God valued Industry, she would no longer waste the Sabbath walking all the way to church. What she didn't say was that church, like the dances, was fraught with danger, that each time the young men smiled at Alice, she saw her father handing her the apple. That she feared that they would go together and she would leave alone.

Still, she couldn't avoid people altogether. When Abigail, the sleeping child of their school days, turned overnight into a blushing flirt and soon was married, they were invited to the wedding. Dancing started shortly after noon. In the barn, crowded with whirling couples, Mary waited for an eternity, while young man after young man passed her by. At last, one of them approached. She felt her heart leap. But he was looking for her sister. Might she know . . . ?

Alice had gone off walking with Amos Crawford, the oldest son of the town fence viewer. When she returned, Mary told her she was leaving, and stomped off with a switch of beech, slashing at the goldenrod and fern. Alice followed at a distance, bemused by the theater, until, ahead, she saw a paper-wasp nest, and then her sister's quickening gait. "No!" she shouted, and ran and caught her hand.

That night, a great storm came. Thunder sounded up and down the valley, and sheets of rain fell against the house. Staring out their bedroom window at the forest, they watched the lightning strike the valley. Each tree stood out against the hillside; the high peak glistened; they felt as if they could see the fleeing stags, the bear, the catamount as grey as stone. Wind poured down the slope; the house creaked; water streamed from the long roof. The storm swept past. And then they looked down to see that they had gripped each other's hands so tight their thumbs were white.

The storm had nothing to do with Amos Crawford, Alice told herself, and yet it seemed as if the heavens had registered their objection. At her side, Mary was thinking the same thing.

Later, as they lay in bed, moonlight streamed in through the window. When at last Alice drifted off, Mary sat up in bed and looked down upon her sister's sleeping form, framed perfectly within the glowing rectangle, and thought how she had everything she'd ever need.

There were other dances that season, but the harvest was approaching, and so they turned their attention to the orchard. There they climbed into the highest branches to complete the pruning, inspected for pests, applied shellac to limb wounds. They trimmed the coppices and weeded, built fences to keep the deer away, and hunted the marauding partridge that had grown too bold.

They were there, in May of their nineteenth year, when their uncle came riding up the road with news of Lexington, and their father's new commission; and in February of their twentieth, inspecting the damage from an ice storm, when Rumbold came riding back alone.

❊   ❊   ❊

They erected a stone for their father in the orchard, and the following summer found his remains in a war cemetery in Pennsylvania, dug him up, and buried him high on the hill, looking down over his trees. They held no ceremony, for Patriotism had swept across the valley, and everyone knew which side he'd served.

For the next three years, they battled outbreaks of canker and tent caterpillars, attacks of waxwings, and accusations of Loyalism. The first was vanquished with applications of vinegar, the second by vigorous smoking, and the third and fourth by the placement of two scarecrows in redcoats to scare the birds and mock the Crown. Then, fearing this would not be sufficient to placate their neighbors, Mary arranged a generous donation of each year's harvest to the local Revolutionary garrison.

At first Alice objected. The scarecrows made a farce of their father's memory, she said, and with the disruption of the war, they couldn't afford the donation. But Mary reminded her that Loyalist farms were being confiscated across the valley, and the true betrayal of their father's memory would be to lose the Wonder. And as far as the books went, she'd kept a close eye on their yields and, assuming the coming into fruiting of the newest saplings, they'd get by.

Alice had to listen. She had little mind for numbers, and had long ceded business matters to her sister.

Also, she had found a suitor.

Arthur Barton was a potter, originally of Greenfield, who'd lost his foot in an accident at his garrison, and come to work in his uncle's shop. They had met in the General Store on East Street, when she had gone to look at the newest napkins, and he to buy rope for a bridle, though the truth was that he usually bought from Lem's, and had just followed her inside.

She was carrying a shopping basket. Despite his crutches, he offered to hold it for her, and when she was done with her purchases, asked her if he might walk her to the edge of town. He'd been a drummer before the accident, and as they walked, he tapped out a string of paradiddles, ruffs, flams, and charge strokes. He spoke of the ways the cannonballs came hissing down the field of battle, the sergeant saved when a British cutlass was embedded in a turnip he had stolen and hidden in his hat, and how he'd seen Howe at Bunker Hill but missed his shot. He'd lost his foot when a gun belonging to a baker from Cambridge went off at half-cock during training exercises. He said that he was lucky, given his profession, that he hadn't lost a hand. Then he told her about salt glazing.

He didn't ask her many questions, though when she told him her name, he exclaimed, "Like the apple!" Twice, he looked over and said he'd never met anyone so pretty, and though Alice wished that he might ask about her family, she was conscious of her father's service on the wrong side of the conflict, as well as the vague sense that her sister was a threat best left unmentioned. And, after all he'd seen, he should do the talking, she decided. His shoulders were broad, he wielded the crutches at a swift clip, and showed her the leather pads he'd crafted for his armpits and his hands.

They parted at the crossroads before the entrance to the valley, where he asked if he might hold her. At first, she thought he was just referring to her shopping basket and hadn't finished his sentence, which confused her, because he already was holding it.

"No, you!"

Other than at a dance, she had never been held by any man, and, with a vague thrill, worried that she might end up like Mrs. van Hassel. But they were in broad daylight, he had gentle eyes, she pitied his wound, and around them, the trees were full of courting songbirds; it was the general condition. Yes, they were virtually urging her! *Kiss-ee-him, kiss-ee-him, kiss-ee-him.* So she nodded. He put the basket down, took both crutches in one hand, and put the other around her waist and drew her close. He kissed her cheek, and she kissed him back, just a peck on the mouth, and then he smiled and pressed his cheek to hers. For a long time, they stood like that. Then she whispered, "Someone might come!" and pushed him away, but gently, for she feared he would fall over. His face was flushed, and he was grinning stupidly, and she realized she must look the same.

He left her with a handful of wild sweet williams that he gathered from the wayside. It was eight miles home, but Alice felt like she was floating. She took out her fife, and as she walked, she played "Come Thou Rosy Dimpled Boy" and "Ye Belles and Ye Flirts," and "Haste to the Wedding," before pulling up short with embarrassment. Oh, but how beautiful the day was! The lady slippers seemed to have blossomed since that morning, violet butterflies swam through the sunlight, and how the birds were singing—yes, they were really going at it—she'd never heard such jubilation. She wanted to tell someone, but when she thought of Mary she felt the day grow dark.

But why? she heard her sister asking. Why, when we have each other?

Alice wished her father were alive. How she missed his irreverence, his sweet tooth, and his pungent curses, the way he flirted with the village girls. For *he* could reason with Mary, argue that a second love didn't diminish the first. Even Anne, their former servant, could have spoken to the virtues of marriage, but Mary had dismissed her during the war, when expenses tightened. She could even imagine telling Rumbold, good, loyal Rumbold, but he'd left for Canada after her father's death. There was a tradition in the valley to whisper secrets to the bees, but others said one should only speak to them of mourning. So she waited until a loud wind to say aloud, "I love him!" And she felt the same rush of warmth within her as she had upon the mossy bed and in the potter's arms.

She flushed, and suddenly was crying, grateful that she still had miles to go.

She reached home in the early evening. "Flowers!" said Mary, when Alice handed her the basket, and for a moment, Alice worried Mary could read everything in the way that they'd been arranged, the stems bruised by a hand broader than her own.

Instead, Mary went through the basket with a critical gaze, approved of the candles, asked whom Alice had bought the cowbell from, and hoped aloud that she hadn't paid too much for the cheese.

Then she stared for a moment at Alice's face as if she saw something, though Alice had already checked in the mirror and knew that no evidence of her tears remained.

All day, all week, Alice thought of Arthur Barton, his callused hands, and how they must wet the clay and knead the clay and spin the clay, how the pot swelled as he worked the gravid billow in his fingers. Pressing the asters, one by one, inside the pages of the *Fifer's Companion*, she wondered when he would show her his leg, and imagined touching it tenderly, seeing his shame at first, and telling him that it meant nothing, that he was a hero, a brave man, and his wounds made her love him even more.

When the next market day came, she announced, as off-handedly as possible, that she would like to go to town.

"But we don't need anything," said Mary.

Alice said she thought they could use a new cider jug.

"There is nothing wrong with our current jug," said Mary.

Alice disagreed. She thought it smelled musty. And she had seen one in a shop. Or if not, maybe a cream pot?

"Which potter?" asked Mary.

"Barton," said Alice, as calmly as she could.

"With the crippled nephew?" said Mary.

Alice paused. "I . . . Yes . . . the soldier."

"Maybe I should go and look," her sister said.

And Mary could not be dissuaded.

Alice tried. For what good would it do for them both to go to Oakfield! There was so much to do on the farm, and the road was terrible.

Then, on second thought, perhaps she didn't need anything.

But Mary was insistent. "First you want a jug, and now you are against them," she said.

"I am not against jugs," said Alice. It just didn't smell so musty after all.

"Well, that's good," said Mary. And she offered to go alone.

Alice knew that Mary couldn't be dissuaded. So, on Saturday, they laced up their boots, put a nose of bread in their blouse pockets, tied their bonnets, and set out.

It was a warm morning. Rain had fallen the night before, and droplets matted the snakeroot that spread across the forest floor. Mary walked swiftly, as was her custom. The two said little, and when they passed the Minister's Jenny, they walked only a way with her before Mary said they must be pressing on. When they reached town, shortly after noon, Alice made a point of wandering through the market, lingering by the cutlers and the drapers, with the vague hope that her sister might be distracted.

"Enough with this loitering," said Mary. "I want to see the jug."

Arthur Barton was outside his shop, talking with a customer, before a row of urns set out for market day. Struggling to keep up with her sister, Alice saw him see Mary walking toward him, saw his bright smile when he recognized her, his smile fade when it was not returned, the brief register of surprise when he saw them both. Alice hadn't mentioned her sister, but she assumed he knew, like everyone knew who had fits and who was widowed and who had lost a leg.

And he knew, he just hadn't been expecting . . .

"My sister," said Mary, reaching him first, "has expressed interest in pottery."

By then, Alice had come to her side. She wrung her hands. For perhaps the first time in her life, she had no idea what Mary would do next.

The other customer scented the makings of a scandal and moved away, but not so far away he couldn't listen in.

Arthur Barton looked between them.

"Hello," said Alice.

"She is looking for some crockery," said Mary.

"Well . . ."

"You have crockery, don't you?"

"Well . . ." And he looked confusedly at Alice, who tried at once to warn him with her eyes, and to distance herself from what might pass.

Mary pushed inside.

Alice followed. It was her first time inside the shop, which was cool and smelled of damp earth. There was, as she might have expected, pottery everywhere. Great kegs and urns were arrayed about the floor, and on the shelves were lines of bone-colored butter pots and pitchers, while a row of chamber pots sat modestly upon the lowest shelves. Apart from a few dishes glazed in burgundy, the only color came from cobalt fish and deer or flower decorations. And the stamped name BARTON, in tiny letters on each neck. Instantly, Alice felt a surge of pride for Arthur, made even more tender by the unspoken threat.

"May I?" asked Mary, standing before the highest shelf at the back of the room, and reached up to take a jug before Arthur nodded. It was a large vessel, with a decoration of a sad-eyed stag. Her face was hidden in her bonnet as she turned it roughly. As she tried to put it back, Alice realized she was trembling.

Arthur also must have seen. "Here, I'll take it," he said.

"You'll take it?" said Mary, her face still hidden, but now her voice also beginning to tremble. Terrified, Alice looked for the other customer, hoping, futilely, that he had followed them inside. But they were alone, and in an instant, she became aware of the magnitude of all that might be broken, saw, in her sister's bent and trembling form, the fury that could, in one sweep, send the entire shelf of pots crashing to the floor. Please, she thought, please, don't. She could recall the moment when she'd stopped her sister at the wasp's nest. Now she feared that if she reached out to touch her, it would only set her rage in motion. At her side, Mary took a sharp breath and handed back the jug. As she took another, Alice saw tears brimming in her sister's eyes. Now, fearful that she would cry, would drop one of the vessels, she touched her. "Mary, please, let's go . . ."

But Mary didn't even seem to hear her. She passed the vessel to the potter, took down a milk pot, turned it roughly, and then put it back. Another. Then a cream pot, decorated with a rose.

"Mary . . ."

"Quiet, Alice!"

Now she grabbed a twin pair of cake pots graced with little birds, looked at them dismissively, and thrust them into Arthur

Barton's hands. He looked between them, eyes begging Alice to stop what they both now feared would pass.

"Mary, please. Let's go."

But she wouldn't listen, and Alice was too shamed even to meet the potter's pleading gaze. She wanted desperately to leave, to be home again; wanted to put her arms around Mary and apologize, to turn from Arthur forever. For how could she leave her sister? They had lost a mother and now a father, and still they had built a life of joy and meaning. And now *she* had threatened it. *She* had been the one to roughly handle something delicate, risked its falling through her fingers. She understood.

But Mary wasn't ready, and it occurred to Alice later that Mary, for all her fury, had not come to end things but, in her tensed and coiled fury, had not actually decided. Rather, she had come to see for herself, to weigh, in one hand and then the other, whether the life which one of them desired was a life the other could endure.

A tear ran down her face. She handed Arthur the final vessel.

"We don't need one," she said at last.

In the years that followed, there were other suitors, young, then older, men who appeared briefly in their lives before they came to recognize the futility of their petitions.

The cousin of Lucretia Parsons, who kissed Alice in the darkness outside a barn dance, and pressed his hand against her breast. The young doctor who had come to attend to Mary when she was sick with pleurisy, and returned for Alice two weeks later. The soldier traveling home from his Albany garrison, who spied Alice walking along the road and asked if she would join him in the field.

And Alice yearned.

In each stolen caress, each quiet conference held in the shadowed parlor while Mary lurked about the house, each bold proposition, she sensed the ghost of Arthur Barton, who, she learned, had died the summer following their one-day courtship, from ty-phoid fever contracted at the Springfield fair. She dreamed again of being folded in his arms, and wished that he'd been bolder, drawn her off the road into the meadows, amidst the boneset that old Joe Walker once prescribed for heartbreak. The memory of the van Hassels braying, once so risible, now came to pain her, and she dreamed about what might have happened had she led the potter onwards, up into Brocéliande, to lift her skirts, and let him press her down into the moss. And then, maybe, she thought, had she presented her sister with the inevitable, a son, a *scion*, they would have found a way forward. There would have been no scene at the pottery, and Arthur would have stayed with her instead of travel-ing to Springfield. She dreamed then of the bounty she would bring him, *them*, and in the wanton of her fantasy conjured up a brood of six, of eight or ten. Yes, ten would be the perfect number, she thought, watching the big bustling families that overflowed the hay carts at market, but she would be happy with eight, with six. She would be happy with one.

Occasionally, when she couldn't help it, she'd betray an attenu-ated version of her yearning to her sister, and wonder why they couldn't find a pair of brothers who would take them both.

But Mary, who knew, perhaps better than Alice, the force of her sister's desires, gave no concession to her daydreams. No, she did not think the rattle on sale at Lem's was darling, and to dress a child with such a bow was nothing but a frivolous waste. And in the same place in her heart where Alice kept her list of children's names, Mary kept a different list—far better referenced and anno-tated—of all the local husbands who got drunk and beat their wives.

Other times, she liked to speak off-hand of mothers who'd died in childbirth, and when their cow calved one summer morning not long after the barn dance, she looked down at the wet, bleating creature, and said, "Not so easy in a woman, that." And she'd give examples. Hattie Martin's baby had presented with a single hand, got stuck, and died. Hattie too. A hand, just sticking out, said Mary, waving like a drowning sailor. And Zipporah Putney, who'd behaved unchastely in the buttery . . .

"But I know!" said Alice.

"But you don't," said Mary. "Else you'd stop wishing so."

And the years passed, and they grew old.

Still, Alice dreamed at times about another life and what might have happened. When she was alone, she went to the woods, though she no longer pressed her skin against the moss. High in the trees, the woodpecker drummed its flams and paradiddles, and she imagined it was the ghost of Arthur Barton come to serenade her. By the brook, on the beech, the letters of their names grew thick and dark. The orchard thrived. In the spring of their thirty-ninth birthday, they began to experiment with hybrids, and a decade later, when the apples fruited, they discovered to their delight, above their father's grave, a dappled, pink-fleshed varietal, which they immediately agreed to propagate that spring.

To celebrate, they went to Oakfield, and ate dinner at the tavern. A family was dining nearby, and the father kept looking at them, until he leaned over and asked if they were the Osgoods, "as in the Wonder." "The very same," said Mary proudly, while Alice recalled how Arthur Barton asked the same thing years ago. When dessert came, Mary, who'd mysteriously vanished that afternoon, presented her sister with a pair of identical painted silhouettes, facing each other, which she'd sat for by herself.

Time began to work more steadily upon their bodies. At night, on days of heavy work, their joints ached, and Mary, after falling from a tree at fifty and breaking her femur, was left with a limp. Reading of the benefits of tobacco for rheumatism, they took to pipe smoking. In the winter, when their skin grew dry and cracked, they rubbed each other's heels with a mix of lanolin and beeswax, and because both agreed that walking in stockings led to unnecessary darning, their feet left oily prints out of each side of the bed and down the stairs into the kitchen. They visited the parlor only to compose their songs.

If one was angry, she would take her pillow to the foot of the bed and sleep head to toe, and so anger came to smell of sheep and bees. But, no matter how they fought, they never slept apart.

And fights were rare; they knew the contours of each other's grievances too well to expect any kind of resolution. Alice slept late, forgot the ladder in the orchard, cleared her pipe with her finger, wore her blouses unbuttoned at the top, gave away too many samples of the apples, spent her money at the market on ballads when she could write her own, and sometimes let the deer graze on the garden, just so she could watch them.

And still she had a habit of wandering off. And Mary, who did the mending because Alice took too long and always added flourishes of lace or ribbon, wondered at night if she might stitch her sister into the covers, and in the mornings let her out.

As for Alice, her grievances were less specific and less spoken of, for they included Mary ruining her life. For there were times when she suddenly felt the need to run. The cold mornings she would wake to Mary piling wood in high twin domes, though they had more than enough to last the winter. The nights she found her sister practicing her penmanship with proverbs, or studying her almanacs, or sharpening the old axe well past what was needed for a tree. The day she learned that Mary had declined a wedding invitation from Rumbold in Canada. And then there was the matter of the sheep.

❊ ❊ ❊

The matter of the sheep had first arisen shortly after their fifty-first birthday, when Mary, in Corbury Junction, saw a prize Spanish Merino called Cristobal. It was hardly the first sheep to find its way to the valley: much of the country had been converted to pasture. The sisters even owned one back in their thirties, a swayback ewe called Sukey who gave sour milk and hid in bleating terror at the time of the rut. But Sukey was like sandpaper compared with Cristobal, and Mary, in Park Square, ran her fingers through the samples of fabric with nothing short of lust. The problem was that the cost of a single lamb was more than they got from a year of apples, for the Spanish Crown kept an embargo on exportation. So, that night, Mary added to her prayers the fruitfulness of Cristobal, and the defeat of the Bourbons. And while Cristobal could do no more than nature allowed him, Napoleon heard her prayers and invaded Spain.

When, three years later, the first Merinos arrived in the mountains, it was Alice who spoke reason to passion. One: the price of wool was too low. Two: sheep were still expensive. And three: their orchard was flourishing, and would provide until they died.

"We don't need one," she said with a shiver of revenge, recalling her sister's verdict in the pottery so long ago.

But Mary persisted.

Within a year, Alice's first objection was taken care of by the declaration of War against England, and the new tariffs against English wool.

The second was settled incrementally by the natural concupiscence of the ram.

As to the third, in late April of their sixtieth year, the sisters woke to a strange violet tint to the sky, and over the next few days, they watched the sun dim to a flat red disk, and sunspots flicker across its surface. Suddenly it grew colder. Frost fell overnight and burned the apple blossoms; snow fell on the 6th of June and killed the strawberries and a second frost in August froze the corn while it was in the milk.

For the first time in their lives, they feared they might go hungry.

Up and down the valley it was the same. Mold seized the wilted crops and people slaughtered their milk cows. In the markets, the price of oats rose fivefold. Down in Oakfield, wagons and oxcarts piled with swaddled children went west toward rumors of Ohio. Daily, Mary grumbled. If they had had sheep to pasture, if Alice had listened, if they hadn't relied so much on apples, this might not have happened. By the time spring rolled around again—a real spring this time—Alice relented.

And so they set about becoming sheep farmers.

But they needed pasture, and the small field their father had cleared to graze their cow and horses wouldn't suffice.

Together they followed the paths they used to take as children. Up the Giant's Staircase, and over the ferny perils of the Danger (slower now; they were no longer seven), stopping at the river, unable to resist the water, stripping down to swim, white limbs yellow in the amber water. Then on again, up through the Fire of London to the outcrop. But this was all too steep and difficult to clear for pasture, and they continued down through Merlin's forest. "Well?" asked Mary. "Well, what?" said Alice. And she knew that her sister had set out not to scout a pasture, but to prove to her that they would need to clear Brocéliande.

She wondered then if her sister had known about her secret visits to the forest, and the mossy bed where once she had conjured up her ghostly lovers. Was that what Mary wanted: to destroy this final refuge of her imagination?

No, this couldn't be. It was too complex, too calculated. They needed pasture. That was all.

"But . . ." was all she managed. And she thought of old Joe Walker and wondered if the feeling that she felt deep within her chest was the breaking of her heart.

"But you agreed," said Mary. "I've already paid one hundred and twenty dollars for the sheep."

Alice said that she'd agreed to sheep, not murder.

"Another year like last and we'll be finished," said Mary. And wasn't Alice tired of mending her own boots and using old bed-sheets as her skirts?

Alice was tired of a lot, but neither of these were what she was tired of. But she knew when she had lost.

They hired five men from Oakfield to help them clear ten acres. Mary joined them, for she could wield the axe as well as any of them, but Alice found reason to be away. The sound of the trees falling sounded to her like screaming, and she was unsettled by the vehemence with which her sister worked, her sleeves rolled, her face wet with sweat and specked with wood chips.

Nor did she like the way they trampled everything, for her father had taught her to walk softly.

She said this.

"Then go to Ohio," said Mary. "Go, pack your cart."

Alice didn't answer. It felt like silence was the only weapon she had left. "Father had to clear the woods to build the orchard," said Mary, and though this was true, it did little to appease her sister. Nor did it help when Mary reminded Alice of the acres and acres that stretched back beyond the pasture's edge. But I don't know those woods, thought Alice. With Brocéliande she felt as if she had made a pact simply by her presence, but she knew that if she said this, she'd be met by mockery. A pact? she could hear her sister answer. And did you sign it? And did the forest sign it? And in what? In mud? In sap?

And something new and dark settled on the sisters and their life.

In the savaged field, the fallen trees were rendered of their bark, left pale and moist and animal. The stumps they burned, and Mary set about to gather stones to build a wall around the pasture. She worked fiercely, hauling twice as many stones as any of the men, heaving the wheelbarrow through the August mud and dry ruts of September. She worked straight through the October rains, and came in at night, steaming like haystack, as if she might combust. Her old fracture pained her, but she said nothing, and Alice said nothing, though she saw her sister wince. They both knew, without saying it aloud, that it was Mary's penance, just as they both knew that, once the field was cleared, her penance would be complete.

❊　❊　❊

Winter passed, then spring. Summer came. The apple trees fruited as if making up for the lost year, the sheep bleated in the pasture, and in July, shortly after their sixty-first birthday, a man came walking up the road.

He was short but held himself erect, and looked about the place as if he were trying to refresh his memory. His coat was too black for a farmer, but on his head was a floppy felt hat, and in one hand he held a walking stick. He introduced himself as George Carter, the Minister's son.

His son! they both thought. For they remembered the runty, jug-eared boy who used to show them, among nature's many wonders, bear dens and blueberry swamps.

Alice went inside and returned with water and a plate of wild strawberries, and Mary dragged a third chair to the shade beneath the elm planted by their father. When George sat, he removed his hat and wiped his brow. "Some heat!" he said.

He told them his story, half of which clearly was fiction; the challenge, they realized, was to recognize which half. After his father died, he'd gone off to live with relatives in Boston, went to Harvard thinking he'd become a minister, then fought in the war and surely would have been shot down in the field, were he not so short. Once, he'd laid his cloak across a puddle for Abigail Adams, only to hear her say, "This is America!" and walk around the side of it. Then he'd set out to see the world. He'd been to London, then Paris, where he was "caught up in the Revolution," and had barely escaped with his head. He'd spent the last fifteen years in the West Indies and Brazil, where he'd seen a chess-playing pig and a horse with cloven feet like the devil, and had cured a man of a madness by pulling out his teeth.

"Brazil!"

And he'd become a bit of a botanist, traveled in the Amazon, written a treatise on the Brazilian cacti, and settled in Rio de Janeiro, where he'd spent the last years working on a philosophical tract on freedom and the rights of man, and stirring up trouble.

By stirring up trouble, he meant that he had been turning slaves against their masters.

"Couldn't you have done that here?" asked Mary, who subscribed to two abolitionist magazines, and contributed a dollar a year to a collection for Simon, the town ward, who had escaped slavery in Georgia, and had consumption and three children to support.

"We think alike," he told her with a wink, though he didn't elaborate further. Last fall, he'd received a letter from a lawyer saying that his uncle was thinking of claiming the property, and decided it was time to come back. For he had always had dreams of returning, to end life as he'd begun it, in the country.

"And your wife and children?" asked Mary.

He laughed. But he was a bachelor!

For some time, the sisters were silent. Then Alice reached up and brushed a loose strand of hair back beneath her bonnet. "Well!" she said.

After that, George Carter came often.

For he was inept. The Minister's Jenny still lived in a small house on the far edge of the property, but she was in Springfield with a sick sister. By the end of the first month, the rats had emptied out his grain stores, George had set a fire in the kitchen, and he couldn't bring himself to kill a pig, not even a chicken. Then his climbing beans were eaten by the deer, the turnips by rabbits, and a pair of porcupines made quick work of his peach saplings.

"He will not make it the winter," said Mary.

"He needs a wife," said Alice. Lately, she had been remembering Arthur Barton, and Amos Crawford, and the cousin of Lucretia Parsons, and the impudent soldier who invited her to join him in the fields.

"I think a servant would do just fine," said Mary.

When autumn came, they took him to the orchard and showed him the apples, leading him along the paths between the trees.

Alice cut him slices. The juice ran over her hand and down her wrist.

"They haven't changed," he said. And he told them how he recalled the rainy day when he led the Major to the apple, while his tall, thin batman waited with the horses by the road.

And Alice cried, "That was you!"

For he had become part of the mythology.

"Do take some home with you," said Alice.

"I really shouldn't," said George Carter.

But it just so happened that he had brought a sack.

From then on, instead of weekly, he came every other day, to help Alice with the harvest. When she picked, he held the basket, and when she climbed the ladder to reach the highest branches, he held her waist so that she wouldn't fall.

And Mary watched. One night, after a harvest, as they lay in bed, she said she thought he was a lecher.

"I think he is a gentleman," said Alice.

"He is an old lecher," said Mary. "A man's hands on you like that! Why, if I didn't know any better, I would think he was inspecting you for milking."

"Was far from the milking parts," said Alice.

"But heading rapidly in that direction," said Mary.

Alice smiled. "Milking days are over," she said. "He can try all he wants."

"There is a word for letting a man try all he wants," said Mary. "Anyway, I don't know what makes you so rosy-cheeked. His mouth doesn't look much better than his barn, I say."

Alice laughed now, relieved to have an opportunity for levity. "We aren't so toothsome either," she said.

"But I'm not courting," said Mary, and almost said, *Have never been.* "That's the difference." And if you had to choose? she thought. Would it be me or him?

Instead, she said, "Anyway, what does he need so many apples for? A man can't eat that many himself."

"I have my suspicions," Alice said.

Her suspicions were confirmed two Wednesdays later, when he came walking up the road carrying a jug of foamy amber. "A trade in kind," he said.

"How gracious!" said Alice. But when she went into the kitchen to get glasses, Mary stopped her. "The Osgood Wonder is not a cider apple."

"Oh, Mary," said Alice. "Come now. It's hot out. It will be delicious." She smiled. "And George seems practiced in the making."

Mary didn't find it funny. "You know that Father didn't plant this orchard to grow cider apples. It's in his letter. You know that."

"Father's dead. The orchard is fruitful, and I don't think the apples will mind to see a few of their number end up in George Carter's cider. He was the one who found the tree, after all."

They both knew that she was right, but Alice saw how red her sister's face was, how she was trembling, and she recalled the fateful day at the pottery so long ago. She said, "I will tell him, dear, that they are best if they are eaten. But this time, it would be unneighborly to refuse."

"Well, I won't join," said Mary. And so Alice went down to the tree alone, and she took the seat that George Carter offered her, and smiled as he poured cider into the glasses. Then he raised his, and she hers, and they drank. For a long time, they sat out beneath the tall elm. And whenever Alice finished her glass, George Carter filled it again.

From up in the window, Mary watched them. She had a sense that, after all her years of making a life where no one would have thought two lone women could have made a life, of raising an orchard and a flock, of guarding against disaster, she had come almost to the very end, and now this man had arrived and threatened to destroy everything.

She watched until she couldn't any longer. Then she went around to the back of the house and sat and stared out at the orchard, and when Alice came and said that George Carter had invited them both to dinner, she didn't reply.

So Alice set off alone with George Carter. It was afternoon, and though it was a warm day, a cool breeze was coming up the valley. The trees had begun to turn, and chickadees flitted in the branches, and in the distance she could hear a hawk. She was giddy from the cider and she should have been entirely happy, but deep within her she could feel sister's misery.

George Carter seemed not to notice that her thoughts were elsewhere.

Instead, he spoke of his travels in Brazil, and his work with the Abolition Society, and an important meeting he would attend in Philadelphia later that year, where he would share one of his essays. At a clearing, he saw a patch of boletes, and gave a little whoop of joy, for he'd developed a fondness for them in Italy. Her father had always warned them against mushrooms, but George seemed confident, and she untucked her blouse to help him gather. When he looked through her collection, he extracted a small while toadstool. "Not unless you are trying to poison Mary!" he exclaimed, and she didn't know whether to laugh. When he was little, another child had died from eating nightmaids; it had nearly turned him inside out.

This story made her somber, and she was relieved when they continued on their way. When the road turned muddy and slippery, he offered her his arm, and she didn't let go until they reached his house.

Then he said, "Well, you've caught me in a fib." For he didn't have any dinner to give her. Just the mushrooms, and some berries and bread that Alice had baked him the week before. That was it. Alice offered to cook something, but he said it wasn't necessary, he wasn't hungry. If she liked, he would go and pour her more of his cider. Yes, she said, for she was nervous. And while he was gone, she looked at her reflection in the window, and had the same impression she always had when she saw her own reflection, which was that she was looking at her sister. She was glad when he came out again, and they sat down together on the porch, and for a quiet moment stared out at the darkening night. He crushed the berries directly into the bread and passed it to her. Then he asked her if she remembered his father, and their classes, and the days they would escape to the woods. She did, she said. He said that he had thought of her when he was away. In the decades that passed, there were moments when he would think back on his life in Massachusetts and wonder what it would've been like had he not left, but stayed, with her.

She was quiet after he said this. Then, after a time, he said, "I hope that I haven't misspoken."

"No," she said.

"You aren't angry?" he asked.

And she turned to him, feeling the tears brim in her eyes. "But why me?" she asked, for she felt that she was the recipient of an undeserved bounty. "Why me, not Mary?"

"Because you are you, and she is she," he said.

Bats flitted past in the lowering darkness. She slapped a bug against her neck.

"Even the mosquitoes find you bewitching," he said.

She ignored this.

"Would you like to go inside?" he asked.

She looked off, in the direction of her home, where her sister was waiting.

His house was spare; it was still the house of his minister father. On the mantel, the stern face of the old man looked down upon her as it had in school. There was a portrait of the family too, father flanked by son and long-dead wife. A shelf of books covered the wall, and on the table, there were plates, and untended glasses, and stacks of other books as well. She wondered if one was George's book on cacti, which she had heard of but never seen.

But she didn't want to delay what was going to happen.

Together they climbed the creaking stairs up to his bedroom. There she let him lift her blouse above her head, and helped him undo his buttons.

His chest and shoulders were surprisingly strong for a man who was so bad at farming. She let him lower her skirts, and then she helped untie his trousers. They stood facing each other. She was aware of the darkness of her hands, the burnt plunge where she left her blouse unbuttoned, the paleness of her breasts.

"'Em's humans today," she said softly, laughing. He looked at her quizzically, not remembering, but she just smiled. Then she touched his face, his shoulder, and he placed his hands upon her hips and drew her close.

The next morning, he asked to walk her home, to protect her from the wolves and catamounts. She laughed. "But they've been hunted off." For she was mostly scared of Mary.

"Not *all*," he said.

He winked. She took his arm. But when they were about a quarter-mile from the house, she asked to go on alone.

"And when can I see you next?" asked George Carter.

"Oh dear," she said, for she saw so many complications. But she felt that she was young again. Her skin was alive, as if she had just come from the river. "Look," she said, "you have no food. I will bring you dinner this evening."

"One kiss!"

"Quick!"

As she turned up the road, she had to resist the urge to look back, for she knew that he was standing there, watching. She looked back. "Go home!" she said. She sensed a swing in her step. For, oh, she was the wanton! After the initial surprise of it, she'd performed quite deftly, and by the third round, that morning, when he'd collapsed in exhaustion, she'd laughed in triumph and pulled him close.

Now, as she approached the house, she felt reality come down upon her. There, somewhere, was Mary. No matter how well she knew her sister, no matter how many times they had fought, there had never been such a rupture. She didn't know which was stronger: her happiness, her sudden shame, or her anger that Mary could cause her to feel regret instead of joy.

She went through the front door, expecting to find Mary in her rocking chair, but the living room was empty. Nor was she in the kitchen, and upstairs, the bed was neatly made, as if it hadn't been slept in. She was aware of the contrast between the old smell of the house, and the scent of George and sweat and spilled cider on her body. No, the consequences of her actions were greater than she had imagined. She could no longer return to life as it was before. And she must tell Mary this, and hope somehow Mary would understand.

It was then that she became aware of a hammering coming from the hill. She went to the window, and pulled back the curtains. Something had happened to the orchard, and it took a moment for her to understand what she was seeing. All along one row, and halfway up the other, the light was different, like the wool of a sheep partway through its shearing, and at the inflection point, between the fallen trees and those that remained standing, she saw her sister swinging the axe.

With a cry, she ran downstairs and up the field and into the orchard, stepping over fallen branches, carnage everywhere, the air thick with the smell of crushed apples, stunned birds scattering confusedly, crying out as if in outrage. "Mary!" she cried. "Mary! No!" But her sister didn't turn, and Alice ran closer, crying, swearing that she was sorry, that she would never see George Carter again, that above anything she loved her sister, that they would be together until they died. She was running when she reached Mary. Her sister turned, and with a single swing, she felled her, and the only sound was a sharp gasp of shock.

"They are not for cider," said Mary, standing alone in the orchard, the savaged trees around her. The birds had returned, hopping about the chips and stumps. Alice lay on her back, hands neatly by her side, legs oddly crossed, like a shepherdess relaxing in the grass.

For a long time, Mary stood there. She felt that there was a voluptuousness to time, as if it had been bestowed upon her in abundance, as if she might remain there in the orchard for the rest of existence, unclaimed by death. The day passed. The shadows of one row of trees drew off her, and then the shadows of the facing row climbed up her legs. She sat, still holding the axe. At dusk, deer came from the forest, looked at her, and sprang away. A red beetle landed on her arm and crawled up until it reached her sleeve and then took flight. She looked out at the stone wall that she had built, and then down at her sister. She felt a need to say something, but couldn't bear the silence that she knew would follow. Flies had begun to mill about the wound, and she shooed them away with a wave of her bonnet.

Night fell, and still she didn't move from that spot, and it was only with the sunrise, and the sound of someone knocking at the far side of the house, that her reverie was broken.

There was, of course, only one person it could be. She rose, brushed the dust and chips from her blouse and skirts, and entered the house from the back, stopping briefly at the mirror to arrange her hair and check herself for blood. She felt, as she often felt, like she was looking at Alice, and it occurred to her that she might take the place of her sister in this man's arms, just as it occurred to her that she might go back and get the axe and dispatch of him entirely. But when she opened the door, she found not George Carter, but the son of the Oakfield baker, who had tied his horse to the hitching post and was holding out a letter. It was for Alice, he said, from Mr. Carter, and Mary thanked him, and when he left, she stood in the hallway and, with a trembling hand, tore it open, and read that George would always love her, but that he was an old bachelor and stuck in his silly ways. He had realized, over the course of his sojourn in that country, that the farming life was not for him. By the time she read the note, he would be on his way to Boston. He'd be back in the spring or summer, for he saw a use to the old house yet. Maybe they could see each other then.

He did not invite her to Boston with him.

Mary set the note down on the table, and then, thinking better, folded it, as if she were afraid that Alice might see it. She felt such love for her sister, and a great relief that she had spared her such sadness.

Then she went back outside. Alice lay there, peacefully. What should I do? Mary wished to ask her. She could dig a grave near their father's, but the thought of life alone inside the house was all too painful, so she carried Alice inside and stripped and cleaned her and dressed her in one of the two pink dresses she had made so many years ago.

"How pretty," said Alice, when Mary showed her sister their reflections in the mirror.

Mary turned to the body in her arms, then back to the face in the mirror. She didn't know how to answer. There was a lot to consider.

"What happens next?" Mary said, at last.

Alice shrugged. "I don't know," she said. "This is also new for me."

Mary kissed her sister's cheek and led her across the living room to her rocking chair. Gently, she lowered Alice down and went to get a shawl to wrap over her shoulders. "Thank you," said her sister, and the chair began to rock and didn't stop.

Five years passed.

The fallen trees gave out new shoots, and then new apples. Each autumn, Mary took them to market alone. The townspeople felt sorry for her when they heard the news of the death of her sister from apoplexy, and didn't haggle when she told them the price.

The winters were hard. More and more her joints ached, and sometimes she would do nothing but sit in the living room with Alice, singing their favorite ballads and writing new ones, about animals and country life. Then, one morning, she awoke with a stitch in her side, and when she pressed there, she felt something as hard as a knot of wood. Briefly, she felt her heart flutter, but then she felt only gratitude, for she had worried that death would take her in the woods or the garden or the road to town, take her from Alice.

After that, she didn't leave home except to let the sheep in and out of the pasture. Inside, she walked through the rooms, looked at their books, dusted them, and set them neatly on the shelves. There was the old Bible among them, the one that had been discovered by her father. She had forgotten it after so many years, and now she brought it to her bedside to give her comfort, but left it sitting there, and ended up reading from *The Pomological Manual* instead.

She felt the thing inside her growing larger, until it was like a small baby. An immaculate conception, she thought: it didn't frighten her. She felt even a pity for it, as if it still thought that it could consume her, and not die, stillborn, within the prison of her body.

As the days passed, she ate less and less, and spent her hours sleeping. She had thought for a long time about what she would do when the end came. She could dig the two of them a grave, but couldn't fill it, but she also didn't like the indignity of someone finding their bodies in their bed. In the pantry off the kitchen was a space set beneath the floor where they stored corn for the winter, covered by two loose, wide boards. It was the best that she could do, she thought, and one morning, she summoned up the strength and gently laid her sister deep inside.

She paused, looking down, then went and got her sister's fife, and the thick book of ballads they had written together over the years. For the days would be long, she thought, and the nights, and it would be good if they could keep composing.

She wound the clock one last time, went out, pastured the sheep, opened the gate, and wished them godspeed. Then she went and put on the other pink dress that Alice had made, returned to the pantry, locked the door, nailed one of the boards in place, and, taking two apples and the old axe as an eternal reminder of her penance, she squeezed through the opening and lay down next to her sister. She had attached a ribbon to the second board, and when at last she was settled, she reached up and took it in her hand.

"It is about time," said Alice, but Mary hushed her with a kiss.

Then, wrapping her fingers in the ribbon, she pulled the floorboard shut.

The farmer joyful now brings home the corn,
The yellow ears his well-filled house adorn,
The husking party jocund at the pile,
Strip off the husks, and laugh and sing and smile.

M. D.	W. D.	Day br'k h. m.	Days' length h. m.	Days dec. h. m.	D south. h. m.	☉ F. m.	D A. d.	Agriculture, Husbandry, Domestic Economy, &c.
1	3	4 32	11 36	3 34	3 26	11	19	The first week or two of this month is generally pleasant
2	4	4 34	11 32	3 38	15	11	20	and agreeable weather, and fa-
3	5	4 35	11 28	3 42	5 2	11	21	vorable for business of most
4	6	4 37	11 26	3 44	5 52	11	☾	kinds, either in the city or
5	7	4 39	11 24	3 46	6 41	12	23	
6	F	4 40	11 20	3 50	7 30	12	24	**SABBATH XL.**
7	2	4 42	11 18	3 52	8 19	12	25	country. Farmers may find
8	3	4 44	11 16	3 54	9 8	13	26	enough to do ; threshing grain,
9	4	4 46	11 12	3 58	9 58	13	27	harvesting, ploughing, build-
10	5	4 47	11 10	4 0	10 47	13	28	ing wall, and sowing and har-
11	6	4 49	11 6	4 4	11 37	13	●	rowing in winter grain, will
12	7	4 50	11 4	4 6	ev.34	14	1	afford plenty of profitable em-
13	F	4 52	11 0	4 10	1 32	14	2	**SABBATH XLI.**
14	2	4 53	10 58	4 12	2 30	14	3	ployment in the field or barn,
15	3	4 55	10 54	4 16	3 31	14	4	while spinning, weaving, and
16	4	4 56	10 52	4 18	4 33	14	5	knitting occupy the industri-
17	5	4 58	10 48	4 22	5 32	15	6	ous housewife and her amiable
18	6	4 59	10 46	4 24	6 28	15	☽	daughters within doors. The
19	7	5 0	10 42	4 26	7 18	15	8	diligent mechanic is busy in
20	F	5 2	10 40	4 30	8 10	15	9	**SABBATH XLII.**
21	2	5 3	10 36	4 34	8 55	15	10	preparing the necessary tools
22	3	5 4	10 34	4 36	9 43	15	11	and implements and other
23	4	5 5	10 32	4 38	10 27	16	12	matters for his customers, and
24	5	5 6	10 28	4 42	11 11	16	13	all things go on in harmony if
25	6	5 8	10 26	4 44	11 55	16	14	they go on right.
26	7	5 9	10 24	4 46	morn	16	○	
27	F	5 10	10 20	4 50	0 39	16	16	**SABBATH XLIII.**
28	2	5 11	10 18	4 52	1 24	16	17	As you treat your land, so it
29	3	5 12	10 16	4 54	2 11	16	18	will treat you. Feed it with
30	4	5 13	10 12	4 58	2 59	16	19	manures liberally, and it will
31	5	5 14	10 10	5 0	3 49	16	20	yield you bread bountifully.

The CATAMOUNT, or a True Relation of a Bloody Encounter that Lately Happen'd; a song for VOICE and FIFE, to the tune of CHEERILY and MERRILY

O, heard ye of the bloody beast
That came down that October day
And made the flock her bloody feast
And chased the lucky ones away?

Was great, they say, of eye and tooth,
And withers grey, and hungry jaw.
With hissing scream, her leap foretold
No mercy from her claw.

To emptied house, she came that night,
Where roam'd in day the blatant sheep,
Now pasture silent, barnyard bright,
The flock within the barn, asleep.

They did not hear, until she came
Into the sweet place of their rest
And into ewe and lamb did sink her teeth,
And tore the life out from their breasts.

And still the great cat stalks the hills
O'er bracken, brook, and stone.
Lock up your doors at night, my dears,
Keep lad and lass at home.

The screams they rose, the bloody screams
The owl lifted from her beech
As 'cross the valley, came the plaints:
The lamb's soft wail, the ewe's beseech.

Their white eyes wide against the dark,
They crashed through trough and blackest water
To flee the fangs that found their mark,
Drunk on the lust of wanton slaughter.

And when the deed was done and good
And silence fell again,
The cat look'd up from all the blood
And heard afar the night's reclaim:

A howl, for scent of blood had lured
The last wolf of these hills.
And went the catamount a-prowl
To find a place to hide her kill.

And still the great cat stalks the hills &c.

From stall to stall she paced in vain,
Then toward the yellow house did glide,
Where paw'd she at an unlatched door,
And so slipped quietly inside.

And there she prick'd her dagger'd ears
And held her lamb-warmed breath
And sniff'd, but from the House of Maids
Came but the smell of Death.

Through silent hall, the great cat slunk,
Her whiskers taut, her eyes ablaze.
The moon through window cast its glow
And lit the halls' besilenced maze.

At shelves she paw'd, and overturn'd
The books that by the bedside sat,
Paused at the hearth where once the fires burn'd
And chimneys sniff'd the blacken'd fat.

And still the great cat stalks the hills &c.

Alone was she, but keen to he
That now loped down the mount.
With yellow eye and curdling bray
His plundering announc'd.

Then swift to barn the great cat raced
To broken lamb obtain,
And drag within the shelter of the house
Her sorry quarry slain.

First one, then two, and three and more
Did haul the fearsome beast
To grow the mount upon the floor
From which to draw her feast.

And still the great cat stalks the hills &c.

And then across the broken walls
And pasture thick with mud
The last wolf of the hills approach'd
That house scented with blood.

But howl he might and growl and bay
With threat and plea and fearsome vows,
Still his petition went unanswer'd by
The Mistress of the house.

For days engorg'd upon that bloody fruit
Did panther rule her kingdom small.
Domestic was our fearsome brute.
On couch she curl'd, and bed she roll'd.

Until the day the dark woods call'd again
To hunt within their gloom.
And so she left for creek and glen
And lonely march resumed.

And still the great cat stalks the hills &c.

From "Proverbs and Sayings"

WHEN the sheep are gone, comes the quiet of the pasture.*

---

* But lo! For while there is wisdom to this old saying, what now rises in the field is not a gentle return to some ungrazed Eden, but, rather, the irruption of a strange, besieging army that has been lying in wait.

For this particular pasture, the invasion can be said to have begun one autumn morning two centuries before the birth of the Merino Cristobal, when a ship departs from Yarmouth on the Isle of Wight. To keep steady through the North Atlantic, the sailors fill the hold with ballast from the wastelands near the Yarmouth docks. There are stones and loam and sand, insects and earthworms, bird bones and crushed snail shells, roly-polies, and tufts of grass that wilt within the darkness beneath the deck. There is a half-decayed mole, and a live one, broken jugs, a Roman coin that will be rediscovered by a young boy walking on the shoreline 317 years later, and another, a "crown of the double rose" bearing an image of Edward VI on horseback, that will sift down into the silty depths of Massachusetts Bay and disappear forever. There is a beaded necklace dropped by a longshoreman's wife during a moment of indiscretion, a splintered lens from a bookkeeper's spectacles, stray curls blown from a barber's market stall by an offshore breeze, peach pits, rotting broadsheets of forgotten songs. And there are seeds, uncountable, scattered in the humid load: red clover, groundsel, spurrey, trefoil, meadow fescue, dandelion, hedge parsley, nonesuch, plantain.

The voyage takes two months. On landing, the ballast is removed and dumped into the harbor. Much of it—the stones, the shells, the beads, the spectacles—sinks to the bottom of the bay. But the seeds, many of the seeds, enough of the seeds, rinsed loose of their swaddling earth, are freed into the breakers and float to shore.

It is warm; within weeks, they have germinated, begun to grow, to flower, to set seed of their own.

Then, one by one, and by the millions, they make their way west.

In the felted boots of a young girl, traveling to Albany with her mother: hedge parsley.

In a hemp sack, dropped by a Dutch settler, after his murder on a lonely road near Hoosick Falls, and then on the wind: common groundsel.

In feed sold one late September to a farmer passing through the Deerfield market, who spills some from his carriage: meadow fescue.

In the ticking of a mattress discovered by a minister to be the locus of his wife's betrayal, fury-scythed to pieces and released into the Plymouth fields: Scotch thistle.
In the pocket of a milkmaid who had thought it was a carrot: Queen Anne's lace.
In the cracks of an old shoe, and the hem of a skirt, and the stockings of a soldier:

The seeds that to the soil take,
will presently our pasture make.

One by one they nestle in among the native grasses, some so swiftly that it will seem like they have always been there (for it is hard to imagine there was a time before dandelions, before thistle). Others creep up the valley slowly, field by field, until they reach the yellow house. Where they grow, unnoticed, humbled by the constant grazing of the Merinos, waiting in the soil for the cat.

Four

IT was early November when he reached the mountains. Grey
stubble filled the fields, and the remnants of a heavy rain glistened
in the furrows. At the edges of the pastures, in the thin strips of
forest that persisted between the farms, among the bare birches
and maples, oaks and beeches clung to their leaves. Flocks of sheep
were everywhere, grazing at the margins of the low walls, clustered beneath the sagging awnings of the feed sheds, clogging the
roads.

Since Springfield, he had endured eight hours pressed between
a fat man in purple velvet trousers, and a newlywed couple who
passed the journey feeding each other butternuts from a rattling
tin. The coach was crowded, its four rows packed with more people than seemed possible, their luggage lashed to the roof in a
creaking tower that strained against the ropes. In the facing seat
before him was a young doctor, and next to him, an old man who,
having discovered his neighbor's profession, spent the ride from
Bettsbridge elaborating on the many ailments he had suffered
since eating a rotten salmon six years before.

The day had started cold, and as they rose into the mountains,
grew colder, but the warm press of passengers more than compensated. The fat man tried, in the early hours of their journey, to
make conversation with Phalen, inquiring with a twist of his bulk
where he had come from and the purpose of his travel, until, finding his seatmate terse and tired, he joined in with the general dis-

cussion about the salmon, awaiting his turn to remove both shoe and stocking and ask about a problem with his foot. Indeed, by the time they reached the Junction and descended for a meal, the young doctor had offered advice to every traveler, save Phalen and the newlyweds, who were too young, too healthy, too intent.

The doctor, whether because he had business in the Junction, or because he had tired of dispensing consultation without compensation, did not board when they continued. But whatever hopes the passengers had for breathing room were dashed by the last-minute entry of a young circuit preacher, who nimbly landed on the middle seat and launched, with little provocation, into a sermon. For two hours, he spoke of the sins of dancing teachers and the evils of the apple tree which gave man drunkenness, as interesting to Phalen as the complaints of croup and chilblain. It was only when he began to speak of the evils of slavery that Phalen shifted his attention. Then the man was speaking of a boy born free and plucked from his life in New York by kidnappers, and the brave men who had freed him. For had not Job once said, *And I brake the jaws of the wicked, and plucked the spoil out of his teeth?* On he went, his voice filling the coach, until, at last, a distant bugle sounded, and the coach began to rattle over cobble, and the crowded evening street of Oakfield drew up outside the window. The passengers began to button up their coats, and arrange their hats and scarves, and it was then that Phalen leaned forward and complimented the man for his fine speech.

"Obliged," said the preacher. It was good to meet another righteous traveler. It was hard sometimes to know whose side one's fellow man was on.

❋   ❋   ❋

That his quarry was hidden somewhere in the mountains that rose up above the Oakfield valley was a conclusion that Phalen had come to slowly over the two weeks since he'd arrived in Massachusetts, ostensibly to sell insurance, a business of which he knew only enough to weary an inquisitor, but one which gave cover to his curiosity regarding homes and their inhabitants. But there were few inquisitors; insurance salesmen, unlike physicians, are not besieged in stagecoaches. In the inns where he lodged, he duly entered his true name in the registers and was forgotten. His face was lean and common, his hair pale and grey enough that one would have been hard pressed to describe its color. He wore his coat loose to hide his physical strength, and his light-brown hat of felted beaver with a light-brown ribbon low over his face.

The guise was hardly accidental, but, rather, one refined over two decades in the profession. Indeed, so unassuming was he that he often had to reassure a client that he was prepared for force. Force, however, he was proud to say, was rarely necessary. For he placed a great premium on caution. The law was on his side, prohibiting any interference in the retrieval and restoration of another's property. But such was the fervor gripping the country, that local passions could inflame, complicating his task and bringing unwanted attention to both himself and his employer. Yes, he had colleagues in the trade who made no effort to dissemble—looked the very pirates painted by the abolitionist press: ugly men of mean education and easy violence. But such men called too much attention, Phalen maintained, even in places sympathetic to Southern business, and certainly among the hypocrites of the North. Indeed, as with his current mission, deep in enemy territory in Massachusetts, only perfect discretion could hope to bring success.

Discretion, of course, came at a price. When he presented a potential client with his fee, he was accustomed to a protesting whistle or a quiet curse. But it was one thing to send a gang of local toughs with dogs and shackles into a nearby swamp, and another to pursue a lost cause on the far side of Mason-Dixon. And while there were some who ended the discussion soon after his appraisal, his reputation meant that his rates were usually accepted, even when the cost of his services far exceeded the value of the slave.

In the case of the girl and child that had brought him that November into the hilly, snow-dusted country of Massachusetts, he knew not what motivated his employer, a long-necked, low-shouldered Maryland planter with two dozen men and women in bonds. That the fugitive was female raised the obvious suspicions, though the client had taken pains to emphasize his chief concern was of a spreading outbreak of flight. She was the third he'd lost that season, and he must make an example for the rest.

Of course, thought Phalen, that the enslaved would weigh even the most severe "example" against the horrors of their bondage was what kept his business brisk.

He did not say this. That day, seated before the planter, he just took a single sip from the whiskey his client had set before him on the table and let the old man speak.

The girl, Esther, age eighteen, had vanished three weeks prior with her infant child; a search party sent across the border into Pennsylvania had lost her. Her motives were plain, her owner told him. He'd sold off the child's father months before, but the man escaped from a ship at Boston. He'd been recaptured, then escaped again, the planter heard, to Canada. He had little doubt that the girl was trying to reach him. *How* she knew his whereabouts, how such information might make it back to her across five hundred, six hundred miles—this perplexed him, though he knew there must be ways.

Phalen listened. Yes, there were ways, networks, routes of word and passage. But he had his networks too. There were more than enough men and women in the North who resented the law-breaking of their abolitionist neighbors. Who had Southern clients who purchased their gears and rivets, Southern suppliers of their cloth.

She was small, said the planter, darker than most, with a sharp nose, and still had all her teeth. Her hair was short; they'd been plagued with lice that season, and he'd made her cut it. But she was comely and strong, could read some, could do a man's work in the field. As for identifying marks—and he paused a moment, as if he had to work to find the memory, though Phalen knew he needed no such effort—there were the usual lashings, and a broken finger on her left hand, for she'd escaped, or tried to, once before.

The planter had offered Phalen a room for the night, but he declined. A three-week lead, an unknown destination, a trail already cold: all this placed him at a considerable disadvantage. Nevertheless, he had worked with less before, and still brought back his quarry. Indeed, given the vastness of the country, the meager descriptions offered by his clients, the growing defiance of the fugitive laws, he was still, after two decades, surprised how easy it was to locate his object. In this case it had taken him but two days to hear of a girl matching Esther's description come through a known station in Trenton. From there, after false leads along the lower Hudson, further intelligence brought him to New Haven and Springfield, where her trail grew cold again.

It was late October then, and he considered, after a week, returning to Maryland, for he had come to know when both his time and his client's money were being wasted. But in a Springfield tavern kept by a man sympathetic to his purposes, he'd been introduced to a farmer from Shadd's Falls, who prided himself on keeping tabs on the area's blacks. He'd seen the girl and child, yes, and wandering freely. That night, Phalen joined him at his farm. For a week, the farmer led him about the country, introducing him to other men who shared his commitment to the nation's laws, until Phalen began to worry that such company would get him noticed by precisely those he hoped to move among discreetly. Then, one night, word came from a teamster in the next town over, that such a girl was spotted traveling in the company of a free black with connections to the railroad. The teamster, who'd heard of Phalen's search, and was hoping for some recompense, had followed them to Oakfield, from which the free man had returned alone.

It was testament to the insolence of the state of Massachusetts, he added, that the girl was traveling in broad daylight.

"And where do you think she is in Oakfield?" asked Phalen, sitting with the others in a tavern run by another sympathizer.

The teamster and farmer exchanged glances with each other.

"Familiar with the name George Carter?" the teamster asked.

Phalen nodded. Hard not to be familiar with Carter, who penned a constant stream of anti-slavery screeds under the pen name "Democritus."

He had, the teamster said, a house in Oakfield. The coincidence, it seemed, was just a bit too much.

"You think she's hiding there?" asked Phalen.

Again, his colleagues exchanged quick looks. Well, just that spring, the teamster said, some people from New York—friends, you might have called them—had grown tired of Carter's disrespect and set fire to his house. But old Democritus had plenty of local acquaintances sympathetic to his troublemaking.

The teamster asked the tavern keeper for a piece of paper, drew a rough map of the town and surrounding roads, and wrote out a list of names and addresses.

"I'd be pleased to take you," the teamster said, but he was known there, as were his sympathies. Which was how, the following morning, Phalen found himself on the westbound stage, squeezed between the fat man's purple trousers and the cooing newlyweds, watching the sheep part slowly in the road.

He found a room on the market square, announced his business at the post office and the general store, and, for the next four days, went house to house offering insurance policies that didn't exist, making sure his route took him to the seven houses marked with little X's on his map.

It was poor country, but lovely, and the fact that he knew that he was getting closer made it lovelier still. Frost silvered the tops of the mountains, the winds shook the leaves from the branches, and each morning, the woods seemed thinner, as if the country were slowly showing him what lay within.

The houses on his map were widespread, and his path took him through the town and up the valleys that fed down into Oakfield. Farmers greeted him at the door to their homes, listened patiently as he described the risks of storm and fire, the workings of the policy and the protection it might offer if disaster struck. Many of the farms were already insured, but the farmers, whether out of thrift or country manners, allowed him in to see the property and offer his assessment, even if they knew that they would stay with Vermont Fire, or Western Massachusetts Property and Life. They were good New Englanders, as cautious as they were industrious, and all knew a story of an errant cow and lantern, or a candle placed too close to the drapes.

And each welcomed him with hospitality. On wobbly chairs and sheen-worn settees, they brought him freshly buttered bread, and chestnuts, and coffee in tin cups, and after feeding him, they led him over floors pitted by hooves, past crackling hearths, and rough-hewn tables. Did they find it strange that the agent seemed so interested in all their houses' nooks and crannies, asked to see each attic, hayloft? Inquired about the servants' quarters, and whether the land held other domiciles, distant camps? A fire could start anywhere, Phalen told them, and often it was a maid or farmhand that was careless. And if the six men and single widow who were listed on the little map he carried in his pocket had asked their neighbors of the agent's visit, they might have learned that he had searched their farms a bit more thoroughly than others, seemed a bit more curious about the help.

The truth was, Phalen knew that if they were hiding someone, they'd never take him there. What he was looking for was not the

attic door they showed him but the one they didn't, or just a simple moment of hesitation in the manner of his host.

On the walls, sun-faded portraits of high-collared, thin-lipped
ancestors watched him as he ducked and climbed the creaky stairs.
In the dooryards, children tumbled in the leaf-fall, and late-
blooming asters shed their thin purple petals on his pant legs.
Each day, he came to understand more of the country. The same
faces drove the higgledy pig-herds, the same cast came tromping
to the town each morning, the same washerwomen labored by
the clotheslines, the same drunks lolled out in the square. Even
the colors grew familiar. Chimneys of a dull-red brick, and in the
graveyards pale-green ranks of marble from a quarry just beyond
the highway, near-translucent, dissolving easily in the rain.

Sometimes the clouds would come in low over the valley, so that
it seemed as if he'd crossed into a different realm. The roads grew
thick with fog, travelers appeared without warning, then all at
once the wind would come and lift the mist, the hills appeared, the
slope so clear, the little huts across the valley so close that he
could see the tiny pigs and felt as if he might reach out and touch
them. On his fourth day, a young wife served him, in leaded green
glass she said came all the way from Holland, a cup of water of
such clarity and sweetness, that he wondered for a moment if he
might stop his search and find a patch amidst the hills to call his
own. And part of him would surge up that hated the dirtiness of
the business, hated the greed of the men who pushed their slaves
beyond breaking, hated the pettiness of the shipowners who kept
tabs on each sad black to cross their docks, hated the blacks who
ran away and disrupted order, who forced him to deceive, to pretend at being a man he wasn't. Who fought him until the very end,
while others went with him so quietly. But then, standing in the
bedrooms of such righteous people, he'd see the muslin drapes and
calico skirts, and to his many hates, he added that for the pious

who preached the slave's equality, but wore cloth made with his sweat.

Walking through the hallways, sitting in dooryards with a cup of fresh-pressed cider, he listened, for distant creaks, or coughing, watched for fleeting figures in the attic windows, searched faces for signs of suspicion or concern. Who, he asked himself, was hiding her? And one by one, he crossed the houses off his list.

His break came on his sixth day, and not from any direction he expected. It was a market day, and he'd stayed close to the inn, to watch the coming and going of the people, out of the hope that here, deep in free country, and lonely for the presence of others, she might feel bold enough to come to town. The day was dark and cold. A fine rain fell intermittently, but still the streets were crowded with coats and hats and skirts of many colors. Factory girls followed a traveling peddler of neckerchiefs and hairpins. Harvest rattled on the drays, and cartwheels splashed in muddy puddles. At the edge of the square, he noticed a crowd milling about a small girl selling apples. There were many apple vendors, though for some reason, she clearly was the favorite. When he approached, a single fruit remained there, nestled in a box of shavings.

Ghost apple, she called it when he asked, but it was dark red and green, and anything but ghostly, and when he asked her why the name, she told him that the orchard it was from was haunted, and when he laughed, she said that even she herself had seen the shadows moving behind the curtains of the abandoned house.

She wore a grey shawl over her head, wiggled a loose tooth with her tongue, and stared back with light-blue eyes, as if defying him to disbelieve her.

It was a nickel for an apple.

For the orchard's location, a mile up past Old Man Carter's

place, she charged a dollar, because, despite Phalen's reassurances that he was only interested in the supernatural, she was convinced that he would pick the last fruits for himself.

And so, for the second time in seventy-five years, a child's apple led a grown man to the north woods place.

He had yet to take the winding road that led up the valley. The cart path was narrow, low branches hung across the road, and sprawling brambles caught on his clothing as if trying to retain him. Crows called from the treetops, as if in warning, and he had to tell himself that such calls were common, and would mean nothing to the girl. Still, he stopped his horse at Carter's house, and tied it to a hitching post that seemed to be the only thing left standing other than the fireplace and a bed that must have tumbled from the second floor and landed beyond the consuming flames. All else ashes. Good old American wrath, he thought. And if this hadn't taught old Democritus, perhaps arrest for hiding stolen property would.

He continued on foot, and when he spied the yellow house far in the distance, he entered the woods to keep from being seen. It had occurred to him, back in town, apple in hand, its heavenly taste flooding his senses, that he might go back to Shadd's Falls and bring companions, but he decided against it. There were many reasons for this. It would be at least two days before he could return, and there was nothing to say Esther wouldn't continue northward. And just as his associates in Shadd's Falls knew the local abolitionists, the local abolitionists would surely recognize his associates, and not only would this serve to warn her, but he was ashamed to think of the acts of hospitality that had greeted him throughout his stay.

The final reason was that he was impatient, and didn't need two other men. Only if he saw that she had friends would he get help.

But it was soon clear she had no friends. A wind was stirring the leaves as he stopped at a low stone wall from which grew young trees thick as his forearms. Beyond this was a pasture, now abandoned, overgrown with bramble, ferns, and lithe, swaying birches. He squatted. When Esther emerged, she had a bucket in one hand and her baby on her waist, and she looked around cautiously as she walked over to a well. She was frightened—he could see this even at a distance. When a crow called, she startled and stared into the woods where he was waiting, then went back to drawing water. She was so small and thin, that, for a moment he was struck simply by the physical asymmetry of the whole endeavor, the collective mass of all the men who'd helped him track down someone no larger than a child. And yet she hauled the bucket from the well without putting down the baby, and carried it full and sloshing with a single hand. Caution, he thought. But he had a pistol, and she had the disadvantage of a child to defend.

She went back inside. He waited. Night fell. He heard her singing softly, saw the flickering of a candle, and then the light went out.

The clouds parted and flooded the house and fields with moonlight. When they closed again, he hurried softly through the ferns until he reached a pair of woodpiles, thick with moss. Again, he stopped, waited, listened.

The front door was locked, but a door in the ell was open. Inside, he let his eyes adjust to the darkness. It was a small room, the size of a hunter's cabin. A butter churner lay on its side by a fallen shelf of pots. Carefully, he made his way into the dining room, where a table sat before a hearth.

A chair was pulled out, and cleared of dust, as was a corner of the table. From there, footprints in the dust led into the kitchen, then the living room, before stopping at the base of the stairs. There, about the foyer, scattered, were the bones of a sheep— a spine, a rib cage. Had Esther killed it? he wondered. But they were old bones: bare, and the remaining flesh had hardened to leather. Cautiously, he stepped over them. The first stair creaked. He stopped and waited, listening for movement. Then again he began to climb, pistol before him, ready in case she was waiting on the landing.

She wasn't waiting. There were footprints everywhere in the dust, and two doors, and he chose the one to the right.

The room was empty save the bed, its blankets rumpled. On the floor, more bones. What kind of charnel house was this? he wondered, his eyes taking in the room, senses alive to the hunt, gloriously alive, thinking how mad he was, just two days before, drinking sweet water from the Dutch glassware, to have considered giving up.

"Esther," he said.

No answer. The whole house seemed to be holding its breath.

"Esther, come with me, come home, and no harm will come to either of you."

A creak. He swung around, prepared to see her fleeing, but there was no one. Another creak, but he could not tell where it was coming from. It was as if the house, having waited in suspense, was now settling in the cool of night. Sounds came from the walls, the ceilings above. Another sheep lay at his feet, its mangled rictus gleaming in the moonlight. She was close, he knew. He crouched to look beneath the bed, hopeful, thrilled even, by the thought of a scuffle, alone in the house, with no angry mob outside, no screeching abolitionist's wife.

But nothing. No eyes staring back across the darkness; no hand over a baby's mouth. And in the closet, nothing, and in the bedroom across the landing, nothing, the bedsheets smooth and trimly tucked.

By the bed was a spill of books, and on the floor a bare, gleaming rectangle in the dust. Had she taken it? he wondered. But he didn't have time to ponder. A rustling on the landing, the sound of footsteps. He followed swiftly down the stairs, tripped on the bones, and hit the ground heavily. He cursed her; she must have dragged them into his path. Then he was up again. Into the living room, the kitchen, where he saw a smaller door he hadn't noticed earlier, found it locked, and called to her again.

He didn't wait for an answer, but broke it open with a kick.

A storeroom, empty. But there, on the floor, the unmistakable outline of a trapdoor.

"Esther," he said.

More sounds in the distance. He turned, wondering if he had missed her, when he heard a cough beneath his feet.

He straightened out his hat so that it lay at a jauntier angle, as if he were about to make a lady's acquaintance.

There was a gap around one of the floorboards, and he used it to remove the board. There was a ribbon on its undersurface, and, knowing then that he had found her, he grabbed the next board with both hands and pried it off. *And I brake the jaws of the wicked, and plucked the spoil out of his teeth.* Darkness below. He lit his match and crouched over the space, not understanding at first what he was seeing, the flickering light upon the fife, the pink, frilled dresses, the open pairs of eyes, the axe.

Alice and Mary Osgood blinked and looked up at the figure above them. A cold draft came from the shattered door. Mary turned her head from side to side, wincing at the crackle, for her neck had always bothered her, and it had been thirteen years since she'd last moved it. At her side, Alice was pressed against her like a hog in a wallow, taking up more than her half of their resting place, as usual.

But this could wait addressing, for the intruder needed reckoning first.

"I don't believe our guest invited you," said Mary, rising, as Alice clutched her fife and closed her eyes so not to see what happened next.

The doleful account of the OWL and the SQUIRREL; or HOW THE LAND CAME TO BE FORESTED AGAIN, being a New Winter's Ballad; written by a pair of GRAVE sisters, for CHILDREN. To the Tune THEN MY LOVE AND I WILL MARRY

A squirrel, autumn-stout and fair,
Stopp'd in the field to muse.
For winter's chill was in the air
And time had come to choose.

Throughout the woods, the trees had bloom'd,
And from their boughs did spill
A bounty of most splendid nuts
Strewn all across the hill.

The waxwings paused along their course.
The woodfrog dug into the mould.
The monarchs left the goldenrod,
And flutter'd south beyond the cold.

The pastures long abandon'd were,
And in their place did bramble rise.

As fern and sapling fought to raise
Their arms into the skies.

And I do sing that Winter's come
With bitter frost and winds most cruel
Come close, to hear this tale about
The owl and the squirrel.

'Twas in this brush the squirrel ran
And o'er it, the owl soared.
And found the squirrel secret spots to hide
His carefully collected hoard.

A hundred chestnuts he had claim'd,
A hundred acorns more:
The autumn bounty that would last
Until late April's thaw.

Thus He that favors Providence
Rewarded our fair chap,
His nutty fund, his daily bread
Straight to his lover's lap.

And I do sing that Winter's come &c.

Then all around, Hunger came down,
The buck grew thin, his sweet doe too,
While hungry martens through the valley slipp'd
Along the trail of vole and shrew.

And in the woods, the hungry grouse
Scavenged beneath the ice,

And listen'd to the hungry peeps
Of chickadees and mice.

But the squirrel, still he feasted
With his bonny little belle.
Went out each day to check the stores
He'd scatter'd 'cross the dell.

And I do sing that Winter's come &c.

At last one day, a great snow came
And fell throughout the night.
And turned the thickly brambled fields
To sheets of silken white.

Now through the corridors of snow
Did dash our little beast
While high above the owl turn'd
And listen'd for her feast.

Until at last, her moment came:
When from the white, she heard his breath,
And striking, left upon the snow
The feather'd silhouette of death.

With squirrel gone, the stash remains,
Entomb'd within the snows,
Where they'll survive, 'til spring arrive
And burst their husks, and grow.

And I do sing that Winter's come &c.

Letters to E.N.

December 18

Dear Friend,

A note to say I have arrived. Dreadful, glorious journey—
snow all the way, city jacket worthless in this cold. Remind me
again: whose idea was it to travel in December? But winter is the
only season one can find workers, and the roads mire with the
summer mud.

Midnight by the time we reached the house. Moon full and the
world aglow—we walked to the entrance without lanterns. Of
course, inside it was a different story, dark as catacombs, and it
was dawn before I could take my bearings. More on that later—
suffice it to say that if Katherine had come with me, we'd be back
in Boston as fast as the train could take us. Five months to pass
muster—will see what can be done.

Lovely country, I should say, sleepy grey fields, low walls fret-
ting the swell as far as one can see. Must have been giants of men
who moved such stones. One could build a small cathedral with
what they hauled out of my fields alone. Extraordinary to think
this all was forest once. Now it seems like I am in possession of
the sole untouched tract of woods.

And cold. Did I say that? Tried to light a fire, but there's
something in the flue, and I had to open the windows else I
choke. Squirrel nest most likely, says Trevors, though sometimes

the panthers use the chimneys to store their prey. Turns out he was serious: when the Register first came to inspect the property, he found windows broken, furniture overturned, the floor littered with dead sheep. Catacombs indeed. Will see what kind of bones come tumbling down.

Now I'm sitting at the old dining table, looking ever the country-man, in an old be-ribboned hat of felted beaver I found on the floor. Two blankets over my shoulders, still in my gloves. Cigar damp and useless, though in the candlelight, my breath pools thick as smoke.

Did I say it was cold?

Will write anon, when my fingers thaw.

WHT

❊

January 17

Dear Friend,

Have been meaning to write for nearly a month now—very much appreciated your letter and the city news. Odd how one wishes to get away from it, but once one's gone, even the slightest gossip is seized upon greedily. The reception for your *Travels* is of course deserved to the fullest—the "American Goethe"! Oh, dear—now the fame will go to your head and you will forget your friend in his winter woods, fall under the spell of some golden-locked publisher's daughter. Likely she is reading this now, over your shoulder. *Sotto voce:* Mademoiselle, he is a *lout.* Ask him about Rome and Naples, how the courtesans still whisper of his feats. Run while you can, or at the very least promise that you will share him.

I jest, but not really.

Kind of you to mention my painting, but I haven't lifted a brush since arriving. My promise to Katherine is that I'll have the house ready by the time she and the children arrive, but I can hardly use this as an excuse—Trevors and his boys do everything, and at best, I've been a hindrance. Trevors would like nothing but to scour the place and put all the old junk to the bonfire, but this feels sacrilegious, and despite broken windows and the bird's nest in the chimney (no panther kill, alas) and the dust everywhere, it's hard not to feel that someone is living here still.

You asked about the prior owners. According to the Registry of Deeds, it was an English Major who first built the house after the French and Indian Wars. Found his gravestone in an overgrown orchard high up the hill out back—soft marble and already barely legible—never imagined I would have my own cemetery. Next transfer of title to the Major's daughters during the Revolution. They are my immediate predecessors if one ignores the sheep, and the venerable Alice and Mary Osgood seem to have run the place until they packed up and moved away. No one knows when or wherefore—much of the county was abandoned in the '20s and '30s, and when they eventually sent a Land Agent up here, he found it empty. The next owner, *in absentia,* was a nephew in London, who sat on it until his death. It was *his* son who sold it to me, though other than clearing out the ovine massacre, no one has laid a finger on the place since the sisters were here—so Trevors assures me and I've got no reason to dispute him. Save the beaver hat (gentleman caller?) it's just skirts hanging in the closet, and if that wasn't enough, they even left their portraits: each dressed in a pink lace so bright that I had to blink when I wiped away the dust, and each holding an apple in her hand. Think of the Cranach *Eve* we saw in Florence, but with more clothes. Given that there are two other portraits *only* of apples, I think that it is fair enough to assume a certain connection to the orchard, though half the trees are sprawling suckered messes. Storm calamity, I gather. Great gale of '37, says Trevors: wander in the forest and you can still see the ranks of fallen

trunks, all pointed in the same direction—north-by-northwest—
a crowd of savages before the grand mountain, a fitting God-
head.

Anyway, the apples have all been swallowed up by birch and
pine now, while oaks and chestnuts rise from the stone walls. I
can already hear Katherine whetting the axe, though I'll do my
best to secure a stay of execution until we can taste the fruit. If
they fruit.

Of course, there is a mystery attendant in all these plates and
portraits and folded skirts: where did they go? Trevors finds my
curiosity *curious*—says there are but two places they *could* have
gone, and accompanies this with an eye roll to the heavens and
down below. But the place is *rank* with Time—why shouldn't I
wish to scrape away the strata? At night, I have a choice of
whether to curl up within the northern dent of Alice (Mary?) or
the southern half-moon valley left by the side-sleeping Mary
(Alice?), or whether I'll sprawl over the crest between the two of
them. How rare to see a life abandoned *in medias res*. Reminds me
of our Pompeii (*locus amoenus*—I at garden easel, you writing at
your desk; that lovely fishmonger with the volcanic eyes; soft sand
of the shadowed coves). But, then, what was their Vesuvius? Storm?
Pestilence? Or some grim malady that took first one and then
the other? If one ignores a few overturned books and chairs
and the stains left by the panther's orgy, it's all so organized,
so neat.

A journey, then? But to where? To be cared for in their dotage
by a spinster cousin in New Haven? Possible, *likely* even, but how
dull! *La Floride?* Better—certainly more alligators. No, I know:
one dispatched the other. A fight over a man, some handsome
young horse trader who has been tupping one, then the other, in
the barn. Hardly knows which one he's with, but of course the
old girls keep score. I peg Alice the murderer. Buries Mary
somewhere in the woods and runs off with her lover, settles in

San Francisco, where her guilt consumes her, sends her into a tailspin of drink and debt. Maybe she is still there today, one of those deathless madams, forever enticing fresh-faced laundresses into a life of vice. Too dark? Very well: how about a tour of the Continent? In *our* footsteps, in high-necked calico, apples in their palms, slipping through the Canals of Venice under the spell of a handsome gondolier. Alice with her easel, Mary recording her *Travels* to be lauded the Goethe of her time.

My serve. Now volley back a version of your own.

So to your answer: *that* is what I have been doing with my time—nosing about and daydreaming, and hatching stories so that one day you might tell them to the world. Most of the belongings I brought with me still sit in crates in the ell, and Annie, the girl we hired to keep house, asks daily when we are going to move in. I know that I just need to say the word, and all of it—bed, clothing, ashes, and dust, in sum the very mortal coil of Mary and Alice Osgood—will get carted off to the ragmongers, but I haven't quite yet gotten up the nerve to wipe them from the earth.

Yours, WHT

P.S.: Hints of warmth this morning. Still snow everywhere, but the sunlight had an insistence which is unmistakable. Trevors said this was mad, promised me that it will be April before the flurries pass. By evening the world had sided with Trevors, and I woke to fields so white, so smooth, that it is impossible to look upon them and not recall, in certain swells and swales, the alabaster curves of those most immodest Venuses. Only a matter of time before our reformers start preaching the dangers of the untouched snowfield. Walking through her felt an act of violation. All day I wished that I might erase my tracks.

❅

March 18

My Dear Nash,

Two days ago received your letter of the 27th, the sole welcome note in a twined bundle of tedium that has been sitting at the postmaster's since my last foray, two weeks prior. The tally: a reminder from CM that I finish her *Sunset at Easterbrook* before this summer's party season, a solicitation for an article in *Crayon* for my opinions "on the current state of landscape painting," a note from Prescott justifying, with his perplexing mathematics, why this month's receipts don't quite add up. In sum, the kind of thing that I had hoped to get away from. I'll be struck down for saying this, but there is something almost obscene about how much they are willing to pay me—were it not for this house, and its way of consuming money, I'd say I was almost sick with it. *The Cataract at Flores* is apparently still up at Tenth Street, illuminated by gas jets, admission a quarter a head, and yet they say the lines continue out the door—they've had to put a pair of guards out to keep the old ladies from scratching the canvas with their lorgnettes as they strain at the long loins of the savages who gambol in the falls-mist. Regret sullying the scene with such homunculi, but Prescott insists that no one will come to see a painting of "just" a river and some trees. Just! Big fight over this last time I saw him. Said RP (railroads) wanted some settlers in my painting of the Merrimack. Nearly told him that if he wanted the human, I'd paint a wigwam littered with the poxed corpses of Indian children, a settler lying spatchcocked in the fields, scalped head winking like a ruby. The beaver gone, the bear gone, the panther gone.

Didn't say this.

I am, of course, guilty of ingratitude, of biting the hand that feeds me, &c, &c, but I seem to have become utterly incapable of painting anything that is *demanded* of me. Nothing is more likely to make me abandon something than to be told to do it.

I enjoyed your description of the dinner at the Farrows'. Kind of Mrs. F to speak so highly of me, and I won't be mad at you *this time* for repeating it, but this is the kind of straitjacket that I worry most about. It isn't praise, it is a command. When they compliment the cook on his potatoes, it's just an order to cook the same thing again. No one is worse with this than CM, who, having bought more of my work than anyone else, told me *Flores* is "a mistake" because it is too large for the drawing room. Makes me want to paint her entire townhouse green with leaves.

Write again, swiftly, often.

WHT

P.S.—just read this over and I see it is nothing but that which I swore I *wouldn't* write about. And you asked why I left. Very well, an answer: here, the banks are lined with fantastic ice—columns like organ pipes, bulbs straight from the glassblowers, thin sheets through which one can watch the rising bubbles. Indeed, I have become a connoisseur of ice these days: the sleet that falls like hissing sand, the white that coats the roads like baker's dustings, the crystalline mesh, thin as spun sugar, that shatters with the passing of my hand. Ah, the whimsy of a God who would deliver water to the earth in the guise of such fine powder! On certain misty days, the clouds leave coats of ragged rime upon the leaves and every single bobbing stalk of winter weed. If only I was so thorough with my canvases.

✻

May 12

Nash,

Spring, suddenly warm. Trees announce themselves with miniature leaves. The two white mounds outside the barn turn out to be a pair of ancient woodpiles, now nearly rotted to soil. Green pushes out the brown everywhere. A kind of amnesia sets in: wasn't it always so? If I didn't have my paintings, I might not believe that once this all was snow.

How do I spend my days? you ask. Rise well before dawn, before Annie's bustling ruins the silence. Slip out through the old apple grove, just beginning to flower. Stand a moment at the forest threshold, until the birches grant their permission. Then into the woods. The low branches gently unhat me; twice this happens before I understand that it's a precondition, my host insists. Off to the river, now roaring with melt. Easel on my back—no more sketching just in service of a later canvas: this would mean running the world through the sieve of my perception, and I wish to paint what *is*. Scramble over boulder until I find my spot and then try to paint, an effort, for the theatre is such that one just wants to sit and look. Yes, "threshold" was the right word—I leave the world and cross into this enchanted place.

Woods, from the Old English *wode* . . . also meaning "mad."

But we've just started. Brave dip in the falls once I get the nerve up—bracingly cold and rocks slippery, but it's a vice now—makes me feel as if a layer between me and the world has been stripped and everything is clear and fresh again. Then stretch out on the rocks like some mad Adamite and stare up at the lattice of leaves and sky.

Attend to the dragonflies, newly arrived. Agate last week, emerald the week before. Turquoise creatures now, *damsels* I think one calls them, delicate as a grass blade and positively bold. Yesterday, a warm day, I was lying out after a swim and one landed on my knee, fluttered up to my thigh, sat for a while as if aware of the eros attendant in her trajectory, and then demurely took to the sky, only to change her mind and return to land low on my belly. Heart pounding then, my world reduced, incredibly, to that faint tickle, astounded at the ludicrousness of my arousal, and yet completely alive to her. If a girl could become a tree, a heifer, who's to say some nymph might not grow such glassine wings? Hummed past my lips. Shoulder, breast, then thigh again, where she seemed to lick my skin. Damsel indeed!

Paint again.

Stumble home only when it grows dark, squinting to find the hickory that waits patiently with my hat.

WHT

❋

May 28

My Dear Nash,

Brief note. Letter from Prescott yesterday. Usual gossip, nothing worth the ink, except a mention of the review of your book in the *Journal*. Four pages! No praise is going to be sufficient, but still I wanted to see what they had to say.

Problem was of course that P didn't send a copy—he must think that the whole world has access to the same indulgences as in the city. Well, my bookseller in Oakfield usually *does* stock a few issues, but this week his supplier in Boston is ill and hasn't gotten around to sending them. Then he told me that Crane's in Shadd's Falls also subscribes, and since I was already down-valley, I decided to go there. Two-hour ride, broken by a sudden downpour during which I found shelter at a farmhouse, took tea with the farmer, endured his ramblings about the coming slave revolt spreading up into the North, as if *his* flocks might be carried off. Then on my way again, pausing for a moment in the road to take in the abandoned farms, the low brush slowly reclaiming a former pasture. What was I doing there? Ah, the *Journal*! Onward! Another hour to Shadd's Falls, shop closed: Crane apparently is in New York on business. Now I was in for it—sixteen miles from home, and nothing to show, when it occurred to me that I was but only *eight* from Bettsbridge, where the general store is a miracle of supply: often stocks the journals for the summer crowd. Anyway, you can see where this is going—I went rambling across half the county and had to spend a night at an inn in Corbury Junction. Bed unfit for a sailor. Shared a plank with some pungent heathen. Downstairs, drunken revelry, and not the good kind. At breakfast: fly wing swirling in my coffee. Beat a defeated retreat before the mist had lifted, stopping at the post to discover that P had sent a copy after all.

Cursed P. Found a dry spot beneath an elm and read it there, in the Square. Obscene it was—not a review, but a love-making. Your words "no less than ravishments"? "The reader feels the warm breath of Filomena on his own lips"? Oh dear! Not signed . . . Well, common enough, though here I think the reviewer need not fear reprisal from you but from your wife.

Of course, none of the praise gave me the same joy as simply seeing our names together in print. "Mr. Nash's travels on the Continent with the painter William Henry Teale, a journey which gave us not only the former's *Travels*, but the latter's grand canvases of sunsets at Vesuvius." How often I wish that I hadn't come home early to attend my father's illness. Still, I can't forget our sea journey, those first weeks along the Italian coast.

Here, news from Katherine is that she will come the second week of June, as planned. I'll admit I will miss my damselfly days, but if I wait any longer, the children will have forgotten who I am. K is eager to have guests and asked whether I might consider inviting you and Clara if the house is done this summer. I had to read my reply twice to make sure I didn't sound *too* eager. You have bewitched her, too, I think. You know she finds most of my artist friends tedious—"unwashed men with easels"—but every time I mention you, I catch a faint fluttering of her lashes. She'd read your *Dido* when she was fourteen, when novel-reading was cautioned against if not forbidden. Said it did to her everything her mother feared—taught her that a woman could be an active agent of love and not simply the wooed. In other words: gave language to longing. I'd have you come sooner, but she'd be appalled to learn the great Erasmus Nash ate with anything but her best silver. Still, the place is nearing shipshapeness, so expect an invitation. She'll promise a well-appointed country room, the most gracious comforts. I promise nothing but the bittern, the spring onion, the morel—in sum, the whole freshness of June.

WHT

P.S.—On the matter of archaeology. You will recall my description of the house—five bays, central chimney, long descending roof in back—standard stuff, save for the odd little shanty off to the side. Well, one of the workers pulled off the siding today and discovered a stone wall (the Osgood house is post and beam). *Very* old construction, Trevors thinks. So *someone* was here even before my Major. Who? If I close my eyes, I can see him. Old Nehemiah, son of Eleazer, son of Adonijah, son of Fearing-God. Tilled the land, kept the Sabbath, and every fortnight, washed his hay-stained hands, pulled back the bearskin, and roused his snoring Prosper from her sleep. No, I can do better: a murderous trapper, who stabbed his partner, made a stew of him. Or better yet, a pair of lovers, who, casting off their Puritan yokes, absconded to this place. He with fair hair and dreaming eyes, a restlessness. She of long black tresses. This their private Arcadia, no one else around.

P.P.S.—not such a brief note. I'm getting starved for conversation.

※

June 15

My Dear Nash,

Well, so long to solitude. Katherine and the children arrived on Monday—lovely to see them, but the house now bustles with such noise that it seems they have brought the entire city to the mountain. Linen is unfolded from crates, hats materialize, chinaware replaces the pewter. K at first pleasantly surprised. For the past year, I've endured such protests over the move, accusations that I put my art before my family, that I will condemn my children to savagery, &c. Only the news that both the Fitzroys and the De Groots have bought homes in the county seemed to have placated her. Never mind that I would go mad in the city, that I had reached the end of my rope—it is the Fitzroys and the De Groots who have convinced her that one might consider leaving the dust and crowds.

I should have known that it would only be a matter of time before the honeymoon ended. When we bought the house, she'd told me it was too small. I'd prevailed upon her to wait a season, get used to its country charm, but now I know that I was destined for failure—the only uncertainty was *what* would become the target of her wrath. My wager would have been on the parlor, which is too small for more than a single family to join us, but instead, the culprit is the chimney. Yes, poor soul, its crime is that it sits there, as most old chimneys do, *plop* in the middle of everything, blocks the entrance, denies her a grand hallway in which to greet her guests. She's right, of course, but were we to remove it, the whole affair would come tumbling down. The solution is therefore what I feared from the start—we will build another wing, and this summer. Never mind that the workers have gone back to their fields—Trevors brought a gang of Irish brothers up from the city and will have it done in *weeks*. So he says. Positively irritating in his enthusiasm, is Trevors. Clearly, patching up an old two-story excited him about as much as painting a portrait of Mr. La-di-da's ugly little daughter excited *me*. But now he has his project. At least they won't be tearing anything down: you know how affectionate I feel for my ghosts. Out here, no one tears down anyway—one just adds upon, *agglutinates*, house to house, shed to shed, like some monstrous German noun. Everywhere one finds these rambling masses: new wing goes up, old one becomes the servants' quarters, old servants' quarters become the barn, old barn becomes the carriage house, and so on. They molt, these houses! As the centuries go on, I would not be surprised to find them traipsing about the country, leaving a trail of former incarnations in their path.

But yes, the bustle: my Arcadia has been transformed, birdsong has been replaced by hammers, bootstep, the scrape of dressers, the unfurling of rugs, the hushed murmurs of the workers as they debate whether they should confess to Madam that they nicked the dresser on the doorjamb. I escape to the woods if I can, and if not, hunker down within my woodsman's stone cabin (now back behind new siding), where at times a child wanders in, gazes with mild disappointment at some painting of a tree or fern, and then dashes off to shred the real thing with his hickory saber. Only Ottilie ever pays me any compliment—my studies of the glen are "nice," the old *Landscape with Two Figures* is "sad," and my cataracts earn a puzzled, chicken-y tilt of the head. Were critics so generous!

WHT

P.S.—Ants ate the envelope glue so I hadn't sealed this yet, and then, last night, just happened to pick up your *Travels* again and opened to your description of the twilight as we left the Azores, the sense of oneness with the world—of dissolving away. Now I wonder if this is what I seek when I paint—a disappearance *into*. Maybe that is what I had come to hate about my grand canvases. Always *I* was at the center of it. Not *literally*: no little WHT, peering backward over his shoulder, *sensu* Cole in his *Oxbow*. But the very act of *composition*, in that specific sense a painter means when he speaks of the act of bringing together various parts into a harmonious whole—this act of cohesion naturally places the *subject* front and center. Cole is a good example: all meant to be wild nature, but there is no doubt that it is man's eyes we are looking through. This is not to doubt his skill. But he is always there, and *my* most exquisite moments are ones of dissolution. But what does this mean anyway? Can there be art without the human in it? Maybe that is what I wish to capture: beast as seen by beast, tree as seen by tree.

I jest, but not really.

✳

July 18

My Good Nash,

Your letter was handed to me on the road to Oakfield by our cheese-man's girl. Apparently, it had been mixed up in a stack de-livered to Mr. Halfpenny, the lawyer, who gave it to one of his farmhands to bring back to the post, and Billy, thinking he might be helpful, instead turned it over to his sister who works at the butter mill where we buy our cheese. But the silly girl forgot, and it wasn't until her mistress found it scattered among the but-ter pots that it resumed its journey. Upshot was that I was on my way to Oakfield when I was hailed by fair Willa, breathlessly fumbling with her bosom in search of the letter, which, understandably, had curled up in those warm recesses and did not want to come out. Eventually she found her quarry and handed it over, blushing. Ran off while I read it there on the road. I still have it before me, translucent with the butter from her fingers, heavenly fragrant. If only every letter were so thoughtfully conveyed.

Much to write, but I'll cut to it quickly: yes, visit. Drop everything. Run, swim, fly. Hurry out on the first train, worry about nothing, bring only yourselves. There is a stage, but I will get you at the station. Katherine will protest that the house isn't finished, that it is not properly appointed, &c., but Trevors has truly worked magic. Wish you were here to see it. Frame, roof, all walls, and half the flooring. Carried the barn over so that it might serve as a carriage house. You read that correctly: *carried.* It's an art here—mastered back when they were rolling logs out of the woods. Woke up one morning to find he had the barn up on screw jacks, then twenty-two oxen, snorting like the cattle of Geryon, come rumbling up our road. Barn groans, protests, creaks across the yard—until they settle it snug against the cabin wall. Well, not quite snug—we had to build a short hallway to connect them, and by "we" I mean the Irish do all the work. But now my quondam barn serves as carriage house, and one may walk, without being touched by a single drop of rain, from carriage, through cabin, old house, and into the grand rooms of the new. Of course, this means that the cabin can no longer serve for my studio, at least if I should want any kind of silence. Instead, I'll take the old servants' quarters in the back—a bit dark, but we have added a veranda so I can look out onto the old orchards and the chestnuts in their creamy glory. North-facing, so I'll freeze in winter, but for now at least it feels more part of the forest than of the house. Sketch enclosed: I should have thought of this first, should have painted the place *before*, so you could appreciate the after. Try this: place your left hand on the barn, your right on the big house, and you'll have a sense of how I found it, seven months ago.

Of course, what you *can't* see is what matters: there is a room for you and Clara, and a separate one for the children, and if some walls aren't papered, and if the shelves are empty, I have confidence that you will find a place of comfort and calm. Note that I have a vested interest in your pleasure, lest you dislike it and not wish to come again.

WHT

P.S. The country! Apples beginning to fruit. Wild strawberry fruit*ed*. Mushrooms broad enough to give one shelter. The goldenrod bobbing as I pass—my nodding acquaintances. Slugs leave hieroglyphs on the beech bark.

Final observation. A heron in the treetops—really, do they perch so high? I'd always imagined them swamp-walkers. But there, above, I have my answer.

❊

August 20

My Dear Nash,

First apple. Nothing to say save that I wished to race into town with it in my hand, raising the crows with my *Hallelujahs*. Henceforth, it shall be forbidden to call anything else an apple. Oh, Atalanta! I used to think she was a fool, but I too would have given myself up to any suitor to taste such gold. Never again shall I chuckle when I pass those portraits of Alice and Mary with their *La Joconde* smiles and their Eve-fruit. Henceforth, every portrait of me will also show one in my hand.

I nearly wept to think that I had wasted half my life before I tasted of it. Let us tear up our Almanacs, date this life from before and after.

My first thought: I will send my city friend a bushel, two, in haste, so that he might know its freshness. But what fisherman hands off his lure? Second thought: come so that you may taste it from the tree. If that can't entice you, I don't know what will.

WHT

✣

September 8

My Dear Nash,

Well! Was it the apples? I know, I know: you were planning to come, regardless, but, ah, the coincidence seems awfully suspicious. But I am not offended—I would travel halfway across the globe for them. Anyhow, confirmed: September 13, the evening train. I will be waiting for you, eagerly. Have told no one, lest the local papers spoil the privacy of our celebrated visitor. Wear your hat low.

WHT

✣

September 19

Nash,

Grab your pipe, take your chair—this is a long one, but there is no other way.

How bittersweet your departure! Trust this will find you safe at home after your journey. We cannot decide what mood we find ourselves in, whether to bask in the lingering glow of your presence or to mourn your departure. Ottilie and the boys sulk about the house in search of their playmates—only the promise of your future visit can rouse them. Katherine, meanwhile, alternately reads the copy of *Travels* you inscribed to her, blurts out, "That *was* lovely, wasn't it?," and frets over the rustic state of your lodgings, unmoved by my assurances that she made a fine host.

And I? Allied in sentiment, I think, to my children.

Such joy that your sweet company makes
Does leave a shadow in its wake.

To think that you were here but a week! It felt both a minute and a lifetime. You are like no one else I know, have ever met. My sole consolation—and it is a great one—is the realization of my life's fortune in your friendship. For it is *Fortune.* To think of all that had to happen so that we might meet, and all that might have happened to prevent it. Had P never held his party, had one of us been taken by the fever circulating that summer . . . had the rains detained one of our carriages . . . had one of my melancholies led me to turn down his invitation! Or: had I come, but had we not, on that excursion up Green Hill, found ourselves in such proximity, and talked. How I remember that, and the envious eyes of all upon me, and my incredulity at it all, the agony that came with that sense that at any moment you would find me dull and move on to someone else. Yes, I'd found, I knew, my Life's friend. How our words tumbled upon each other! I could see others watching—I knew that they wondered what it was we could be speaking of—what magic might have engaged us so. But it *was* so, and I count from that moment a joy that I have known nowhere else. Well, I hardly need rehearse this history—but I think now how little has changed, how instant our friendship was, how it grew throughout our Tour.

And yet that is where the mystery in all this lies, for I *should* be content with this joy, pleased as Katherine is pleased, satisfied as after a good meal. But a meal satiates. You remarked—just yesterday!—that I seemed not myself. If I was not forthcoming, it was not because I intended any deception, but was simply the victim of my moods . . .

I fear I am beginning to write in circles. Dear friend, might I offer a confession? When we parted after Herculaneum, it was not, as I said, because of a letter from home, my father's illness. It was something else—both the joy I had felt until that moment, and the sense that there approached, before us, a precipice which I was afraid to cross. Am I too vague? I cannot help but think that you know the moment I speak of—the evening after our supper in La Spezia, when we returned together up the winding alleys above the Gulf, and at the crossroads to our chambers, bid good night. We had fallen silent—rare for us. And in that silence, I sensed between us something which had been there since Green Hill but had lay slumbering, unable to make itself known before we threw the heavy fetters of Society off. Precipice . . . slumbering creature . . . Erasmus, I mix my words, but I trust you might find meaning in them. In sum: *that* was why I came home: my wish to preserve the wonder of our friendship, and not risk those perfect days by asking greedily for more.

A malady in the family, but not in the person I might have led you to believe.

Or this: sometimes, friend, I even wonder if I moved to these north woods not for peace and silence, but that I might get away from you.

Dear Nash, the inner life lies beyond my ken, perhaps you can put words to it. Were I able to paint what I am trying to say, it would be a simple canvas, two linked spirits in a glen more beautiful than ever I have painted.

There: I have said what I can. Know that I ask nothing. If anything within offends, please rest assured that I am most capable of resuming our friendship, *as is*, in perpetuity. When you write back, you may write of the books you read and the parties you attend, and the places you wish to travel. You may ignore these ramblings of affection, knowing simply that I remain,

W

P.S.! (And never has the world known such a postscript!) Ah, Erasmus. Brought this, my letter, to the post, only to find *yours* waiting. Snatched *mine* back from the postman, horrified at my indiscretion, for suddenly I was certain I would find some quiet note signed by you and Clara thanking us politely for our hospitality. Shame instantaneous—how close I had come to betraying myself with feverish ramblings!

Went outside—I was trembling and didn't want anyone else to see me. Read your letter standing there in the middle of the street, twice nearly run down by carriages. Read it again—there was no world left beyond your words. Let the critics debate your greatest poems, for me there will be none other than your letter. In answer, I enclose the above, written at my desk, while you wrote at yours.

To put a reply to your query: in one week's time, Katherine will take the children to Albany to spend the final days of September with her mother, and I will be alone.

✷

September 29

Friend, I send this in haste, for you have just left, but there is still so much I feel that I must tell you. The world is of a different color today—azurite sky, canary sun, tumbling streams of malachite. Van Eyck has painted my leaves, the green moss wears a sheen of gold, and even pewter gleams like silver. I wish to stop each long-faced citizen and grab him by his shoulders and shake him, demand that he look around and marvel at the trees, the blue stone, the white cusping on the river. Whence come you,

Erasmus? How is that I have been granted such a benediction? The blanket which we brought with us will go unlaundered for as long as I can hide it from Annie without suspicion. Twice on the road I brought it to my face to inhale your memory. I had thought the Falls a sacred space enough without your presence. Now I fear that I might betray myself by shaking hand and reddening throat, should I take another visitor there. All questions about impossibilities vanish, shame vanishes, never has life been clearer. The necessary duplicities we spoke of seem but trifles, and earthly ones, and easily solved. For aren't all men, to some degree, liars? In sum: I can live like this, and if I must endure the distance, it is as one can live through winter knowing spring will come.

P.S.—You have left a jacket.

✿

October 3

My Dear Friend, In haste, pseudonym to pseudonym. The peril you describe concerning Clara's near discovery of my letters drew me up short. To think that I have risked everything fills me with remorse. I should have learned this after my own close call with Willa's buttery fingers, back in that time *before* this madness struck us both. Write back to me care of G——, at his tavern. He is discreet, will suspect a dalliance, make some winking joke about a Boston maid, but cherishes his reputation as a keeper of secrets.

Anon, W

✿

October 10

Dear Friend,

Received your letter of the 8th. How kind of the Muses to grant you inspiration. Hope your writing *me* does not arouse

their envy—I am not certain what they think of works with au-
diences of only one. I, of course, am grateful, flattered to think
that I might have played a role in the "poems of friendship" you
are writing, but you know that the genius is your own.

Here there is nothing but splendor. You have lit a fire beneath
me and made me feel, if for an instance, that I am equal to the
gauntlet thrown down by these woods. For how, indeed, to capture this? Gone the slow and cautious gilding of the birches, the
faint yellowing of the sugar maples, this inching into autumn: no,
now the forest plunges headlong into it. Yesterday it was the
hornbeam, today the chestnut—I'd hate to see her tailor's bills.
There are times I'm sitting in my glen (our glen), before my
river (our river), and I am certain that the low beech who drops
her branch across my vision has changed her hue over the course
of minutes. That the high maple behind me blushes more deeply,
that the little rim of fire had spread a little further around the
scalloped feathers of that oak. Ha! I want to shout at them. *I saw
you.* It is like a game I used to play with O when she was very little, when she would slink from hiding place to hiding place, moving very slowly, as if this meant I wouldn't see. But I *do* see.
There is a way-faring tree who greeted me this morning clothed
in crimson, and yet, as the day went on, revealed a distinct pur-
pling. I caught my breath when I first saw it happen: one leaf and
then, above, a second, and then, at once, the rest. Began the
morning cursing at the limits of my cinnabar, only to discover
that what I needed was a deeper blue.

In sum: I can't keep up. I had sworn to myself that I wouldn't
paint any more from sketches: no more winters troubling over
autumn's memory. But this was a conceit of summer, when the
days seem to pause for a moment in their cloaks of green. But the
sun doesn't slow for the painter of sunsets, so why should my
woods? Might you find, somewhere in your city, some Hindoo-

god of a contraption, of a thousand arms and thousand brushes
with which, by means of some many-jointed lever, I might capture all I wish? Yesterday, I was but a stone's throw from the
house when I found a parade of little mushrooms, rising from the
leaf-fall. Easily overlooked at first, but upon closer inspection,
creatures of such a pale blue as I have only seen in alpine waters.
Had I been painting, locked up in my room, I would have
missed them, for by afternoon they had begun to blanch, and
by nightfall, were as white as brides, with lacy veils descending
from their caps. Death and the maiden—by morning they were
gone.

Such is my predicament—it is all happening too fast. Yes, it
will come around again, next year, and after that again. But one
feels the lurching of the minute hand. I propose a new calendar:
not one autumn but twelve, a hundred. The autumn when the
birches are yellow but still have their leaves; when the beeches
are green but the birch leaves have fallen; when the oaks tint to
the color of ripe apricots and the beeches yellow; when the oaks
turn a cigar brown and the beeches curl up into crispy copper
rolls. And so on: I've missed a few. But to call it all just
"autumn"!

P writes again, asking if I am progressing, if I have anything
new. Dashed off a letter that I now fear was a bit flippant, but I
will paint what I paint and not answer to their bully whips.

Almost forgot: yesterday, O, playing in the orchard after the
rain, turned up what seemed to be the head of an old hoe. And to
think that, in all its shifting, the earth decides to offer this up
now. Which of my ghosts? Alice? Mary? Dull old Nehemiah? I'd
like to think that even he wasn't immune to the charms of the
place—perhaps he took old Prosper up to the falls and let her
feel the rumbling of it. Bathed up there, rubbed the ice in his
armpits, and splashed snowmelt on his chest until, one day, the

heart couldn't take it anymore and he pitched gloriously over into the stream, where he's been dissolving ever since.

That's how we'll go: heart to heart, thump thump, churn around each other like wood shrimp in the tumbling water, deliquesce, and flavor the tea.

WHT

✻

October 24

Dear Friend,

Katherine again to Albany. Annie in Boston with her sister, who is ill. You, cursed you, have returned to other claimants. Solitude here, *'mongst boughs pavillion'd*. Prefer, of course, the *highest bliss*. November 5—your promise, blood-sworn. With this knowledge I can take my stand and endure the crucible of time.

Still giddy. Nature doing her best to draw me into her cloak of melancholy, but I have the memory of my friend. A week of cold wind: days when I must bind myself in blankets, when the paint is too cold to spread. Wander, then. Over the logs, fungus-feathered like turkeys, the moss where we once pressed our silhouettes. On a flat blue stone, a pair of beetles, even darker blue, and iridescent as cantharides—so absorbed in flagrant delectation that they ignored me as I lifted them. Farther: an old ash, dead, wearing its loose bark like an écorché figure that holds his own flayed skin.

The frogs seem to have vanished. I might go on, but am exhausted from a night spent yearning.

November 5.

Write.

WHT

P.S.—Last apple of the season—my consolation. And a mystery: a worm hole leads in but not out of it. What am I to make of this? Do they follow their own trail in exit? Transform into the very apple's flesh?

❊

November 4

E—very well—I understand. I am prisoner to the calendar: the 15th, then. Will wait, will ever wait. You can come— Katherine will be back here, but she will think nothing odd of your needing some country air. Still miles of country where we can be alone.

W

❊

November 12

N—another note, to your home address, as I am not certain that my prior letter reached you. Greetings to Clara and the children. First snows here. The beeches and oaks have yet to lose all their leaves, and the sight of the white snow on the brown and red is exquisite—am working on a smaller canvas trying to capture what I mean. My family joins me in extending an invitation—even if the color is gone, I think that you will find much to inspire you in your new work. All are invited, though if Clara cannot join you, you are welcome to come yourself.

WHT

❊

November 16

E—fear I have said something wrong. Please come. Please write.

WHT

❊

November 21

Walking in the woods yesterday after a rain, I found myself
before the silver stump of a fallen birch, whose smooth skin and
two tapering roots looked so much like the torso of a statue that
it took my breath away. Suddenly I understood what it must have
been like for the young Greek shepherd whose wandering flocks
turned up the abandoned pelvis of a marble Venus, and who, for
one blessed moment in his life, before he whispers his secret at
the tavern, before the world converges on his little wood, has her
to himself.

❊

November 30

Dear Friend,

I do not expect a reply. You are aware of my situation. Katherine has gone to Albany to be with her mother. I will remain here,
with my ferns and my mountain. No words to describe the tears,
the fury—truly, I hadn't thought her capable of it. Nothing can
placate her, despite my insistence that what I have with her and
what I had with you exist on different planes. She would be my
wife always, never did I think otherwise, never did I hope to
cause such pain. Oh, but whom am I arguing with! Will *you* convince her, Nash? You are banned, you know this. The threat is
very clear—your career *will* be ruined, and so your life. I suspect
mine already is—career that is; I will live on—but the more I
think about it, I think my career ended when I came here,
stopped painting for them, and truly tried to *see*. But you are too
great for the world to lose you. Oh, the dream circles me that
you might give up the accolades of men and come here, vanish
with me among my fugitive leaves. But you are made of some-

thing different—the world needs you, not only I. Such is my jus-
tification, though I know I have been left without a choice.
Sadness, only.

So: no scandal, no pleading. I will follow at a distance, and
content myself with the knowledge that one day I might find
myself within your pages. Should in the future, on a pleasure trip
to these mountains, your carriage pass my port side, have no fear:
I promise I will look to starboard. I ask only one thing. If your
harridan wife has not destroyed my letters, I humbly request that
you return them to me, as I here return yours. There are things
there I wish to hide from the world and recall only to myself.

WHT

Five

NOT to his daughter, for she knows his secret had been kept from her deliberately. Not to her sister in Boston, for she would be disgusted by the sin, condemn his memory for its godlessness. Not to her family back on the island, too distant. Not to her friends— though there are so few now—for they wouldn't understand what love had driven her to do. Not to his neighbors, for he has a right to be remembered as the person he pretended. Not to the priest—oh God, no. Not to the sad, stumbling Oakfield drunks, whom she imagines as more understanding, but less discreet.

Not to William, for he cannot answer. Though she dreams he answers. Though it is his forgiveness that she needs.

Late December, and she haunts the house he left her. Rises in the morning and walks its rooms, its stairs and corridors, opens doors, just looking. Ghosts everywhere. She senses them, knows that there is no such thing.

Sometimes seeks his presence.

William, are you there?

Is that you, William? I saw the curtains shifting, I heard rustling. Just say so, and I'll tell you everything, I will explain.

Just a signal.

Puff of vapor on the mirror.

Dent in the pillow.

A word.

But the whole house breathes, always has. Creaks and tilts. Cracks and whispers with the cold.

A whole chorus, but in none of it is him.

In the mornings, she walks outside, where once they walked together. Wears his jacket, his scarf, his mittens. The snow knee-deep in places, but it doesn't stop her. Before, she carried the two of them through worse.

She goes because it is the only place where she can bear his absence. Because the cold, the treacherous path: they make their own demands, distract her from her secret. *Two* secrets: his and hers.

Everywhere the tracks of little animals, the deep steps of the deer. The snow renders their passage legible, reveals the long night's silent maps.

Would they listen, the animals? She smiles ruefully, imagines the chipmunk scolding from his oak confessional. The gossiping chickadees. The wolf's summary revenge.

No.

Not to mouse or marten. Not to the river. Not to the earth.

But maybe?

Stops there in the forest, and looks about her. Then she's on her knees, digging into the snow until she strikes the moss beneath it. Throws off her mittens, digs again. When she hits the frozen earth, she grabs a stick and scrapes the gravel, the fine roots. Black loam crumbles. Deeper now. Until she can press her face into the hole.

Inhales it, the sweet, cold smell of moss and soil. Whispers into it and feels the warmth of her breath rise back to her. Looks down to where she'll bury it, and then presses her mouth into the hollow and begins to speak.

❊　❊　❊

She had come to work for him after his seventy-fifth birthday, when he had fallen on the road outside his house and fractured his leg.

She was fifty-four. *Temporary* was what the daughter told her. *Temporary assistance in matters of everyday life.*

House a bit run down too, could use some tidying up.

Three hours by train and another by sleigh, and she had never been more than ten miles from the ocean. No other help, the daughter told her, besides his neighbor, Lund, who did odd jobs and brought his meals.

December, and already snow across the country. Many reasons to say No.

Yes.

Because her niece's family was growing, had no space left for their spinster aunt.

Because her last client had passed away that autumn and she felt she was no longer necessary to the world.

Because there was no returning to the Azores, to that hunger.

Because of something in the daughter's story. *A painter, once renowned, until he disappeared into the woods alone.* Something in the life that needed answering. Something in his solitude which reminded her of her own.

She arrived there one week later, snow-dusted, smelling of the bearskin blanket on the sleigh.

He up in his room, tall and pale, with a sparse white beard. Nails untrimmed, brace on his right leg beneath the sheets. The sharp shin of the left.

His hair matted to his head by sleep-sweat. A pair of ladybugs upon the hand that lay outside the blanket, at first she thought they were two drops of blood. She looked over at the daughter.

A temporary assistance?

For she'd nursed the old for twenty-seven years, knew the leg

163

was just the culmination of a chain of troubles, a waypoint on a road he would have continued down had she not come. When she shaved his beard that night, she found a face of such fine, translucent flesh, she felt as if she held his skull.

He was knobbly-elbowed, rail-chested, and scars showed pearly over his heart and flank. Low on his coccyx, she found the pink sheen of an impending ulcer. How long had they let him languish? If the skin had given way, there would be no turning back.

And outside, grey deer, blue snow.

And the house, the tumble, the mazy skein of its rooms.

The beds dusty, spotted with mouse droppings.

The ashy, unemptied hearths, the sooted lamps.

Four roofs, ten fireplaces, eighteen rooms, and all but three abandoned. The rest filled by his life of scavenging. Strips of bark and withered clumps of fungus. Bones of animals. Piles of porcupine quills. Dried grey tufts of goldenrod, cracked pods of milkweed, fern fronds, jars with insect specimens. Antlers, turtle shells, and bird eggs, lined up along the mantelpieces: lemon yellow, blue, and charcoal black.

And stones by the hundreds, and feathers by the hundreds, and the gourds. Birds' nests on the shelves, and branches everywhere, great piles of bark. Walnuts chiseled by the squirrels, each with the same exquisite butterfly design.

And the daughter, as if sensing the question: they were studies for his paintings.

As if this could explain why he'd kept them, why he didn't throw them out.

Was it then that she had fallen in love with him? Presented, as she was, so instantly, with the evidence of her necessity?

Or had it happened later that December, when she'd taken him outside to feel the falling snow against his face?

Or January, when he'd yielded to her nagging, and allowed her to gather up the old leaves from his shelves? When he mentioned, gently, as if in passing, the children's sleigh beneath the clutter in the barn. When she hauled it out and set him on it, pushed him to the meadow, where they could look back on the house.

Or was it February? Walking through the yard with her arm around his waist, and his over her shoulder, something thawing between them. Listening to him tell how he'd found the house so long ago. In an orchard deep within a wood.

Or was it when the brace came off in March? And the doctor, up from Corbury Junction, peering over his handiwork, at the withered leg with muscles knotted by contracture, extracted from his bag a piney balm and showed her how to apply it to the stiffened ligaments, watched her as she scooped it, worked it into the muscle, softly first, then harder, running on the thick bands around his knee and hip. Muscles yielding, the pale flesh growing pink and warm. William grimacing, gripping the sheets, eyes closed, lips pinched between his teeth.

Was it then?

Or later, when he took a key that he'd kept hidden, led her into the wing he'd built and then abandoned. Up the stairs (and though he used a cane, he chose to lean on her). Through rooms empty of everything but canvases. Hundreds of canvases. Stream and forest, tree and stone. His woods. But there among them: a vision of the place she'd come from. For he had stopped there long ago, during his travels. Painted the cliffs, the waterfalls. The little children on the shore.

She froze: but was it possible? Had their paths crossed once before? How astonishing to think she could be one of the little figures in the breakers, but when she looked closer, the forms dissolved to brush-strokes. Still, to think that he had seen her people, heard her gull cry, breathed her air.

Or April? For he could walk without his cane, but chose to take her arm along the river that had begun to bubble up beneath the ice.

—

In May, the forests of his paintings appeared to her a second time.

A green cathedral, oaken apses alight with moss.

And now they shared stories, slipped in and out of conversation. Like thinking, she thought: it came and went so gently. He spoke of the woods, the trees, the spring birds. It was like being with a child, all this naming, like being with Adam, and all she had to do was listen and he was glad to speak.

He told her about his childhood in Connecticut.

The painting lessons paid for by his uncle.

His early apprenticeship with a portrait painter in Hartford.

His first landscape paintings.

His Grand Tour and early exhibitions, canvases of island peaks and lush, abandoned ruins. The crowds that lined up outside the galleries, the noise and clamor. The blessed silence he had found up in the hills, the raking light, the rushing clouds, the streams, the ecstasy and wonder of it all. He had fallen in love, he said (and her heart quickened), fallen in love with the house and bought it on a whim, only to find that what he loved his wife did not.

And his wife had left for Boston with the children, and he, succumbing to the worst of many episodes of melancholy that had plagued him since his youth, had tried to take his life.

He had paused then, and she looked up.

He said he hoped he had not shocked her.

No.

You seem—

I just—

Fists clenched to keep the tears back.

But she had known. Had read the scars upon his chest and back, the darkening that surfaced sometimes deep in his eyes.

The months missing from his sketchbooks.

—

She rose early the next morning, before him.

Took the horse down to the general store, summoned the clerk, and pressed three dollars of her own into his hand.

It took two weeks for the paints to arrive from Boston.

June now. Together they made their way up to the glen. He walked alone, which pained her, but on her back she carried his easel, canvases, and paints, and settled near him when he set to work. Before this, she had never cared for painting. Perhaps, at times, in the other houses of her employment, she would stop and look at the works that lined the hallways, but it seemed as if she had never really thought of them as something created by another person. While now, with William, she felt as if she were discovering the world again.

She watched his eyes and wondered what he was seeing.

The shape of stones and shadows, the thousand greens attendant in the mosses, the muscles hidden in the tree limbs.

Watching it all appear upon his canvas. Thinking, I repaired this.

June.

Temporary, the daughter had said.

In the beginning, she had slept on a small cot at his bedside, in case he needed her during the night. Still she slept there, just within his reach.

And the house, the tumble, the mazy skein of its rooms.

She'd cleaned the beds of the mouse droppings.

Emptied the hearths and cleaned the lamps so they shone brightly.

Sorted the scavenging. Threw out the goldenrod, for it was back in season. Returned the withered clumps of fungus to the woods.

Kept the antlers, because.

And some of the stones and gourds and some of the birds' nests.

Quietly carried the others out through the meadow, and left them like little offerings by the river's edge.

Kept the bird eggs, but gently dusted them.

Arranged the disarranged, placed the displaced, unraveled the raveled.

Still called him Mr. Teale, but in her mind: William.

Before you came, he said, it had been three years that I had scarcely left my bed.

❀   ❀   ❀

All of which she tells the earth. So the world will know, because of what came next.

❀   ❀   ❀

When it was summer, and the days were long, they lingered in the forest for as long as light would let them.

When it was autumn, also.

When it was winter, they read.

Dickens. Hawthorne. Wordsworth. Poe on the darkest nights. Camões—for her, he said, asks her what it would have sounded like in Portuguese. Erasmus Nash, whose works he had in number, who once had been his friend. Choose any, he had told her, and she had gone into the library, taken down a title, brought it to him.

As she did the next night, and saw the bundle tucked behind.

Immediately she recognized his handwriting. *Letters to E.N.*

As if never sent. As if returned.

They were his; she had no right to them. She read them, standing in the dim light of the lamp.

Dear Friend, A note to say I have arrived.

❀   ❀   ❀

Which is the first part of the secret. His. The part that he kept hidden from the world and her, and she kept to herself.

Stops.

Lifts her head and looks about the glen. To her astonishment, she realizes that more snow has fallen, dusted her jacket, gathered in her hood. Forehead cold from where it's been resting on the frozen soil. Touches the hole where the words stir, still warm with her breath.

❊ ❊ ❊

Had he wanted her to find the letters?

Had she known already, seen the hollows in his story?

And his wife had left for Boston with the children, and he, succumbing to the worst of many episodes of melancholy that had plagued him since his youth, had tried to take his life.

Was she to tell him that she'd found them?

That she'd felt such anger surging through her? And the scenes that rose up before her? Vulgar scenes, of sad, shifting men in Boston, who coursed the alleys off the docks?

That she had given her life to him, found him frail, and carried him up?

❊ ❊ ❊

Which, lying on the frozen soil, she tells the earth.

Tells the root and earthworm and frozen beetle.

For she'd given up her life for him.

Which they must remember when she told them what happened next.

❊ ❊ ❊

Winter still. A brief hiatus from the snowstorms. The week before, they'd gone on an excursion to the lake at Bettsbridge.

Walked out on the frozen body, listened to the groans and pops, the deep thumps from the depths beneath them.

Too cold to hold a paintbrush, but his eyes keen to the white and slate grey of the ice.

She beside him, thinking that this was how she wished that it could be forever, together, suspended in the middle of that great expanse. Around them, at their feet, lay stones thrown onto the ice by village children, resting, suspended between the water and the sky.

Later, she walked outside his home, their home, while William remained inside, painting. In the distance, Mr. Lund, their neighbor. His arm raised high and waving a letter: he had been in Oakfield, to the post office.

For Mr. Teale, he'd said, and ambled on his way.

She turned it in her hands, now puzzled. For William had no correspondents, and there was no return address. Now puzzled, for she loved him and there should be no more secrets.

Dear Friend, it said.

She had to pause to catch her breath.

Dear Friend,

    It was with emotion that I received your note from January. I too have thought of you these days, though in truth I have thought of you my entire life, have wished that summer might have continued, *ad infinitum*. I am an old man now—we are old men. Clara, as you might have heard, passed away last year after a long illness. There is much to say . . . but you asked me a question. The short answer is Yes. I would love to come. I await only your response to tell me when.

E.N.

In the trees above her, a cardinal shrilled.

It was with emotion that I received your note from January.

But how had William written?

She made his meals, slept at his bedside, walked him through the pathways of the snowy orchard. Couldn't recall a single time that he had penned a letter, even to his daughter. If so, she would have seen.

And here was proof.

And when the man arrived, what would become of me? she thought.

This man, whose words she'd read to William in his convalescence.

She who had found him so, and carried him up.

❈   ❈   ❈

She says, gathering the earth with which she would inter the story.

❈   ❈   ❈

A bright-blue sky above. Mr. Lund disappearing down the road. William in his studio at the back of the house.

Around her rose the woods, the mountain, the silent trees that William had taught her to love so deeply.

No, she thought. They did not need somebody else.

A squirrel joined the cardinal in his alarm.

The decision simple. Once, long ago, he'd erred and then lost everything. Now he had her. Would need her in the end.

She who found him so.

She tore the letter into strips. Slowly, crumpling the shreds into her hand. Inside, a fire was burning in the stove that would receive them. She hurried, for he was waiting, had been waiting a long time.

A DECEMBER Song. Another Ballad by a pair
of GRAVE Maids, to the Tune of When Phoebus
did Rest, &c. FOR FIFE and VOICE

Now sing us a December song
To ease the cold of winter night.
The year, we fear, is not for long,
As is the day, as is the light.

From summer's blaze, the days contract,
Their pleasures shed, which night obtains.
Our waking hours thus subtract,
Become our sleeping hours' gain.

So winter comes down from the north
And seizes all within its clasp.
The trickling rills, the quiet earth:
The bee, the moth, the paper wasp.

The burrowing toad in leaf-fall yields
To winter's iron will.
As does even the robin
Once so lusty with his trill.

And comes the freeze that leaf embalms
In crystal rattled by the breeze.

The stones, the ice does upward heave
And grips the walls, and sash and eave.

And seizes moonlight in the well,
Entraps fish in icy wreaths.
And gels the pond with torquing swells
While great black bubbles move beneath.

And seizes: deep, the privy's turd,
The worm, the grub that bird escaped.
The buried bodies long interred,
The ribs in roots enwreathed.

And seizes now the very cold:
The glass bulb cracks, the mercury spills.
As even sunlight turns to ice
While Time itself goes quietly still.

Ra ta, ta ta, Ra ta, ta ta
Ratata tilitata

Six

IT had begun the usual way, in the parlor of the big house, on three upholstered chairs arranged around a small circular table, the lights off, the curtains drawn to keep out the glow of moonlight on the snow.

Anastasia Rossi, born Edith Simmons, sat upright, her bulk filling the chair to its arms. She was dressed in her typical costume for a séance: silk kimono trimmed with cambric, loops of jet beads cascading down her bosom, "Pocahontas" headband with its diadem and ostrich plume. To her right sat Mr. Farnsworth, a tall, bearded man with russet eyebrows, to whom she had made love that morning beneath a rearing stuffed panther, lips (the panther's) pinned back to show her fearsome teeth. To her left, her thin fingers trembling in Anastasia's ample palm, was Mrs. Farnsworth, a slight, hysterical woman in a neck-high blouse with bishop sleeves. It was she who had first heard the ghosts that August, and for whose relief the séance was being conducted.

Anastasia had arrived at the house two days before. It was never her practice to stay so long with a single client. She preferred swift visits, for greatest psychological effect. But the storm had begun when she was halfway up the valley, and by the time the carriage reached the house, the snow was coming down so heavily that she couldn't see the tracks behind her. And Mrs. Farnsworth, essential to the proceedings, after revealing the particulars of the haunting, had fallen into another of her attacks.

In retrospect, the delay was fortunate, not only because it had facilitated coitus, which, despite her initial dislike of Mr. Farnsworth, had turned out to be unexpectedly satisfying, but for reasons professional. The case at hand was a tricky one, at the bounds of her abilities, and it was useful to have time to study both family and house.

Time was always useful. It was often not so easy to persuade her clients that the words she whispered in the darkness were in fact utterances of their departed loved ones. And though she was a great student of people, and though she brought (and she truly believed this) immense relief to clients and their families, she was nonetheless aware that, strictly speaking, her séances were but theatre and the voices creations of her imagination. Indeed, her entire persona was a fraud, from her "shamanic amulets," to her claimed ancestry of Russian and Mohican Indian, unless by "Russian" and "Indian" one meant third-generation Irish.

That a charlatan could find her way into enough parlors of upstate New York and Western Massachusetts in the early years of the twentieth century to provide a comfortable living, was not, in itself, remarkable. Anastasia, however, was, in the spectrum of spirit rappers, table turners, and ectoplasmic spinners, a practitioner of such ability that on some level, she decided, what she did was a kind of magic of its own. She'd come to the profession by way of her sister, who had correctly sensed that the pale, wide-eyed girl possessed a certain affinity for the extraordinary, and had brought her to a séance, where Edith, perceiving that the medium had affixed a scrap of iron to her boot to tap out the spirits' "answers," decided, in a moment of pique, to out-channel the star, tossed herself upon the carpeted table, and arching her back and tearing at her bodice, cried out in the voice of a Roman emperor named Augustus Titus.

What possessed her? It wasn't Augustus Titus, whom she'd invented in the moment. Nor any familial tendency. Her mother worked in a textile mill, her father peddled hair pomades. Devout people, yes, but of a dull, predictable devotion, loyal to their quiet church. She had no true interest in the afterlife, except that she was a person whose hunger for the world was greater than what the world provided. Transcendence lay in theatre, pantomime, burlesque.

And once she started, nothing could hold her back. Oh, the joy of it! She saw universes in a ball of crystal, extracted wispy reels of cheesecloth from her mouth and called it ectoplasm, tapped out spirit messages with a weight hung by a plumb line to her garters. It was rich business. The families of the war dead, despite the decades, remained unflagging in their credulity. And all the promises of the bright new century seemed to send more people scurrying into their superstitious, benighted past.

For five years, she'd worked alone, and then one day, a young man who'd watched her twitching in the parlor of a wealthy Albany couple, met her in the hallway and, without a word, reached down her blouse and removed the cheesecloth on which she'd painted ghostly faces. She swung to strike him. He caught her wrist. His name was George Rossi, he was the family chauffeur. He'd seen a lot of hooey in his time, he said, but none so beautiful. He took her walking, laid out his philosophy, their future as he saw it. That night, leaning back on the carpet of the family's carriage, she put one leg on the sill and the other on a footstool, lifted her skirts, and showed him where she attached the plumb line to her thigh.

She was no stranger to a tumble, already had a lover who'd left one morning for Ohio, and hadn't expected the driver to stick around.

But George soon quit his job to manage her. It was his idea to change her name to Anastasia. Monsieur and Madame, together they blew across the district. Spirits followed her, drawn up from the teeming shoals to manifest in marbled halls and humble sheds alike. She loved the challenge of it, the pageantry, the cool sound of her rings circling the crystal, the smooth bills she collected at the end of the strange, damp nights. She took on any client as long as they could pay; she was American. She had no compunction, nor need for any. Unlike mediums who whispered the names of winning horses and hightailed it across the Hudson before the races, she made no promises unless in astral currency, redeemable in the beyond.

And she grew fat on it. Her mass lolled across settees when she fell back in mesmeric ecstasy. Stones mushroomed on her fingers, her earrings jangled, the hubbub of her torques and pendants announced her presence before she swept into a room. She knew that on some level she was a caricature of herself, a grand parody, the kind of circus mystic that a certain class expected. But there was an honesty to such a costume, for it made clear that what would happen was, on a fundamental level, theatre. If a grieving mother could not abide a crystal ball belonging to an "Egyptian" magus, she was unlikely to abide the séance either. Nor would she be comforted by the vague utterances that Anastasia drew from the darkness at the height of her exquisite jest.

What she hadn't expected was that, as time went on, there came the sense that her gift was sharpening, approximating that at which it pretended. The magic that amazed, she had come to realize, was less the gauzy wraiths she drew out from her mouth than the secrets she could glean by carefully watching the living. For the clues were all around her: in the clothes they wore, the photos on their mantels, the stories that they told her, the way a voice could break. She would have made a fine physician, she thought, and sometimes, purporting to read a palm, she rested her fingers on a wrist and read a pulse instead. She wondered what would happen if one day, surrounded by her clients in a curtained parlor, she truly came to hear the murmurings of a ghost.

Given her gift of reading others, she was surprised how long it took her to learn that George, while enjoying her receipts, had shifted his affections elsewhere. When he announced his imminent departure to Florida with the wife of her milliner, she'd indulged a maelstrom of vituperation. But the truth was that by then he'd dulled to her. What was this little man to someone who spent her hours communing with such resplendent fantasies? At least there had been no children. This had been her election, for her stomach turned at bringing another soul into such a deceitful world.

She was alone, then, when she received the letter begging for assistance with the management of *rowdy spirits* across the state line. *Rowdy* was enticing, certainly, and yet her first impulse was to decline the offer. The letter's tone was frantic; the wife, the one afflicted, seemed, even from the brief description, crazy. The place was far, the season inconvenient. And more importantly: rarely, very rarely, did she take hauntings. If she were to weave her magic, it was crucial that she was the only one to hear the ghosts.

At the same time, she was growing tired of the endless trail of parents weeping with the reassurances of their departed children. She relished a challenge. And the county was a place of grand estates, the letterhead belonged to a man whose company made the very buttons on her shoes, the fee was ample, and her appetite was great.

❖   ❖   ❖

"This is Eden, Madame Rossi. The Serengeti of Massachusetts. A sportsman's paradise. Look at the walls around you. White-tailed deer. Black bear. Bobcat. *Moose.* Each one of these animals was taken within these very woods. Oh, people will tell you that they have been hunted to extinction in New England, that you must travel far away if you ever have any hope of shooting anything but rabbit, but it goes to show you that man has a gift of ignoring that which is right beneath his nose. Speaking of which, another serving? My wife won't eat any of it. She lives on air."

It was the evening of her arrival. They were in the dining room, at a table overhung with mounted heads. Before them, on the damask cloth, a hunter's stew. The husband, in a dinner jacket, ruddy with wine and warmth and the exertions of conversation. The wife, as pale as porcelain, and just as still. Somewhere in the house was a girl child, of her mother's skin and father's hair, seen fleetingly at the doorway before she was shooed off. It was a matter for adults.

"Yes, please. Thank you, Mr. Farnsworth."

With a flourish, he slopped another gleaming mass upon her plate.

The piney tang, he explained, was porcupine.

"Where was I?"

"Eden."

"And I knew it the moment I saw it, Madame Rossi. We were coming back from the Adirondacks, and decided to take a detour through these mountains." He paused, and gestured broadly toward the windows. "Just imagine: August, the forest a lush green blanket. We had crossed over the ridge and found ourselves looking down upon this valley, and I knew that it was preordained. Inquired at the Registry of Deeds and learned the owner had passed away seven years before, and his heirs had yet to find a buyer. He had gone in over his head—tried to build a second wing but fell on hard times—and no one was mad enough to repeat his folly. Too grand for the locals, and too far for the New York crowd; the only person living here was his old nurse. Well, *I* saw the potential. Not just as a summer home but as a private lodge. High-end, you see, quality people only. Beautiful bones on the place. Bought it for a song, let the old gal keep what she wanted before we sent her packing, and then hauled out all the junk. Finished the rooms that had been left unfinished. Each one a different theme, a different animal—you'll be in the marmot room tonight. Forest a mess of useless, tangled apples, took two months just to carve out space to play croquet. Already placed the adverts in the sportsman's magazines. Full page—The Catamount Lodge." He took a mouthful of the stew, and pointed with the fork. "And it gets better. I know a man with connections to the President—I know, I know, everybody has connections, but my guy and Roosevelt go back years. I've invited him for our opening season, and let's just say, between you and me, that the answer I got back was . . . encouraging." He grinned and cracked his knuckles. "Can you imagine? The Presidential Suite."

He threw his hands over his belly and leaned back. A great-eared man, with green eyes and a nose suggesting some faint history of fisticuffs, he had a napkin tucked into his collar, his sleeves rolled up, and for a moment seemed the very picture of satisfaction. Then he looked over to his wife.

"And now we have . . . this."

"Oh, Karl, but it isn't proper!"

They were the first words from Mrs. Farnsworth. She sat across from Anastasia, lips half parted, eyes half lidded, her long black hair plaited and pinned with a tortoise comb. A different species from the male, entirely. Fingers resting indecisively upon the table. On her shoulders, a scarf of white voile so light it seemed to flutter with other people's movements, threatening to settle in the carmine stew.

But there was no concern, for she had refused a serving, and on her plate sat a single piece of untouched bread. Yes, a different species, and yet they once had crossed.

"Emily . . ." her husband answered.

"But it *isn't*. We will be the laughingstock of New England."

Mr. Farnsworth looked back across the table to Anastasia. So now, at last, they had come around to the reason she'd been hired. The wine, the food, the fire: she had so succumbed to the pleasures of the feast that she'd half-forgotten she was there on business. Beneath the table, she'd removed her shoes and was massaging a corn against a claw foot of the table. She sat up.

"We are speaking, I assume, about the ghosts?"

Mrs. Farnsworth turned to her, eyes brimming. "Oh, yes."

There was a long silence, during which Anastasia looked at Mrs. Farnsworth and then at Mr. Farnsworth, and Mr. Farnsworth looked at Anastasia—looked at all of Anastasia—and then back to his wife.

"Tell her, my pigeon," said Mr. Farnsworth.

Mrs. Farnsworth shook her head. "But she has seen the letter. And all this talk of hunting makes me ill. Might I rest? Maybe tomorrow I'll have the strength."

"Nonsense, my dear! I will remind you that it *was* your idea to bring her. She has, I suspect, many other clients."

Still a bit drunk, pleasantly puzzled by Mr. Farnsworth's unabashed appraisal of her bosom, sensing her cue, Anastasia leaned forward and gently touched the woman's hand. She did her best to put on her most earnest expression. "In the letter, your husband mentioned that there are spirits, unwanted ones. But that was all." She looked to the husband, who nodded in encouragement. "Perhaps," she asked, "you can elaborate?"

"Oh, Madame Rossi. You will think I'm mad."

"I will think nothing of the sort, Mrs. Farnsworth," she answered. "It is a well-accepted fact that, even in the firmest substances, the atoms do not touch. There is ample space for other worlds." She paused. The fat from the stew was a little thick on her lips, and she stopped to lick them. She thought that she might like another serving. Something to wash it down. Piously, she said, "Only those of us who experience the other plane can know the power of the messages it brings us. It is both a privilege and a burden."

Mrs. Farnsworth shook her head violently. "Oh, no! It is not a privilege at all. It's vile!"

Again, Anastasia looked to the husband, who, seeing her plate empty, filled it. But no further explanation was forthcoming. So, she thought, shifting so that she might loosen one of the ties in her corset to better accommodate this newest portion, it wasn't going to be easy. She took a bite. "And is this the first time you have heard such sounds?"

"Oh, yes!"

"That's a start." She paused. "And a good sign too."

"Yes?" Mrs. Farnsworth lifted her face hopefully.

"Yes. *Often*, yes. It suggests the trouble is not . . . personal. Rather, a trouble *of the place*. Indeed, that your problems began here simplifies our task immensely." She paused, aware that too much optimism risked disappointment. "And these spirits, you have heard them since the beginning of your time here?"

Mrs. Farnsworth looked down. She began to knot her napkin around her fingers. "Not immediately . . . But it didn't take long."

Anastasia had struck a rather intransigent piece of gristle, and took a moment to work on it while she waited to see if Mrs. Farnsworth would continue.

Mrs. Farnsworth did not.

"And how long is *that*, Mrs. Farnsworth?" Anastasia asked.

"Some weeks."

"Summer, then."

"Yes."

Another chew. "And were you . . . alone?"

"Oh, yes. Alone."

"Good." Chew. "And *where* were you, Mrs. Farnsworth?"

"In . . . in our bedroom. I . . . Oh, I can't!"

"You *can*, Mrs. Farnsworth." She leaned toward the woman, affecting a somber, caring gaze of motherly concern. "You were in

your bedroom—very good. It was morning, afternoon, evening . . . ?"

"Afternoon. I had just woken from a nap. I thought at first it
was just the dogs, but Karl had taken them hunting." Her voice
grew louder. Anastasia had the sense of a shy creature beginning
to unfurl itself from a defensive stance. "Lily—our daughter—was
with our maid, in the garden . . ." She trailed off, a look of pleading
in her eyes.

"Very good. And *what*, then, was it you heard?"

"It was . . . Oh, I cannot say!"

The little creature drew back into its shell.

Anastasia took a deep breath, and moved ever-so-slightly forward, bending to try to see the woman's downcast face. "A voice?"

"Not just a voice."

"No? Then *what*, Mrs. Farnsworth?"

"I cannot say it."

"Please."

"No."

"Then I must go, Mrs. Farnsworth. Your husband is right—
I have other clients." In bluff, she placed her napkin on the table.

"Please, don't!" said the wife, who seemed to have forgotten the
miles of road now two feet deep in snow.

"But we are getting nowhere."

"It . . . it rhymes, madame."

"Yes?"

"The word. The word for what they were doing. It rhymes . . .
with . . . pottery . . . with bonhomie . . . with *psalmody*."

"Sorry?"

"Psal . . . mo . . . dy . . . , madame. Vile, vile psalmody." She looked
up, her eyes now wide.

"I am so sorry, Mrs. Farnsworth, but I don't . . ."

"Madame Rossi, don't torture me! I hear *laughter*, if you must
know. They . . . laugh so! They discuss . . . *painting*. They read to-

gether. They read, madame, *love poetry*. There is a painter and a poet, and they are so . . . *delighted* in each other's presence." Mrs. Farnsworth straightened, almost defiant now. "They are *men*, madame. Two men."

"Reading together."

"And sighing, and moaning, Madame Rossi. There! If you must know!"

There was a moment of silence. "Of course, ghosts do sigh and moan," said Mr. Farnsworth, helpfully.

Mrs. Farnsworth turned, with violence, to her husband. "Oh, shut up, Karl. You know that's not the kind of sighs and moans I mean."

And she buried her head in her hands.

It was over. Anastasia felt various contradictory emotions; the most prominent was gratitude for the gristle, which, true to the idiom, gave her something to chew on and kept her from breaking out in laughter. Mr. Farnsworth was stroking his wife's lacy shoulder. "There, my pheasant. There, my ptarmigan. You can see, Madame Rossi, the problem this presents."

Anastasia turned to him. Despite his terms of endearment, several of which were mounted on the wall, his manner betrayed his frustration. Ghosts or not, he had a thorny situation on his hands. And as if this needed clarification, Mrs. Farnsworth sobbed "There will be no lodge! There will be no *Presidential* Suite! Can you imagine if *Teddy* were to hear it?"

There was a long pause as Anastasia and Mr. Farnsworth considered both each other and the question. Several possible responses occurred to Anastasia: That the President was a man of worldliness and likely had heard such revelry before, even in the White House. That the ghosts, mindful of his eminence, might decide to keep it down. Even she, a great shouter, would keep it down with Roosevelt downstairs. One could always bite a pillow.

Of course, what she wanted to say was that they really should have no worry, because Mrs. Farnsworth was insane, and the President was not, and would hear nothing but the whispers of the mountain wind.

Instead, she said, "*Mr.* Farnsworth, have you also heard these acts of . . . psalmody?"

He shook his head. Looking cautiously at his wife, he said, "No, Madame Rossi, I have not."

The lace shoulders trembled. "You hear creaks, Karl! You hear footsteps."

"Yes, that's true. I do hear creaks and footsteps."

Anastasia nodded. *Creaks and footsteps.* In an old house.

"And your daughter?"

"God have mercy, Madame Rossi, Lillian knows nothing, save that I am vexed."

Anastasia looked down into the stew, which had, in the short time, in the cold, begun to settle beneath its fat. She drummed her fingers thoughtfully against her cheek, and registered, deep within her belly, a borborygmic protest against her gluttony. The couple waited. Certainly, they were expecting a verdict, some plan of action. But she liked nothing about the situation. Already the fine warmth of the wine was but a memory. A headache was coming on.

"You see, Karl?" said Mrs. Farnsworth. "She *can't* help us."

"My owl . . ." He stroked her again as he addressed Anastasia. "Madame Rossi, I have heard such praise. Mrs. Turning says you found her boy forty years after Antietam. And Tom, my associate, said that one could *smell* the smoke when you conjured up his poor burnt Gerty, and that you had channeled the spirit of Mr. Franklin, our Founding Father, and King Philip the Indian, who was so very helpful. Surely . . ."

Did she hear skepticism? She waved her hand. "Thank you, Mr. Farnsworth, but your wife's concern is warranted. I *am* fortunate to have been blessed with these gifts. But normally, I *take* a message. In this case, you wish to *ask* the spirits something. It is quite distinct." She paused to assess if her audience was following. For even ghosts needed rules, and her clients came with different preconceptions of the landscape of the spirit world. How many times had she been asked to explain what was essentially a metaphysics? Why was one house haunted while its neighbor wasn't? Why did only some of the dead return? Could ghosts take material form? Did they eat? Did they age? What about dead cats and dogs? (This was a favorite of children.) When the deceased rode horseback, was it on living horses, or only ghostly mounts?

There were almost too many possibilities to think of. But she loved making the stuff up, and the story that she had settled upon over the years was that which, frankly, enabled what seemed to be the best compromise of narrative possibility and constraint.

She expounded. "Let me put it another way: The dead do not go away. The world *teems* with their spirits: *a thousand angels on a blade of grass.* What keeps the commotion down, so to speak, is that they must *wish* to contact us, and, frankly, most of them do not. Now, *why* they appear is a matter of debate. Love, revenge—these are the most famous motives, of course. Other spirits might see a wrong committed, and so be moved to redress. And there are the perverse ones, the insolent who take joy in chaos, pot banging, fits of sneezing, unhitched horses, hidden house keys, et cetera. But to take physical form requires some effort, and—I suspect—is not always approved of by their ghostly peers. In other words, a decision not to be taken lightly . . ." She paused in her recitation. "But I am ahead of myself. *These* ghosts, for now at least, have remained within the auditory realm. Though this might change, if the problem is not addressed."

"I'm sorry," said Mr. Farnsworth. "*What* might change?"

"Well," said Anastasia, "for now, you, Mrs. Farnsworth"—and she looked to the wife—"have only *heard* them. They have not sought to make their delights known to you in the flesh."

With the word "flesh," Mrs. Farnsworth became so instantly

still, so pale, that the possibility occurred to Anastasia that she'd just killed her, and they were just waiting for her to topple over. Hastily, she added, "I would say that this is *good* news, actually. For they do not seem to be malicious. Incautious, maybe. Maybe too enraptured in their celestial marriage . . . their *frequent, repeated* celestial marriage, apparently, which of course should not surprise us. For ghosts do not grow old, they do not tire . . ."

"Then what do you suggest?" interrupted Mr. Farnsworth.

Anastasia turned to him. "What I always suggest. That we put the question to *them*. After all, you are their guests."

"Ha!" said Mr. Farnsworth with a little snort. "*Guests?* That's nonsense. We bought the house three years ago. The title, as they say, is free and clear."

"In the *corporeal* realm, perhaps, Mr. Farnsworth. But the dead do not use the Registry of Deeds. This *is* an old house. Three years means nothing in the spirit world. There has been a long succession of owners, God knows how many competing claims."

Mrs. Farnsworth turned to her husband. "I knew we never should have bought it!"

Anastasia held up a hand. "That is not what I am saying. All homes have histories. What I am saying, rather, is that there just need be a mutual understanding between all interested parties. A *realignment*, if you will. You must, when the time comes, make your case to this . . . painter, this poet. Appeal to reason, sympathy, common interest."

"But *how?*" the couple asked, at once.

It was then, looking beyond them, that Anastasia became aware of a single eye, belonging to the Farnsworth daughter, who had cracked open the door and stood watching from the darkness. For a moment, Anastasia felt exposed, as if her deceit were something that a child, who better knew the rules of the pretend, could see. She stiffened, lifted the cup of wine, and swirled the dregs. Now she felt that she was performing an act of confidence for not only the haunted woman, but all of them, the husband, child, ghosts.

"It is late. Tomorrow night will be the séance. That is when we will find out."

❊   ❊   ❊

"Catamount, Madame Rossi, *Puma concolor,* known also as the cougar, the mountain lion, the panther. Extraordinarily rare these days. She has been stuffed as I apprehended her, in the moment of the attack."

They were in his study, a grand room in the new house, crowded with animals. By the window: the panther. On the dresser: a large, four-tusked creature that she had first thought to be the whim of a taxidermist, but which Mr. Farnsworth had explained was a warthog, and one that had also attacked him. He would show her the scar, but it was a bit high on the leg. He was sitting on the edge of his desk, smoking a pipe, dressed in an olive hunter's jacket of worsted wool. She below him, on the couch; a zebra carpet with a raised head lay between them. On the desk: a tray, a decanter of whiskey, two glasses, a knife, a pheasant, a ruffed grouse.

For the past two hours, he had given her a tour of the premises, during which they had discussed the history of venery ("such an odd word, that means both the hunt *and* conjugal pleasure"), differences in hunting rules and regulations in the states of New York and Massachusetts, the grouse (it really had been lovely, followed him like a puppy), how long a man could live only on rabbit (not long) versus opossum (fattier, thus longer), and the Indian practice of polygamy, a topic on which he'd made some study (he had a manuscript in progress, should she like to see).

She listened patiently, mostly seeking anything that might be useful for the séance. But the tour of the home had yielded little by way of archaeology, for he'd kept but some dressers from the prior owner, a grandfather clock of Revolutionary vintage, a kitchen table, a bed.

"Ah?" For a bed, at least, was germane to the troubles.

"But the ghosts, Madame Rossi, hardly confine themselves to the bed."

And he had shown her the new ceilings of printed metal, the William Morris wallpaper, the Turkish rugs. The chimney needed mortaring, and there was still a draft in places—they would need to reframe the windows. He hoped that this had not disturbed her sleep.

The only thing that had disturbed her sleep was the porcupine.

"No celestial couplings?" he asked.

She recognized the lidded gaze that had passed over her figure at the pitch of last night's feast.

"No couplings, Mr. Farnsworth. It was a very deep sleep."

She wondered how early he had started on the whiskey. Drinking was not unreasonable, given the situation. His wife had taken ill after last night's conversation and, despite her bromides, passed much of the small hours assaulted by another ghostly performance.

One of the dogs stirred by the fireplace, rose, and trotted over. Mr. Farnsworth bent to feed it something from his pocket, then resumed his regal posture. "It is all in her imagination, isn't it?"

Anastasia was unprepared for the directness of the question. "Sorry?"

"This bacchanal. The voices."

"Oh, I do not know yet, Mr. Farnsworth."

He waved this away. "Nonsense. She's crazy. You know that."

"I've said no such thing."

He pointed with his pipe. "But I can read you."

Anastasia watched the dog return to settle by the fire. "If I may, Mr. Farnsworth. I am surprised. Last night you seemed a man open to the possibility that our material realm exists within a greater fabric. Of the communication between worlds. When we discussed your colleague that had recommended me . . ."

He waved his hand. "Oh, *please.* You know as well as I do that it was all for my wife's benefit. I can hardly keep track of all the lies that I must engage with to keep this house together."

"The sounds you mentioned. The creaks, the footsteps."

"Old houses creak."

"Old houses also have ghosts, one might be inclined to answer."

He studied her for a moment, before he forced his most charming smile. "*Madame Rossi.* For a moment, please drop the stage show. I understand the necessity for *therapeutic* purposes. You'll be paid, I assure you, but don't treat me like a fool—I did not build my factories by being tricked by other people. I know flimflam when I see it. I've been to séances. Turnips that grow up from the carpet! Dancing vases! The ghost of King Philip! If I were the ghost of King Philip, I'd use the opportunity to finish what I'd started and massacre the lot of you lunatics."

He stopped and drew heavily on his pipe, found the embers dead, and poured himself another glass of whiskey. Anastasia watched him. For all his bombast, she did not dislike him. A proper adversary. At the same time, one did not need to believe in an afterlife to feel some outrage at those who so swiftly cast away the past.

"And you do not think that, with all that *I* have seen, I'd be mad *not* to believe?"

"Bah!"

She followed his gaze to the window, where a pair of crows had settled in the branches of the tall, magnificent elm that rose in the dooryard. "I am surprised, Mr. Farnsworth. If you think that I'm a fraud, and that your wife is merely ill, I would suggest that you consider consulting a physician."

He took a gulp of whiskey. It was meant, she knew, to show resolve, but a slight trembling betrayed him. "Oh, don't think I haven't tried. But do you really believe that she would tell her doctor about such angelic buggery? She says her stomach hurts her; he sends us home with liver pills, or syrup for her nerves."

"A stomachache," said Anastasia, "would not be my diagnosis. Nor liver pills my cure."

Another gulp. "It is good to know that we agree on one thing."

"More than one thing, I think. I'll grant you madness too. But the mad hear ghosts as well."

He turned back and began to speak, but she held up a hand to stop him. Her bracelets clattered down her wrist. "I know what you will tell me, Mr. Farnsworth. But I don't wish to go in circles. One believes the world is enchanted or one does not—it is no use trying to convince another person otherwise. If I might suggest something more productive? I have been conducting séances for nearly thirty years. If there is one thing that I have learned, it is that apparitions do not occur by happenstance. They come at certain times of—how might I put it—opportunity. That is, they tell us something about the situation in which they appear."

He sighed. "Madame Rossi, you are asking me to believe, when I have told you . . ."

"No. Please. Believe nothing. No ghosts. Let's just say it's madness, only. Might you have a hypothesis of why your wife might be afflicted?"

"A *hypothesis?*"

"A soldier, Mr. Farnsworth, with nostalgia, develops a palpitation when he sees a serving girl who reminds him of his beloved. A widow wakes to find her husband lying in the bed beside her. A bride loses the use of her legs the day she must walk to the altar with a wealthy older man she doesn't love. Such cases are well known . . ."

"Oh!" He waved her away with a look of disgust. "Gibberish. Heredity is my hypothesis. Her mother was like this. There is a weakness of constitution."

"A weakness, or an openness?"

"I don't know if I see any difference."

She took a deep breath, and didn't let her gaze fall from him. "This home. Its purchase was her idea?"

"I'm sorry?"

"You suggested madness. I am seeking to better understand. It sounds as if you had a lovely life in Hartford, near your factory. The decision to come here, it was made together?"

"The germ was mine. But it was one that she embraced whole-heartedly."

"She ventured no objection?"

His eyes narrowed. "If you are suggesting that she is fabricating this to deliberately undermine . . ."

"Fabricating, no. Nothing of the sort. If you insist, I am sure she wished to move here. She seems quite dedicated to you."

"She is."

"You are happily married."

"Of course!"

"She is provided for."

"Sorry?"

"Materially. She is materially provided for."

"She wants *nothing.*"

"Spiritually."

"Every Sunday, we go to church."

"Socially."

"We have more friends than you can fathom, madame."

"Excellent. And sensuously, then?"

His face turned dark crimson. "Madame! What! How dare you bring up . . ."

"*Venery,* Mr. Farnsworth? Celestial marriage? It was *Mrs.* Farns-worth, I believe, who 'brought it up.' She hears *love* poetry. Enough of it to make us mortals jealous, frankly. Indeed, someone within these walls seems to be enjoying themselves immensely. But that is not my impression of the corporeal inhabitants I've met."

He stood, and she stood so that he could not loom over her. His flush was nearly purple. Oh, she'd struck a nerve, she thought. Yes, the anger proved what she'd suspected: a problem with the marital bed.

He said, "You're not suggesting . . ."

"Not suggesting *what*? That the topic of preoccupation is often transferred from the terrestrial to the heavenly realm?"

He was close to shouting. "I have never had a woman speak like this. It . . . it . . . is . . ."

"Yes?"

"It's whorish!"

"Whorish! This from a man who leers at me across the table while his wife trembles in terror! Who makes vague insinuations of his books on Indian marriage and tells me of his warthog scars? Ha!" She felt her neck warm. She hadn't argued so forcefully, so honestly, with anyone since discovering George's infidelity. It was magnificent.

Mr. Farnsworth's hand went to the whiskey. It shook as he poured. "You are a fraud," he said.

"Yes, you said that before. A fraud and a whore. I am glad I have your esteem. You should be happy that the storm will end, and I can leave you alone with your menagerie, in this home of such unbridled joy."

He made to speak again but clenched his jaw. For a moment, she thought that he would grab one of the knives from the desk. Very well: she would grapple with him! For she didn't care now about the séance, the fee—it had been worth it, for one moment, not to pretend. He rose and walked to the fire, jabbed the ebbing backlog with a poker, and then threw it, clanging, across the floor.

In a mirror above the fireplace, she could see herself between the panther and the pheasant. She was not unpleased by the color in her cheeks, the hourglass into which her half-turned posture had shaped her. Karl Farnsworth strode to the door, put his hand on the knob, and opened it. A draft swept in; the fire flamed. He stopped, and then he slammed the door shut and threw the bolt. Anastasia dropped her arms. Outside, the snow fell heavily; the crows had departed. The house was utterly, perfectly silent. He was standing at the door, and then he turned swiftly, and with two steps seized her around the waist and drew her toward him.

❊   ❊   ❊

"What we have before us, friends, is a question of interpenetration, the passage between the corporeal and the spiritual. The boundaries we perceive are merely illusions. The eyes are dismal organs, formed in the darkness of the womb. But there is a third eye, an organ of extraordinary power, once open for our ancient priests, the shamans of the Arctic, the Indian powwow. That it has atrophied in modern man is undisputed. The evidence is before us in our willful blindness. Yes, willful! Can we fault those who do not wish to use it? All around us is a world of howling souls, a terrible place. But blindness has its costs."

They were holding hands around the table. The parlor was dark, save for the light of a single candle, which flickered in the crystal ball and cast three shadows against the wall. In the corner of the room, the stove hissed softly. Anastasia's beads clacked as she turned from side to side.

The speech was the same one that she had given countless times, with the minor addition of the organ of extraordinary power in honor of her paramour. Since the prior morning, while Mrs. Farnsworth lay in her sickbed, Anastasia and Mr. Farnsworth had met and separated four times: twice in his study, once in her quarters in the marmot room, and once in the old kitchen, her hands braced against the low lintel of the ancient fireplace. They had been interrupted when Mrs. Farnsworth had teetered to the top of the landing and called out weakly to her husband. Anastasia was searching for a button, torn from her bodice (the tearing off of buttons apparently a particular delight of the great manufacturer, proving yet again that eros is but a condensation of the general psychic state), when her lover returned to share the news.

The wife had regained her strength, and she was ready for the séance to proceed.

"This woman has suffered," said Anastasia, lifting the limp, cold hand that lay in hers. "A fragile creature, who in another day and age might have been a temple priestess, she has heard voices most foul, seen sights unmentionable . . ."

"Oh, remember, I didn't *see* any sights," whispered Mrs. Farnsworth. "Please, don't encourage . . ."

Anastasia ignored her. "She has *seen* and she has suffered! Gazed upon the lineaments of the Immortal Coupling! Felt the angel's warm breath upon her lips! Sipped from the trough of celestial pleasure and felt the burning fire in her throat!"

Lying in Mr. Farnsworth's arms, propped on Mr. Farnsworth's sofa with his face buried in her breasts, shooing Mr. Farnsworth's dog away with her foot, riding Mr. Farnsworth like a saddle upon the splayed zebra with such momentum that they inched right past the fireplace, Anastasia had given consideration to the means and mechanism by which she would conduct the séance. She had brought all the necessary equipment: the ectoplasm and the weights and lines to simulate the rapping, the sleeves with hidden pouches. She had considered automatic writing, the Ouija board, divination by molten lead in water. And she'd dismissed them all. For what a mess she had gotten herself into! What a glorious mess! As if the madwoman weren't enough to contend with, now she had her besotted husband. "My elk! My sea lion!" he had cried to her. He had been convinced that he could get her to admit she was pretending. But she'd resisted, and her resistance drove him into deeper frenzy. He must know, must conquer! And after each grappling round, she'd left him defeated. But there would be a final reckoning. So she decided to forgo the sleight of hand and work her magic without spectacle. For she—clairvoyant, clinician—had seen to the marrow. She must drag it into the light.

She blew out the candle. In the darkness, she could sense them watching. She closed her eyes, waiting for the sense—honed over so many years—that hypnosis was ready to begin.

"I hear something," she said softly.

The wife's fingers were rigid. She began to gasp in quick sharp breaths. "I hear it, too."

"I hear it," said Anastasia. "It is coming closer."

"Yes!" said Mrs. Farnsworth. "It is terrible."

"There are such colors," said Anastasia. "Such goodness, but also such anger, such betrayal."

"Yes!"

"Such love, but also hate."

"Yes!"

"Closer now, I feel it coming," said Anastasia. "A man. I see him; he wishes to speak."

"Yes!" cried Mrs. Farnsworth.

"My God, there!" said Mr. Farnsworth.

In an instant the eyes of both women sprung open. The room was no longer dark. Instead, a single winking light appeared above the ball of crystal, and then, nearby, a second.

"It is them!" said Mrs. Farnsworth.

Brighter they grew, and began to twist around each other.

"There! There! Speak to them! Oh, speak to them!"

But Anastasia couldn't even move.

"Madame Rossi, it is them, I tell you!"

"Look!" cried the husband, spellbound. For the lights were growing taller. Now two cold flames danced about the table, ducked and slid, coalescing into silver forms suggesting hands and faces.

"My God!" said Mr. Farnsworth, as the flames fell on the seated trio, passed along their necks and arms, and gathered in the center of the room. Anastasia, terrified, transfixed, could see a pair of half-formed beings, one of pure white light and the other of a thousand shifting colors. Tumbling, playful, luminous creatures. She wished to go with them. She wished to scream.

"Speak!" said Mr. Farnsworth.

"Yes, speak!" said Mrs. Farnsworth. "Madame Rossi! Ask them what they want!"

But Anastasia's tongue was frozen. She closed her eyes and opened them. There they were. Still. Waiting as if in expectation.

And then they spun together, tapered into a single point, and they were gone.

The room was dark again.

"What—"

"It was them!"

"Emily!"

"Karl, it was them! You saw them!"

"I saw them, Emily! It was extraordinary."

"But what did they want? Why did they go?"

"I don't know!"

"Madame Rossi!"

"Madame Rossi!"

But she was too astonished to answer.

At once, and as if in coordination, they dropped her hands.

"Madame Rossi!"

And she was ready to confess. That she had never heard a voice, never seen a spirit, never received a single message from the beyond. That tomorrow, before she left the house, she would abandon the crystal ball, the rings, the muslin, deep in the forest, and not divine again. That she was of this world, entirely. A baubled fraud. Flesh and only flesh.

That rushing past her now were the faces not of ghosts, but of the people she'd deceived.

"Madame Rossi, what did they say?"

It was then that she was aware that the room had once again

begun to brighten. This time it was a single point, pale and blue, that didn't split apart but grew before them, until it glowed so brightly that she could see the tears that ran down the cheeks of Mrs. Farnsworth, the ruddy face of Mr. Farnsworth, the man and wife now holding each other close as they stared up. All along her back, she felt an exquisite chill.

"Wait," said Anastasia. "I hear it."

And she did. From far away, she felt it ripping through the sinews of the cosmos. A whisper, at first imperceptible, but then louder, growling, terrible, the figure taking form as something brash, irate, and martial. She closed her eyes. The light and words entered her.

"He asks," she said, "what you have done to his apple trees."

Seven

WHAT happens next can be said to be the story of two winds.

By now a century has passed since the catamount laid waste to the Osgood sheep, setting in motion changes that transformed the land around the house. Pasture gave way to bramble, bramble to brush, and brush to birch and pine, while oak and beech and chestnut rose from the nuts abandoned by the squirrel killed one winter morning by the owl's strike. Over the years, smaller clearings have been dissected from this second forest: a kitchen garden, a meadow from which to paint the passing clouds, a croquet lawn for guests who never came. It is at the edge of this lawn that a beech tree—weakened by a fissure wrought one morning by a sudden freeze, by the assault of sapsuckers, by leaf miners who carved out cryptic runes upon the leaves—is shaken by a whipping wind, and breaks in two. Falling, it strikes a neighboring chestnut—not hard, but enough to tear a branch and leave a long thin scar of pale-brown pith.

This is the first wind that matters.

The second comes just four months later, June. A warm wind, and wet, splattering the western Appalachians. In its gusts it bears a broth of little beasts—birds, beetles, spiders tethered to their skeins of silk, seeds in forms of puffs and parachutes. As it sweeps across the hills, it gives and takes away, and in a wood north of the Susquehanna, it oversoars a forest of a hundred thousand chestnut trees. For generations, the chestnuts have given sustenance to

Mohawk and Oneida children, German settlers, militias of the Revolution, farm boys, not to mention deer, horse, bear, moose, pig, bird, worm, squirrel, porcupine, and slug. But now the trees are dead, choked by creamy, filamentous waves of blight that struck the previous decade. Yellow tendrils curl from pinhead blisters in their bark, while microscopic flask-shaped fruiting bodies gun their ammunition to the wind.

It is one of these bullets that now concerns us.

During its brief existence, the spore has never left its host tree. Shaped like a blunt spindle, bisected by a thin septum like the scoring on a pill, it has lived forever in the damp depths of its chamber, arranged with its brethren in orderly rosettes. Release, therefore, when the west wind comes sweeping sheets of spores off of the ruined forest, brings about a transformation that is nothing less than ecstasy. Loose, tumbling, it rises above the death around it, departs its host's crown, skims the canopy, swirls through the tugging eddies of a waving summer pine, and is sucked into the sky. High into the belt of grey-black cloud, and giddily down, it leaps the Catskills, spans the Hudson, whisks up the Taconics' flanks. The wind is swift. The spore can feel the tug against its membrane. For a blessed moment, it seems as if it might dissolve into the air or soar so high it won't come down again. Briefly, the pleasure—for what else can we call such chemistry?—is almost unbearable, until, within a cloud, it strikes a gathering raindrop.

Now again it is falling. The raindrop warps, flattens. Little waves roll through its surface as it gathers moisture from the cloud. Down and out above the spinning forests. The air warms, the raindrop grows. Falls faster.

It lands in a field by the yellow house in the north woods. It is morning. The grass is wet. The water's weight is formidable, but the day is warm, and when the storm moves on, a dog rolling in the grass gets the spore upon its fur, and shakes. With a puff, the spore is airborne once again.

Small thermals rise from the grass. The spore floats into the woods and settles on the chestnut with the pale-brown gash left by the falling beech.

It is not the first time that the blight has passed through the forest. It has been almost twenty years since it began its march, and by now half of the chestnut forests of New England lie decimated. Billions of spores have swept through on the wind, and billions more have waddled through on bird and bug and mite. But it is not so easy to destroy a forest. The right spore must find the right breech in the right tree's defenses, must germinate and find the corridors through which to spread its choking fan inside the chestnut's bark. It must evade the cankered bulwarks that the chestnut heaves up against the onslaught. Must launch its poisons, dissolve the barricades within the wood.

And so, until now, this forest has been spared. Each summer the chestnuts fill the canopy with lambent plumes so bright that it is said that they are lit by private sunshine. Each autumn, mast covers the forest floor with nuts. In the spring, the leaves are soft and green, with hints of russet. They are thriving when the inoculum sets down.

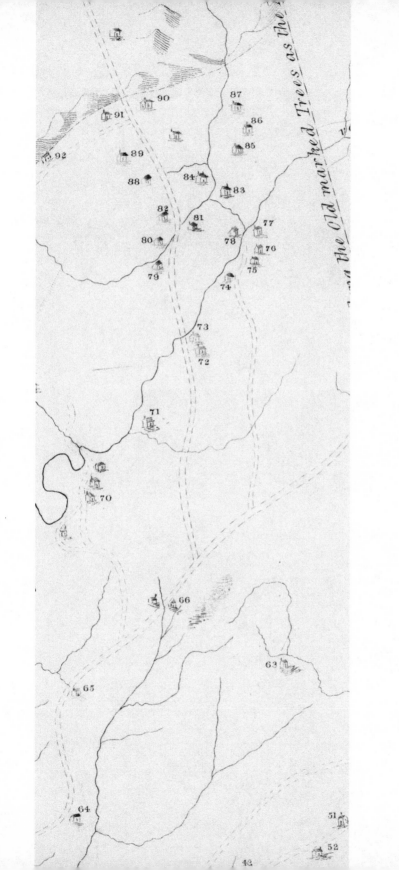

90

87

91

86

89

92

85

84

88

83

82

81

77

80

78

76

79

75

74

73

72

71

70

66

63

65

64

51

52

… and the Old marked Trees as the …

43

Case Notes on Robert S.

THE mother, Lillian, comes to the consultation alone and provides the history. She is forty-three, a widow, the husband having died from appendicitis when the patient was six. The patient, Robert, is the older of two children; his sister was conceived shortly before the father's death. Mother raised both siblings by herself in Boston, though she cohabited for some time with a dancing instructor, a relationship which ended bitterly. She is vague as to the reason, does not answer whether he was rough with her and whether this might have been witnessed by the children, though she is adamant that they were never touched. Patient attended school, performed well, though had few friends, spent most of his time reading science and mystery magazines. The family had once been one of means, and although much of this was lost following the Crash, they retained some income from a button manufacturing patent belonging to the grandfather. Able, during this time, to live comfortably if modestly. Employed a Finnish woman, who helped with chores and with the boy.

Family history mostly negative, save unspecified "visions," and "nervous exhaustion" in the mother's mother. Mother's father died due to complications of alcoholism, otherwise was healthy. Paternal grandparents of "solid Dutch stock." No other known insanity in the family other than one cousin with general paralysis. Lillian herself is "unhappy" due to "life's difficulties," at times uses a bromide to fall asleep.

Development proceeded normally in the patient. All milestones met. No major childhood illnesses, other than a fever at the age of twelve that lasted two weeks and progressed into pneumonia. Played sports and games reluctantly, occasionally seemed "frail," but his mother denies concerns beyond the "typical concerns of a mother for her son." She is not aware when masturbation commenced, or how often it is practiced, though evidence in the laundry suggested nocturnal emissions around thirteen. Other markers of puberty as expected. Has not had relations with females to her knowledge—"How could he, if he is so terrified of people?"

Regarding the current troubles, the first disturbances were noted when patient was fifteen; he would become anxious at bedtime, and ask if his mother had seen anyone in the apartment. Began to check the locks on the doors and windows, claimed that he was being watched by someone, worried about his family's safety. Came home from school in the middle of the day as he was certain his mother had been harmed. Behavior began to have an impact on his schoolwork, and in his final year of high school she was contacted by his teachers and told that he was no longer attending classes. Returned to school, then dropped out again. At eighteen, he was arrested for threatening a couple in Boston Common, after he'd "overheard" them plotting to rob him. Evaluated at the jail, and sent to the hospital. This first admission lasted three weeks and was followed shortly by two more. On each occasion the diagnosis was schizophrenia, either paranoid or hebephrenic type. He improved enough to return home with her, but remained suspicious and confrontational, would claim that he was the subject of a conspiracy, the neighbors were listening through the plumbing, lying in wait, etc., etc. Spoke of shadowy figures who followed him everywhere and who were plotting violent revenge for crimes he was certain he had committed, but never could describe. By then, behavior had drawn the attention of some neighborhood boys—twice he was set upon and "left with a few bruises," though not seriously hurt. But it was "just a matter of time."

In addition to the manufacturing patent, the patient's mother had inherited a country estate that her father had tried to convert into a hunting lodge, though, following the Crash, he'd been forced to sell much of the land behind it to the state. She'd spent part of her childhood there, and at times she considered returning, but the house was not only remote, but suffering from a decade of neglect.

Back in Boston, trouble with other boys continued, Robert stopped sleeping, would wander for hours, then neighbors began to complain that he would wait on the landing, menacingly. Never hurt anyone, but landlord began to threaten legal action; eventually, this was too much, they decided to move but retained the Finnish woman, who, besides his mother, seemed to be the only person the boy did not implicate in one of the infernal plots.

Moved in the summer. Seeing the impossibility of rehabilitating the place with only the Finnish woman, the patient's mother sought help from J., a married man, who "developed an interest" in her, unreciprocated, but "necessary to endure," for he knew the area, helped with repairs, etc. About two years ago, J. prevailed upon her to sell off a significant portion of their remaining wood lot for timber. Robert received the news terribly, disappeared, and was found the following morning only after a long search involving police and several neighbors, immobile, refusing food, speech, squeezing his eyes shut and resisting every entreaty. The crisis persisted for a month, and relented only after the potential buyer suffered an accident during the survey and assessment, and the offer was withdrawn by the heirs.

After this, they lived simply. J. had left after the debacle, but the Finnish woman remained, and they had managed. Mother says the patient improved when left alone, but would walk in the woods

for hours, and could only be engaged on the topic of his persecu-
tion, the details of which she defers to my meeting him. States the
following year was uneventful. He stayed clear of the neighbors,
and she could let him wander. Says he is a great rover, that he has
taken off for days at a time before returning on his own. Sometimes he is picked up by the police or concerned citizens. Has wandered as far as Boston, Quebec.

More recently, on one of his walks, the patient got in an alterca-
tion with a surveyor, the sheriff was called, and he was sent to
Longridge, where he has been for the last four months. Mother
finds it terribly depressing, but the patient doesn't seem to mind,
is given latitude to roam the grounds.

Mother holds out hope that he may return to the person he was
before the illness. In January, she read an article about our clinic
and our surgical success.

On the surface, case seems appropriate for the procedure, indeed ideal if we are to expand its use into the chronic psychoses.
Mother aware that it remains in its early stages, reviewed the risks
with me, etc. I will be up at the asylum next week to consult on
other patients and can see Robert then.

February 13

To Longridge today. Met with Robert in the afternoon. He is a
male of very pale complexion, narrow-shouldered, and generally
ill-appearing, consistent with someone accustomed to institution-
alization, poor sleep, and constant distress. Physical exam conducted. Height 5 foot 9 inches, weight 155 pounds. No nystagmus,
strabismus, ankle clonus, or Babinski. Other reflexes brisk and
equal. Pupils are reactive. No stigmata suggesting paresis. According to asylum records, the Wassermann is negative. Speech is
normal, soft generally, though he becomes voluble when on the
topic of his delusions. Multiple mannerisms: when he is not speak-

ing, he pulls on his right ear with his right thumb and forefinger or strokes his left jaw with his left forefinger, then taps his forehead with the same. Lungs and heart negative save a faint systolic murmur over the apex. Abdomen mildly distended, with stool palpable in the left lower quadrant consistent with constipation, noted by the hospital staff. Pulse 80, blood pressure 134/78. Denies any pain or discomfort, but says he suffers *"mouches volantes,"* "borborygmus," and "antalgia," terms which he appears to have learned during his hospitalizations. Believes these symptoms are caused by his persecutors, and thus cannot be treated.

On mental examination, he is mild-mannered, guileless, superficially friendly, save moments of obvious suspicion. He gives the impression of experiencing ongoing auditory hallucinations, stopping at times to consider a message, or shaking his head and laughing in a silly manner. He makes poor eye contact except at times when it is very intense: the eyes widen so that the sclera is prominent, and he appears to be staring directly through the interviewer—this is often followed by haughty laughter. He appears unaware of his own person, flecks of saliva appear at the angles of his mouth, and when we walked in the cold, he did not wipe his runny nose. He is malodorous, will not bathe unless compelled. Insight is poor. With regards to the nature of his hospitalization, he says that he is there to get rest, explains that he is under constant assailment by a gang he calls the "Harrow," who began to torment him in Boston. The world, civilization, etc., exists in a state of constant threat of a "Rupture," which he, and only he, can repair through a series of ritualized walks. Calls these pilgrimages his "Stitchings," as if his footsteps are literally the needle that repairs the earth. Such "Stitchings" have become the very reason for his being. If he fails, the suffering that comes will be indescribable: it is he alone who can keep war from breaking out, who has saved countless creatures from extinction. Poor weather, bouts of illness—none of this matters. He cannot rest.

As to be expected, he possesses no insight into the possibility that such torments might be the product of a disease, worsened by isolation, and that the act of walking might serve in essence as a form of *therapy*, albeit an incomplete one. Even the mention that exercise and sleep are regular treatments for his condition makes him angry. To him, there is no doubt as to the reality of the Harrow. They are beings of particular cruelty: for his past failures he has been bound, raped, chiseled, skinned, and so on. Indeed, his tormentors appear to have employed much of the armamentarium of American industry to effect their torture: the bandsaw, the boring machine, the dump rake, the welding torch, the steam-powered thresher, the grindstone, etc. He has "physical proof," shows me "scars" on his wrists and heels where he has been flayed and reassembled. When I say these are normal creases, his voice rises, asks if can I hear it, the murmurs, the screaming, accuses me of deafness, says sound—all words, all winds, all birdsong—does not disappear but remains about us. Begins again to touch his face, calms after a while, clearly listening to something I cannot hear. When we continue, he says that, since he arrived in the country, there have been others he calls "Soul Heirs," vaguer, more benevolent beings, whose identity and purpose he has yet to puzzle out. Voices clear, their forms less so. Sometimes tries to sketch or photograph them, wishes he had a machine that might record them, has written letters to film studios asking that they help him out. Gets increasingly agitated when he sees I don't believe him, until he abruptly stands and walks away.

Consistent with earlier assessments, the patient exhibits a classic schizophrenic process, with delusions and hallucinations in addition to motor stereotypy and episodes of frank catatonia. The history of the "nervous exhaustion" in the grandmother suggests a possible hereditary component. The mother is exceedingly anxious, hysterical even. I would not discount a latent paranoia, especially given the history of *her* mother. The prognosis is poor; the current course, despite the respite offered by the removal from the stimulus of urban life, is clearly dementing. All evidence suggests that he will continue to deteriorate. Despite no history of violence, the possibility of vengeance against a perceived aggressor cannot be discounted, as is the likelihood that one of his long pilgrimages will result in exposure, injury, or death. Already he has been found collapsed due to sheer exhaustion, though fortunately this has not occurred beyond the help of his fellow man.

That he is a good candidate for our procedure is self-evident. I would expect rapid cessation of hallucinations and superstitions, while the docility which we commonly observe would have the added benefit of keeping him from wandering off.

I communicated this at once, and forcefully, to the mother, who responded immediately by breaking into tears. She has been given the dire prognosis before, and this is the first time anyone has offered any hope. But when I mention our schedule, the brief open window this month before I travel to Philadelphia for more demonstrations, she becomes hesitant, asks for time.

February 22

Had scheduled a meeting with Lillian at the end of the month, but to my surprise, she arrives today at the office, insisting that she see me. There has been a setback. Robert, it seems, has been told of the procedure by a fellow patient at the asylum (K.P.). Now he has correctly divined the reasons for my interview and has become antagonistic. There has been an extension of the persecutory complex: in a meaningless scar of another patient, he claims to see the marks of a barbaric saw. The mother is distraught, angry at me (though I have told the patient nothing), and must be reminded that our approach does not leave any visible mark, that K.P. has *not* had the surgery, is not even a candidate. When I calm her at last, she insists I see Robert again and try to reason with him. I remind her that this is not necessary; she is his guardian, she may make the decision alone. She begins to weep, asks how we can carry out the procedure if he does not go willingly. I make the mistake of answering this question literally, which only sends her into further distress. Again, asks me to return to the asylum. I agree, though I'll admit a reluctance. Am beginning to see the extent of her fragility, and I have no shortage of patients. And yet something about the young man (the severity of symptoms, the potential for rehabilitation, the tragic mother?) is compelling.

Lillian has just left when there are loud voices in the waiting room, and Zenobia comes to tell me that the mother of S.B. has returned and is demanding to see me, starts screaming that she wants a "reversal," that I've turned her daughter into a "drooling piece of meat," etc. All quite horrible: I am as distressed as she is, did not wish for this outcome, but I have also seen that, for one S.B., I have fourteen other patients well enough that they can live at home. I don't dare remind her that her daughter had twice attempted to take her own life—there is no winning this argument. Unlike last time, the distraught mother will not be pacified by conversation, and I must threaten to call the police before she at last agrees to leave. It is late, and I am shaken.

February 23

To the asylum to see Robert. The nurse tells me he is in the jacket, that he has been given barbital, is sleeping. Dr. Barnes comes. He is new to Longridge, but has heard of me, makes no attempt to hide his disapproval, says that I am "shooting fish in a barrel" by coming there. I must remind him that the Board of Overseers has sanctioned my visits—that they have an interest in trying all means to help the most chronic cases. He changes his tactic, reminds me of my age, his experience, etc., claims that he has read deeply about our procedure, believes that it does nothing to relieve delusions, but works entirely upon the will. That, while he sees such potential in cases of chronic manic excitement, he has little hope for any substantive improvement in a patient who must already make such an effort to form a coherent understanding of the world. My argument that such fantasy is the product of an *excess* of mental association does not move him. For some time, we go in circles. The conversation is civil but tense, the mutual antagonism clear. He is of a generation that has resigned themselves to stasis, monotony, who will cheer when a young man of once-great promise can learn to darn a sock.

At last, the nurse arrives to tell me that Robert is awake, and I can see him. He is still in the jacket, which I ask to have removed. She demurs—this can only be ordered by Barnes, I must wait, etc.—and she leaves me with Robert, who, despite the lingering effect of the barbital, has returned to a state of agitation, says the Harrow has threatened him with worse torments if he lets the doctors "hack up his brains," though doesn't seem to register that I am the one who would be doing the "hacking." Asks me to inspect his foot, which he says has been injected with poison, with semen, with radio wires, that he can hear them speaking from his heel, "listing the names of the dead." When I point out that the "lump" on his ankle which has precipitated such distress is but a small varicosity, he accuses me of being incompetent, says I am not a doctor, that he is the doctor, etc. The picture is of severe disorganization, though one is compelled to listen, as there are flashes of coherence that seem at first insightful, even poetic. But no thought is carried out to its conclusion, it is exhausting, his desperation to be believed is palpable. I make no headway in convincing him, see no point in trying, as it only seems to agitate him again. I leave in low spirits, not only from the spectacle of such sufferings, but from the lack of courage in those who seem content to consign the boy into a state of raving.

February 24

Received a message from my office that Lillian returned again, wished to speak to me, did not say why, though my suspicion is that she has made a decision—why else would she bother to make the trip?

March 8

A third meeting with Lillian. Dressed elegantly today: beret, muskrat coat, kid gloves. To my surprise, she arrives with a copy of my address to the Society from last October—got her hands on a copy of the *Proceedings* from the asylum library. She has read it carefully, she says, and passes it to me as if *I* might wish to read it too. I see she has underlined sentences of more rhetorical effect— "The mind, man's <u>most precious possession</u>," "our sentimental attachment to the <u>memory of who a person was</u>," "a <u>restoration of the whole person</u>," etc.—while seeming to have skipped over the technical sections. She has come to tell me that she has decided definitively against the procedure, that she wishes to thank me for my time, but that she will not be coming back.

Of course, this is quite odd—it is a two-hour journey by car from her home to my office. My suspicion is that she remains ambivalent, wishes me to convince her. She tells me that her son has improved noticeably, that Dr. Barnes has allowed him to go home, has made two house calls, takes the boy on walks in the woods. Robert still talks incessantly about the Harrow, but he sleeps— she thinks—and there have been no more "catonic (sic.) episodes" (I disagree with Freud about most everything, but such mistakes regarding a word that is hated/feared are hard to ignore). I do not argue with her. She has come prepared to dispute me, but it is evident that she has doubts—else why would she come? I thank her, wish her well, and tell her that she may always return.

Predictably, she hesitates. She wants to know if I agree with Barnes's approach—if there is not a better way. I tell her that I am glad to see that the boy is no longer in a straitjacket, that Dr. Barnes clearly has a salutary effect on him, that perhaps this is all that can be hoped for. Yes, she says, perhaps that is all that can be hoped for. I hand her back the paper. I have another patient who is waiting, I tell her, which is true. She says she wonders whether I might come see her son again. At her home? I ask. She clarifies: just a single consultation, to assess if I would still recommend the surgery. She knows it is far, she is willing to pay for the travel expenses, etc. I ask her what Dr. Barnes would think of my visit. Ah! But it isn't necessary for me to come on a day when Barnes is there; I would just need to speak to Robert.

And so, as expected, I will visit Saturday. I suspect it is a waste of time—she will change her mind again, etc. but I feel as if a gauntlet has been thrown. It is as if a worldview is being tested, of which she is the jury. Reason, pragmatism, even basic arithmetic suggest I shouldn't bother—I could see six patients in the time I make this fruitless trip.

March 11

Drove today to see Robert. In my haste, did not consider the challenges of the weather—a warming spell had left the road awash with icy slush, and I had to abandon the car, dig my boots and raincoat out of the trunk, and cover the last mile by foot. Sprawling yellow house, quite picturesque—wasn't sure which entrance I was to choose from, but after some ringing, was greeted by someone who could only be the Finnish maid. Had the strange notion that I might ask *her* what she thinks of the boy, that somehow the flinty old girl in her apron and kerchief might offer an insight into the case.

Anyway, there is no time for this, for Lillian follows swiftly behind her in a state of high anxiety—she had told Robert the night before that I would visit and he agreed—it seemed—but this morning, she awoke to find him missing. Of course, she has grown used to such departures, but she is afraid that she will waste my time. She leads me to the living room. I sit, and she sits close to me. She says she has been sent signs to help her with her decision: a silent owl in the oak, an unfamiliar button salvaged from between a pair of kitchen flagstones. I am struck for the first time by her beauty, which, in the old house, takes on an almost fabled, tragic dimension. There is something very different about seeing her here, and I am aware of the men who drifted through her story—dance instructor, neighbor, and now—I suspect—Barnes. Does she know the effect she has? Or is it unintended, a habit of survival? Thankfully, the Finn brings tea. We talk of the roads, the weather. Lillian wonders about Robert, nervously tries to fill time by showing me some heirlooms: a portrait of her father, a stuffed bird, a scattering of unremarkable antiques. She grows silent, rises, leaves and then returns, says she thought she heard something.

It is nothing. The clock chimes the hour. A figure descends the stairs, stops, but it is the sister—Lillian introduces her—Helen, sixteen or seventeen—she eyes me warily, a look of exhaustion and resentment in her eyes. I can only imagine what it is like to grow up in the shadow of all this turmoil.

At last, I ask if we might look for him. I do not say it, but if we can't find him, I will leave.

She agrees. She leads me out through the kitchen and into a field. Snow is falling, but it is still possible to see footprints that lead off up the hill. Everywhere are fallen trees—chestnuts, she tells me, each storm will bring another down. They used to be magnificent, she tells me—when she was younger, she could gather basketfuls of nuts. It is one of her fondest memories of childhood, and it is hard not to feel that somehow the blight, and Robert's illness, are part of the same process—something sinister that attacked them from within. Could he also have been infected? she wonders. I tell her no one knows the causes of his illness, but I have never heard this hypothesis. Anyway, she says, there is a single grove remaining—sometimes he goes there. Yes, I say: he believes that he can save it, he told me this. He told you so much, she says, he is not so open with anyone else.

I don't know how to answer her, so I just follow, past an old wall, as the trail steepens and we enter the woods. Everywhere is ice and slush, she holds her skirt in one hand, slips and reaches out and grabs my arm to keep from falling, does not let go. Am I wrong to allow it? It would be unkind to brush her off. The forest closes in, the footprints branch, return, vanish at a stream which trickles around blocks of frozen snow. We follow the river, though I see no prints, no sign of passage. Still, she insists—there is a glen where she often finds him, amidst the old trees, where he digs to listen to the words he says are buried in the earth. But Robert is not there, and she begins to cry again. Around us are the chestnuts he spoke of, extraordinary—it occurs to me that I haven't seen a chestnut since I was a boy.

She is very close, her cheeks are red, as someone with a fever. She begins to speak, again. Do I have children? She has seen my ring. She imagines that my wife is so lovely, perhaps in another time, under other circumstances, they might be friends, she and my wife. I say nothing, but I offer no objection. To correct her, to remind her of the professional capacity of my visit, would seem unkind, scolding. We walk back. She drops my arm when the path narrows, and I hasten so that she may not take it again.

Back at the house there is still no sign of Robert. Helen still upstairs—I could see her in the window, watching us before she let the curtain drop. Evening is coming. Lillian asks if I wish to stay. It is not an unreasonable offer given the weather, the roads, but I am aware of certain vulnerabilities, of all parties, and I do not wish to be drawn in.

To leave with Robert missing seems negligent, but I have been there for nearly four hours already. I remind myself that he has vanished many times. She offers to walk with me to my car, says that Robert sometimes goes that way—it is in the line of one of his "Stitchings." I must be careful, she says—there are animals in the woods. I joke I'm not afraid of squirrels, but she doesn't laugh. I accept her offer. On the road, she takes my arm again. I am worried about being seen like this, am certain for a moment that I see another traveler, pink- or scarlet-coated, but no: just the flutter of a cardinal. Lillian speaks of Robert, admits that there are times that she is frightened of him, feels that he doesn't recognize her, that his loyalty is to something else. The fallen snow has erased my footsteps. We walk for some time, but I do not see the car; I tell myself it must be farther, but the woods are the same in all directions. We reach a farm with a grand barn I recall driving past. Somehow, we must have missed the roadster—but how? It is impossible, one does not simply misplace a sky-blue DeLuxe. We circle back; this time I recognize my parking place. The car is gone.

It is the boy, of course. There can be no other answer. Back at the house, the Finnish maid tells us that Robert is home, but there is no sign of the car. In truth, I do not care. I just wish to leave. Then Robert comes out, tells me I should not be there, the "Soul Heirs" have warned him of my intention, that if I know what is best, I will go and not come back. We agree! But Lillian wants me to stay, says it is too late, the roads aren't safe, etc. I remind her of my family. She says my wife will understand, that women understand each other. She seems unsurprised by the theft of the car. I can make no sense of this; I just want to be gone from this house. I ask for her to drive me. She demurs, says we will not make it through the snow. I say I must get back home, that I have consultations tomorrow morning. I am adamant, I do not like the house, the boy, the sullen sister, the Finnish maid (might she have stolen it?). I wish to go.

Lillian consents. We go to the garage, the old barn, now connected through a mudroom. Her Ford requires half a dozen tries before it starts.

We make it perhaps two hundred yards before the road banks and we slide off into the verge and into a slope of snow-covered ferns. I am certain this is deliberate. Lillian is in tears again, apologizes, knows that I came to help her and she has made such trouble for me, seizes my arm and begins to kiss my face, my neck, climbs onto me, legs clamped to either side of mine. She is smaller but she is wedged between me and the dashboard and I am pressed into the door and at first I cannot push her off. I register only shock, then, briefly, in my confusion, I am swept up by the warmth of her mouth, the cold of her cheeks, the weight of her body, and I reciprocate, but only very briefly, and then reason comes, I find the door handle, and we go spilling into the snow.

I stand. We are both chastened. She apologizes, I bow stiffly. I must go—she is not to follow.

It is very far to Oakfield by foot. Fortunately, after an hour, I flag a passing truck. Along, I pass the farmhouses, once picturesque, now threatening. In which barn would I find the DeLuxe? I have the sense of being watched by hostile creatures. Behind the weather-beaten doors, I see the pinch-faced natives of this region, each harboring a sinister son.

March 22

Leaving the office late last night, and who meets me on the street but Lillian? I startle at first, am afraid that she will make a scene there on the street, but she has come to apologize. She was not

well, has not been well, had not meant to draw me into her troubles. It is her burden, she says; she knows she must bear it alone,
and yet at times, this happens . . . others are drawn in. Others! But
I do not ask. Anyway, she says that she's relieved to see that I am
safe. The car, she asks, has it been found? I know she knows it
hasn't. The police have been notified, and if I am to believe them,
the neighbors have been interviewed, without resolution. I ask
what it is she wants of me. She says she wishes to forget the moment of indiscretion and continue where we left off.

The boy, she says, now wants the procedure.

Ha! I do not believe this, suspect some trick. Perhaps by Robert,
more likely by his mother. But why?

And Barnes? I ask.

Dr. Barnes will no longer see Robert, she says. Dr. Barnes confused his professional duties with his affections.

Affections? I ask.

He tried to force himself upon me, she says coldly. In the house.
While Robert was out.

Given the events of earlier, I do not believe this either. Does she
say the same to him of me? It occurs to me that I should bury the
hatchet with my colleague, align against this woman's tricks.

And yet it is impossible not to feel, on some level, a kind of victory. She is here. She has one son, and for the first time, she has
fully agreed to turn him over. Victory, but what strange spoils?

I notice that she has come closer since we began speaking. I fear
that she will weep, that she will try again to kiss me, that someone
will see us, in early evening, on the street alone, and perceive, in
our postures, an intimacy. I am certain then that I will not rid myself of her until we go ahead with the procedure; else we will travel
round and round. Will it free Robert of the demons that torment
him? Without doubt it will silence him. No longer will she worry
about him roaming their woods, guarding his chestnuts, defying
the conspiracies that rise like vapors from the earth. A "drooling

piece of meat"? . . . Well, I hope not, of course I hope not, but if there are unseen consequences, she will manage better than others. She has her home, her Finnish woman, the silence of her woods.

If I say No, this wound will only fester, she will be back, she will cajole, threaten, and tempt.

I operate on Thursdays, I say: tomorrow. They can come in the evening, after the others, as the day's last case. After that there will be a follow-up visit; this is standard. One, only. Then they will leave me alone, free of complications, with those that I can truly help.

VIEWS OF THE SAME TREE, TAKEN ON THREE SUCCESSIVE YEARS, 1909, 1910, AND 1911 RESPECTIVELY. WYNCOTE, PA.

[The branches have been cut off as fast as they were killed. The tree will die this summer (1912).]

Eight

NOW a second plague comes to the house in the north woods. And while the first was brought by wind and spore, this time the mighty finger of Blame points clearly toward the interstate, the Girl Scouts of America, and eros.

Many years ago, on the boundary of Natick and Weston, on the north shore of Nonesuch Pond, was a property belonging to the Scouts, a pleasant, quiet country area, where some fifty-two campers and sixteen to twenty counselors and staff convened each summer to enjoy swimming, boating, archery, arts and crafts, nature study, drama, and music. It was, according to all who visited, a unique property, "ideally adapted to . . . the charitable and educational uses of giving wholesome rural recreational and educational opportunities to groups of young city dwellers."[*] It was also in the path of the Massachusetts Turnpike, which paid three dollars in compensation for the seizure, an amount deemed by the jury before which the Scouts brought suit to be woefully inadequate, even for a region with a long history of underpaying for land that belongs to other people.

Among the various consequences of the purchase of the land, in addition to the loss of privacy and sense of remoteness enjoyed by the campers, was the destruction of a small forest through which the highway passed. The trees, the bulk of which were oak, birch,

---

[*] *Newton Girl Scout Council v. Mass. Turnpike Auth.*, 335 Mass. 189 (1956).

and pine, also included a group of fourteen elms that had lined the camp entrance until their deaths from Dutch elm disease. The Turnpike Authority, in a goodwill gesture to the campers, had processed several of these into firewood, neatly ordering them in woodpiles near the off-ramp, where, one February morning, a pair of newlyweds on their way to a ski vacation pulled off so that the wife might answer the call of nature.

As the wife peed, the husband, Tom, vaguely aroused by the thought of his lovely bride squatting over the cold, snow-scattered field, turned his mind to the cabin he had rented, and the acts of intercourse he had planned. For this man, who appears so fleetingly, and yet so crucially, in these pages, had a thing about fireplaces. It was not clear what in his past could have given birth to such a fetish. There was no early seduction by a campfire. As a child, he had indeed been witness to the so-called "primal scene," but his parents had been in the laundry room, far from the family hearth, and laundries did nothing for him, sexually: they were neither good nor bad, just neutral. Distantly, he recalled reading a naughty book about a scullery maid who seduced an earl before the open fire of the kitchen. But she had also seduced the falconer in the hawkery, the ostler in the stables, and a visiting baron in the dungeon, and none of these places elicited even a shiver of erotic association. And yet desire consumed him when he thought of fireplaces. The word itself was enough: the voiceless labiodental fricative giving way to the growling "r" and "pl" of "please" and "pleasure," before it ended in a hiss.

Having entered his marriage a virgin, Tom had since enjoyed many acts of coitus, but had yet to consummate his dream. How he imagined it! The warm light flickering across his wife's bounding breasts. The bodies tumbling over a fireside rug (bearskin, or "Persian"). The moist lock of her crotch as if a kind of second flame. O savage ritual of sacrifice and purification! Such thoughts had only quickened (dare we say, burned brighter) since he had learned of the cabin from a colleague. In Boston, they lived in an apartment with a steam heater, which was not the same.

We should not, then, be surprised by what went through his mind when, waiting in the former woodlot of the Girl Scouts, his eye alighted on the remnants of the turnpike woodpile. Certainly, the cabin would be well equipped with firewood, he reasoned, and yet it was a fair guess that most guests did not appreciate a flame as he did. What a crisis it would be to arrive at last, and find his dreams thwarted by a stingy host!

No one was around. There was still space in the generous trunk of their Chevy Nomad. It wouldn't hurt to take a few logs from the pile.

His wife returned, and they continued on their way. They reached the cabin in the evening. What followed was everything Tom had imagined. For five days, he found himself brought repeatedly to the heights of ecstasy. How the light of the fire shimmered in the sheen of sweat that collected on the neck of his beloved! And the shock that ran through him to feel her fire-warmed haunches! Watching the shadows of their cavorting forms upon the cabin walls, he felt at times as if they were not mortals, but two beasts rutting in the burning ruins of a post-apocalyptic world. They also went skiing.

As it turned out, stealing the firewood was unnecessary—the cabin had enough. And so, when the day came and the couple reluctantly climbed back into the Nomad, they left behind some logs of elm, and in the elm, the larvae of a scolytid beetle overwintering within the bark.

Our attention now turns to the beetle.

Had the young couple paused even briefly in their mutual enjoyment, and pulled back the bark of the log on which Tom had found that he could place his feet for better purchase, they might have wondered how such an exquisite work of art had come to be.

For the larval chambers of the elm bark beetle are nothing short of masterpieces. What might we compare them to? Etched Viking labyrinths? The facial tattoos of certain Pacific Islanders? A giant centipede? But they are nonpareil. Such symmetry, such grace! Other beetles, in comparison, are mindless stumblers, leaving winding, drunken squiggles in their wakes.

But what would have astounded our young lovers even more, would have been to learn that only six months prior, this winding maze had been a pleasure palace like their own.

With regard to the beetle, the romp began, as sex romps often do, with carpentry. A female beetle, slightly smaller than a rice grain, had found herself, one summer afternoon, wandering about the logs that lay beside the off-ramp. Do not ask me how she got there; she came from another log, as did her mother before her—it is logs and beetles all the way back. But she was hungry, and so delighted to have found the elm wood that she gave her hairy little rump a shake. For some time, she scurried over the bark, until she found a place to make her burrow. It was her first burrow, but the work came instinctively. She bored inside, excavated a smooth, straight corridor, tidied it, settled down, and released a siren's plume of pheromones that drifted through the empty chambers and out into the air.

And what perfume! Threo-4-methyl-3-heptanol! Alpha-multi-striatin! Alpha-cubebene! Can we fault then the young swain who, flying by, paused mid-flight, swiped the air with his antennae, and made a U-turn toward her borehole? Shivers of lust passed through his elytra as he found her scent grow stronger. And beneath the bark, within the gallery, what heaven! The scent was overwhelming—it was as if he'd walked inside her genital chamber itself. He purred and dipped, so befuddled by her smell he nearly mated with a mite. The mites cleared out—they had long learned not to get between a pair of scolytids in heat.

From there our little stud advanced along the corridor unimpeded. Did he stop to appreciate her handiwork? Unlikely. For, despite the darkness, he could sense that he was getting closer. If only we could know the things he said to her as he approached her sanctum, and what she answered in her own lascivious purr. He dipped his head—he did not know why he did this, but such moves were coded in his serum. He touched her. First her frons and then—oh, God—her epistome. Rubbed his setae on her abdomen. Sensed a stirring of his aedeagus: during his fourteen days of earthly existence, he had wondered what the thing was for, and now he had his answer. Her genital chamber opened, his aedeagus extended, retracted, extended again. He had never known it capable of such agency. It was as if it possessed a mind of its own.

He mounted.

And then she threw him off, smashed him against the wall with such aggression that the peeping mites went scurrying in fear.

Puzzled, he cowered in the corner of the scented room . . . But why? How? Her smell! Her hushed clicking of encouragement! Her open genital chamber! And then to greet him with such violence! Was he not welcome after all? But to leave, well, it was not so easy: try turning around inside a corridor the width of a rice grain with your aedeagus hanging out. The mocking twitter of the spying mites grew stronger. Damn the little fuckers, he would try again.

He scuttled forward, gently tapped her sides with his antennae, hummed and ducked his head, awaited her attack. But this time she didn't strike him. Tentatively, he lifted his gaze and again approached her. Another tap, and then she turned. Before him rose her coxites. Halloo! His palps shook. His feet did a little dance in place, but then, recalling his first failure, he restrained himself. Gyrated for a bit, waited for his aedeagus to retract, then swiveled and pressed against her, back to back, as his member swelled again and slid inside her, and she pulled him deep into the scented den.

The product of this congress was the raft of eggs she laid in nooks carved in the wall of the main gallery.

The next spring, the larvae hatched. Creamy little baubles, each as plump and pampered as an emperor's favorite child, they turned from the central chamber and began to chew in parallel ranks. By the time they reached their fill and stopped to pupate, they'd carved that Viking maze of such sublime design.

But we have forgotten something. The galleries within this slab of elm aren't empty when the larvae awake, but carpeted with the very fungus that had killed the tree before the turnpike chopped it up.

The story now shifts again, from the first beetle and her mate, to her scion, the seventh beetle on the right, who chews *her* way to freedom one April morning, long after Tom has left. The cabin is dark when she emerges, and it takes a moment for her to orient herself within her new, cold universe. Her antennae tap, her head pivots. Laden with fungal spores, she flies up into the rafters of the cabin, where she spies a gap. On the roof she pauses, then takes flight.

She does not set out to find that particular elm tree planted by a retired Major of the British Army to shade his dooryard. The scent of elm is everywhere. Live elm, sick elm, dead elm, wild, planted; in addition to the forest, nearly every town and city in New England has used the tree to line its avenues. Lubricant spreads over her mouthparts. For the first time in her short life, she has an inkling of the appetite of which she's capable. But the wind is stiff, and now she finds that she is soaring higher. It carries her over the woods and fields and streets lined with a feast that she cannot reach. Up a valley. When at last she fights her way down, she is floating over a yellow house.

She is going very fast when she strikes the chimney and tumbles down two shingles, then rights herself and probes the air with her antennae. The fungal spores still coat her wings in streaks of silver. Twelve feet away, the scent plume of an elm is unmistakable. A great tree, nearly two hundred years old. It is a short flight to the spreading canopy, where she pauses, bids goodbye to daylight, and begins to eat.

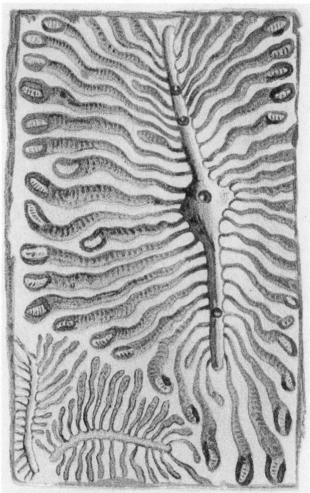

Brutkolonie des Fichtenborkenkäfers.

Nine

SHE had signed up for the prison pen-pal program soon after joining the Women's Benevolence League, a nondenominational association devoted to the creation of a better future through friendship and good works. She had been invited by Agnes Taylor, the town librarian, who sensed, she knew, her isolation. The group met weekly, at different houses across the county, sometimes almost two hours away. But she didn't mind the driving—it was a welcome distraction, and gave her a reason to be out of the house, and in the world.

There were twelve other women in the county chapter, and it was the responsibility of the host to set each week's agenda, though this varied little. They began with minutes, proceeded to important announcements, progressed to readings and special topics, and then moved on to outreach. Over the years, outreach had depended on the personal interests of the participants, and consisted primarily of immigrants, prisoners, and children. The programs for children had been suspended after accusations that the Benevolents were pagan, though this couldn't have been further from the truth. No one was keeping such close tabs on either immigrants or prisoners, so those programs had remained untouched.

The monthly pen-pal program was organized by Professor John Trumbull of the Community College, the eldest son of Mrs. Trumbull, one of the founders of the county chapter. For nearly a decade, Professor Trumbull had taught a literature course at the state prison in Concord, part of an education and rehabilitation initiative. The course was called Captivity Tales, and surveyed the long history of first-person accounts of prisoners across time—from the Bible through the recent writings of Martin Luther King Jr. and Aleksandr Solzhenitsyn—most of which were included in a volume, *Captivity Tales*, edited by Professor Trumbull himself. The initial intent of the pen-pal program was to have the Benevolents and the prisoners write to each other about topics from the course, but from the beginning, the Benevolents had trouble keeping up with the reading. So the prisoners wrote about the readings and the Benevolents wrote about . . . Well, they wrote about anything that came to mind. Professor Trumbull, they all decided, was qualified to speak on *Little Dorrit*. He could elevate the prisoners with his gift, while they would serve the equally vital role of friendship.

Almost immediately, Lillian had proved to be the most prolific letter writer in the circle, or, as Professor Trumbull described her, "the star." She was proud of her success, and it relieved both her loneliness and her growing worry that something was happening to her thinking. She could not say exactly when she had first noticed the changes. She had always been a little flighty, and she had endured so much hardship that it was understandable, as Agnes once told her, that she might, from time to time, find herself a little out of sorts. But lately it seemed that she was forgetting more than usual, such as which groceries she needed, or even the name of her dog, a feisty terrier that had been a gift from the other ladies in the chapter. And with the new street signs they were putting up everywhere, and the old farmhouses coming down, and more and more dirt roads asphalted, it was easy to get lost. Worse, though, was the sense that she was having trouble following the meetings, or that the others were having trouble following her. Once, even,

Agnes and Sally Garfield had approached her when the meeting was over and asked if there was anything the matter. Of course not! she'd said, perplexed and angry, but then she'd gone out to her car and found herself uncertain of where she was going, and Agnes and Sally were tapping at her window. She'd ended up in the hospital—in the end, it had turned out to be an infection in the bladder. Imagine that! A bladder infection causing such confusion! But when it was over, her mind still didn't feel the same.

Perhaps this was one reason she liked the pen-pal program. For she could write and she didn't worry that the prisoner would be bored by her, or misunderstand her, and if they did, they were forgiving, and grateful to have contact with "the world." And they knew that not everyone always made the best decisions. Just as they knew that, if one was simply patient, a friend's true essence would emerge in time.

There were six prisoners participating in the program when Lillian joined. Three were regulars who had been there since the beginning, and three were recent additions. The process was simple. Each month, Professor Trumbull would deliver the letters to the Benevolents, and collect the letters to the prisoners in turn. He did not read them—it was important, he said, that the prisoners felt that they had a real correspondence—though the group was encouraged to share highlights from the prisoners' letters with one another. Not *secrets*, said Trumbull. His students (he did not call them "prisoners") had come from worlds where trust was in very short supply.

This was the first rule. The second rule was that one should never ask a prisoner about his crime or his release date, unless he mentioned it first, and even then, one should not show undue interest in such matters. The third rule was never to question a prisoner's protestations of innocence. The fourth rule, which seemed to Lillian to be a contradiction, at least in spirit, of the second and third rules, was that one should only use one's first name and never include one's home address.

In her nearly five years as a pen pal, Lillian had had fourteen correspondents. Several of them had ceased writing without explanation, but others had become regulars until circumstance interfered. Her most recent regular, her all-time favorite, was called Henry Jones. Henry was halfway through an eighty-year sentence when he signed up for Professor Trumbull's course. Lillian had inherited him from Gail Turner, who had been a lackluster correspondent—unimaginative, judgmental, and always slow. Lillian knew a lot about Henry, because Henry wrote a lot—he was, in the taxonomy of the Benevolent pen pals, a "confessor," a word that had thrown Lillian at first, as she had understood it to refer to the person who heard a confession, not the one that confesses. Henry told her everything—he had a lot to get off his chest. He was seventeen when he took part in a robbery in which a man and woman had been killed, though (as he told her many times, and promised that the court records would back him up) he hadn't been the one who'd killed them. The plan was to hold up the couple for some spending money, but then things had gotten out of control. It was not his fault, he wrote. He'd only been a kid. Too young to know any better, but old enough to be tried and sentenced as an adult.

Despite the passage of time, Henry had been quite angry when they first began their correspondence. But with the counsel of the other Benevolents, Lillian, in her third letter, had encouraged him to focus on the readings and seek the positive in his life. After this, he hadn't written back, and Lillian regretted her injunctions, which in retrospect seemed insensitive, even insulting: Henry's father had been killed when he was a baby, and his mother had died of drink when he was twelve. But then, to her surprise, a letter came, with an apology—he'd been sick with a kidney infection and had been taken to the hospital. As for her question about the positive in life . . . Well, that would have to be his younger sisters. He thought about them all the time, he said, as one had a son who was on the same path that had landed him in prison, while the other, a spinster, suffered terribly from a disease that caused her knuckles to grow crooked and laid her up with pain for weeks.

In addition to classifying the prisoners, the Benevolents also had their own taxonomy, of which Lillian was a "discloser." While, for some, disclosure was an ideological stance, for Lillian, it was somewhat less deliberate. She had always been a discloser; indeed, sometimes she was so drawn into other people that she ended up in trouble. She'd fallen for her husband with such force that it had terrified her, but it was scarcely a month after his death that she had found herself with another man, and after him another. Each time, she had the sense that the man could fill an emptiness, almost impossibly vast. Of course, she didn't tell this directly to Henry Jones, whom, she realized, she was also in love with. Instead, she wrote vaguely of how one must be careful with one's responsibilities, which, in her case, almost all involved her son.

For all her tendency to open her heart to other people, it had taken her nearly five months to share with Henry what she had come to understand to be the defining circumstance of her life, which was her son's illness. She didn't know how much Henry knew about the disease called schizophrenia, she wrote, and went on to explain how, since his late teens, her Robert had suffered from this condition, for which he had been hospitalized many times. It was for this reason that she had not married again, she told Henry. Robert wasn't dangerous to other people, but the full force of his disease was terrifying to observe, and the few people who drifted into her life were frightened by him, and by the rituals he undertook to prevent the calamity he believed would come upon the world.

As it turned out, Henry had some knowledge and opinions

about the condition, for he had a cousin who suffered from schizo-phrenia, and in Professor Trumbull's class, they'd read a book about a man in an asylum who'd had part of his brain cut out and become a "vegetable." It was not an easy burden for a mother, he'd written, there was no doubt about it, but a mother's love was what kept her strong. She knew that he was writing in part about his own mother, or the loss of his mother, and for a week or so, she had worried that Henry would get jealous hearing how much she had cared for Robert. But she couldn't hold herself back. She wrote about the Harrow and the Stitching and the Soul Heirs, and when this sounded too strange, she made sure to tell him about the good things too. For he was so smart, her Robert, he knew history and science and could tell you the name of every plant, every mush-room, every bird. He kept notebooks, hundreds of them, on every-thing he found.

As far as the surgery that Henry mentioned, well, long ago she'd almost gotten it for Robert. But on the day of the procedure, another mother caused a commotion, and when the doctor went to deal with her, Robert stole his case notes from his desk. She still had them! And it was lucky that he had stolen them, for the doctor had written terrible things. Had they proceeded, Robert might have been left like the man in Henry's book, or worse. It was one of the times in her life when she'd been certain that someone was looking out for her, for him.

Deus ex machina, Henry wrote back, for he'd learned the term from Professor Trumbull's class. It was what every prisoner, in his heart, believed in: that one day his captor would be struck dead by a greater power, or the prison walls would tumble down.

The doctor had marked a change, wrote Lillian, for after, there was no one she could trust. All that seemed to help her son was to let him wander in the woods; their land backed onto the state for-est, and one could walk for miles. Sometimes he would go off for days. In the beginning she was scared, but then she'd come to trust him. A wandering man, Henry had written: a rambler. But that wasn't Robert, thought Lillian. A *rambler* suggested a free spirit, while her son, bearing his terrifying burden, was anything but. He didn't want to wander, she wrote, he *had to*. And then, last summer, shortly before she and Henry had started writing, Robert had disappeared.

Over the weeks and months that followed, she tried to find an explanation for his disappearance. The strange thing was that he was healthier than he had been in years. They had a maid, Anneli, who had been with them most of Robert's life, and moved with them to the country when he'd fallen sick. The year before, Anneli had gone to the doctor for a lump in her neck and returned to say that she'd been advised to go to the city for treatment for cancer. But she didn't want treatment. The doctors said it would give her a few more months but also might make her sicker. She had come to love the house in the woods and decided to die there. For years she had taken care of Lillian, and in the end, it was Lillian who cared for her.

What was most amazing was what happened to Robert—it was as if the demands of the real world had brought him back. Throughout the spring and summer, he stayed and helped with the cleaning and cooking and relieved her at Anneli's bedside. He had been with Anneli when she died one summer morning, and he rose to tell his mother what had happened. Then he went out walking, and by the time he came home, something seemed to have changed. She worried that the Harrow was back, for he sat on the couch with his eyes closed and his face moved like someone who is hearing screaming all about him and can't shut it out. But the next morning he began to write. He kept a notebook with him, and over the months that followed, he spent hours writing, even corresponding with his sister, Helen, a professor in California. And then, one day, like any other, he'd gone out and hadn't come back.

As it was summer and she was used to his long walks, she didn't call the police until three days had passed. But the police were tired of Robert—they'd been called many times over the years, by Lillian and by neighbors who'd seen him stalking their woods, talking to himself. They spent a day with the dogs, but said the trail was faint. She knew this was a lie: those dogs could find anything. It was their way of saying they were giving up.

Dearest Lillian, how you have suffered! Henry had written. For the Lord took away my mother, and the State took away my freedom, but even a childless man like me knows there is no punishment on earth worse than losing a son.

Henry had come from a family of devout Methodists, and his belief had grown even stronger in prison. Perhaps she might find comfort in church, he wrote her. He had profound respect for the good deeds of her organization, but no work was possible without the countenance of God.

She did not write: Sometimes, when I go to the woods, Robert's woods, I am so shaken by his absence that I pray, I kneel down before his trees. I lift the earth up and I speak to it. I ask it to bring him home.

And why not? she thought. Sometimes he'd heard the soil whispering. Maybe, if she spoke to it, it'd let him know.

What she wanted, she wrote, was someone to care for her again. She thought of Henry Jones, imagined him holding her, saw his body beside hers, broke the second rule and asked if they might ever grant him parole.

He did not answer this question, so the next time she wrote, she asked again, and he didn't answer, and she asked again, and only then did he write that they would not consider it, no.

She was in a low place. It was shortly after her bladder infection, and then, that October, she'd woken in the night to a howling, and she'd gone to the window and looked out on the wind whipping through the forest, and heard the creaking of the old elm outside the house. Rain was falling, and the field shimmered, and she had a sense of the earth coming loose and rocks turning in dark water. She was going mad, she thought, and she threw open the window to show herself that it couldn't be so. The force of the storm knocked her down, water crashed through the open window, the wind sucked at the curtains, and papers whipped into the air. As she rose, she heard a tearing, as the whole house seemed to heave, and the pictures fell and the lights went out.

She awoke the next morning on the floor beside her bed, wrapped in wet blankets, amidst the scattered papers and puddles. In the mirror she saw abrasions on her face, and her hip hurt and her wrist hurt, but to her relief she could still walk. The storm was over, but outside the world was almost unrecognizable—everywhere, there were downed trees, and rills coursed through the upturned earth.

The terrier—Charlie, that was his name!—was barking, so she let him out and walked outside, still in her dressing gown, to where she could survey the damage. She hadn't dreamed the tearing sound. A great limb of the elm had fallen, crushing the chimney and part of the "grand" wing of the house.

It was then that she realized that it was still raining. She called for Charlie, but he had found something in the tangle of fallen trees and would not come.

The police arrived later that afternoon. There had been damage throughout the valley, and they were checking to see if people were okay. She greeted them warily, worried they might judge the house unsafe and take her from there. She'd get the roof fixed soon, she promised. But she was fine. She rarely went to that part of the house anyway, for there was a horrid mounted catamount belonging to her father—yes, he had hunted it himself—but she understood the urgency, she told them, and she would get it fixed. She knew the officer well from the many times people had complained about Robert—he was from an old family in the area and always had given her son the benefit of the doubt. She thought of offering him tea, but she hadn't cleaned in a long time, and she was afraid of the picture that it would present.

The next day was Professor Trumbull's visit to the Benevolents. She had three correspondents then: Henry; a second with the vaguely familiar name of William Blake, who sometimes went by Will; and a third called Edward Kelly. Neither Will nor Ed was a correspondent quite like Henry, but they were better than most, and she knew a lot about their tribulations, and had shared hers with them as well. She'd already written that week's letters, and wondered if she might add an addendum about the storm, but she worried that one of them would tell her she should consider moving. Only to Henry did she add a postscript. *I have been feeling very low,* she wrote. *I have come to believe that I will never see my Robert again.*

The meeting was about an hour's drive away, but it took longer because of the downed trees, and she was late, arriving just as Professor Trumbull began. He had letters from two new students, he told them, one of whom, named Harlan Kane, had requested Lillian specifically. There was a murmur when he said this—for all her reputation, she'd never been requested before—and Trumbull made a joke about her growing fame among the prisoners. Then they turned to that week's reading, written by an anonymous woman who'd been captured by Indians, which Professor Trumbull had edited himself in spelling and grammar. Lillian had read it, found it difficult, and wondered what kind of "edits" Trumbull had made, because she found the spelling still no better than a child's, though she agreed with Agnes that it added "flavor." Mostly, the woman's baby made her think of Robert. The woman also had endured many tribulations, and though they were different from Lillian's, in some ways, they both were trapped.

The account was a mystery, Professor Trumbull told them. No

one knew who had written it—it had been found scrawled in the margins of a Bible belonging to a colored family in Canada, handed down over the generations. The story's end, the killing of some English soldiers, had puzzled historians, he said, and it provoked a heated discussion among the Benevolents about justice that left Professor Trumbull in a state of almost orgasmic pedagogical bliss.

Lillian listened as if from a distance. Mostly, she was thinking about Harlan Kane and the letter that was waiting in her purse. The name was strange, but there were many strange names these days. There was only one explanation, she thought, and that was that Henry or Will or Ed had been talking and told another prisoner of their friend Lillian and how they had found such comfort in her words. Just when she thought she had reached the bottom, here came a reminder that she was needed.

She was so lost in thought that she scarcely noticed that the discussion was coming to an end, and Professor Trumbull was preparing them for that month's reading by Boethius, a great favorite among the prisoners, a home run. When he left, there was a snack break. But Lillian could not endure the mystery of Harlan Kane any longer, and she opened the letter as quietly as possible, so as not to draw attention to herself. It was double-sided, filled with writing to the edges. When she read the salutation, the world around her disappeared.

He had been arrested about a year ago, shortly after Anneli died and he left home. He had traveled for a while and then "borrowed" a car to drive back to Oakfield, when he was in a crash that led to the destruction of some property, and when the police came, he'd tried to run. "Harlan Kane" was a name he'd taken for reasons he would explain later—but it was him, Robert. He was sorry for not having written earlier, but the Harrow hadn't let him. They'd been vengeful after his arrest. Every night they tortured him until he was raving, and the doctors at the prison had to shoot him up with all kinds of drugs to make the raving stop. Then, even when the Harrow got quieter, he was too ashamed by his predicament to write. But last summer, in a therapy group, one of the prisoners was talking about the pen-pal program and a lady who wrote to him and how her son was missing. He hadn't believed it at first, but then Henry—that was the friend—had shown him the letters, everything she had written about him, about them. He asked her to excuse his penmanship. He had broken his hand a few weeks earlier and had to learn to write with the other, but it didn't matter. What mattered was, he missed her, and in February he was being released.

She did not make it through the remainder of the meeting. Not for Agnes's presentation about the Boston chapter's gardening program for refugees, or Sally's legendary sponge cake. She murmured something about forgetting something and something for Charlie and threw on her coat and hurried out.

Her first impulse, of course, was to head out to Concord and show up at the prison. But Robert, in his letter, must have known this. I know you'll want to see me, he'd warned, but, please: you must not visit. He was ashamed about being in prison, and wished to close this chapter of his life. He knew how hard it would be to wait for him . . . Perhaps she could write to him directly? It was hardly practical to go through Professor Trumbull, especially if he was getting out in February, just four months off.

She was so lost in thought that she didn't remember driving home, and when she pulled up at her house, she realized to her chagrin that in fact she *had* forgotten to let Charlie in, though the dog was merrily gnawing on a bone and hardly seemed to care. The house was frigid—she'd left open the door to the ruined wing—but she didn't even bother closing it, didn't even remove her jacket, just went straight to the table, and began to write.

She began by telling Robert how she forgave him, she understood what he had been through, that the past was past and all that mattered was that he was coming home. She, too, had endured so much. Did Henry tell him that she'd been in the hospital for an infection? And sometimes she found herself forgetting, and then, just this week, the house had been damaged in a storm. She began to write about the old elm tree, and all the destruction in the forest, and what a mess it was, but stopped. What if Robert changed his mind? Home should be a place of refuge and comfort. So she wrote of his favorite spots, things he would miss, the late autumn's colors, the owls in the woods. And the mushrooms, Robert! She was careful not to eat the ones he'd warned her of, but all summer, she'd found chanterelles and hedgehogs and hens blooming beneath the oaks.

It was nearly midnight when she stopped, and she was so tired then that she didn't change into her pajamas. She wrote "Harlan Kane" on the envelope, as he'd instructed. How strange it was to see those words, and how thrilling, as if she were conspiring with Robert against the world. She slept. In the morning, she drove the letter straight into town, though she might have left it in her mailbox at the bottom of the road. She didn't want to take any chances, not with her son so close.

So the letter went out, and she waited, and she could hardly think of anything but him. She felt the world was bright again. She began to clean the mess that had accumulated in Robert's absence, and hired a girl, who came twice a week to help. Every day she drove down to the mailboxes. But then a week passed, and she began to worry that Fortune had changed her mind, or that the warden had reversed his decision. Maybe Robert had fallen sick! What if he had stopped taking his medication? She'd write and tell him that he must take it—maybe he didn't think that it had made the difference, but it had!

Ten days went by like this—it was torture. But then, one after-noon, while she was waiting in her car down by her mailbox, his answer came.

As opposed to the long letter he had first sent with Professor Trumbull, this one was only a page and rather vague, but she read it over and over. It was still strange to see the unfamiliar name on the envelope, but he signed it "R," and each time she read the un-familiar hand it looked more like his own. If only she had someone to share her joy with! But he specifically asked that she not tell anyone that they were corresponding, not even Henry Jones, be-cause Henry couldn't keep a secret. And not the Benevolents ei-ther: once word was out that Robert had spent time in prison, people would always think of him as a criminal.

The girl who came and helped her clean was from the next val-ley over, and a churchgoer, and Lillian decided that she could be trusted with a secret. Harriet listened to the story with tears in her eyes. "You must have prayed," she said when Lillian finished, and Lillian, recalling the feeling of the soil against her lips, said she had, though she didn't say to whom.

She wrote back immediately, told Robert how lovely the woods were. She'd hung suet out on the cherry, and they were visited by chickadees and cardinals. In the evenings, a barred owl sang: *I-wait-for-you . . . I-wait-for-you-too.* Even the deer seemed to linger a little longer, as if they were expecting him.

Again she mailed the letter in town, and again she went to wait each day at the mailboxes. This time it was nearly two weeks be-fore his letter came. But it did come, though it was even shorter and vaguer than the letter before. How unlike him! she thought: he who filled the shelves with notebooks! Had the drugs done this to him, or was it simply the labor of writing with his unaccustomed hand? And he must have foreseen her doubts, because in his next letter he apologized for not writing more. Sometimes the staff read the prisoners' letters, he wrote, and she knew how much he valued privacy. He asked about the house, and how she was managing without Anneli. Did anybody come and visit? He preferred no strangers, he hoped she understood. Just her. Well, she wrote, there was a girl who came, but Harriet was just temporary. When he returned, they'd manage on their own. And Helen? he asked. Please don't tell Helen I am coming home.

Lillian knew better than to argue. Strangely, she was even a little relieved to encounter some of his familiar paranoia. For, as winter deepened, she'd begun to worry about what life would be like now with Robert's changes. The life she'd come to know was that of illness, densely populated by his ghosts, dictated by their insistences. What would happen if he no longer felt compelled to walk the woods, or fill his hours with his writings? What would happen when he came and saw his cluttered room and wild screeds? After so many years of wishing otherwise, she'd come to accept this life, had learned to recognize the wise, gentle boy inside the madman suit. But had *he* resigned himself to such a loss? What would happen when he returned and saw the evidence of so many wasted years?

And so a new fear came: that he would return to her and, seeing the remnants of his prior life, the damaged roof, the shattered winter woods, he would want to leave again. Oh, why couldn't it be June? she wondered. Why couldn't the woods greet him in their green glory, with their birdsong and rushing brooks?

Into her letters, she let this doubt creep, but gently. She hoped, she wrote, that he would not be disappointed. And he replied that there was nowhere he would rather be than home.

December turned to January. When Professor Trumbull met next with them, he didn't even notice that she didn't have a note for Harlan Kane. Perhaps this was because of the discussion of Boethius, which, despite high expectations, was even livelier than anticipated. Or perhaps because he was nervous about how he was going to frame the next month's reading, which was from the Marquis de Sade. Given the events with Robert, Lillian hadn't read the passage from Boethius. So she sat quietly through the conversation, with what she hoped was a "thoughtful" expression on her face.

To her irritation, Sally and Agnes were at it with their meddling, and found her after the meeting. Was she feeling well? they asked her. She seemed awfully quiet. Not everyone has to love Boethius, she answered. But this wasn't what had bothered them, for they said she was wearing just one earring, and her lipstick looked . . . Well, had she used a mirror to put it on? And was she eating enough? Maybe they could come and bring a meal.

She waved them off, for they were being silly, though when she passed by a hallway mirror, she was puzzled by the way her lipstick went outside her lips, if just a little. Well, Agnes sometimes had runs in her stockings and Lillian didn't harass *her.* And Sally had a girl to help her, hadn't cooked herself a meal in her life. Anyway, she didn't need them. When Robert came, she planned to tender her resignation to the Benevolence League. She would keep writing to Henry, and Will and Ed if they wanted, but she could do this on her own.

It was February when she received a final note from Robert. She had offered to pick him up, but he declined—he worried about her driving on the winter roads. This was nonsense, she thought, but there wasn't time to argue. He would be there that Tuesday. There was a train to Corbury Junction, and a bus to Oakfield, and he told her he would walk from there. He insisted; it would be good to stretch his legs.

So soon! she said to Charlie. When Tuesday came, a snowstorm blanketed the house and woods, but she was so happy that she couldn't stay inside. Together with the dog, she walked through the fields, looked up at the mountain and down at the house, and tried not to count the hours. A wind was coming from the west, and all around her snow began to fall again in heavy flakes. How lovely it was, she thought, but as the evening drew on, she began to worry. Did Robert have the right clothes and boots to keep him warm? It was a long walk up the road. Of all days for there to be a blizzard! She sat at the window and looked, but the only living creatures she saw were a pair of white-tailed deer.

That night, she heard on the radio that the trains were delayed. She spent a sleepless night and rose the next morning to see that even more snow had fallen. What bad luck! she thought, and tried to tell herself she had waited over a year, and could wait another day. The table was set. She'd bought a chicken, and mashed her own potatoes. When the snow stopped, she put on her snowshoes and walked with Charlie down the road, but she scarcely went a quarter-mile before she found that it was blocked by a fallen oak. She cursed, quite out of character. In the distance, she saw Mr. Irving, her neighbor, who approached her with a saw. He'd been trying to clear another treefall just down the road. Seemed like the moment he cleared one, another came to take its place.

Oh! she thought, for she felt as if the snow, the forest, were conspiring to keep her son from her. She went back to the house, and started a fire, and closed her eyes to rest, and she must have dozed off, because when she opened them it was dark, and Charlie was barking at the door.

"Robert?" she said aloud, but when she went to the window and looked out onto the moonlit fields of snow, she didn't see anyone. Had he let himself in? "Robert?" she called. She went up to his room, but it was as she'd left it. Now, downstairs, the dog was really going crazy. He barked at the door and then ran down the hall into the grand wing and back and down the hall again. She followed, she opened the doors to show him nothing was wrong. But something strange was happening; there was something different about the house. Cold seeped from her father's old study, the window was broken. Had this happened when the tree fell? Except it wasn't her father's study, because that hated catamount was gone. Did Anneli move it? Where *was* Anneli? she thought, standing, turning, puzzled, and then she was brought back by the sound of the dog barking at the front door, then racing toward the back and growling at the window, as if he couldn't decide which side needed guarding. "What is it, Charlie?" she asked. "Silly dog!" she said. "It's just the snow." And then, to show him, she caught him by his collar with her left hand and, with her right, opened the door. The wind nearly knocked her over. The snow was piled high against the door and blew in across the rug. "See?" she said, dragging Charlie toward the door. "See, it's nothing." But the terrier was whimpering now, almost wailing, and with a lurch he pulled so hard she fell. "Christ, Charlie!" she cursed as he went scuttling into the living room, where she heard him slide beneath the couch. "It's just the woods," she said, but then she heard it, or smelled it, or felt it, she didn't know what. The door was wide open and snow was blowing, and she could sense it, circling in the darkness beyond the house.

Murder Most Cold

What happens when a trail runs red? A Jack Dunne exclusive!

> We Englishmen never cut throats in cold blood.
> —Smollett

SO March is upon us.

Readers of TRUE CRIME! will know that I reserve this column for only the most terrifying, bone-chilling accounts to cross my desk, and this month is no exception. But get ready for something different, friends. Whereas I usually take you into the underworld of our great metropolis—her alleyways, her flophouses, her gambling dens—this case, one of the strangest I have encountered in my thirty-seven years as a reporter, brings us deep into the mountains of Western Massachusetts.

A place of extraordinary wealth . . . and backwoods poverty.

Gilded ballrooms . . . and clapboard shanties.

Summer retreats of artists, poets, captains of industry . . . and dark forests where the hunter stalks.

If this was the tale of a single murder, that would be enough. But prepare yourself, for I give you not one, not two, but *three* cold-blooded killers. That's right: three! Start digging in the woods and who knows what you'll turn up!

There's quite a body count awaiting you, my friends.

A Mysterious Tip

It was a normal Thursday morning, and I was sitting in my office, reading through the galleys for my newest thriller, *Death Takes a Vacation* (on the stands in October!), when I received a call from a tipster who lived up in the county of which I'll speak.

We had never met, this tipster and I, but he was a loyal reader of my columns, and had learned, over the years, how to spot a good story when he saw one. There had been *a murder most foul*, he told me. A body had been found in a tree. That was all he knew. There had been a snowstorm, and not even the police had made it up to investigate. If I wanted to know more, I should go to the town of O——.

Now, I was doubtful, even a bit suspicious of this tipster, who wouldn't give me his name. But the story was irresistible. A body in a tree? An untouched, snowy crime scene? I'd been stuck in the city for weeks and could use some fresh air. If I hurried . . .

Friends, I wasted no time. I grabbed my coat and hat, called my girl, and told her to put dinner away. Then I caught a cab to Grand Central, where the noon to Albany was just about to depart. In Albany, I hired a car to take me up into the mountains. Luckily, they had cleared the roads, and I had a crack driver, who made good time up a dark and winding road to the small police station in O——.

Now, unlike New York City, where my access to the crimes you have become familiar with is the fruit of a long association with the brave officers of our city, I knew no one in these mountains. And so the first native I encountered was the station secretary, lush and sulky, dressed in a tight sweater that showed off a figure that could turn even a city boy's head.

I paid her said compliment, but she was in no mood for flirtation, and met my introduction with a gaze that could silence a wolf pack, then rose and went to find her boss.

I readied myself for disappointment. Of course, I hadn't called ahead—it's too easy to say No to a nosy reporter over the phone. But odds were still ten to one that I was about to get a foot to the keister. And by the looks of the captain, it was going to be quite a foot: a burly old fellow named Doyle, 6′4″ if he was an inch, with a thick red beard that made him look more the lumberjack than an officer of the law.

I spilled my story, and to my surprise, a smile lit the cop's face. You see, the captain was as much a fan of TRUE CRIME! as you are, and had read my novels for years. Well, I'll admit it was a bit embarrassing to see such a behemoth as excited as a schoolboy, but he'd just finished *Pray for the Corpse* and *A Gun for Cinderella** and he was full of praise for the chilling crime, the mind-bending mystery, the sizzling romance.

Now even Beverly (that was our siren's name) allowed a curious arc to her eyebrows as Doyle pumped my hand and led me to a lounge in back.

He'd tell me everything, he told me, provided I kept the name of the town secret, though the truth was that he knew little more than I.

They had received the call that morning. The storm had just begun and two hunters, coming down from the mountain, saw the body. They hadn't looked too closely. It was about a dozen feet up, there was no easy way to reach it, and . . . well, it wasn't the kind of thing one wanted to get close to. A lot of men like to act big when they are hunting animals, he said, but ask them just to take a little peek at a corpse in a tree . . .

Did he know anything about the hunters? I asked.

He shook his head. "Anonymous call." Then he paused and added in explanation, "Not hunting season."

---

* Available from TRUE CRIME! Print Editions, with Free Shipping and Handling; see order form at the back of this issue.

Of course, he had a good mind who these fine citizens were—it was a small town. But an officer won't go far by fining poachers. Miles of woods and six police to cover it all, he said. One needs all the help that one can get.

I nodded. Ask any city cop and they'll tell you the same thing.

Anyway, they'd left him a good description and he knew the spot—he also hunted up that way. But he hadn't been yet, because, by the time he got the call, the road was covered in heavy drifts and no one could get through.

They would head out in the morning, on horseback, he said. If I wanted, I could come along.

Horseback. By then I knew my instincts for this story had been right.

Doyle offered me a spare cot. I didn't want to abuse his hospitality, but he said that it would be easier than fetching me at the only inn in town. I agreed, and he called Beverly.

It was late and I would have thought she'd left. Maybe she'd like to stick around a little longer? I asked, as she handed over a folded blanket.

I didn't even get an answer. She led me down a hallway. "Make yourself at home."

Which is how I spent the night in the only jail cell of the little mountain town of O——.

A Trail in Scarlet

It must have been something about the mountain air, because I slept deeply, and was jolted awake by the sound of knocking at my cell. There would be four of us heading up to the crime site: Doyle, myself, and two sergeants, Burke and Flynn. Straight out of the flicks: Burke with a pugilist's jaw and wiry little devil-browed Flynn—you could have cast Bogart and Cagney in their place.

They had brought the dogs along, German shepherds twice the muscle of our city hounds.

The horses were stabled at the edge of town. It had been a long time since I had ridden, but I settled in quickly. I could see why they were needed: the snow grew deeper with each step.

It was farmland at first, all fields, but then we joined a long road and the forest closed in. Now there were few signs of habitation, save scattered farmhouses and ramshackle barns. What kinds of secrets did they hold? I wondered. I had the sense of certain city neighborhoods, where the locals watch the police from behind curtained windows, and hold their secrets close.

As we rode, we talked. Doyle wanted to hear about the plot of *Death Takes a Vacation*, and I'd be lying, readers, if this man of the law didn't say he thought that it would be my most whipping tale yet. I, in turn, wanted to know more about the land. Know the land, and know the killer. Man's a product of his environment, and that's true for the upright and the sickos alike.

Well, Doyle gave me a bit of a history lesson right there. His family went back in the town three generations, all police. Land had once been fertile farming country, but it had fallen into a kind of decline about a century ago. Grand mansions moved in next, only to be forgotten when the robber barons turned their affections elsewhere. Only recently had it been rediscovered by city folk, which led to some tension with the locals, but all the building had brought jobs along, and it was hard to complain when you were drinking from the trough. The land had been cleared and then abandoned, cleared and then abandoned. Now they were converting the abandoned fields to lawns again.

Used to be that he was busy with horse thieves and village drunks. These days he filled the coffers ticketing out-of-towners who drove too fast. The woods where they had found the body was one of the few stretches of untouched forest, which was what made it such good hunting.

By then, we had reached the end of the road, where a driveway veered off toward a sprawling yellow house. We continued, into the forest. There was no path now, at least none that I could see, but Doyle and his men clearly knew the woods.

The dogs were on their own, bounding through the snow, charging off, and then circling back. Boughs low; twice the trees doffed me, as if I were some schoolboy who'd forgot to remove his ball-cap in respect. Silence everywhere, pure white pillows on the stones and branches, a true winter wonderland, so pretty that it seemed impossible the earth was rank with death.

The hounds stopped and began to bark.

It was only when we drew closer, and I followed their muzzles skyward, that I saw the corpse up in the sky.

(Any readers faint of heart might want to skip the next few paragraphs, because, while I have seen some grisly crime scenes, this one made even *my* steel stomach turn.)

Imagine, if you will, a tree coated in blood.

Five yards up, in the crook of a branch of the old oak, the snow-covered body had disgorged its contents down the trunk. Blood coated the bark, filled the crevices, and hung in scarlet icicles. In synchrony, Flynn and Doyle made the sign of the cross.

And this was even before we brought the body down.

Normally, one takes great care at any crime scene so as not to disturb the evidence, but the situation didn't leave us many options. Flynn had a camera and took what photos he could, and then, pulling a rope from his saddle bag, tossed it over a high limb and scurried up the far side of the tree. A whistle came from above, and then the fatal words.

"There's only half of him, boss."

(Actually, the squeamish may wish to skip a little farther.)

The body didn't want to come down, of course—it had been frozen to the branches by all the gore. It took some pushing and pulling, and then they passed a hatchet up to Flynn, who began to chip away at the frozen blood, sending bits of pink ice down upon us. At last, he succeeded in getting it loose, hooked the lasso over its chest, and lowered it down, where it settled against the trunk like a hiker taking a midday siesta, if that hiker had forgotten his lower half at home.

For a moment we stood and stared at the man. He was dark-haired, with a broom moustache and a six-o'clock shadow. Broad-shouldered, and healthy-looking once you ignored the missing part.

"Well, I'll be . . ." said Doyle.

"You thinking what I'm thinking, boss?" asked Flynn.

"I don't know what I'm thinking," said Doyle.

"I'm thinking that it might be time to believe them rumors," said Flynn.

Doyle shook his head. "Nah."

"Then how do you propose he got up in the tree?"

Doyle walked around the trunk. "Could have climbed."

"With just his arms?"

"Could have climbed, and then whatever was chasing him got his bottom half."

Flynn considered this. "All right. I'll grant you the possibility. But it still doesn't tell us who was chasing."

Doyle didn't answer.

I'd been following this with some confusion. "Rumors?" I asked.

Doyle turned to me. "Catamount," he said, and then he added, "That's what they call mountain lions around here. Half the county claims to have seen one or know someone who did, but Fish and Game says that there hasn't been one in New England since old times . . ."

"That's not what they say," Flynn interrupted. *"No native population* is what they say. But every decade or so, they find one, wandering far out of its range." He paused. "Other folks think they're here and watching."

"Folks like Flynn," said Doyle.

Flynn smiled. "I'm with the rumors. Heard too many to doubt."

Just then one of the dogs started barking again, and we followed it to a snow-covered log. Except it wasn't a log, and when we'd cleared the snow from the gory leg, it was hard not to agree with Flynn. For I could see it with my own eyes—the scratch marks, the cut of the fangs, and there in the ground, frozen beneath the snow, the unmistakable print of a paw.

Flash! The camera snapped again.

Well, loyal readers, what do you think? Big cat or something equally sinister? I'll tell you now that when Fish and Game eventually weighed in, it was to say that a catamount attack was "unlikely," that the only mountain lions east of the Rockies were "stuffed ones," and that even if a cat had made it back into New England, the chances of an attack on humans were next to nil. Of course, those "experts" didn't have a better explanation, save to suggest that a citizen as fine as Mr. Drawn-and-Quartered must have left plenty of human enemies in his wake.

So I'll hand it over to you, friends: write to us, and tell us the answer. Maybe you can solve the crime!

The Foul Fiend

Now, such a verdict was still days away, and there was still the matter of the corpse. Back at the body, the upper half, Burke handed over a wallet that he had found in the man's jacket. Inside there was an ID card with the picture of our corpse in a happier time, and the name Harlan Kane.

Had a mean kisser on him even in life, Kane. Something told me that he wasn't one to live on the right side of the law, and I wasn't wrong about that. Two days later, my man at the Feds called me up with the goods on Half-a-Man. Indeed, it looked like our feline friend got a taste of some authentic New England con: Kane had been in just about every slammer north of the Connecticut line—extortion, kidnapping, blackmail, even a couple of murder charges that never stuck. Before his last stint (robbery), he'd been charged with the strangling of a hat-check girl, but the case was bungled by a rookie who misplaced the prints.

Well, it sounds like our panther had a taste for justice, and between you and me, might have done the people of Massachusetts a favor by removing this piece of scum off the earth. As in literally. As in up a tree.

Of course, I think the murderer will get off this time.

But I'm getting ahead of myself, because that's two days out, and I was still standing in the woods looking up at the bloodcicles.

I had promised you three killers, and I've only given you Kane and the beast. So here's where the story gets stranger. By now you must be asking what I was asking: what was our con doing out in these woods in the middle of February? So we take another look at his billfold. It's thin—guy's got two dollars to his name, the ID, and a piece of paper with an address on it. Doyle knows the address—it's the old house at the end of the road, belonging to a widow, Mrs. S.

We decide to pay her a visit. Flynn and Burke get our crunchy morsel in a body bag and throw him on the back of the horse—apparently, that's how they do hearses in these parts—and we set off back down to the road. Kane is frozen stiff, bag bounces with each step of the horse.

Good thing it's nice and cold, I thought.

On the way, Doyle tells me a bit about this widow. She's got a story too, mostly to do with her son, a *bona fide* nut case—Doyle'd been getting calls about him for years before he disappeared last summer. Old lady would always fight for him, took him home each time the state asylum gave her the chance. Doyle confided that when he first heard of a body up this way, he wondered if this

"Robert" had something do with it. But the madman had never laid a finger on anyone, and, sure enough, I later learned that the police found Robert at a jail in Minnesota, where he'd been serving a few months for breaking and entering, alibi as tight as a Minneapolis cell.

Of course, none of us knew this then. And over the years I've seen enough of the work of psychopaths so that I was none too eager to find myself in that old house in a winter wood, no matter that I had three of Massachusetts's finest to guard me.

We arrived. I'd not given it a good look on our way up, but now that I laid my eyes on it again, I felt a shiver run down my spine.

It was not because of the cold.

A Mother's Shock

Imagine, if you will, four different structures under four separate roofs, all stuck together. Papa and Mama Bear with two li'l ones in between, and then imagine that someone came and took a bat to Papa's head, because a tree had fallen and a good quarter of that house was collapsing on itself and fit to be condemned.

Now, I don't believe in ghosts, but the state of the place had me thinking twice about entering. I was so certain that it was abandoned that I was shocked to see one of the pale-blue curtains move and a suspicious old face appear in the window.

We knocked. By the look on that face, I expected her to come out with a shotgun at the ready, but the door creaked open and Doyle tipped his hat.

"Robert's not home," she said.

"Of course, ma'am," said Doyle. "But it isn't Robert we are here about. Can we come inside?"

She hesitated.

A dog appeared at her feet and growled until she slapped it.

"I can't be much of a hostess," she said, and from the soaked carpet beneath her feet and her disheveled clothing and uneven makeup, it was hard to disagree.

"Oh, no problem, ma'am. Just want to ask a few questions. See if you can help us out."

She nodded. We dismounted and tied the horses up at an old hitching post, and followed her inside. We took our seats in a living room cluttered with stacks of magazines and old pieces of taxidermy.

Mrs. S hobbled off and came back with some tea, and though the cups were dirty, I was cold enough that I was happy to have some warmth. The dog wandered back with a big flat bone in its mouth.

For a minute or so, Doyle and Mrs. S exchanged some country platitudes, but then Doyle cut to the chase.

"A body has been found in your woods."

Her face went so pale, her eyes so wide, and for a moment I thought she'd keel over on the spot.

"Robert . . ."

"No," said Doyle.

"My Robert!"

"I said 'No,' ma'am." He paused. "Man named Harlan Kane . . ."

"Oh!" She gripped the chair. "But that *is* Robert!" She slumped from the chair and onto the floor. Now she was babbling. "He said . . . he said . . . his name . . . I wrote . . ."

Well, you can imagine the confusion but Doyle knew the son well, and that dead man wasn't him. Of course, this was a few weeks before they found her boy alive in Minnesota, so we couldn't be of much comfort, and the old gal was in such a conniption I was near certain we'd soon have another corpse on our hands. Doyle must have thought the same, because he sent Burke and Flynn hurrying back out to get the old hamburger himself.

For a horrified minute, I imagined that they would bring the carnage into the living room, but, thankfully, they just stopped at the front window, holding up the bloody torso of the real Harlan Kane between them, like a drunk supported by a pair of friends.

Now, I don't know about you, but I think if I saw a gnawed-on demi-man outside my front window, I'd be worse for it, but color seemed to come back into the face of the good widow.

"That's not Robert," she said, with confusion and relief.

"See?" said Doyle.

He waved, and the men trundled off their grim companion.

It took some time, and the widow had to go up to her room to get the letters, but after about an hour, we'd puzzled it out. Turns out that the widow was of the idealistic type, joined some letter-writing program with the criminals at the state prison, and had been conned by this fine pen pal, who pretended he was her boy. Pen as in penitentiary. Sweet talker (or writer!) he was, and from what I learned later about his exploits with the hat-check girl, I think our old Mrs. S just missed meeting her maker.

But the sad thing, dear readers, was that she was *disappointed*, because she'd been expecting her son.

That's a mother's love for you.

So now I've got one killer lion and one de-legged strangler who'd come within a cat's breath of adding this old lady to his collection, and the sun hasn't set.

But I thought there were three! you say.

I get it. You've paid your dime. Hold tight. Now's when it gets hot . . . or cold.

Remembrances of Murders Past

So we are in the living room. Doyle tells old Mrs. S to be careful, can't trust anyone these days. She thanks us, asks him to tell her if he hears anything about her son. Of course he will, he promises her. Then, as we are filing out, Burke bends over to pet the dog, who nearly bites his hand off. Mrs. S is horrified. "Charlie!" she exclaims. Says he's been like that since he found the bone.

That's when we all look down and, for the first time, really notice what he's munching.

Now, I'm no coroner, and the little terrier had done a fine job chewing it up, but this was part of a pelvis if I've ever seen one. And Doyle must have thought the same, because he asks where it had come from. Storm brought it up, says Mrs. S, and explains that ever since the wind knocked the trees down, the dog's been nosing about in the mud.

"Bear, I think," she added, but Doyle shook his head. He and his boys had been hunting and dressing their own kills since they were kids and knew their bones. And me—well, I just had to reach down and touch my waist to confirm some basic measurements.

It would be another week before we began to get our answers.

Of course, my first thought was that it was a piece of Harlan Kane, but I knew this was wrong the moment I thought it: the bone looked old enough to be a fossil. Mrs. S didn't have an explanation. Said her Robert once had found an old gravestone up the hill, but that was far away from where the terrier had done his digging. How many bodies were there in this place? I wondered, but Doyle was unfazed. If he got excited about every gravestone, he'd have to tear up the entire country. His business was in the unaccounted for.

It was late in the day, and there was too much snow to do any digging, and so we returned the next morning with equipment, and Doyle's crew went out behind the house and turned up a femur and some ribs and part of a skull. By then, they had realized the age of the bodies, so they had to notify the State Archaeology Section and soon the place was swarming. I stayed up another week, rooming in my little jail cell, and Bev—well, let's just say she found a soft spot for this old scribbler that made my return to city life a little bittersweet.

I heard the rest of the story from Doyle: Three bodies had come up by the time they were done. At first, they thought it was an Indian site, but by the bits of clasps and buckles that they found, they figured they were English. Wish we knew more, but the secret, I'm afraid, will be lost to time. A waylaid hunting party? A family grave?

Only the woods know. And the trees aren't giving up their secrets, save for one chilling detail:

When they looked closely at the skulls, they found two with an axe scar, and one with a bullet hole.

I promised you more bodies, right? Well in this case, I think the killer will escape justice, just as the panther did.

Some dark centuries in crime, my friends.

Ten

IT was raining when her flight arrived in Boston. They'd been in the clouds since Lake Superior, and when, at last, the plane broke free over the neat houses lining Boston Harbor, she found herself above a landscape of muted blue and grey. Thin ribbons of water streamed over her window, broke into loose threads, and rewound themselves. As the tarmac approached, she could see the swiveling reflection of the world in the runway puddles—cloud, horizon, terminal, and waiting planes.

It took a long time to taxi, and by the time they reached the gate, the sun had begun to set, and a new darkness had settled on the day. As she disembarked, she could hear the drumming rain against the din of tugs and service dollies, carrying in the familiar smell of diesel and the sea. Farther along, it fell in sheets against the windows of the terminal, gusted through the levels of the rental garage, beat down upon her windshield as she entered the city traffic, left the city traffic, joined the turnpike, and headed west.

She was tired. The quarter had just ended, and she'd passed the flight working through a stack of papers from her graduate seminar. She'd slept poorly the night before, the whole week, really. It would have been reasonable to spend the night in Boston or out in Wellesley, see old friends and colleagues. But she was anxious to be done with what she'd come for and go home.

—

She had received the call a month before, in February. The officer who called had been the one to find him. A neighbor, who was used to seeing Robert on his daily walks, had noticed his absence, and found him just outside his house. The body was currently at the medical examiner's office. The officer gave her the number and asked her to call them for instructions. He didn't know the autopsy results yet, but there was no reason to suspect foul play.

Helen thanked him. She had no concern about foul play either. He'd been unwell for several years now, often mentioned a cough, difficulties breathing, but refused to quit the cigarettes he said kept back the voices in his head. Had never seen a doctor, because of an incident earlier in his life.

She had thought the officer would bid goodbye then, but after a pause, he asked if she knew what she intended to do with the house, given—he paused—its condition. The county said her brother had died intestate. If she was next of kin, she might want to think about the property. He didn't want to be disrespectful on the heels of such sad news, but the property, it was . . . neglected. The town hoped she might come soon.

Soon! It was the middle of the quarter, and in addition to her graduate seminar, The American Romantic, she was teaching an undergraduate survey of nineteenth-century literature, and had the usual mix of dissertation and committee work. She took a deep, slow breath and thanked the officer. When she called the medical examiner later that morning, he told her with some irritation they had already held the body for a week while the police had tried to locate her. The autopsy had shown severe emphysema and a fist-sized cancer in his lung. As for next steps, there was a small cemetery in town. His sister was the funeral director.

Robert had never spoken of his wishes for his body. Their mother had been buried with their grandparents in Hartford, but Robert had no connection to Hartford. She decided the town cemetery was the simplest solution. And barring burying him herself in his beloved woods, it was the closest she could imagine to his wishes.

She might have contacted a realtor then and sold the house, paid for an estate liquidation service. She had no connection to it any longer. It had been nearly twelve years since she had visited, and she had no idea what kind of detritus had collected there across such time. Well, she had an idea: a vast and indiscriminate accretion, like the strata in a geological basin where sediment accumulated. Ingress without egress.

But then her swift decision to bury Robert without ceremony began to weigh on her. It seemed ungenerous, and dismissive of his life's substantial struggles. In a month, spring break would be upon her. Saul, her husband, had a conference in Seattle, and Michael, her son, was in medical school and not planning to come home. She owed Robert, at the very least, respect for the material remains he'd left behind.

For most of her life, it had been impossible for Helen to separate her brother from the house and the woods which surrounded it. He had first been diagnosed with schizophrenia when he was eighteen and she twelve, but it seemed as if he had been sick forever. Always, he'd been odd; always, other children had avoided him. If the relentless bullying that erupted when he arrived in high school surprised her mother, it hadn't surprised Helen. For what child tolerates such stutters, the jacket sleeves crusted with snot, the winter boots worn even in summer, the recesses spent stalking the far end of the field? Later in life, it hadn't been hard for Helen to find compassion, even fascination, for his strange obsessions. But as a girl, she'd had no patience, not in Boston, and certainly not after their move.

From the beginning, she hated the yellow house. Hated its distance from town, the town's distance from the city. Hated the darkness of the forest that surrounded it. Hated the low ceilings, the creaking floors, the dusty rooms of garish wallpaper and mounted animals. She had hardly been a week at Oakfield Middle and High before the whole school knew about her brother, and those friends bold enough to make the long trek up the valley did not come there again. And who would, she thought, with this strange boy pacing beneath the remnants of her grandfather's ghastly harvest, speaking of the bestial counsel in his head?

She had a single friend, who lived in town, and tried, when possible, to spend the night there. It was easier to get to school, she told her mother, which was true, though no one—not her mother, not her friend's parents—doubted her real reasons. There were weeks she didn't see her mother because she was with her brother at the hospital, months she took her meals alone.

In the end, she'd studied her way out, enrolled at seventeen at Radcliffe. The autumn when she left for Cambridge, Robert had just been discharged from the asylum. It seemed as if her mother didn't even notice her departure. She met Saul in the summer of her sophomore year, when he was on furlough from the army, and married him before he left.

It was three hours according to the good people of Rand McNally, but with the rain and lowering darkness, she missed her exit, took a local highway she thought would return her to the interstate, got lost again, and found herself in Corbury Junction, a town she remembered only vaguely for its rival high school. From there, according to the map, a road should have taken her into the mountains, but the asphalt soon gave way to dirt, dead-ending at a long driveway flanked by those twin heralds of American hospitality, PRIVATE PROPERTY and BEWARE OF DOG. By then, fatigue had set in. She realized that the airplane lunch was now nearly seven hours in the past.

There were three hotels in Corbury Junction, each of which

seemed intent to outdo the other in the remoteness of its historical reference: the Jonathan Edwards Motel, the King Philip Motor Lodge, and the woefully landlocked Mayflower Motel and Spa. The King Philip was the only one with a vacancy. There was no one at the reception desk, which was still hung with bunting commemorating last summer's Bicentennial. She had to ring the desk bell several times before a wheezing woman in a bathrobe came lurching from the back, sucked on a cigarette, and took a seat. Yes, there was a room available, the sign said so, didn't it, sweetie? The HBO had been canceled, and the heating was broken, but she could bring an extra blanket and give Helen ten dollars off.

Helen didn't care. Was there a diner somewhere?

There was, but it wasn't open. Not since Mabel left for Worcester, and Earl's whole thing.

This was not an invitation to ask about what Mabel was doing in Worcester or Earl's thing, but a statement of galactic fact. There was, however, a vending machine in the hall.

She thought she would sleep, but once she was in the room, her body, now that it was no longer girding itself for annihilation beneath the wheels of a hydroplaning big rig, remembered it was only 7:00 p.m. in California. It took another trip to the front desk to get change. Back in her room, she settled before the stack of term papers, blanket around her shoulders, two packs of Nut Goodies and a Good & Fruity on the desk.

Sixteen papers, and somehow, on the flight, she'd read just two of them. Now she shuffled through the rest.

"Painted Words—Cross-Genre Influences in the Antebellum North."

"Eros, Deception, and the American Séance."

"Materializing Memory: The Function of Phantasm."

"'Bold Bug': Erasmus Nash's 'The Damsel' and the Desire of the Demure."

She took this one from the stack. At least someone had written on Nash. His *Eclogues* were her favorite of that quarter's readings: a "hot Walden," to use the felicitous phrase of one of her undergraduates, and a decisive rebuttal to the general attitude that somehow the current generation had discovered sex. One of her cherished pedagogical experiences was to recite, say, Nash's "Galatea" to her undergrads, as innocently as she might read "The Song of Hiawatha," keeping a curious eye upon them as the odes to oak and wren steamed up.

Touch of skin as smooth as stone / and stone as skin . . .

Mossy notch and eager lip . . .

The heat with which her Dryad's womb embraced . . .

By the time she'd reach the fifth stanza (*She clutched the roots that clutched the earth*), the tension would be palpable, and when, at last, she finished, she would raise her eyes to find the group reduced to silence, a blush upon the face of even the most reluctant chemistry major taking the course for distributional requirements ("Arts and Letters").

During her assistant professorship at Wellesley, there had even been a complaint: a poem about a man who makes love to a treewoman didn't meet the standards of the institution, and she'd had to wait until she reached the corrupted wilds of Berkeley before she taught it again. Even there, it felt like a kind of transgression. As was Nash's copious correspondence with his wife: if not quite a Joycean level of uxorious smut, still thick with desire. It didn't hurt that, in their portraits, Nash looked a young Brando, and Clara seemed to smolder with a glow that was decisively postcoital. It put *your silhouette pressed in the moss* in context, it did. ("Anyone want to guess what he is referring to here? Anyone? Come now, let's not be prudes, people, these are the seventies. No-

body?") Of course, what delighted her the most about it all was
that, for all his brookside pleasures, Nash himself was famously
city-bound; after an early tour to Europe, there was not a mention
in his journals of a visit to the countryside, save a single sally to
Western Massachusetts before the war, which merited but a complaint about the heat.

"Bold Bug" was by a second-year graduate student named Natalie Birch, who had once asked Helen to read the first draft of a
fantasy novel she was writing, a gowny, spelly kind of book with
so much scrying that Helen had been moved to warn her of the
limits on the use of crystal balls in fiction. But Natalie had redeemed herself in seminar, and now the thought of the diminutive
girl with thick glasses and a bit of a lisp writing on the hot-blooded
Nash was a joy of its own kind, even if her thesis—that Nash's
"Damsel," with its frank scenes of "inter-species eros" between
man and damselfly, represented but a translated tumble with
Clara—was hardly original. But Natalie cited dutifully, and it was
hard not to indulge the palpable pleasure she had taken with the
poem.

B+. A few words of encouragement, a suggestion to look more
deeply. Maybe at Lafcadio Hearn's discussion of dragonflies in
Japanese Miscellany? And it seemed one could not discuss insect-
human transformation without confronting Kafka, no? Yes, it was
a seminar on *American* literature, but Kafka was part of the univer-
sal marrow. By then it was midnight. She finished the last Nut
Goodie, and took the remainder of the stack to bed.

She slept poorly. She always slept poorly in hotels, but the bed in
the King Philip was of a vengeful discomfort. Sometime in the
night, she'd given up, washed down a sleeping pill, and turned
back to grading, making her way through the promisingly titled
but ultimately disappointing *"Was a Farmer, Had a Dog*: Animal
Husbandry in American Popular Song," and the less promisingly

titled "Does the Heart Really Ask Pleasure *First*?" until at last, despite the sound of Emily Dickinson screaming in her grave, she fell asleep.

When she awoke, the rain had slowed to a drizzle. The diner was still closed, as was the cheese and furniture shop beside it, but there was a gas station in the next town over with fresh coffee and supermarket pastries sealed in cellophane. In the parking lot, a historical marker commemorated, "with gratitude," the site of an old English fort, "abandoned after an Indian massacre." Dead weeds in the stonework. Amber curls of shattered glass. A quote from Isaiah.

Because the palaces shall be forsaken;
the multitude of the city shall be left;
the forts and towers shall be for dens for ever,
a joy of wild asses, a pasture of flocks . . .

She ate as she drove, Rand McNally open on the seat beside her. She thought of her last visit, with Saul and Michael. A November, the woods bare and dark, the house still heated by firewood. Her mother, sixty-nine, and beginning to show the signs of impairment that would soon bloom into a full-blown dementia, still a child of the Depression and worried about wasting fuel. Robert was unwell, spent much of the day on one of his "Stitchings," and when Helen asked if she might go along, she found him lost in his own world. Michael, age thirteen, was unnerved by his uncle's long stares, and they were all appalled by the dirt and the cold, and they left two days early.

As if in penance, she paid to have a new boiler installed, but Robert had refused to let the contractor in. Called to tell her that the "Harrow" would just use it to harass him, wouldn't let them put a machine like that inside his house.

It's not crazy to think your boiler is conspiring against you, said Saul that day, when she cradled the receiver in frustration. She let the matter drop. Winter passed, and no one froze. Summer came, and then, one day, there arrived a letter from her brother. She was perplexed; she could not recall receiving mail in the past. Six pages, words crowding the lines like a clichéd film prop of a madman's manifesto. Her first thought was that her mother was dead.

But her mother wasn't dead. Later, she would learn that Anneli had died, but Robert never mentioned this. Instead, he was writing because he had finished a book, *an explanation of things that happened.* He was aware of the dangers of sharing this information, but he was getting older. His knees hurt, and his chest hurt and he got short of breath, and couldn't continue his Stitchings forever. He needed others to know, to carry on when he could no longer walk.

He would like, he wrote, for her to help him publish it, in hardcover, or in serial in a magazine.

The next two letters, arriving in quick sequence, said the same thing, with increasing urgency.

She'd called. The line was disconnected, phones being another object of intermittent technological distrust. So she wrote a brief note offering to read anything he'd send her. She said nothing about the odds that a professor with two academic publications that had sold a total of 384 copies could help him find a publisher. For now, she saw an opportunity to build something from what she'd come to assume was an irreparable loss.

The package had arrived two weeks later, wrapped in three brown paper bags, and sealed with duct tape. Eight hundred pages, entrusted to the post office by a man who didn't trust a boiler. She could see how he had struggled to impose some order on his story. There was a table of contents, a haphazard index, two rambling chapters about the kindly "Soul Heirs," the persecutions of the

"Harrow," the permanence of sounds. Mostly, though, he wrote about the "Stitchings," giving utterly precise directions of his routes.

After the fifth maple, you will pass a white stone with tufts of
    grimmia moss . . .
The place where the brook turns toward the oak with the hollow like
    a tall, thin heart . . .
Above the view which lines up the beech with the carved initials and
    the pine with the branch that curves up, then straightens like a
    sickle . . .
At the yellow birch with high, arced root . . .

"Soul Heirs," "Harrow," "Stitchings"—where did it all come from? The book was massive and terrible and untethered, and as a reader who prided herself on not slinking before difficult texts, she found herself in awe at its sheer strangeness. Diabolical tools, a ruptured earth, words which froze in winter: were it a poem, not a disease, she might find it fascinating. But his suffering was far too close.

It was also unreadable. Before the package arrived, she'd entertained the fantasy that he had written something that might redeem his illness and provide some kind of triumphant coda to his life. But there wasn't a single person interested in the enumeration of what seemed like every single tree and stone on some little postage stamp of Western Massachusetts soil. To submit it to a publisher risked not only rejection of the book but outright mockery of his life.

She tried, as she always tried with her students, to respond as generously as possible. *It is an extraordinary effort,* she wrote, *a testament to your unique experience.* She could picture the woods, the paths he walked, with utter clarity.

And how was he? And how was their mother? *Are you sure I can-*

not help you with the heating? I worry about Mom trying to cut wood. And you, if your knees and chest are hurting so.

But, no, he still didn't want a boiler. He'd already explained this. He wanted her to find a publisher for his book.

She wrote that she would think about it. She reminded him that she was an academic. The only editor she knew was her own editor at the University of Massachusetts Press.

Then send it to your editor. He didn't understand why she was delaying. If it was a matter of author's fees, he had money he'd saved up.

She tried a different tactic, which promised, at least, to buy her time. Might he consider revising it? Perhaps shortening it a bit, and placing it in the context of other nature writers? Had he read Thoreau's essay "Walking"? In some ways, she said, it reminded her of his work.

But he'd have none of it. Of course, he'd read "Walking." What idiot has not read "Walking"? He'd read Thoreau's entire journals, all fourteen volumes. There was nothing similar at all.

I am under the growing impression, he wrote, *that you don't comprehend the urgency of the situation, what will happen if you delay.* She'd lived in that house. She'd heard the Harrow—he knew she had, *they* told him that she had, it was why she fled. *I too would have left if they let me.* But that was immaterial now. What mattered was that time was running out. *Please,* he wrote. If she—a university professor!—were to tell the world that it was true, people would listen. He was sick of people telling him that he was mad.

You told me you believed me. Now I'm beginning to wonder if you lied.

She had never told him she believed him. But she saw then how he had misconstrued her warm reception. How her good intentions had gone astray.

She wrote a letter, tore it up, then wrote two more, trying as hard as possible to reframe his accusations.

I have no doubt, Robert, that this is what you think.

No: *what you experience.*

I truly believe that it is real to you.

But he would not accept this either, and so, at last, she wrote the truth. She did not believe in the "Harrow" or the "Rupture." She never heard the voices, never saw the "Soul Heirs" in the shadows. She did not believe that he repaired the world by "Stitching" with his footsteps. She was sorry that he had spent his life so burdened by these responsibilities. She could only imagine how distressing it must be. But she couldn't lie to him. She believed that he had an illness, and there was a name for the illness and treatments for the illness, and that if he accepted this, perhaps he could get better. She loved him dearly. She was happy to have him in her life again. This also was the truth.

She dropped the letter in a mailbox while she still had the courage.

He did not write back.

When, at last, she reached her mother, she learned that he had left and not returned.

What had happened after Robert's disappearance was never entirely clear to her. She blamed herself and called the police, and when they couldn't help her, hired a private investigator, who also turned up nothing. A year passed, more, and then her mother had called to say that Robert had written, from jail, that he was coming home that February. But then February passed, and her mother told her there had been an error. And Robert had been found in Minnesota, arrested for breaking into a trailer to sleep during a storm. Hadn't touched a soul, her mother said, and the trailer was unlocked, but there was a child sleeping in the room. He'd done his time, and now he was home.

He even came to the phone. Made no mention of their correspondence or what had precipitated his departure. But he kept saying something very bad had almost happened and he wouldn't go away again.

He didn't. He stayed until their mother's death, four years later, and when he lost the income from her Social Security, he accepted Helen's offer to pay his bills. He still went through periods of paranoia about the phone lines, and when the water pump had broken, he refused to have it fixed, and started drawing water from the well. *The old way.* But he never mentioned the "Soul Heirs" or his "Stitchings" or any of his troubles, save to say from time to time how hard it was to breathe.

It was shortly after noon when she reached the town of Oakfield. Little had changed since her last visit, save a few new buildings at the edge of town—an auto-parts shop, a dollar store, a mums-and-cider operation, boarded up, presumably, until the fall. A few trucks moved slowly along the main road, but the streets were empty.

From there she headed up the valley, past the turnoff to her old high school. It was still raining, the road was soft and rutted, and she had to hold the wheel tight to keep the car from veering.

How she remembered this season, the bare trees, the mists, the mud like folded slabs of potter's clay. The winters had been terrible, and yet even her sullen teenage self could find beauty in fresh snowfall. But her memory of late March was of uncertain, unstable earth, and grey days that lurched between spring's promise and winter's stubborn persistence. Banished to the forsaken house, at the literal end of the road, she had felt as if the sun would never find them. The arrival of the birds would do little to assuage her— they too seemed deluded, singing in an empty forest without leaves or flowers. As if Robert had failed, and the Rupture had already come.

Robert, she thought, suddenly. Because one needed friends to be a Bobby or a Bob.

Farmhouses, low and dark. In the woods, a scattering of maple-syrup pails. Beer cans in the verge. She passed the Hopkins house, where classmates gathered before the dances, and then the farm belonging to the Irvings. In their yard, a figure wrapped as thickly as a Russian peasant slowly raked the dark-brown earth.

When she reached the house, she scarcely recognized it. Its yellow paint was worn, its roof beset with moss. The damage caused by the falling elm was patched with tarp and tin. Around it, the young saplings she remembered from her childhood had matured into a forest of their own. Nothing like the old woods that lay beyond the stone wall, but still remarkable, this sense of reclamation. She recalled the dwindling grove of chestnuts that Robert guarded so fiercely. By now, she knew, the blight would have destroyed them. She could only imagine his anguish, his sense that he had failed.

The rain had turned to a fine sleet. She was tempted to get back into the car and drive back to Oakfield, or Corbury Junction, or Springfield, or Worcester, walk into the nearest real-estate office and put the house on the market. *As is.* Certainly, there was someone who would see that the value of the land was worth the costs of salvage, though the memory of all the abandoned homes she passed suggested this might not be so.

She had a key, but the door was unlocked, and she knocked either out of habit or superstition, or to give an overwintering animal fair warning that the quiet hours of its hibernation were about to be disturbed. No one answered. The door creaked as she went inside. Her immediate impression was that everything seemed smaller: the windows low, the tin ceiling now just beyond her reach. To her right, the old furniture was piled with boxes, as was the dining table. As if someone had been there before her and begun to clean it out.

But no one had been there, of course. It was all just accumulation. She knew then she couldn't complete the careful inventory she had intended. If there was something worth retaining as a keepsake, it would have to be extracted. She walked slowly, through the dining room, into the kitchen, back into the living room, and up the stairs. And everywhere was junk. Old copies of *Good Housekeeping* (her mother the housekeeper!), empty jars and commemorative chinaware, used clothing. She was struck by the discrepancy in meaning the belongings presented. That death meant not only the cessation of a life, but vast worlds of significance. A candle that might have once provided comfort in the winter darkness, a shawl gifted by an erstwhile suitor, a pheasant that recalled her poor lost grandfather. Old brass, old rag, old bird.

Newsletters from a local dog club, copies of the county advertiser going back well into the sixties, chairs with torn rush seats, circulars of the "Benevolent Society" of which she vaguely recalled her mother was a member. In her mother's bedroom, a few books— *One Day in the Life of Ivan Denisovich, Little Dorrit,* a Modern Library edition of Boethius—Boethius, really?—and a well-thumbed anthology of prison narratives by a John T. Trumbull of the local community college. Nothing of value, no jewelry in the dresser, but she knew her mother had sold it long ago.

Empty-handed, Helen went downstairs and followed the hallway that led to the guest wing. Once, she'd lived upstairs, as far away from her brother and her mother as possible. But the floor that led to her bedroom was rotting from exposure to the elements, and she didn't want to risk a cave-in. Instead, she wandered through the old "ballroom," which Robert seemed to have transformed into a kind of syrup house—there was a stove and woodpile, and stacks of buckets and recycled soda bottles, some crusty with dry crystals. Dead ladybugs everywhere. Old electronics on the floor and tables—a film projector, a generator, the innards of a pair of televisions. Her grandfather's old study almost unrecognizable. The zebra carpet piled high with boxes, the once-resplendent peacock upside down behind a couch. Half of a 1929 *Encyclopædia Britannica* edition piled on the pedestal where the catamount once stood. So it, too, escaped.

Papers everywhere, books everywhere, miserable, half-decaying books that he'd collected from yard sales, old *National Geographics*, *Life* magazines. Stacks of phone books, broken along their spines and filled with newspaper clippings, weather forecasts, sports scores, obituaries, the names all unfamiliar. No rhyme or reason she could ascertain. Sound and fury, she thought, signifying nothing. Or signifying something, but something lost.

She found the closet at the far end of the room, the door secured with a pair of combination locks. It occurred to her then that it was strange that, of all the emotions that followed her throughout the house, fear wasn't one of them. Sadness, exhaustion, regret, but not fear, despite the abandoned rooms, the dusty animals with empty eyes. But now, faced with the locks, she felt uneasy. Water had run down the wall, the paper was peeling, the frame seemed to have rotted. She pulled on the handle and saw the hinges yield. It took just two more tries before the bolts broke from the decaying wood.

It was a small closet, three shelves, each stacked with lurid yellow cases of six-inch reels of Super 8 film. She stood there, unmoving, thinking of the clutter of cameras and projectors that an hour before had seemed so innocent. Pornography? she wondered, but inherent in the secrecy was something far more sinister. Robert had never touched a soul, she told herself, and yet she felt a wave of nausea. Had she, in her pity for him, missed something? Nervously, she brought down one of the cases, on which he had written ALICE? in thick black marker, followed by a date. She paused, puzzled by the question mark, then took another: MARY + ALICE. Let them be adults, she prayed. A scene rose in her imagination, of two sad local whores enticed to ply their trade before the camera. Had Robert filmed it? The penmanship on the case was unmistakable—she had eight hundred pages at home. But the thought of him engaging in something so corporeal, so *human*, seemed impossible. Not her brother, with his endless exegeses on the ways of beetle and moss.

But of course he wouldn't write to her of such a . . . hobby. She took another down—again MARY + ALICE. Then a doubtful ALICE, RIVER? Then NURSE ANA. She stacked them on the floor.

NURSE ANA, POSING FOR WILLIAM, QUALITY POOR.

Quality poor. She could only imagine.

WILLIAM + ERASMUS—well, *that* was unexpected. She never would have thought . . . but, then, she couldn't imagine Robert interested in women either. And any actor named Erasmus deserved a little credit—she couldn't decide if it was more amusing if he'd been named for Nash, or just for the author of *In Praise of Folly*. She could see the paper now: "The Influences of 19th-Century Pastoral Poetry on Amateur Sex Films: A Review." "*Hot Walden*" indeed.

Three more reels of WILLIAM + ERASMUS. Two with a "?" and one without.

Then NURSE ANA, VOICE ONLY.

Oh dear.

The next was THREE PURITANS.

Well!

But what to do with all of it? she wondered. Straight to the fire? Or to the police? But why to the police, if she didn't know what they contained?

WILLIAM + ERASMUS, TEASING NURSE ANA, ONLY VOICE.

FIRST LOVERS.

ALICE, ON FIFE.

Oh, no.

FIRST LOVER, WITH CHICKEN.

No, no, no.

CHARLES OSGOOD, DISCUSSING APPLE CULTIVATION, ONLY VOICE.

She stopped. Apples? She turned the reel over in her hands, but the case said nothing else.

The next four were similarly labeled.

C.O., VOICE ONLY, ON DAMAGE FROM WAXWINGS.

C.O. ON GRAFTING TECHNIQUE.

C.O. ON OTHER VARIETIES—WITH MARY—DISCUSSION OF PRUNING, PORCUPINES.

The whores stood up, put on work shirts and overalls, and picked up a ladder and a basket. Looked at her accusingly: What kinds of sick thoughts did you have?

C.O.—MEMORIES OF THE FRENCH AND INDIAN WAR.

Now her unease had yielded fully to her curiosity. She dragged the projector to the living room, as far as possible from the generator, and slid the reel out of its case.

C.O.—MEMORIES OF THE FRENCH AND INDIAN WAR opened in the forest. She didn't know the spot, but it might have been any of a thousand in the woods around them. It was late fall or early spring: almost all trees were bare, the leaves upon the ground were brown and indistinguishable. There was a smooth, pale marble gravestone, letters illegible. Beech and birch trunks rose among a rank of weathered, knotty trunks she did not recognize. On the right, a log pointed toward a beech sapling, its fluttering leaves so pale as to be nearly white. Spring, then: now she remembered how the beech leaves faded. Other than the swaying of the camera caused by her brother's labored breathing, this was the only movement until the wind blew through the grove. A pair of leaves rose into the air and circled each other like butterflies. And that was it. The reel finished; the celluloid released, slapping at the projector as it continued spinning.

Perplexed, she removed the reel, and loaded another—CHARLES

Osgood, on Pruning (she was not quite ready to risk First Lover, With Chicken yet). This time, the scene was winter, and it took her a moment before she realized that she was looking at the same scene as the previous. Snow covered the forest floor before her. The leaves of the small beech were darker. This time a light wind was blowing, the only sound.

A third: Charles Osgood, His Orchard. Summer, and she recognized the beech and birches, and now the old, weathered trees, their new shoots full of blushing fruit.

Memories, then, of the wild apples growing on the hill.

The forest was in full leaf, the floor alight with ferns and small white flowers. A brown bird, unknown to her, flew into the frame and settled on a log, then vanished, and then a second—robin— landed upon the apple's branches and sang its wobbly song. *Cheerily—cheer up—cheerily—cheer up.* In the distance, a squirrel disappeared up one of the trunks.

The reel reached its end.

Mary + Alice showed a ferny boulder before another beech, this with what seemed like scars slashed in its bark.

Mary: oaks growing from an old stone wall.

Nurse Ana: a muddy beach beside a river pool.

William + Erasmus, Poor Quality, Voice Only: a bed of moss and lichen, beetle lumbering across the frame.

And on. Each reel was the same; by the time that she reached Alice, on Fife, she had no fear of what she'd find. A bird, a passing squirrel, a pair of deer were the only signs of life that weren't vegetable. And yet she was riveted. She had never been drawn to the woods as Robert was, but now, in the shambles of her old home, the same forest, flickering upon the cracked plaster beneath the stairs, seemed rich with meaning. It was as if she were attending a video installation at a museum, and yet she knew her brother could not have intended it as art. What, then? And why the names, Mary, Alice, William, Charles Osgood? "Osgood," in its strangeness, vaguely familiar from her brother's tales of "Soul Heirs" long ago. And then she understood, and with this understanding came a sense of the void across which her brother lived.

He had tried to capture his hallucinations. She had disbelieved him, and he had spent his final months trying to record what he had seen and heard, and offer them to her as proof.

She watched every reel without stopping to sleep, and when she was finished it was late morning. She stood. There were still shelves and closets to explore, but she knew that she had seen enough. She found some old grocery bags and filled them with the reels and carried them out and put them on the back seat of the rental car. She had no idea what she would do with them. Likely, she would store them among her belongings, and one day—when she died, when the small beech had grown, and the lumbering beetle had turned to glittering dust, and the ruined apples had finally given up their ghost—Saul or Michael would find them. Find them, puzzle over them, and then perhaps hunt down an old projector, unafraid, for the possessions of an old lady were not the same as those of an old man. Then, there, in the room of her empty house, or the archives of the library where one could still find such forgotten equipment, they would watch the screen light up before them—robin, sapling, eternal beetle—the images stripped of all their prior meaning, signifying nothing but the gentle motions of a forest that no longer was.

An Address to the Historical Society of Western Massachusetts

WELCOME, everyone, and what a lovely spring day.

It is an honor to give our illustrious Society's seventh annual "Mitch" Harwood Lecture. As you might know, Mitch was a dear friend of mine, and though our falling-out over Worcester cabinetry is well known, he was a grand aficionado of mystery and intrigue, and I do think he would have enjoyed today's address.

I also wanted to thank a few people whose aid and counsel have been of inestimable value. On more than a few occasions, Ed Franklin has lent me his MetalQuest 3000, even after I accidentally broke his first one. For those of you who have wielded that puppy, you know you are in command of the true king of the hand-helds—try to find a Puritan shoe clasp at the Chicopee Exxon with a Detecto F25 or a Pinpoint WS10! *[Pause for laughter.]* Hat's off to you, Ed. I'd also like to thank Carol Watkins of the UMass Press: Carol, doll, even though you are not here tonight, I'm taking your advice to heart and will try to cut some of the "personal touches" from my next submission. Promise!

Finally, I am aware—we are all aware, I think—of the circumstances that led to my temporary suspension from the Society. The past year, as you also know, has been one of loss for me, and while this does not excuse the, well, enthusiasm with which I dealt with my grief and loneliness, I do appreciate everyone's generosity in taking my circumstances into consideration. This group is family to me, and I cannot fully express my gratitude, especially to our fine Chairman, Leonard, for welcoming me back within the fold. I hope that today's talk will serve to rehabilitate me, not only as a historian, but as your friend.

[Pause for dramatic effect/glass of water/applause.]
Let us begin.
[Spread hands in "panning, scene-setting" motion.]

On April 3, 1951, on the windswept shores of Halifax, Nova Scotia, Robert Jorgensen, Professor of History at the University of King's College, stood at the lectern of the Library Auditorium, much as I stand here today, and delivered a public lecture on "Indian Captives in Canada," before a packed, enthusiastic audience.

Drawn from a chapter of his recently published *Our Canada*, it was, by all accounts, a resounding speech.

"The crowd rose to its feet," reported *The Weekly Advertiser* the following morning.

"PROF CAPTIVATES," proclaimed the arts page of *The Chronicle-Herald*.

"For two hours, Jorgensen regaled his audience with knuckle-biting tales of men and women carried off into the wilds," wrote the *Gazette*.

And how could he not regale? Yes, friends, from the earliest days of the colonial era, readers have been transfixed by accounts of Europeans taken from the sanctum of their homes and spirited into the realms of the Iroquois, the Mohawk, the Abenaki. Perhaps you have your favorite? *A Narrative of the Captivity and Restoration of Mrs. Mary Rowlandson*? Cotton Mather's "Notable Deliverance" of Hannah Dustan? The *"Sufferings"* of Zadock Steele? Yes, history offers a veritable smorgasbord of abduction. Pity the poor eighteenth-century reader who spent his hard-earned shilling on *The Redeemed Captive*, only to be tempted by *A Very Surprising Narrative of a Young Woman, Discovered in a Rocky-Cave*! Was he no different from today's housewife in thrall to her daily soaps? A captive of Captivities!

[Pause for laughter.]

[Panning, "marquee" motion again.] Let's picture the moment. Outside, a cold breeze comes off the Atlantic, while indoors the boilers hum merrily. His talk complete, Jorgensen basks for a moment in the fading applause before he begins to gather up his papers. He is accustomed, after his talks, to find a small crowd assembling to ask him questions, but, to his mild disappointment, he sees no one. The crowd files out, and he is also moving toward the exit, when he is approached by a black man in a trolley conductor's uniform, who introduces himself as one Isaac Hill. Would the Professor have a moment? asks Hill. It has been a fascinating talk, truly enlightening. He knows Jorgensen is probably eager to get home, but he has something that might be of interest. For once his family had owned a Bible, brought by his great-grandmother to Canada. Nearly three hundred years old and with minuscule writing in the margins, telling a story that sounded very much like those accounts the Professor just described.

It's late, and Jorgensen is tired. As a historian, he's often approached by some old man or woman with a story to tell him; rarely do they prove more than family myths. But this, he senses, is different. Even before the conductor opens his satchel and withdraws the photographs. The Bible itself was lost in the city fire that followed the explosion of the SS *Mont-Blanc*, says Hill, but his father, the Reverend Jeremiah Hill, with foresight, and at no small expense, had the six pages of the fragile volume photographed and enlarged some years prior to the fire, so that he might better decipher and transcribe them. He has brought this transcription as well.

May I see them? the Professor asks him, and the old conductor beams.

Friends, I do not need to repeat the tale that Jorgensen read that night. We all have read Anonymous's "Nightmaids" Letter, so called for the unidentified mushroom which was used to poison the trio of English soldiers. We have all felt the terror of the young, nameless mother. We have seen her fear soften in the presence of her mysterious host. We have recoiled at the violence of her brethren, cheered her revenge, watched with sober sadness as she buried the four bodies. Imagine the way *your* heart raced when you read it, and now imagine our fair Professor reading the careful type of Reverend Hill.

For how the heavens open above our Professor Jorgensen! All his life he's labored over the classics of the genre. He has analyzed the variations in spelling in the later editions of Mary Rowlandson, fretted his fingers along the twine-bound spines of Cotton Mather's sermons, tallied changing Biblical quotations and the increasing use of *Job*. Yes, he's made steady contributions to our understanding. A specialty is the influence of diet on captive assimilation; he has a monograph on pemmican. And yet deep down, he dreams—as all historians dream—of a text so pure that reading it would be a form of time travel. For he knows that most accounts are, on some level, propaganda, shaped to outrage the colonial imagination, and to sell.

But until that day, his reveries of treasure chests of untouched diaries and letters are reveries and nothing more.

He is sixty-three. His hip is troubling him. Slowly, he can feel his mortal coil shuffling off.

An instant friendship is formed. Further conversation reveals that Jorgensen knows of the Hill family and their long presence in Nova Scotia, their engagement with the historic New Horizons Baptist Church. He cancels a trip to speak in Newfoundland and dedicates himself to confirming the minister's transcription. Sadly, Isaac knows nothing about how his great-grandmother came into the book's possession, save that she once fled slavery in Maryland, said the volume sustained her in her flight, loved it so that when she traveled to see a daughter in New Brunswick she would bring it with her like a talisman. She knew it forward and backward—was legendary for this, says Isaac, knew the Bible better than her Reverend grandson, even as she lost her sight. And yet she never mentioned the marginalia, as if it was a secret she felt entrusted to defend.

He was grateful, he said, that she had died before they lost it in the fire.

A hundred questions remain, of course. Jorgensen wants to know where she found it, who had brought it there, who else had held it their hands. And while all of this is lost to time, there is more than enough material to publish a pamphlet containing the text, a history of the Hills and their contributions to the civic life of Halifax, and an essay by the Professor placing the narrative in context. A small exhibition is mounted at the University Museum. Jorgensen prepares a longer monograph, but then Infirmity, who has been kind to allow the old men their moment, decides He's waited long enough. Jorgensen is diagnosed with Lou Gehrig's, declines quickly, while Hill suffers a fall from the trolley, and moves to Toronto to be cared for by his son.

For a decade, the narrative is forgotten. Then, in 1962, a hitherto unknown American professor of English named John T. Trumbull comes across the pamphlet at a library yard sale, and includes an edited version in his 1964 anthology *Captivity Tales*, published by the University of Rhode Island Press. The anthology is a success; a second edition is assigned in high schools in both Massachusetts and New York. The canon has opened her doors. It seems at last the "Nightmaids" Letter has taken its rightful place.

It seems.

[Pause.]

It seems . . . for, as we all know, with fame comes scrutiny. Tell the world you've found a 1662 Massachusetts Oak Tree Twopence at a Quabbin boat launch, and every detectorist in Massachusetts

will be out there the next weekend, asking how you know it's gen-
uine, and trying to find one of their own.

Yes, even the pros must face the heat, and almost immediately
come challenges to Trumbull's blithe acceptance of the Jorgensen/
Hill text. Who was the narrator who was so compelled to tell her
tale? Why record it, and for whom? Didn't her sympathies seem,
in retrospect, perhaps a bit too modern? Why was there no corroborating evidence, no contemporary reports of her disappearance, no archaeological remains? For, unlike famous accounts like
that of Mary Rowlandson or John Williams, confirmed by multiple sources, the "Nightmaids" Letter stands alone. And why, some
people begin to ask, should we trust those six photographs?
Wasn't it a bit convenient that the famous fire happened to destroy
the book? Might such a story not have served the civic aspirations
of Reverend Hill, who ran for City Councilman the following year?

[Meaningful glance.]

Indeed, without a context, without a single artifact, the tale
seemed more and more like fiction. The third edition of Trumbull's book includes a clarifying paragraph, acknowledging historians' doubts. And while I must admit *I* wasn't bothered either by
the fact of our narrator's confession (for secrets burn when they're
kept close), or by her growing sympathy for her captor, or by the
absence of any corroborating accounts (for who would publicly
admit the murder of her countrymen?)—I have spent too many
hours sweeping the earth for campfire lead to trust anything I
can't touch with my own hands. Yes, in the heart of every detectorist there lives an archaeologist. I needed to see the bones.

Such were my thoughts after stumbling upon several copies of
Trumbull's anthology at, of all odd places, the yearly sale for the
Prisoners' Reading Fund at the Massachusetts Correctional Institution Library in Concord. I bought one and took it home, and
likely would have forgotten it if, one month later, I hadn't come

down with a cold—bear with me here—and found myself perusing an old copy of a very different kind of text.

[Pause. Hold up issue of TRUE CRIME!*]*

I will now admit to you a little secret. Those of you who know me best may be aware of some of my private interests, not just birdwatching, but my collection of ribald pirate songs, my turnpike memorabilia, my work-in-progress on Puritan woodcut erotica. If I have not spoken to you of my TRUE CRIME! magazine collection, it is perhaps because I remain a little self-conscious that this boyhood hobby might continue into old age. But now I confess. Yes, friends, standing before you is the owner of one of the few complete private collections of TRUE CRIME! magazines in Massachusetts, sorted and stored away in the basement of my home. Unlike my woodcuts or my sea ditties, TRUE CRIME! was of pure personal interest. Never did I expect to make scholarship from it. I enjoyed it as a boy, and even today, a dull afternoon might find me thumbing through old favorites. As I was last October, when, beset with the sniffles, I happened upon "Murder Most Cold."

The story was nearly fifteen years old, and part of a regular column written by Jack Dunne, whose firsthand accounts of crime investigations regularly received top billing in the magazine. It was one of Dunne's last stories before he was famously stabbed by his wife, and it described his trip into the forests of Western Massachusetts to investigate a fatal mountain-lion attack—a masterpiece of gore that I highly recommend to all. But it wasn't the kitty that got my attention that rainy afternoon. At the end of Dunne's adventure, he finds himself at a lonely country home, where the chance discovery of a dog's strange bone leads to the disinterment of three ancient skulls, *two with an axe scar, and one with a bullet hole.*

How extraordinary are the ways of Fortune! Immediately I rose and rummaged through the stacks of books I'd bought in Concord. No, it couldn't be, and yet . . . the shoe fit perfectly! The "Nightmaids" Letter lacked a crime scene; the TRUE CRIME! story lacked a suspect. It was just a matter of putting two and two together. Instantly, I understood the implications. Not only did it prove the authenticity of the Letter, but also redeemed the efforts of the Hills, my fellow students of the past.

Of course, in my excitement, I couldn't help but acknowledge one essential weakness in my argument. The *literary* evidence was compelling, but a true historian requires *tangible* proof. Show me the body, I heard my critics whisper. *Habeas corpus.* But how, with a tale so old?

And yet I couldn't let it go. I cleared my table, set "Nightmaids" next to "Murder Most Cold," and once again began to read. I was halfway through my fourth reading of the Letter when I realized that not all was lost.

[Pause/leisurely sip of water/look around room.]

Now, those of you who listened closely might have noticed that I have given you the clue already. Think.

That's right.

Dunne, I said, wrote that they exhumed *three* bodies, but our "Nightmaids" gal tells us she buried *four.* Yes, my dear old friends. Somewhere, deep in the woods in the hills above us, there lies the body of a woman, shot through her good heart, who wore a ring of silver, and a necklace hung with charms of bone and iron.

And where? you ask. Now, Dunne, out of respect for his informants, always kept his locations anonymous.

But in this case, I know where it is.

Eleven

MORRIS Lakeman, birdwatcher, metal detectorist, amateur historian, bane to professional historians everywhere, folded up the draft of his address to the Historical Society of Western Massachusetts, stepped back from the cheval glass (c. 1870), and turned with a look of triumph and defiance to the dresser on which he'd placed a photo of his wife of beloved memory, Miriam.

He was dressed for the occasion in a black tuxedo jacket with grosgrain lapels, a light-pink dress shirt, and a paisley waistcoat. A bow tie patterned with "birds of the world" hung loose beneath his freshly shaved cheeks. He had done his best to arrange his comb-over discreetly, an effort flattered by the angle of the cheval glass, which, he reasoned, given that he stood six foot three, was how most friends saw him anyway. That no one else would notice seemed immaterial for the moment. The reading, as he understood it, conducted *in absentia*, was an act of protest, a ritual before the cosmos. And for a moment, as his final words reverberated in his bedroom, he felt his heart break into a gallop as the cosmos rose in applause.

What the cosmos knew, but Miriam fortunately did not, was that, only three days before, Morris had received final word that his ban from the annual April dinner, due to his violation of the Society's Code for Sexual Conduct, would not be overturned. That an august organization such as the Historical Society of Western Massachusetts had such a code was, until quite recently, unknown

311

to Morris, despite his sixteen years of service as Chairman of the Society's Subcommittee on Relics and Remains. Under any other circumstance, he might have wondered *why* the Code existed; *that* seemed a juicy topic, ripe for study. What was clear, however, was that the obscurity of the bylaw was not sufficient excuse for his behavior. In February, Morris had been paid a visit by his old friend Leonard Shepley, the Society Chairman, who put it in no uncertain terms that chapter meetings were not hunting grounds for seduction, and that the three female members in question, Dorothy Ketterman (Puritan numismatics), Maude Loomis (non-maritime scrimshaw), and Shirley Potter (tin-ceiling design), joined him in the wish that the group return to their halcyon days, which meant—he was sorry—without Mo.

Morris, a CPA until his recent retirement, and thus, by definition, well versed in negotiating with imperium, had of course objected—matters of the bed were the business of the (very) adult Society members themselves—and in defiance of the ban, he'd shown up at Eleanor Thompson's long-awaited presentation on the history of Oakfield salt-glazed stoneware. He hadn't spoken, and although he raised his hand to ask a question, he didn't take it personally when he wasn't called upon. (It was late, and there were a lot of questions.) But he didn't receive the invitation to the following meeting, and no pleading with his former paramours could reveal its clandestine location. He had to hand it to them: Dorothy, Maude, and Shirley, once adversaries for his affections, had united to protect the sanctity of the group.

The approach of the annual dinner presented a quandary, however. Each year, the honor of the "Mitch" Harwood Lecture fell on a different member, which, as fate would have it, this time around was Morris. In vain, he waited for a letter of reconciliation, called Leonard twice, and, when his old friend didn't answer his messages, phoned his office and made an appointment. For Leonard, in addition to being Massachusetts's resident authority on the history of American lithotomy, and owner of one of the state's largest collections of urethrotomes, cystotomes, and lithotomes, was, by day, an actual urologist—in fact, Morris's urologist—and so Morris had the added humiliation of bringing his petition to the very office where, eight months prior, he'd had his prostate checked. To his credit, Leonard was adept at keeping the secrets of his vocation separate from the public responsibilities of his avocation, a necessary practice, given that, as far as urology went, he was the only game around, unless one went to Heinrich Hobbs in Corbury Junction, though once that mistake was made, it was not repeated. Shadd's Falls was an insular community, and one learned discretion. Morris, for example, had done the taxes of half the members of the Society, and knew that Leonard had once deducted a connecting flight to Maui as a business expense, although the American Urological Association had met in Honolulu only. An impartial observer may wonder why Morris did not consider weaponizing such information, but said impartial observer has clearly not lived in a small town.

Sitting in Leonard's waiting room, alone, that early-April day, Morris could not help but consider that, metaphorically speaking, his current, vulnerable position was not unlike that which he was forced to take during his physical. But Leonard, in both settings, was brief and gentle, though ultimately unyielding. He was aware that the "Mitch" Harwood tradition presented them with a quandary, but the bylaws were clear: inactive members were not allowed at any meeting, and he was sorry, truly, Mo, but he couldn't break the rules.

Morris had considered various appeals, running from the procedural (the wording in the Code was vague, and would not withstand the mildest interrogation) to sentimental (he and Leonard had seen one of the last Bicknell's thrushes in Massachusetts together) to frankly tragic (he was a widower, and concupiscence was a natural, documented stage of grief). But Leonard, long practiced in the art of delivering bad news to old men, was used to such men protesting their fates.

Seeing the futility of his petition, Morris did not say that to cut off an old widower from his friends was, frankly, an act of cruelty. That he'd been so excited to deliver the paper that he'd dragged his tuxedo from the attic and driven it all the way to Springfield to get it dry-cleaned. That his speech would be a master class of erudition and suspense. No, Leonard could go screw himself. Morris owed his discovery to the heavens. And so, that Saturday, as those Society members in good standing slowly filed into the Springfield Howard Johnson, Morris, alone in his home, slipped into his tux, placed a cup of water on the mantel beside the photo of Miriam, stared into the very mirror where, not long before, the gartered bottom of Shirley Potter might have been seen flashing in the shadows, and cleared his throat.

Because who needed the Society after all? The amateur historian is no stranger to rejection. Working alone, adrift in a sea of hobbyism, buffeted by the predations of unscrupulous vanity presses, he (or she, nowadays) lives in a state of permanent disrespect. The very designation is an insult. The citizen who does his own taxes is not dismissed as an "amateur accountant," nor the father who pulls a wiggly tooth an "amateur dentist": they are admired for their resourcefulness. There are "amateur musicians" and "amateur artists," but such descriptors are borne with pride and affection, for they suggest a kind of devotion unsullied by the marketplace (*amateur*, from the French for "one who loves"). In contrast, we call the lover of history a *buff*, after the color of the costumes worn by volunteer firemen; hence the name will always carry the sense of someone playing. It should not surprise us then that the amateur historian lives in a kind of purgatory. No matter how fine his scholarship or useful his discoveries, without a Ph.D., he can never escape the stain of dilettantism. No: he may spend most of his waking hours engaging in his passion, he may know more about Vermont philately or the history of slippers than any "professional" (or than he knows about the tax code by which he earns his bread)—never mind—he is an amateur, his interests are hobby-horsical, his discoveries greeted with mockery, if greeted at all.

Such was Morris's fate, and one that he had long ago accepted. For, unlike so many resentful "amateur" practitioners who spent their days bemoaning their disciplinary apartheid, Morris was blessed with one of the greatest gifts that the Deity might bestow on one of His creations: the profound indifference to others' opinions. To put it more eloquently, he had been born not giving a shit, it had insulated him against the taunts of bullies, bestowed stardom on many a Bar Mitzvah dance floor; it was what had so beguiled Miriam Lehrer when she first met him in the UMass library shortly before the war. If his essays detailing a new epiphany went unanswered by Professor Such-and-Such at Harvard, he sent them to So-and-So at Yale, and if So-and-So did not reply, he shrugged, raised his middle finger in the direction of Cambridge or New Haven, and filed his discovery among the many private joys of life.

Given such a blessing, we might have expected Morris to take his ban in stride. But in this case, there was a practical consideration. His hypothesis was bold, his discovery original. Imagine: with nothing but a crime pulp, he stood to redeem not only a centuries-old text, but also the family that had served as its custodian. All he needed to secure his triumph was to find a body. And while he loved digging, lived for swinging the detector over hill and dale, Morris suffered the curse of all Lakeman men, going back to the (ahem, amateur) boxer Moritz Lejman, the "Red Giant of Czernowitz" and Morris's namesake, dead at forty-two from a massive *Herzinfarkt*. He had already been warned by his cardiologist that the pain he felt running down his left arm was not a "pulled muscle," and that his days of unfettered detecting were over, unless he underwent a procedure of uncertain benefit and certain risk.

His "Mitch" Harwood Lecture, therefore, was not merely ceremonial. When he had called out to his imaginary audience and conjured up the dark woods where he was certain he would find his body, he was readying an appeal. Who would join him? And he had imagined the mass of them—Leonard, and Stan (late-seventeenth-century hinges), and Al (World War I valentines), and Ed Ikeda, who was to Japanese-American detectorists what Morris was to Jewish ones—a pioneer—and Dorothy and Maude and Shirley: in sum, all his onetime friends—driving up the road to the abandoned home and setting out together to find the lonely woman in the earth.

Looking at his flushed face in the cheval glass, Morris felt a twinge in his chest, took a nitroglycerin just to be safe, plopped down on the bed, and felt the loneliness of his life come washing over him. God, he missed his wife! If only Miriam still were with him! (Granted, if she were with him, grief wouldn't have driven him into such a rutting frenzy, wouldn't have set the ladies scrabbling over him like Discord's apple, wouldn't have forced the invocation of the Conduct Code.) For his love remained undimmed despite her death, and despite events which would have sent a lesser man into a fit of blinding jealousy—namely, that his dear wife, in what was to be their long-awaited sunset years, had announced one morning that she was leaving him, to take up with a retired realtor who'd picked her up at Stop & Shop.

It had been so improbable that Morris still could not believe it: Miriam, who had joined him in the Historical Society meetings, who had bought him his first binoculars, his first detector, who, in the years that followed, had waited while he wandered over grassy lots and ballfields and listened for forgotten worlds. As for her reasons, she had simply said that she was tired. Morris was a man of such *enthusiasms*, she told him. Perhaps, she needed someone a

bit more conventional. Someone who didn't bring his binoculars when he went to check the mailbox, so he "wouldn't miss
anything" on the way. A gap had appeared between them. And
Rudolph—Morris, who had once *defended* the Disney reindeer im-
agery at Shadd's Falls Elementary as pop-cultural, beloved by the
children, and of no deep offense to his traditions, had the favor
repaid by being cuckolded by someone named Rudolph—had a
country-club membership and a cottage on the Cape. It wasn't
something that she'd expected. But one reached a stage where one
valued comfort, and Rudolph was neat and predictable, with none
of Morris's constant seeking. Look at them: they were nearing
eighty. And Morris wouldn't replace the drafty windowpanes because they were historic, considered visiting the rake collection of
Bettsbridge Farm Museum a "vacation," and cluttered the house
with all the crap that he'd dug up.

It wasn't crap, it was History, and they could wear sweaters if
they were cold—they'd worn sweaters for forty-seven years. Was
it sex, then? he'd asked. Was Rudolph some miraculous lover he
was not?

But no, and yes. Rudolph scarcely touched her, but maybe this
was better. Once, Morris was so handsome, so beautiful to look at.
But weren't such contortions better for the young? There was an
age at which it seemed better to keep one's clothes on. It wasn't
quite so lovely anymore.

"It?" he'd asked.

"You. Me. Us."

There was no more arguing. She slipped off quietly, called him
from time to time to say hello. For she cared for him, she said. It
was too late in life to waste their time with ugliness, and he agreed:
Love made the old do the same dumb things as the young. He had
his hobbies, spent some time sorting his coin collections, took a
trip to Costa Rica to go birding, waited, certain she'd return.

And she did. After the lump was found, good Rudolph suddenly decided that her presence complicated his victory lap. When Miriam called Morris one summer morning, it was to tell him of the cancer and to ask if he might take her back.

And he had, though by then their life had turned into a fog of doctors, treatments. There was no passionate reunion. She felt too sick. The lump was implacable, and it was when she took her second, final leave of him that Morris truly felt the void inside him open, and desire, mysteriously, almost mystically, surge up in the place she'd left.

But neither Maude's dexterity nor Dorothy's surprising, whispered exhortations offered him relief. His beloved daughter, Rachel, a psychiatrist in Philly, had "wondered" if Morris's intent to dig up the Puritan body was not a displaced wish to resurrect pre-Rudolph Mom. But Rachel had never fully understood the joys of history (an interesting failure, when one considered it, for someone who spent her days inquiring—one could say *digging*—into the past). She called him daily after Miriam's death, and never failed to ask, affectionately, if he was still busy with his "hobbies." Had he seen any new birds, found any new treasures? Treasures! As if he were an earring-wearing pirate, prospecting in tot lots for loot dropped by distracted mothers, or pendants dislodged by love-struck teenagers fondling in the grass.

And so it was that April morning found him lying on the bed alone, waiting for the Nitrostat to pry the demon's claw out of his chest. How he had hoped that his discovery, his speech, might have redeemed him, won back his friends' affection and respect. Well, damn them, the lot of them. Once he'd proved his beautiful theory, they'd realize how much they missed him. Alone, he had found three bodies in the pages of *TRUE CRIME!* and alone, in God's forsaken soil, he would find the fourth.

Had Morris been allowed to speak in Springfield that day, what he *would* have told them next was how he'd located the house back in

November. In some ways, it was a discovery on par with his tex-
tual epiphany, but the truth was that it had been almost shock-
ingly easy. The fools in the State Archaeology Section were of no
help—of the three staff members he spoke to, one had laughed
when he had mentioned *True Crime!* magazine, while the other
two interrogated him about his credentials. What was his name
again? Where did he teach? But it didn't matter. For Dunne had
done a slipshod job of hiding sources. Between the Hudson and
the Connecticut there were but two towns beginning with the letter "O," and no fool would travel all the way to Albany to get to
Otis.

It was but a half-hour's drive to Oakfield. There Morris had
considered stopping at the police station but decided it was best
not to call any attention to what he expected might be some
frankly illegal detectoring. Instead, he hastened to the amateur
historian's most loyal ally: the town librarian, in this case the
broad-shouldered Agnes, nearly as old and tall as him, in whom he
sensed—yes, it was unmistakable—the stirrings of a flirtation. Of
course she recalled the catamount story. She knew the house—
how couldn't she? For weeks, they hadn't let their kids play in the
woods.

He had stuck around a bit to chat with her, but duty called, and
soon he was driving up the late-autumn valley, looking for the
"sprawling yellow house" that bordered on state forest, readying
the pitch he gave to landowners who worried that he might cause
some lasting damage to their lawns. "The pitch" was a famous
issue in detectorist communities. Once, Hank Pulaski had even
given a talk on technique, which was funny, because, with his
tinted glasses and Wyatt Earp moustache, Hank looked like a
composite image of the Wanted posters in the post office. Morris
never had a problem. Always handed over his business card. Not a
soul in America who didn't trust a CPA.

Of course, most of the time he was looking for coins and musket balls and buckles. Whoever opened the door for him (and, with the memory of Agnes waving as he walked out past the card catalog, can we fault him for imagining a lonely widow, perhaps also interested in history, maybe with some old button collection belonging to her late husband that she would like to share?)—well, he'd just tell her he was prospecting for treasure. And when he stumbled on the human remains? "Well, hello, and look at that!" he'd say. "It seems we have a body!" Sure, there would be state regulations, and he'd have to call the Archaeology Section (triumphant this time!), but he would worry about that later. They could have the bones themselves.

As it turned out, no pitch was necessary. For when the old, yes, *sprawling* house appeared at the end of the road (still yellow!), it was clear it was abandoned. Dead grass lay in sodden swirls across the driveway and dooryard, sprouting from the roof and fenders of a pair of rusting cars. Broken windows everywhere. Loose tarp hanging uselessly inside a gaping hole that descended from the roof into the siding. Juncos flitting beneath a pair of walnut trees. Robins staring at him quizzically as he stepped out from the car.

He'd brought his copies of *Captivity Tales* and TRUE CRIME! as guides, though by then he knew them both like Scripture. Yes, the place was unmistakable. Here, by the front door, was the window where the "suspicious old face" had looked out on Oakfield's finest. (There even were the "pale-blue curtains"!) Here was the hitching post. Here (and now he peered inside the living room): the couch, the old works of taxidermy. And though he couldn't be sure, about forty paces from the house, there was a clearing, a gap in the forest, now covered by spindly trees and grey, mold-spotted milkweed, where—yes, it must be—Dunne and Co. had brought the bodies up.

He had planned just to survey the site, but once he was there, the opportunity to do some detectoring was irresistible. So he went back to the car and dragged out his brand-new Nautilus, and

slipped on the headphones. Cycled through discrimination settings just to get a feel for how the baby worked. Solid—bit boxy,
but one didn't get this level of mineral discrimination without
some heft. He gave her a friendly pat and, as if in gratitude, she
whistled like a wood thrush. Yes, someone up above was on his
side. Miriam? Feeling bad about the whole Rudolph thing, old
girl? In the months after she died, he'd woken every morning certain that she was lying by him in his bed. We call them *grief hallucinations*, Rachel told him: common, and completely normal. *Of
course*, said Morris, *hallucinations*, though he knew with utter cer-
tainty it was her ghost.

For the next hour, Morris worked his way along a winding,
carefree course. Again and again, the threshold purred for him. He
scarcely went two steps before the detector proclaimed another
find. Pennies, old nail, copper wire. And then the soil hailed in
tremolo: paintbrush ferrule, tube of paint. Yes, someone up there
was on his side.

And yet no guardian angel, no matter how omnipotent, could
do a thing about the weather in Massachusetts in November. Rain
began to fall. The Nautilus Company boasted that its flagship
model was waterproof, but he was not one to push his luck.

He walked back to the car, where he paused to listen to the
pinging of a northern cardinal. He couldn't wait to share the news.
Nothing this exciting had happened to the Society since Vince
Smith had turned up a stash of vintage Epsom salts in his cousin's
husband's grandmother's basement. *And used them*. His curse was
that the season, with the muddy earth soon freezing, was no time
to start an excavation. Well, the body wouldn't be going anywhere. He'd finish up his paper, and come back in the spring.

And then the ban came, and on the evening of the April potluck,
he gave his lonely speech before the cheval glass and Miriam's
portrait, popped his nitroglycerin, and early the next morning
packed a lunch and headed back up the valley road alone.

—

Spring had wrought a transformation on the property. Grass grew up among the dead weeds in the driveway, a bright-green moss covered the stone walls, and a red wash of budding maple spread up the mountain. As he stepped out from the car, there was a scuttling of birds and squirrels, as if the group had been secretly mingling, gossiping, and now hastened along their separate ways.

How loud it was! He stopped a moment, considering how both his passions consisted of not only the search for tiny treasures, but also an act of listening. Tufted titmouse, white-throated sparrow, golden-crowned kinglet. He couldn't see a single one of them, but he knew that they were there.

A bobbing pair of butterflies preceded him as he walked around to the back of the house and set down his equipment. He had worn his lucky satin Red Sox bomber jacket, but the day was already warm, and he hung it on a branch. A flock of robins, who had fled into the trees, seemed to have decided in the interim that the intruder wasn't worrisome enough to interrupt their banquet, and one by one flew back to forage in the grass.

There I buryd them, the men together and my mistress nearer to the house.

If he was right about the TRUE CRIME! dig site, "nearer to the house" meant about a half-acre of ground. It wasn't much to go on, and it assumed the current house stood in the same spot as the original stone one—a risky assumption, given the time that had elapsed. The building was of a "connected farm" style, about which he knew more than a little, for the Society had invited a renowned historian of New England domestic architecture to speak to them some three years prior. Mid-nineteenth-century addition, judging from the Federal style on the larger wing, while the central structure was a classic saltbox, perhaps dating back to the Revolution, even earlier. A whole lot of years lay between him and his captive; it was almost dizzying. But he'd gone prospecting on far more tenuous leads than this one, and if most of them led nowhere, it didn't really matter. Because they often led somewhere else. He'd be a fool not to embrace a lovely spring day, with the whole world to himself.

And it was all to himself. On his way up he had passed several houses, but many looked abandoned, and he hadn't seen any cars at the neighbor's down the road. What if he were to fall, or hurt himself? Should he have told someone what he was doing? But whom? Certainly not someone from the Society. Rachel? And put up with her mumbo-jumbo? Agnes? For all her promise, he did not know if he could trust her yet.

No, it was better that he was alone for now, he thought, and headed up the hillside toward the hollow, flipped on the Nautilus, and let his ears fill with the hum.

While it is a roller coaster of emotion for the practitioner, even the most ardent detectorists will admit that watching *another* detectorist is, frankly, pretty boring, unless it is the girl in the tank top who advertised the Pinpoint P100 on the Shopping Channel. Watching Morris . . . well, no matter how he shimmied to the theremin cry that issued from the soil, let's just say that it was a true sign of Miriam's patience that she had spent so many hours waiting, and it would be unkind to ask the reader to do the same. And so let us skip the pings and crackles of that first morning, the chicken sandwich eaten before the robins' accusatory stares, the cooling afternoon, the reluctant return home to sleep. Let us skip, in fact, the next day too, for it yields up but a crystal ball with its rusted iron stand—a beguiling find, of course, but not a body. Let us skip the dimes and pennies, the old campfire lead, the can-slaw and the pull-tabs (God, let us skip the pull-tabs). Let us skip the second night and the third morning, and the third night and the fourth morning, and let us reconvene amid the flock of waxwings that paused in a small, bewildered crabapple to make swift work of last year's fruit. It is a warm afternoon. Morris is napping nearby in the back seat of the Oldsmobile, his Red Sox jacket serving as a pillow. He is sleeping deeply, not only because of so much exercise, but because there's not a CPA, no matter how many years retired, who can make it through an April night without waking in a sweat. He's catching up. The Nautilus sits in the passenger seat, the window is open. In the grass lies a pile of old nails that Morris had set down yesterday, forgotten, and then run over this morning, and so he wakes to find his tire flat.

It may seem a foregone conclusion that, at some point in this chapter, Morris Lakeman would go inside the sprawling yellow house, but let the record show it didn't need to happen. He could certainly have waited the rain out in the Oldsmobile. In the trunk was a spare tire, and though long ago he slipped his disc changing a tire, that was before three months of Jazzercise cured everything, *ad infinitum*. On his third day, he had seen a truck outside the neighbor's house, and certainly was capable of walking there to ask for help. He had plenty of possible excuses, but even if he told the truth, it is unlikely anyone would care. Indeed (though he did not know this), there was some vague neighborhood resentment that the house's owner, a Californian, seemed sentimentally attached and would neither tear it down nor sell it, though clearly it was a public nuisance.

In other words, Morris didn't *have* to follow the footsteps of the great Jack Dunne and try the front door and find it open. Didn't have to call out, though he knew no one was home. The electricity was off, of course, but he always traveled with a flashlight, and he decided to have a look around.

It was quickly apparent that the larger wing of the house was no longer habitable. Everything was soaked and rotten. Mold laced the walls in arcs as perfect as Spanish fans. Chips of paint covered the floor of the ballroom like parade confetti, shredded curtains fluttered before open windows, and in an upstairs room, broad strips of wallpaper unfurled themselves to reveal, to his astonishment, the unmistakable deep gouges of a pileated woodpecker. In a downstairs office, the shifting walls had opened a seam from which bloomed a lurid crust the colors of a giraffe. Something had devoured the lampshades. In the carpet of a red room, he found a patch of ink mushrooms. He stopped his exploration when his foot punched through a rotted stair.

And yet, despite this, the damage had yet to make its way across the little hallway that connected the wings, and so, for all practical purposes, the main house had changed very little since the last human visitor, seven years before Morris. There were more dead ladybugs now than there were then: the south-facing wall had been discovered by the locals as a warm place to overwinter. Swallows were nesting in the chimneys, but for Morris, this just added charm. The stairs creaked. The landing pitched south at such a tilt that it could send a marble rolling with velocity. In one upstairs bedroom, a broken window (bird strike, indigo bunting; fortunately, he didn't know this) had let in the elements, and so it was in the other that Morris—after wandering for hours with a historian's voraciousness (tin ceilings! wide floorboards! woodstoves! that wallpaper!)—paused. By then it was dark outside. A cold, wet wind was coming down the mountain. Goldilocks tested the mattress and found it firm.

For the first night in a month, Morris did not dream that he has missed a client's filing deadline. In the morning, when he woke, he found that pre-1956 copies of *Good Housekeeping* made for great starter in the woodstove, there was water in the well outside, and the coffee from the tins tasted surprisingly fresh.

In fact, the former owner must have been a terrible hoarder. In the pantry, Morris found enough cans of beans and corn and peas to last for months.

—

And so it was that Morris Lakeman slowly moved into the sprawling yellow house. He began each morning detectoring, before he stopped to eat and set about straightening up what he soon came to think of as his new home. Having once handled the taxes for a rather thorny property dispute, he knew that, technically, it took twenty years of continuous possession for a squatter to make an adverse-possession claim in Massachusetts. But from a practical standpoint, there were only three forces that might interfere with temporary occupation: the owner, the town police, and Rachel. The first two showed no signs of caring. As for his daughter, after a week, he jacked the car and slipped the spare on (and his back felt great, like he was forty again, proving what he had always known: the problem was the mattress), and drove back down to Oakfield, where he called her from a pay phone, and said that he had found a little cabin in the woods. He was taking a vacation. Then he'd driven back and continued with his work. No bodies yet, but this didn't bother him. His days had been distilled into a kind of purpose that he hadn't known in years.

Indeed, it occurred to him that, given the opportunity, he might stay there forever, were it not for the problem of companionship. Walking back and forth through the sodden soil of the late-April meadow, following the winding deer trails, watching the birds flit through the reddening maples, he found himself thinking less and less of history and more of *his* history, and maybe it was the warm April days, or his voluptuous sway—for it is an unspoken secret that the movements of a metal detectorist are a bit like intercourse—or his losses, or the power with which desire had a way of seizing him, but when he thought of his history, mostly he thought of his history of love.

He thought of girls that he had held at dances in his youth, and in parked cars and campfire shadows. His neighbor's cousin visiting from Michigan, who took his hand one evening at the beach in Montauk. The fellow student at his night school who thrilled him with her boldness when she asked him over for a drink. The army nurse who'd cared for him in Tripoli, and left him with a kiss upon his lips.

And Morris yearned.

If only, he thought, I did not have to endure the rest of this alone.

He thought while wandering through the woods and by the stream that tumbled over slate-blue stones and down through mossy channels.

And in the evening, watching the family of browsing deer, the chattering squirrels that gave chase across the catslide roof.

And on the afternoon the Nautilus gave off a high note, followed by a low, slow choppy one.

Cardinal. Owl. Ring of silver, charm of iron. *Hi-hoo.*

He stopped.

In an instant, his reverie vanished. Gone was Miriam at the seaside, '58, slowly removing the top of her two-piece swimsuit, gone the soft lips of his neighbor's cousin, gone the imagined tumble in the linen closet with the long-lost nurse. For he was there, back on earth, on the warm spring afternoon, in Massachusetts, the wind upon his neck, redemption serenading him from the underworld. He looked about. He was at the near edge of his transect, the sound was coming from a gap between a pair of oak roots. Again he did a pass, again he heard it, turned the Nautilus off and on in disbelief. "It could be anything," he said aloud, to no one. A nail, a pull-tab. Odds were . . . But there was something different, something hard to explain to someone who hasn't found a thousand nails and pull-tabs in his life. He removed his earphones and wiped his forehead with the back of his hand. "It could be anything," he said again. It could. And it could also be what he'd been searching for the last two weeks. No, not the last two weeks: his life.

He had left his shovel by the house, and by the time he'd made it there and back, he was out of breath. But the roots presented an impassable obstacle. He stabbed futilely with the shovel, then went back around to the garage and rummaged frantically through a mass of rusted tools, settling at last on an old pruning saw. On his way back up, he broke into a run. He was sweating heavily now. He dropped to his knees and began to saw, until he reached the level of the soil. But he couldn't get any farther, the angle was awkward, he scraped his knuckles, stood, and tried the shovel again.

No luck. Back to the garage. What he really needed was an axe. He began to tear through the junk—chairs and boxes, cans of paint, old electronics. This was nuts—a house in New England without an axe? Behind a stack of boxes, he found an adze—the blade was dull, but it would do. He ran back to the tree, and struck. The adze sank into the root. Again, again, and now the chips flew, and the root broke, and he grabbed it with his fingers, bloody from the scrape, and pulled.

A ripping pain ran down his left arm. He stopped. He heard a fluttering and turned, expecting the robins, puzzled by the sight of what seemed instead like pigeons, but with white side tail feathers, and a paler, almost orange, breast. More like the passenger pigeons he'd seen in natural-history books than any rock dove. He grimaced. Rachel would have a field day. Just like him, in a moment of emotion, to spot something that had gone extinct. He tried to lift the adze again, but by then a vise had gripped his chest.

His nitroglycerin was in the glove compartment. He dropped the adze and began to stumble down the hill. More birds, the sky was black with them; the land around the house had turned the grey of twilight. The air was filled with sound like rolling thunder. But he didn't stop to look, for now, next to his car, he saw another vehicle, a sky-blue DeLuxe Roadster, the flocks above him reflected streaming in the chrome. And someone sitting in the driver's seat—a woman. The house's owner? Morris hailed her, the impulse for companionship now greater than the impulse for the pill. But something heavy came down from the ether and knocked him to the ground. He tried to rise, but he couldn't lift his face out of the dandelions. So it was happening, he thought. He wasn't scared. It wasn't fear he felt, just loneliness. *If only I did not have to do this alone.*

He heard the car door open and then sensed her there beside him. *A grief hallucination.* But he could feel her hands upon him, turning him, lifting, holding him up so he could breathe. *There, there.* Pink skirt settling about her in the dust.

"Oh, you poor, dear man," said Alice Osgood, savoring the warm day, the sounds of the pigeons, the face pressed to her breast. "I think you fell. I do hope you aren't hurt."

Masterfully, toward female.

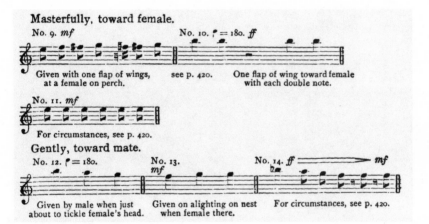

No. 9. *mf*

Given with one flap of wings,
at a female on perch.

No. 10. ♩ = 180. *ff*

see p. 420.

One flap of wing toward female
with each double note.

No. 11. *mf*

For circumstances, see p. 420.

Gently, toward mate.

No. 12. ♩ = 180.

Given by male when just
about to tickle female's head.

No. 13.
mf

Given on alighting on nest
when female there.

No. 14. *ff* ———————— *mf*

For circumstances, see p. 420.

A Cure for LOVESICKNESS, being a SPRING SONG, sung to celebrate the REMEDY of a long Affliction, to the tune of THE YEARNING MAID

A bonny lass, for years had lain
A-yearning in her bed.
Forlorn she mourned the sweetest thing:
The love she never had.

Around her mossy canopy,
The worms they turned, the ants they crept.
While carcassed in her loneliness
Her heart ached as she wept.

Oh, woe! said she. How can it be
A dame of tress so fair,
That dammed within the earth could be,
Like winter's toad, or bear?

About her face, the roots embraced,
The beetle locked his mate in lust.
While our sweet maid, caressless stayed,
Her lips a-gathering dust.

Above, the Almanac's old pages turned,
The snows heaved 'gainst the sills.

And lovers rolled, and fires burned.
But our sweet maid lay still.

Indeed, for years in yearning did
This damsel thus repose
With naught a hug, but from bold bug
That slipped within her clothes.

And why? said she. How can it be,
That lovesick must I keep?
While at her side, Answer replied,
Hush, now, sis, don't you weep.

And then, one morn, as spring awoke
And bird and bee took flight,
Came up the valley, 'pon his steed,
An eligible knight.

And quickened so, her rooted heart,
That songs rose from her fife.
For knew she he but tenuously
Did hold to his sweet life.

So when his soul slipped from his lips
She caught him as he fell.
And to those lips breathed sweeter air
And took his hand as well.

Thus Cure came to our patient maid
And joy replaced the tears she'd cried.
While *he* joined in the common grave, and moved
Her neighbor—grumbling—aside.

3 Bd, 2 Ba

TAKE a step back into the past, without sacrificing the comforts of the future! This is a once-in-a-lifetime opportunity to buy a true New England treasure. For countless generations, "Catamount Acres" has offered peace and tranquility to its owners. Recently renovated and returned to its 18th-century footprint, this tastefully appointed house could serve as either a stylish weekend retreat or a full-time work-from-home abode. The historic 1760 saltbox includes two sky-lit bedrooms, a modern kitchen with walk-in pantry, and a luxurious, yet intimate dining room. All rooms have been furnished with state-of-the-art appliances, are fully wired and smart-home ready. Charming historical details have been painstakingly preserved, from a sub-floor storage space perfect for a wine collection, to the stone hearth, wide plank floors, and Empire mouldings. A new stand-alone garage salvaged from the old carriage house can fit two vehicles, each with its own charging station, so you will never be out of "juice" when you want to explore the many shops and cultural attractions the area has to offer. The surrounding state forest guarantees privacy and serenity, while the 6-acre lawn could be adapted for a private putting green, excavated for a large pool, or both. Come and join the long history of discerning owners who have found sanctuary in the rustic luxury of this peaceful country jewel. A unique offering not to be missed!

May, like *Arabia*, breathes; her morning flowers,
New sweetened with the dew and evening showers,
Send forth a charming fragrance as they blow,
And causing health on every cheek to glow.

M. D.	W. D.	Day br'k. h. m.	Days' length h. m.	Days incr. h. m.	☽ south. h. m.	☉ s. m.	☽ A. d.	Agriculture, Husbandry, Domestic Economy, &c.
1	4	3 8	13 58	5 8	11 29	3	14	In ploughing land for plant-
2	5	3 6	14 0	5 10	morn	3	O	ing, should it happen to be on
3	6	3 5	14 2	5 12	0 27	3	16	the side of a hill, it is best not
4	7	3 3	14 4	5 14	1 29	3	17	to plough the furrows up and
5	F	3 1	14 6	5 16	2 33	3	18	SABBATH XVIII.
6	2	2 59	14 10	5 20	3 35	4	19	down the hill, but across it in
7	3	2 58	14 12	5 22	4 38	4	20	an opposite direction, to pre-
8	4	2 56	14 14	5 24	5 35	4	21	vent the rain that falls upon it
9	5	2 54	14 16	5 26	6 25	4	☾	from running down into the
10	6	2 52	14 18	5 28	7 14	4	23	valley. In planting corn, some
11	7	2 50	14 20	5 30	7 54	4	24	farmers lose considerable by
12	F	2 48	14 24	5 34	8 33	4	25	SABBATH XIX.
13	2	2 46	14 26	5 36	9 17	4	26	planting the hills too far apart.
14	3	2 44	14 28	5 38	9 56	4	27	About two and a half feet be-
15	4	2 43	14 30	5 40	10 41	4	28	tween hills, and three feet be-
16	5	2 41	14 32	5 42	11 22	4	29	tween rows, is far enough, if
17	6	2 39	14 34	5 44	ev.12	4	●	you drop four or five kernels
18	7	2 37	14 36	5 46	1 1	4	1	in a hill. Four stalks in a hill
19	F	2 36	14 38	5 48	1 51	4	2	SABBATH XX.
20	2	2 34	14 40	5 50	2 41	4	3	are enough to grow, and if any
21	3	2 33	14 42	5 52	3 30	4	4	be thinned out, it is best to do
22	4	2 31	14 44	5 54	4 18	4	5	it before the roots get too much
23	5	2 29	14 46	5 56	5 8	4	6	entangled with one another.
24	6	2 28	14 46	5 56	5 54	3	7	If ashes be applied to corn on
25	7	2 26	14 48	5 58	6 41	3	☽	land broken up in the sward,
26	F	2 25	14 50	6 0	7 27	3	9	SABBATH XXI.
27	2	2 24	14 52	6 2	8 20	3	10	it is best to put it on the corn
28	3	2 23	14 54	6 4	9 15	3	11	just as it is coming up. Plas-
29	4	2 21	14 54	6 4	10 9	3	12	ter may be applied at the time
30	5	2 20	14 56	6 6	11 10	3	13	that ashes are, or later, or
31	6	2 19	14 58	6 8	morn	3	O	both.

Twelve

SHE had just entered the bend when the bear appeared in the headlights, huge and shimmering in the falling rain. She braked and swung hard to the right, felt the soft mud yield beneath the tires, the sudden sense of weightlessness even before the car began its roll, once, twice across the road and then down the embankment, crashing through brush and sapling with each lumbering heave, before it came to a rest, wheels up, in the creek. A single headlight shone into the darkness. She hung there from her seat, her hair dangling into the water that was gurgling through the shattered windows and across the ceiling of the car. Slowly, the sounds of night re-formed themselves, the bellsong of the spring peepers, the crickets' trill.

She did not know how long she remained there, stunned, listening to the water, the vision of the great animal still floating before her eyes. The airbags had deployed, and when at last she managed to unstrap herself, she found herself tangled up in belt and fabric, thrashing in the water, as if Fate, which spared her in the crushing tumble, decided to bind and drown her in the car's own knots.

She half-crawled, half-floated out through what used to be the windshield, slipped below the hood, and rose unsteadily in the glare of the headlight. Numb from the shock and the cold of the water, she looked about, but could see nothing beyond the beam. She stumbled to the bank and ran her hands along her legs and arms. Her insulin pump, astonishingly, was still attached. She patted her pockets; her phone was in the car. She stumbled back through the water, reached in through the shattered window, and felt around until she found her knapsack, soaked and tangled in her sleeping bag. Her phone was cracked, wet, and very dead.

Deep inside the car, a circuit shorted, and the headlight flickered off. She wondered if she should climb up the embankment and look for help, but the road was dark and lonely, and it had been hours since she'd seen another person. Luckily, the night was warm, and the rain seemed to be tapering off. She stumbled upstream until she found a bed of moss beneath the shelter of a cottonwood. She had no idea what she should do, so she sat and wrapped her sleeping bag around her, wet, but warm enough to make it through the night.

She had arrived in the mountains a week before, seeking field sites for a study of spring ephemerals, woodland flowers that bloomed briefly in the fleeting sunlight before the trees leafed out and the canopy closed. She was in her second year of a post-doctoral fellowship, paid so little that she slept in her office or the back of her station wagon and ate most of her meals at campus events advertising free food. She had ended a five-year relationship six months before; she spoke rarely to her parents; her lab chief at the Experimental Forest, increasingly absent to attend to unspecified personal affairs, kept handing her one duty after the next. With the summer season yet to start, and campsites quiet, she had spent her days in total solitude. She had never been so happy in her life.

That she, the only child of an insurance inspector and a wedding planner, had followed a path in life that found her alone in the woods that warm May evening, was a surprise even to herself. It was not that her mother and her father were *against nature*, as they told her when she announced her major. Only, like majoring in film studies or Spanish literature, it was a little unexpected. When she was growing up, her family vacations varied mainly by the

342

choice of beach resort, and the closest thing to a forest were the four palm trees that neatly pinned the corners of their quarter-acre Orange County plot. Perhaps, her mother wondered, it had been Nora's childhood surrounded by flowers—the bridal wreaths of baby's breath and pale rose centerpieces that made their passage through their living room. Perhaps, Nora had answered, but held her tongue. For those weren't flowers. Flowers were what bloomed in scarlet ruffles on red maples, shone opalescent in the leaf duff, bowed, in late September, on golden sprays beneath the weight of bees.

If anything, she blamed a book, and an odd one. After high school, she had gone to Amherst, fallen instantly in love that autumn with the changing leaves, and then, that winter, fallen further, into an abyss. Exactly *what* had happened remained, even years later, a mystery. She'd known the word "depression," certainly, but had always pictured it a bit like a sad but sweet and slightly silly Eeyore, whereas the dark winter cloud that came upon her sucked the very air from life. It fell across the once-green grounds where she had lounged throughout the autumn, drew the color from the campus forests, descended over the dining rooms and lecture halls, smothering her the moment she awoke. It had been so total, so physical, that at first she wondered if it was her diabetes. Homesickness, maybe? But it was hard to say she missed her mother's constant talk of bouquets and wedding cakes, her father's grim tales of catastrophe. California, then? The ocean, or the bracing violence of the coastline? The Californian light?

She might have drifted deeper had her RA not noticed and referred her to a counselor, a psychologist from Argentina with an accent so lovely that Nora sometimes wondered if she might cure her patients just by uttering their names. To Luz, she deplored the mercurial friendships of the college freshman, the vacuity of campus parties, the unrelenting march of problem sets and papers, the broader shittiness of the world-at-large. Confessed her fears of being seen as sick, her roommate's request that she keep her glucose strips off the bathroom countertop, the hesitation of a boy who, while making out with her, grew silent after reaching up her shirt and discovering her patch and pump. Dug deeper, back to her only-childhood, the subtle burdens of a mother who sold fantasy and a father whose family had fled Cambodia when he was nine, and who, by his own admission, had chosen his career because of its clear-eyed embrace of disaster at the core of life.

Insights, all, but none of it helped. In March of her freshman year, sleeping fourteen hours a day and still exhausted, she had to ask for extensions on her papers. And then she'd found the book.

It was perhaps presumptuous to give such convalescent credit to C. R. Millman's *Key to All Bark*, when at the same time she had in her corner a trusted therapist, unusual levels of self-knowledge for a college freshman, the lengthening primaveral hours, and six weeks of thirty milligrams of pharmaceutical assistance. (Luz, January: "You know, it might be reasonable to go back to Dr. Arbuthnot, if just to get us *unstuck*.")

And yet she could recall, perfectly, the exact moment when she sensed the dark cloud lifting. It began, as many of her days did, with an act of procrastination. It was during midterms. She had a contract with Luz that she would leave her dorm room every day, and so had trudged each morning in snow boots, parka, and pajama bottoms to the biology library, where she settled into a carrel on which someone—a premed, she assumed—either in a frustrated hormonal surge or a vain attempt at practical magic, had etched a primitive vagina and an emphatically circled, underlined, and highlighted "I want SEX!"

She liked the spot, whether for the sad plight of her co-carrelian, or the view that gave onto a small forest, or the proximity to the vending machines. Whenever she got up to stretch (which was often), she passed a shelf of books whose names—*New England Ferns and Allies, Weeds of the Northeast, How to Know the Wild*

Flowers—promised a kind of simplicity and clarity she felt was absent from her life. She did not know why that day, before her chemistry midterm, walking by the shelf of field guides, she'd chosen Millman (Luz: "Perhaps wildflowers seemed too cheerful?"). But back at her carrel, she'd found herself amused by the earnestness with which the author promised his readers young and old a *revolutionary system to learn the secrets of the woods.* That his *revolutionary system* was basically just a table with columns for ridges, scales, and other bark traits only added to its charm. Reasoning that it wasn't really procrastination if she was doing something scientific, she decided, some eighteen hours before an exam she had yet to study for, that she would put his system to the test.

The last time the book had been checked out was 1957. A light snow was falling as she made her way out to the forest's edge.

Later, in Luz's office, she tried to describe the moment, standing ten feet into the grove, when she felt the sense of hope. Even then, in the warm room, in the deep, soft chair she'd come to love, her mind fast and light again, she couldn't explain it. It was as if she had been made aware of a structure to the world, an architecture which existed beyond her and which her sadness could not consume. She had identified a white oak, three red maples, and an ash (green or white, she wasn't certain; it was hard, said C. R. Millman, even for experts), and she had begun to work through the table to identify a new tree, when suddenly she knew exactly what it was—sugar maple, she told Luz, recognizable by the rough, vertical seams that appeared to open as if something inside was trying to get out. It was then that the winter forest underwent a transformation. As if something she had thought was dull and monotone had revealed itself to be a place of secrets and discoveries. As if the world were restored to what it was meant to be, a place much greater than herself.

"And just like that," said Luz.

"Well, not *just* like that. But that's when it began to break."

And Luz smiled, wonderfully, though in her therapist's eyes Nora thought she noticed something else, a hurt, as if the trees had done what Luz could not. "It seems as if our work is paying off," Luz said, but then she must have sensed the envy in her voice and added how glad she was to see Nora smiling at last.

❖   ❖   ❖

It was shortly after dawn when she awoke to a lusty quartet of robins, who had taken their positions on the axles of the upturned car. Dawn shivered in the creek water. Trillium and bellwort grew on the banks, daubs of spring-green birch and witch hazel painted the understory, and by her head, the fiddleheads were hoary with the dew. A wood thrush sang over a growing chorus of warblers. She listened. Chestnut-sided? Black-throated blue? Black-throated green? No matter how she tried, she never could remember. And now were the days of spring migration, the air so full of sound it was almost impossible to separate one bird from the rest.

She splashed water on her face and sat back on the bank, staring at the car, as if somehow her disbelief could change her situation. She had $315 in her bank account. Her parents, when a recent grant had fallen through, had asked (again) if perhaps it might be time to consider a different path, and she would rather walk back to her lab than ask them for help. The accident would have to be reported, she assumed, though there was the added problem that she was driving on an expired license that she'd been too busy to renew.

Nor would she call Mark. They had broken up after a common academic discussion had spiraled into something very different, when he had taken the position that the salvation of certain trees, like ash and hemlock, required too many resources. He studied ash, should love ash, she thought, and she never could understand the equipoise with which he charted the unrelenting march of the

emerald ash borer as it decimated stand after stand. She had wondered at first, as they argued, if he was simply tin-eared, and didn't
understand that arguing for allowing nature, or disease-as-nature,
to take its course, sounded very different to someone who had
been diagnosed with diabetes at the age of seven and required insulin ever since. It was not that his position on the ash borer wasn't
common, even reasonable. She just wanted him to recognize how
she might hear it, wanted him to assure her that he wasn't talking
about *her* disease.

But there was a stridency to his argument, and though it was
years since she'd seen Luz, she could still hear her gentle questions. *I wonder if there is something else here. I wonder why you're telling me now.*

When she said this, he said that she was crazy. She would have
accepted even an acknowledgment about the complexities implied
by "survival of the fittest." But nothing. Just that she was crazy
and wasn't listening to him.

Except she wasn't crazy, and she was listening very closely. Because they had also been talking about starting a family, and about
the genetic risks of diabetes. And so, after three weeks of listening
to him go on about the fucking ash borer, she'd told him that they
should take a break.

It was all too much to ruminate on now, though. Thank God for
hierarchies of need, she thought, listening to the ghost song of a
wood thrush: she was hungry. For the past week, she'd been living
on peanut butter and jelly, but she'd finished the loaf of bread the
night before, and, beside her glucose tablets, now had nothing left.

She rose. The closest town was Oakfield, which she had passed
many times on other trips, but never stopped to visit. Not much of
a destination, but she could get food there, and perhaps call someone from the lab to come and get her, or find out where she could
catch a bus. She rose and folded up the sleeping bag and stored it
on the bank, shouldered her knapsack, and climbed up through the

scar cut by the car, through crushed fern and banks of barberry and broken birch saplings. On the road, still soft from the rain, the swerving tire tread and deep bear prints gave testimony to the night's events. She wished her phone worked, if only to use the camera. In her winter-ecology courses, she liked to show the students animal tracks that told a story: the deer that stopped to nose the ferns beneath the snow, the squirrel trail that ended in an owl strike. This would have made a nice complement: 1997 Volvo, bear.

While, down below, the creek made a lovely tinny sound as it lapped against the broken hood.

Her current project on spring ephemerals had grown out of her interest in succession generally, the patterns by which one group of plant or animal species replaces another. For no sooner had she learned her trees than she began to understand the degree by which the trees were changing. The forest that she had wandered into that Amherst winter with her Millman was not the same one that emerged after the college closed the pastures that had fed the sheep they sheared to make the coats and socks worn by the student body; nor the same forest that had been cleared to make the fields. To study how it changed seemed but a natural extension of the joy she took in her understanding of the woods around her, only now the understanding ran like a reel through time. The task, of course, was infinitely more complex than simple naming. In the brief, exalted moments when she could picture the grand cinema of the forest's passage, she felt like nothing less than a clairvoyant with a crystal ball.

Here Pocumtuc men and women cultivated fields along the river floodplain. Here the beech and oak rose slowly in the shade of nurse trees. Here the birch shot up after the King's men took pine to raise as masts over their ships . . . It was as if the past were written everywhere upon the land. In the size of stones found in the snaking walls, which told whether the land was used for crop or pasture. In the rotted hemlock that registered its ghost beneath the stilted roots of silver birch. The Eastern white pine that owed its bifurcated form to the marauding of a weevil in its sapling-hood. The many-fingered trunks that testified to browsing deer long dead.

To such evidence, she added more: surveyors' notes on witness trees, botanical collections, pollen cores she drew from lake beds. Sometimes, giving tours to schoolchildren visiting the museum linked to the laboratory, she said her work was time travel. *Witness trees*, she'd tell them. An old term of trade for trees that marked invisible boundaries. Now also used for those that were present at important moments in our history. In other words: the ones that witnessed *us*.

Given her constant search for clues to long-lost forests, it was odd that when she was approached the previous summer about a retrospective at the Museum of Fine Arts, she did not appreciate the opportunity it represented. The MFA had contacted her adviser, but he was busy and forwarded the email on to her. She had just received her grant rejection, and her first response was to be annoyed by the museum's request. She had never heard of the artist, a landscape painter of the mid-nineteenth century who'd been forgotten until the previous summer, when some eighty-seven of his works had been discovered in the attic of a Roxbury home belonging to the family of his former nurse.

Despite her affection for nature, she had little interest in nature painting—she could never get past the freedoms that the artists took, the impossible juxtapositions, the imagined trees, the meadows of flowers that would never be found together. William Henry Teale, however, was something of a revelation—photographically precise and seemingly intent on recording exactly what he was seeing, rather than composing something pleasing to the eye. She could identify at least a dozen species in every work, down to his clubmosses, and his way of painting in the same spot across the years and seasons gave a window into the lost landscape of Western Massachusetts where she had done much of her work. It was as if she had traveled back almost two hundred years to make a species survey of the same kind she made from lake cores and surveyors' books.

Eight rooms were mounted to show the works. Her role had been to identify the species when possible, and to provide commentary from an ecologist's perspective, alongside a discussion of Native plant use by two Mohican descendants who'd been brought there from their reservation in Wisconsin. And so she had described the way the level of the lichen on the trees gave evidence of snowpack, the exactitude with which Teale had distinguished ferns that lost their leaves in winter and those that didn't, the different holes drilled by the different woodpeckers, the clustered sapling oaks that suggested a forgotten squirrel cache. But what struck her most was the vision of a forest she had previously only imagined. How extraordinary it was to look at a grove of massive beeches unblemished by beech scale, hemlock unmenaced by the adelgid, ash before the borer, elms before Dutch elm disease, chestnuts before the blight. At the end of the exhibit was a virtual-reality installation, produced in cooperation with a team from MIT, in which visitors could don headsets and step into a digital re-creation of Teale's *Creek and Chestnuts*. When she first placed the glasses on her head, she found herself within a world she'd known only in data tables. She'd seen many photographs of chestnut trees, but she had never stood beneath one and looked up.

The headsets were so loud that she had to turn the volume down. But this is what it would have sounded like, the wall text told her. Between 1970 and 2019 alone, nearly a third of all birds had disappeared from North America. Once, the forest would have been deafening. In the recording they had layered the songs of

hundreds of birds, not only those she knew, but others now displaced to distant forests—blackpoll warblers, Bicknell's thrushes—
or lost forever, like the passenger pigeons whose melodies were
re-created from musical notations that had been set down before
they went extinct.

And it was then, looking up at the canopy, feeling the birdsong
in her spine, that it had all come crashing down.

She felt as if she had fallen in love with someone only to learn
that they were dying. She could recall the winter day in the forest
outside the library at Amherst when she first began to sense the
possibility of an enchantment. And a decade had passed, and every
day she'd felt the wonder grow deeper, and every day, reading the
journals, attending conferences, she found herself confronted by
the mounting evidence that she was losing the very thing that had
saved her. Standing in the museum and looking skyward, she realized that even she had never really grasped how astonishing these
forests were. She thought of a paper she had just submitted with
her grant application, a dry and cautious study showing the drop
in species richness across three sites in Western Massachusetts,
the neat graphs that she had labored over, the patient, collegial
exchange with her reviewers. She wanted to scream.

The show at the MFA had opened in late April, leaving her but
a few days to gather her field supplies before she went off searching for spring ephemerals. She hadn't received any news about the
project's approval, but the flowers wouldn't wait. She'd begun in
the borderlands of Western Massachusetts and Southern Vermont. Teale country, she thought.

The days were warm and lovely, for spring had come early.
Spring was always coming early. Soon mayflower would begin to
bloom in April. Her time was short. Which was why that warm
evening had found her driving so swiftly through the rain.

❊   ❊   ❊

From the crash site, the road sloped gently down the valley, which widened after a mile into a quilt of pasture and hedgerow. A wash of spring rose up the distant mountains. Garlic mustard bloomed among the dandelions on the wayside, the sheep's sorrel was bright green, and swaths of cuckooflower stretched far into the fields. All European escapees, brought to America for food or beauty. Bluebirds flitted in and out of the windrows, and chattering arose among the sparrows as a hawk settled in a locust that had yet to leaf. By late morning, she had finished the last of her water, and she was contemplating taking a side road to one of the distant farms when, at last, she heard the faint rumble of an engine from the road behind her. She waved it to a stop.

A battered pickup bore the name of a tree-service company. A very old man was driving, dressed in denim overalls and a dirty undershirt, can of soda in his hand. Eyes bright grey, skin pink and sun-mottled, beneath a white mane of uncombed hair.

Briefly, she hesitated before drawing close to the window, aware now of her vulnerability, the risks of asking help from a stranger on a lonely road.

But he was waiting, she had no food or water, and the truth was he seemed too old to be much of a risk.

She told him what had happened: the rain, the bear, the tumbling fall.

"Ah, that was you!" he said. For, he had come that way, had seen the accident, and gone down the bank to see if anyone was hurt.

He had a vague accent she could not place. The cab was cluttered with rusted farm tools—shovel, scythe and pitchfork, coils of corrugated hose. A handleless, partially disassembled lawnmower sat like a passenger on the seat.

"You don't think I could hitch a ride?" she asked, looking doubtfully at the mess.

He didn't ask her where she was going, which was good, because at that moment she didn't have an answer. Just reached over, swept the lawnmower parts to the floor, and heaved the tools onto the middle seat.

Inside, it smelled of cut grass and machine oil, and something very old and dusty, like the mold found beneath a season's leaf fall, or pages of a forgotten book.

"Mr. Pibb?" he asked, offering her the can over the tangled barricade. "Kept these when they switched to Pibb Xtra."

Her doctor had long banned soda. But she was thirsty, and it seemed rude not to accept the local hospitality, so she thanked him and took a sip.

Charles Osgood, proprietor of Osgood's Tree and Lawn, also Osgood's Window and Siding, Osgood's Oil, Osgood's Roof and Chimney, Osgood's Plowing, and Osgood's Pool Service, was at that moment traveling to inspect a ruptured septic tank. It would just be brief, he said, though he'd also been asked to fix the A/C at another property, and then they had to swing by the Erickson place—there was something in the pool, a muskrat or whistlepig. Granted, Janet Erickson often exaggerated, he said, his speech picking up the momentum of someone a bit starved for conversation. Drank a little in the daytime, Janet did. Often called him for something in the pool, but it had always vanished by the time he got there. Of course, he had his suspicions why she was really calling. His voice rose in a falsetto: *Mr. Osgood, however might I reward your services?* Yes, once the rumor got out that a gent's still got some gristle in his sausage, half the lasses in the county had a muskrat in their pool. Nothing new under the sun, though, he said. Oh, there were those who complained how the youth had been corrupted by dancing and fluting, or got their wigs up in a wad when the Fludd boy was apprehended with that ewe behind the Coopers'. As if no farm boy tupped a ewe when *they* were younger! Oh, things were far worse in the olden days, in his opinion, and if anyone disagreed with him, he asked them who'd been scalped of late. And he got 'em there—they just looked at him with the expression of a heifer who'd hit upon a fire beetle in its cud. Yes, he'd take a sheepy congress over a scalping any day, and wouldn't even say the sheep was worse for it. One might ask why Ol' Vic Cooper had sheep anyway if he was an investment banker in the city. An *affectation* was what it was, like the hayfields that he grew to get a farmer's tax break. This was the same man who converted the old van Hassel barn into an indoor pool, so he could swim during the winter, on the four days he was there.

"Can you imagine?"

"No," said Nora, who was beginning to wonder if she should have kept walking. The truck was going sixty, a dirt rake was leaning against her shoulder, and the old man was fully turned to her while he was driving. Had he said "gristle in his sausage"? She tried to place his speech, which now sounded like a Yankee farmer playing a deranged English lord, or maybe a lord pretending he was a backwoods Yankee fahmah, or maybe just someone who'd done a lot of traveling in his time, and was no longer certain where he was.

It didn't help that he appeared not to have a single tooth left in his head.

"Me, I'm a vegetarian," said Charles Osgood.

"Oh . . . yes?" Right: he had been talking about sheep.

"No, not a vegetarian . . . what do they call the other?"

"Vegan?" she offered cautiously, deeply wishing he would keep his eyes on the road.

"The very same. And I'll tell you how it came about. See, once I was courting, and the lass, she was a . . . what do you call the ones with the armpits a wee bit . . . ?" He lifted his arm so that she could see the tufts of hair.

Nora, who rarely shaved her armpits either, was hardly in the spirit for this particular conversation. "I think a lot of women . . ."

He waved his hand. "Yes, yes, I know, I know." He raised a finger. "Suffrage, right?"

"Well—"

"Truly, nothing but the greatest respect for the weaker sex. Know too many men who tell their wives to go render the chicken and then put up a stink when they find a gizzard in her petticoats. A tough lot, they have, the women. And I should know—I raised two daughters, apples of my eye." He paused. "But I was saying . . . ? Yes! This lassie . . . what do you call her? Armpits, lute, sandals . . . Wait, how do you call those sandals with the little Puritan buckles?"

"Um . . . Birkenstocks?"

"Exactly."

"Was she a *hippie*?" asked Nora, trying to speed the story up.

Charles Osgood touched his forehead. "And a bonny one she was. Oh, you're a bright gal. 'Swounds!" He slammed on the brakes.

With a clatter of rake and scythe, Nora slid from the seat and barely stopped herself from striking the windshield.

"Drove right past the place where we were going!" said Osgood with a laugh. He put the truck into reverse, swiveled to look out the back window, and hit the gas again. Again, Nora lurched forward. "Careful," he said, as if it needed mentioning. "No, um—"

"Seatbelts?" said Nora.

He slapped the dashboard. "Very good. Was going to say 'yoke.'"

The truck shot backward up the road. "So," he said. "I was talking about the . . . Why do I keep forgetting the word?"

Her eyes flicked anxiously between road and driver. "Hippie?"

"No, *hippie* I remember. The one where a person only eats raw food . . . Ah, my memory! Plugged operculum, they say. Come, now, what's the word? Milk from the teat, et cetera et cetera . . ."

"Well, I said 'vegan' before, but . . ."

"*Vegan.* Thank you. And, for a while, I went along with it, would go out into the barn and take suck with my hippie, just like Romulus and Remus, until she died of brucellosis."

"I'm so sorry."

"Ah"—he waved—"I've buried a lot of them over the years." A pause. "Ay, that sounded dreadful. Gave you a fright!"

The main reason Nora was now frightened was that she was going fifty in reverse, next to a scythe. "Say," she said, after a while, "I think we are getting close to where we started."

"So I bet you are wondering how a fellow specializing in trees gets into septic," said Osgood.

"This is where you picked me up," said Nora.

"No."

"Yes."

"No."

"Yes," said Nora.

He slammed on the brakes again. "Well, I'll be . . ."

In silence, they waited, dust settling around the truck.

Osgood was thinking, scratching his head.

"Are we lost?" asked Nora.

"Lost? My dear girl! I've lived here forever. But, God, it's easy to get confused . . . Used to be a big oak over at the corner . . . and a stream over here, but then it was diverted for the golf course . . . chestnuts all along the path, but they were dead after the blight . . . elms over by the crossroads, but now it's a General Dollar . . . maples until they cut them down during the Japanese bowling-alley craze . . . And don't go looking for cedars on Cedar Swamp Road or beavers at Beaver Creek . . ."

"You were going to check on a ruptured septic tank. Then a muskrat."

"Ah!"

"And then," said Nora, "you were going to take me . . ." But where? To the police to get cited for driving on an expired license? To a motel she couldn't afford? To call her parents at age thirty-one and admit her life's mistakes? She turned to find Charles Osgood looking at her, and because she had no one else to talk to, it all came tumbling out.

It was amazing how a story that once might have filled the very rich hours of a therapist's company, or the quiet of many an insomniac night, could be distilled to a stranger in less than the time it took for him to down a second Mr. Pibb.

When she finished, he was looking past her into the fields. He didn't answer. Whether for the jostling of the truck, the warmth, or the effort to keep herself from breaking down and crying, she found herself beginning to feel a little nauseated. Usually, her insulin pump kept her sugars under control, but with the stress, or perhaps the soda, she suspected they were off. She looked down at the pump. The number hadn't changed since last night. She tried to turn it on and off. No luck. Screen frozen. She took a deep breath.

Charles Osgood reached for the gear shift.

"Excuse me," said Nora. "But do you mind waiting a moment? I have diabetes . . . I think my pump was broken in the accident. I need to do a finger stick . . ." She began to rummage through her backpack. Inside, it was a mass of wet notepaper and some old food wrappings and a hat and flashlight and a book, and she was suddenly gripped by the fear that she had left her backup monitor and test strips in the car. Trying not to panic, she began to empty the bag onto the seat beside her.

The test kit was at the very bottom. She unzipped its case, relieved to find that it was dry. She felt a moment of self-consciousness as she wiped her finger with an alcohol pad.

But Charles Osgood had reached over the pile of tools, and picked up the pamphlet from the MFA exhibition that had fallen on the seat.

"Pray, what," he asked, "is this?"

She told him as she pricked her finger and transferred the drop of blood. Out of the corner of her eye she could see him squinting as he read the text. The monitor beeped, but the screen said nothing. Now her backup wasn't reading either. She cursed under her breath. She would really need to find a pharmacy.

"Do you think . . ." she began.

But Osgood had put the pickup back into drive and continued along the road. "You asked how a man who begins in trees finds himself in septic," he said again.

It was a long story, he told her, but he'd try to make it quick. He had come to the land back when it was mostly woods, purchased a lot to raise an apple orchard, cultivated a variety he called the Wonder, probably never heard of it, most exquisite thing the world had ever tasted. Made Braeburns taste like sheep dung in comparison, and don't get him started on the Red Delicious—My Red Arse would be a better name. But then the war came and he'd gone off to fight and left the place in the care of his daughters, and after a time, the girls had had a little falling out. By then he'd had what one might call a change in circumstances, and before he knew it the land was someone else's, a woodlot had grown up over the orchard, and the new owners, all six in a row, had their own problems, so it wasn't until recently, when the house was on the market, that he saw his chance again. By then, of course, he couldn't afford to buy it; dollar didn't buy what it used to. But when the land was sold to a new owner—a rather famous actor, he gathered from all the gossip in the neighborhood—he saw his opportunity. And that's when he came out of what one might call "retirement" and left his card. Of course, it wasn't hard to get hired. With all the locals being forced out of the area by the second-home market, there was almost no one left to do the work. When the neighbors learned about how—and he said the name of the actor—had found a guy to do his trees, he started getting asked to take care of other houses. And from trees it went to lawns and pests, and pests to fencing and siding, and on to heating and septic. He could barely keep up with all the work.

Still, his real passion was for his orchard. And that was what he was getting to, the whole reason for the story. He still had some friends in the area, old folks like him, but they were busy with their own hobbies—painting, hiking, archaeology, balladeering, penance, et cetera. As for his daughters, well, with regards to apple trees, one of them had what one might call—to use a word he'd picked up from a book he found at the house some years ago—a "complex," and it was probably better not to "activate it." Best just to let her move her stones around. And the other daughter, well, she was in love with this Hebrew fellow, and making up for lost time, and it had been very difficult to get her to do anything, for fifteen years.

Anyway, he said, he supposed Nora could see what he was getting at. Soon summer would be upon them, and with the apples fruiting, he would have to fix the fencing, else the deer would ruin everything. Could she imagine how many deer there were these days? Made one really miss the panthers. And Nora could stay as long as she wanted, could help him with the orchard. Needless to say there were many lovely—what did she call them?—*spring ephemerals* in his woods.

They had driven quite a way by then, down the long road and into town, then up another road, which snaked past modern homes on sprawling lawns. Nora listened quietly.

"And if *he* needs to use the house?" she asked, a little too awestruck to use the actor's name.

"Ah, but it's been ages," said Osgood. "He purchased the cottage as a second home when he was acting in a summer festival in Corbury Junction. He now comes just once a year, and he always telephones ahead, so I can get it ready. But then . . . Well, how should I put this? Unless you want to meet him, there is no need for him to know you're also there."

Nora, puzzled, looked over at the old man, but for the first time, he was looking at the road ahead, as if he didn't wish to meet her eye. And then she was afraid, not of Osgood, whose presence she suddenly felt she needed, but of something vague and undefined, as if the stakes were suddenly far greater than a roof over her head. Quietly, she thanked him. Yes. Yes, she'd like to stay, until she got back on her feet. There was just the question of getting a new infusion pump, more insulin.

He didn't answer her.

"Is there a pharmacy nearby?" she asked.

Charles Osgood was silent. Outside, as the road rose higher, the season seemed to be changing into earlier stages of spring. The road was lined with swaying, bright-green beeches. The forest floor still mostly bare. At last he turned to her. "I suppose you didn't look inside your car?"

"That's not it," she said. "I have everything. I just think some water must have gotten into the monitor, and I need a new one. Maybe just new batteries."

He shook his head. "I mean today, this morning: you didn't look?"

His face was infinitely kind.

"Well . . . no. Why? . . ." She paused. She felt a cold wave, a kind of seasickness. "Is there a reason?"

He looked at her again. It occurred to her that somehow the rattling had stopped, and the truck was moving so fast it seemed as if they were floating. The trees parted like a great green curtain. And he could see the understanding cross her face.

She wished to ask him how it was and what the rules were. What she had brought with her, and what she'd left. How one crossed the boundaries, whom she'd meet, and would there come another end. But there was time for this, she knew—lots of time to study and learn how this new world worked. For outside, as they climbed higher on the road, something extraordinary was happening. She saw it first in the beech trunks, now unpoxed by canker, and in the elms that rose like fountains above the crowns of hickory and birch, and in the ash still with its skin, and—

"Wait. My God. Those . . . those are chestnuts."

A yellow house appeared at the end of the road. The truck stopped and they descended and began to climb the hill. Rows of flowering apples stretched up toward the forest. Waxwings lifted from the branches. A woodpecker drummed on a tree, and Osgood, not breaking stride, saluted, and continued on his march. A wind came and filled the air with petals, and he led her through the orchard and to the forest's edge. From there, a trail wound through the trees and stones and over fallen logs with high fans of upturned roots. Dozens of tracks broke from the path, and then converged again, but Osgood kept going, until they crossed a glen carpeted with ferns and clubmoss, to where a man was painting, his hat hanging on a nearby branch.

Orchids and lilies and trillium on his canvas. Behind them, before them, walls of birdsong. The man turned, and, without speaking, rose and went to her, and they stood together and looked skyward as the canopy closed.

Succession

SHE stays. In the forest, the canopy grows thicker. Shield and ostrich ferns overgrow the spring ephemerals. Ruby-throated hummingbirds fly in from the south, swallowtails and wood satyrs flit between the dogwoods, and the songbirds find their mates and settle down to nest. In the mornings, in the forest, she can hear the caterpillars eating. Queen Anne's lace begins to sprout up in the orchard, beneath the fruiting apples, while the young deer stare hungrily beyond the fence.

In the house, she sleeps on a large, soft mattress, on the top floor, with a skylight and a view of the woods. She showers beneath a gilded spout, cooks meals of morels and ramps, and eggs she steals from neighbors' henhouses. She does not need to eat, she learns, or shower, really, but she is relieved to know such pleasures remain. Just as she learns that she retains the joy of swimming, of diving deep into the dark water of the mountain ponds, unchained from breath. On warm days, she lies naked on the stones, and lets the sun pass through her, as she does the tumbling water from the falls. She spies upon the famous actor when he comes, sleeps by him in his bed, grows tired of his beauty, the hum of the air-conditioning, a gardener's constant mowing of the lawn. She sleeps in bear dens, in empty tree houses, on the decks of warm, untended pools. Wanders through the fern and goldenrod and Joe Pye weed. Returns after the actor leaves.

She notices. Indeed, she has no demands but noticing. There are no grant applications anymore, no meetings, unless she decides one day to haunt them. No email; along with immortality, metempsychosis, the taste of mushrooms once poisonous to life, it is one of death's great virtues. There is loneliness. Though she has companions, they are no less complicated, no less insufferable than they were in life, especially those who can't remember that they already told you the story about their bayonetting ninety-seven times. She hears the stories of the ones who went before her, the lovers, the captive, the soldiers, the mother and son. Who have returned to their people, or gone farther north to seek another hermitage. Others drift off slowly, to the sea, to haunt the places where they couldn't be together, to tour the country in their roadster, hunting for treasures behind locked gates. Osgood stays.

There are reunions. When the time comes, she goes to meet old friends, her parents, Luz, but she doesn't tarry. She does not wish to miss what happens, the sequence of events.

Three years later, somewhere, far away, a small plane disappears into the ocean. Once again, the Register of Deeds takes down his volume and spreads it open on the table. The succession resumes: the actor's nephew for a season, for eight a local teacher, who sells it to a pair of weekenders. For four years it is the home of a woman and a little yellow dog, who barks at Nora gliding through the hallways. A couple fleeing fires on the far side of the country settle there one summer and rise each day to greet the world in little grids upon their screens. The lines go down after a heat wave overwhelms the local power station. Soon this happens regularly; the couple leaves. They are followed by a doctor with a rural practice. His daughter, her son. A man who sits for hours before a bedside mirror, staring at a darkness even Nora cannot fathom. A young woman, a graduate student in ornithology who reminds her of herself. Who comes one spring carrying a thumb drive onto which she's transferred reels of film belonging to a great-great-grandmother she never knew. Looking for a world that she can't see.

There are meals in the house, of lush greens, impossible tomatoes, gathered from the farmers' markets, grown in the garden, foraged from the woods. There is lovemaking in the room upstairs, and by a pool that appears, fleetingly, for fifteen years, before it sunders and spills its water deep into the earth. In the basement dug for shelter from the heat.

There is a murder. There are deaths from falls, from drownings, from hunting accidents. There is a suicide. There are two births, a wedding—many weddings; indeed, proving that one can't escape one's origins, the house becomes a "wedding destination" until Osgood hears of plans to clear the gnarled apples, and she helps him drag a deer carcass, rich with maggots, and leaves it in the bridal suite.

More skylights pierce the roof. Another ell is added to the eastern wall to make a "theater." The floor is torn up, the windows are replaced. The garage becomes a barn again, the barn becomes a recreation room, the recreation room is subdivided into guest rooms, more walls go up, come down. It is a bed and breakfast, a "Center for Holistic Living," a retreat for poets who convene each night to read each other poems about the last days of the world. It is a strange, bunkered barrack filled with blue-robed men and women who tear out all the wires, smash the televisions, burn them, and entomb the shattered, melted mass inside the earth. Call each other Patience, Perseverance, Fortitude, strip even the plants and animals of their old names. It is a hunter's cabin, until the hunter goes off into the woods and doesn't come back.

The pages of the Almanac turn. There are changes, warned of, and unexpected. Plagues of caterpillar, a thrashing worm, a porcelain fly attired like a gaudy polka-dotted marionette. There are good days, of cool winds, and murmuring warblers, and soft rains that leave the forest lush and damp. Monarchs, still, against all expectations. Many good days, filled with beauty, that give respite from what could be an unrelenting grief.

She waits. One by one the big trees fall. Soon the hemlocks are gone, the ash is gone; some years, she travels to see the sugar maples that hold on in Canada and Northern Maine. The apples still bear fruit, cuttings of cuttings of cuttings, grafted onto root-stock that can withstand the heat. Scarlet oak and pawpaw and sweet gum from the hills of Carolina fight to rise above the ranks of burning bush and multiflora rose until, again, the land is cleared to pasture cattle, sheep.

Sometimes, overwhelmed, she retreats into the forests of the past. She has come to think of them as her private Archive, herself as Archivist, and she has found that the only way to understand the world as something other than a tale of loss is to see it as a tale of change. During her life, she'd dreamed about these ancient forests, but what she finds is glorious beyond imagination. Skies blackened by bird flocks, valleys full of grazing moose and elk. The glens echo with the songs of long-lost warblers (and by now, she's learned them), children singing in Mohican, wolf howl. Rivers so thick with fish that she could walk on them. The ghosts of the damselflies, dryad's saddle, elm trees: a thousand angels on a blade of grass.

Alone, she walks beneath the soaring chestnuts, lies out beneath the thunderheads, and lets the rain fall through her, on her, through her. Watches the wind baffle the once-maples, whip the fluff of milkweed bloom across the meadow, tear, one by one, the shingles from the roof.

Autumns, children—from where she does not know—come to steal the apples, behead the milkweed, and climb on one another's shoulders to peer in windows swiftly vanishing behind the wild grape.

Far away, there are more changes, some terrible, some wonderful. People cease to come. It is not over—it is not so simple—but now these mountains are left alone. No more weekenders, no more ascetics. The few remaining holdouts, barricaded in their shelters, pass away, leaving their cans to rust, their guns to vanish in the crawling fingers of the creeper. When the trees fall on the road from Oakfield, no one comes to clear them away.

Kudzu and honeysuckle succeed the forest and the orchard, overrun the house. The roads grow choked with knotweed, tree of heaven, tearthumb. The apples wither in the darkness, yield finally to the heat.

Of the house, the ant and mold continue what they once began.

Osgood takes a bag of cuttings, kisses her upon the forehead, and heads into the north.

Still, she stays.

And then, one day, far away, someone sets a fire, clearing brush for game.

It is autumn, a dry autumn. They have gone from years of flood to drought, to flood to drought again. Now the flames find ranks of desiccated barberry, dead Callery pear, tangles of smothering bittersweet and privet, pine that once evolved to thrive in burning Georgia barrens. Fanned by the dry, south wind, it comes tearing over the country, consuming the forests that have grown up over the abandoned homes.

She is in the woods when it reaches the yellow house, or what remains of it, the jumble of wood and stone beneath June's fern and snakeroot. She runs down the trail to watch the flames consume it. There is no hesitation. She is accustomed to indifference—it is what one might call the great lesson of the world—and yet she still expects a pause, some kind of recognition or acknowledgment. But the fire doesn't stop. It takes two hours, and the house is gone. For a moment, a stillness hangs over the rubble, and then it all begins again.

Acknowledgments

For their patience, their love of words, their walks in the woods and in the snow: Sara, Rafa, Peter. For my mother and father, for listening to my stories since the beginning. For sharing his awe for the forests of Massachusetts, its ghosts and literatures: Kevin McGrath. For showing me where to dig my wells: Tinker Green. For Josh Mooney for companionship in the mountains. For time travel: Nathan Perl-Rosenthal. For the Ashmead's Kernel: Wyatt Mason. For my family, Debbie and Emma, Susan and Howard, Charlotte and Ed, Sylvia and Aaron, Pearl and Cotton, my nieces and nephews; and friends whose help and wisdom have found their way into these pages, particularly Robert Alter, Lyn Hejinian, Mariko Johnson, Tanya Luhrmann, Jill McCorkle, and Jed Purdy. For Carol Cosman and Heloisa Jahn, who knew this story as a seedling, and remain, today, acutely missed. And for my colleagues at Stanford, and companions in the New England woods: Caroline and Tim, Dina and Jeff, Elena and Eric, Jess and Dan.

For Figaro, for showing me where to dig.

For the planting and pruning: my editors Andy Ward at Random House and Jocasta Hamilton at John Murray. For guiding me down the right trails: my agent Christy Fletcher. And Evan Camfield, Melissa Chinchillo, Sarah Fuentes, Donald Lamm, Katharine Morris, Carrie Neill, Laura Roberts, Kaeli Subberwal, and Terry Zaroff-Evans.

For the means to write and explore: the New Literary Project and the Guggenheim Foundation.

For the work of William Cronon and Tom Wessels, whose words bear responsibility only for this book's education, and none of its mistakes. For the good people at iNaturalist.org and the Merlin Bird app, who have made the natural world more legible. For Clarisse Hart and a tour of Harvard Forest. And for Professors Svihra ("Courtship of the Elm Bark Beetle," *California Agriculture*, 1980) and Nelson ("Mating Systems in Ascomycetes: A Romp in the Sac," *Trends in Genetics*, 1996), for opening my eyes.

Finally, enduringly, for my hosts, in the forests of northwestern Massachusetts and southern Vermont, on Mohican ancestral homeland, in the watersheds of the Hoosic, Deerfield, Housatonic, and Walloomsac rivers: among many others, the ash and beech, the striped maple, the sugar maple, the northern red oak, the hemlock, the clubmoss, the spring warblers, the flying squirrels, the porcupines, the boletes, the dryad's saddle, the ostrich fern, the catamount, the wild apples. And for those human beings who have worked tirelessly to protect these and other forests, and continue to do so today.

About the Author

DANIEL MASON is the author of *The Piano Tuner, A Far Country, The Winter Soldier,* and *A Registry of My Passage upon the Earth,* which was a finalist for the Pulitzer Prize. His work has been translated into twenty-eight languages, adapted for opera and the stage, and awarded a Guggenheim Fellowship, the Joyce Carol Oates Prize, the California Book Award, the Northern California Book Award, and a Fellowship from the National Endowment for the Arts. His short stories have been awarded two Pushcart Prizes, a National Magazine Award, and an O. Henry Prize. He is an assistant professor in the Stanford University department of psychiatry.

danielmasonbooks.com